Legends Lost

Galdin

Nova Rose

Legends Lost Galdin

ISBN-13: 978-0615716480
ISBN-10: 0615716482

Printed in the United States of America

—The Legends Lost Trilogy has taken about twelve years for me to write. A lot of people have helped me in this venture and I thank all of them. But one person I forgot to thank was the angel on my shoulder who first gave me the idea.

Thank you. And I hope it meets your expectations.

Table of Contents

Scales
Rainbow River
Death Valley
Arsa Mountains
Hill's Valley
MurDair
Samara
Crystal Creek
D'arr
Gangas Pass
Unsirth Plains
Whispering Canyons
Lil' Montes

Silvery Seas
Eirey Caves
La'Dar
Belyndril
Swamp Lands
Taliny
Changing Woods
Bluhon
Scales
Rainbow River
Death Valley
Sagils Pass

Mountains

alls Pass

Lil' Montes

Saniga

Keep
of Ebri

Castille

Hemil

Belarnia

Azul p

Sym

Derbi

Esquir Sea

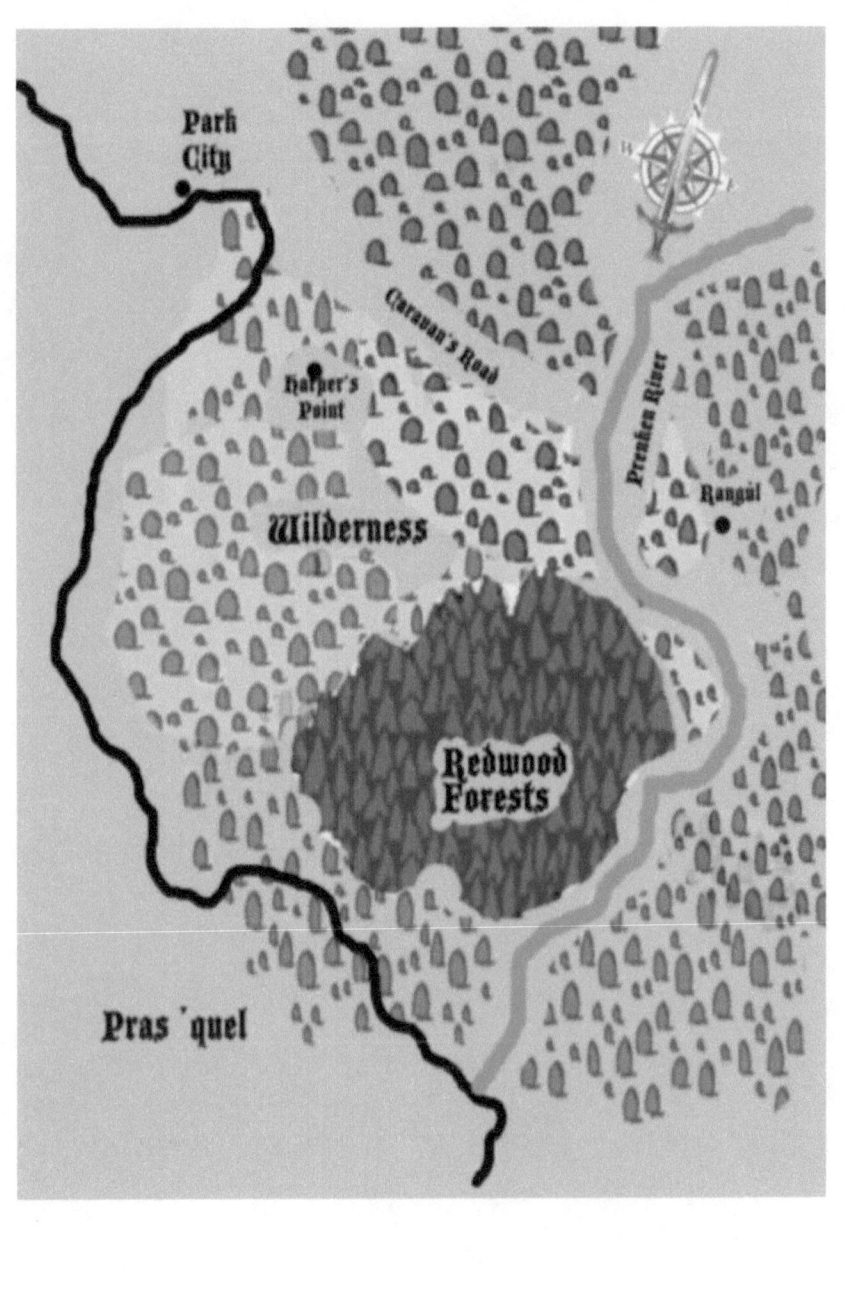

Book One
Dark Shadows

Concealed and elusive as the night;
Darkness abounds invading my plight.

What mystery makes strangers so bold?
Embarking on a journey too great to behold.

Cloaked whispers and secrets abound
While darkness' past is found.

Dancing and writhing in candle's flame
Dark shadows conspire just the same.

Take your whispers and all that is said.
I'll pursue you even after you've bled.

Prologue

Captain Dylan burst through the chamber doors. "We must leave, my lady," he urged.

The sounds of battle echoed throughout the grounds. *Betrayed.* The king was dead. Killed by his most trusted general. Captain Dylan had an oath to fulfill. But it was more than that. To Captain Dylan, the king was like a brother. He viewed the king's family as his own. This would be his final act of loyalty to his king.

"So it has begun," said Kylana.

"General Vasagius has staged a coup. His soldiers have overrun the palace. You and your children are in danger. He has come for them."

"He wouldn't dare."

"My lady, I watched as he stabbed the king not once, but three times."

"Where are the others? Are you the last in which loyalty still resides?"

The castle rumbled beneath their feet as catapults bombarded it. Captain Dylan raced to the balcony and watched in anguish as Vasagius' army stormed the gates; filling the castle grounds with their slaughtering thirst. Vasagius himself issued orders from atop his black, armored horse in the courtyard. Captain Dylan knew time did not favor them.

"My lady, please," he begged with a note of urgency in his voice.

The screams of the dying came closer as death's grasp tightened over the castle. The vile taste of fear crept from his chest to his throat, desperate for escape. Captain Dylan's military rigor refused to let it through.

Kylana remained reserved. The cries of the soldiers grew louder. "Nylana, grab the child," she said to her five-year-old daughter.

"Yes, mother." Nylana hurried to the cradle and gently lifted the baby boy from it. She handed him to her mother.

Kylana rose to her feet. She held her baby close and placed a reassuring hand on her daughter. "Lead the way, captain."

Captain Dylan saluted and led them into the corridor where two of his men stood guard. "This way."

They walked quickly. The battle cries resonated from the stone walls, drowning everything else. The rioting mob drew closer. His heart ached. He longed to be with his men. A soldier belonged on the battlefield, not creeping through dark hallways. Yet, he had sworn an oath. That oath placed him with the queen and in charge of her safety. He stopped them in front of a giant statue. The two guards pushed it aside revealing a dark and damp tunnel.

Kylana approached the tunnel warily. With a glance at Captain Dylan she entered, followed quickly by Nylana. Captain Dylan followed the ladies while the two guards sealed the entrance. His heart pounded as they moved through the dank tunnel, carefully treading on the slimy floor. If caught, they'd be slaughtered. Perhaps this is what death feels like, he thought, endless anticipation of the inevitable. The baby whimpered. He looked back. Kylana skidded on the slime and fell. Captain Dylan hurried to help her up. Vasagius may have succeeded in taking the throne today, but Captain Dylan vowed to protect the true heir so that one day the rightful king would reign. These tunnels would not become their tomb.

Thunderous explosions rumbled above them shaking the tunnel walls. Rock fell over them. They were thrown into the slimy muck on the floor. As the dust cleared Captain Dylan looked around.

"Anyone hurt?" he asked.

The baby wailed in reply.

Captain Dylan scanned the pile of rock. He saw a small hole near the bottom right of the newly formed rock wall. *Too small.* Captain Dylan and his men set feverishly to work widening the hole. Their efforts and slow progress reminded them of time whittling away. Coughing and wheezing filled the air. A distant crash in the tunnel sounded behind them. Wide enough or not, they had to go through the hole.

"Go." Captain Dylan shoved Kylana and her baby through first. Next, went the two guards. "Come on," he said holding his hand out to Nylana. The girl stared at him with saucer sized eyes. She was terrified. Can't blame her, he thought, her entire world had just been ripped away. Marching footsteps echoed through the passageway.

"Come," urged Captain Dylan once more. Nylana pulled away from him as he snatched her and shoved her through the hole.

Once on the other side, Captain Dylan plugged the opening. He pushed the queen onward. He did not like being rough with her, but their survival was imperative. A sliver of light lay ahead. They were close to the tunnel's end. Air brushed their flushed cheeks as they finally escaped the dark underground and greeted the sun's rays. Celebrations would have to wait, however, as they were still far from safety.

Captain Dylan commandeered a hay wagon. He put the queen and her children onto the cart covering them with hay. One guard secured the driver's seat while the other rounded up horses.

"We must cross the river," he yelled. He leaped on his horse and charged for the bridge. It wasn't far. Once across, they could escape in the woods beyond.

A horn sounded in the distance alerting others of their escape. Soldiers lined the castle wall. Others on horseback raced out of the gates chasing after them. Arrows rained down on them. Captain Dylan watched powerlessly as they pierced the hay in the wagon. He turned back pulling out a dagger. He flung it at the approaching soldiers striking one of them in the chest.   More followed.

He chased the wagon. His heart lurched as he watched it bounce a foot into the air upon reaching the threshold of the bridge. Such a wagon was not meant to be driven so hard, or so fast. He hoped it held together long enough to get them to safety. He would not falter now. The wagon lurched again as one of the wheels broke off. A woman's scream pierced his ears. Kylana sat bolt upright as the wagon swerved from side to side before coming to a screeching halt.

"My baby!" she screamed.

Captain Dylan stared in disbelief as the river's current carried the baby away.   There was nothing he could do.   Vasagius' soldiers approached and the baby had reached the waterfall. As Kylana ran to the edge of the bridge, he kicked his horse and rushed to his queen before she could jump in after the child. He grabbed her arm and yanked her onto his horse. She struggled to break free.   He punched her in the jaw rendering her unconscious.

"Let's move," he yelled as one of his men grabbed Nylana.

As he reached the rivers' edge and rode to the safety of the trees sorrow swept over him. He choked it down. The child was lost. Only the queen and her daughter remained. I have failed you, my king, he wept inside.

"Captain," yelled one of his soldiers, yanking him from his self-pity.

He steeled his heart for the moment.   Grief and second thoughts had to wait.   For now, they remained in the vast emptiness of the unknown.

Farther down the river, in the northern reaches of Sym'Dul, a woman lay by a fresh mound of dirt. Tears streaked her soiled face as she wept for the child she would never know. Her sorrow blocked the chill seeping from the wet earth. A flutter of wings sounded overhead. She looked up and stared at the grave next to the one she laid upon, the one of her husband. Two losses within five months weighed heavily upon her.

Cold steel pricked her fingers. She pulled out the dagger she always carried with her. She turned it in her hands. It glinted slightly in the dimming twilight. My salvation, she thought. Not wanting to bear the pain within her broken heart, she lifted the dagger. The sharp point settled on her left breast. Taking a deep breath, she tightened her grip and—

CAW!

The harsh screech of a bird stayed her hand. The woman glared into the sad eyes of a strange bird on the edge of the river. Its brilliant feathers glowed brightly despite the oncoming of night. "Who are you that disturbs me in my grief?" said the woman.

The bird glanced down at a bundle before it. For the first time, the woman noticed it and the tiny hand that stuck out. An infant's cry filled the air. Forgetting her grief, the woman dropped her dagger and rushed to the child. *He's beautiful.* Gently, she lifted the baby cradling him in her arms. Her vision blurred as tears filled her eyes. A small smile crossed her face.

An inscription on the infant's cloth diverted her attention. Galdin, it read. "Well, Galdin, let's go home," she said soothingly to the child.

The woman sang to the infant as she carried him to her home. Her previous sadness remained buried with the fresh mound of dirt. Now, she had a son to care for.

Chapter I
Nylana

Commotion arose in the otherwise peaceful marketplace of Norlyk as a group of heavily armed soldiers dragged a young boy to its center. The boy kicked and screamed as he was thrown roughly down on the ground in front of the sergeant. The soldier grabbed the boy's hand and yanked it toward him, stretching it out. The frantic boy wrenched back and forth in an attempt to break free. The soldier's grip tightened.

"For stealing you are hereby condemned to the loss of a hand," said the sergeant raising his sword high as more gathered within the crowd. "In the King's name, I carry out this punishment."

"Is that so?"

Everyone immediately fell to their knees as a brilliantly dressed lady rode up on a white stallion bearing the crest of the king. She pushed the hood of her cloak back revealing the crown upon her golden brown hair. Lady Nylana towered over the crowd in full glory.

The soldier's sword clattered on the ground as he bowed low before her. "My lady," he stammered.

"It is my understanding that such punishments were outlawed long ago," said Nylana, "And have never been reinstituted."

"This boy was caught stealing," replied the shaky sergeant.

"The law states that he is to be brought before the Magistrate to be tried. Why have you not done this?"

"My lady," started the sergeant, "He—I— "

"Narúl," said Nylana, "Cut off his hand."

A black, muscular man stepped forward, a stark contrast to the pale faces surrounding him. He seized the sergeant with his strong hands and pinned him to the ground. Narúl stretched out the man's hand before him. The sergeant gaped in fright as the roles had been reversed on him.

"No! No! My lady, please," the man screamed.

Nylana watched the proceedings with an emotionless stare. "You were quick to deal out the same punishment to the boy moments ago," she said, "Do not be so hasty to deal out such punishments unless you yourself are willing to suffer the same fate.

"Narúl."

Narúl raised his gleaming sword high above his head. It swooshed through the air as he brought it down. Dust flew as the blade struck the ground beside the sergeant's untouched hand. Narúl released the relieved man and reclaimed his place by Nylana's side.

"Consider this a warning," said Nylana, "To any who dare abuse the law. Bring the boy to me."

Two other soldiers carried the boy over placing him before her.

"What is your name, boy?" asked Nylana.

"I didn't steal anything," replied the boy.

"That was not what I asked," said Nylana. "What is your name?"

"Artryl, son of Atlanyn."

"And where is your father?" asked Nylana.

The boy looked at his feet in answer.

"Your mother?"

Artryl continued staring at his feet.

"I see," said Nylana. "And are you guilty of stealing as is claimed?"

"No, my lady. I accidently knocked over a crate of apples. I was trying to pick them up when the soldiers began chasing me," replied Artryl.

Nylana looked deep within the boy's eyes. Her expression softened. "You will come with me."

Narúl gently placed the boy upon her horse. Artryl held tightly to her waist. Never before had he been on a horse.

"Where is the merchant whose apples were damaged?" demanded Nylana.

A fat, old man stepped forward. "They were mine, my lady," he said. "I apologize for the commotion. I never meant for it—what I mean is, the soldiers had already grabbed the boy before I could say anything."

"You needn't fear me," consoled Nylana. "Here." She pulled a purse full of coins from her cloak and tossed it to the man. "This should pay for any damages."

"Thank you, my lady," said the elderly man. "I've heard tales of your generosity, but they pale in comparison to this. Thank you."

"There are many who could learn from your graciousness. Good day."

Nylana turned her horse and galloped off toward the palace with Narúl by her side. The sergeant glared after her. Anger clouded his face as he refused to learn from his humiliation. "Clear out of here," he yelled at the crowd.

The palace gates opened as Nylana and Narúl rode up. The marbled palace walls shone radiantly in the sunshine, sparkling ever so slightly. Six flags whipped in the wind. Each bore a crest, five of which were dedicated to the five lands of Tesnayr; the sixth bore the crest of Tesnayr himself.

The horse's hooves clopped on the cobblestone courtyard. Artryl marveled at the grandeur of the palace. The courtyard was filled with gardens of plum trees and flowers of every kind. Merchants conducted their business auctioning their wares. Ivy crept up the walls behind the gates.

The heart of the palace itself was set high above the city. Tiers of marbled stone, each with balconies, overlooked the sea and the city. The sun's rays made it shine like a beacon for the entire world to see.

Artryl gaped at the sight. The palace had always looked marvelous from the city slums. But here, it took his breath away.

A stable hand greeted Nylana. He helped Artryl off of the horse as Nylana hopped to the ground. Narúl handed him the reins to both horses giving him orders concerning his lady's mount.

"Artryl, how would you like to live at the palace?" asked Nylana.

The boy nodded, speechless.

"You will work in the stables first. If you work hard, you may one day be trained as a soldier and perhaps a member of the palace guard. Of course, the gates are always open. No one stays here against their will. But for now, Narúl, see to it he has something to eat."

"My lady." Narúl saluted Nylana.

*   *   *

Nylana entered the great hall of the palace. The council ceased their meeting to acknowledge her presence. "Nylana," greeted Krispyn dismissing the council.

"Brother." Nylana stretched out her hands and engulfed her brother in an affectionate embrace. "It is good to see you."

"You see me every day," said Krispyn, "And each day you say the same."

"And should I not be overjoyed to see my brother?"

Krispyn gingerly placed his hand on his sister's shoulder. "I hear you had some trouble in the market this morning."

"No trouble, Krispyn," said Nylana, pulling off her gloves, "A soldier tried to take the law into his own hands by punishing a boy with a barbaric law."

"And the boy?" asked Krispyn.

"I brought him here," replied Nylana.

"Here? Nylana—"

"He can work in the stables," interrupted Nylana, "And maybe he can train to be a part of the palace guard if he proves himself worthy."

"And what of his parents?"

"He has none. And I have been thinking. Perhaps we should open a home for orphaned children. They will have a place to stay and can learn a trade."

"Nylana," laughed Krispyn, "How are we to pay for it?"

"We will rely on the people's generosity."

"No one is as generous as you, sister."

"Then perhaps you should rescind some of your taxes. People are more inclined to give freely, when they have money to be generous with."

"Always thinking with your heart," said Krispyn.

"A man cannot always be a statesman. You must learn to use this—" Nylana pointed to Krispyn's heart, "—in conjunction with this—" she moved her finger to his head, "—before you can truly lead them."

"As you know, in six months' time the council will meet," said Krispyn, changing the subject, "And I still need to find a solution for the problem in Pras'quel."

Nylana kissed her brother lightly on the cheek. "I am certain you will, Krispyn. You always do."

"If only everyone had the faith you do, Nylana."

"Well, we wouldn't want to make things too easy for you."

"I have duties to attend."

Nylana kissed her brother again and departed. She quickly made her way to her chambers. Once safely inside, she released a huge sigh letting her regal demeanor go. She unwrapped her cloak from around her and let it fall unceremoniously on a chair. *The royal lady.*

Her room was the only place where she found comfort and privacy. She moseyed through the tidy chamber among the chairs, embroidered tapestries, and elegant tables. A sheer veil separated the sitting area from where her bed lay.

A boy's voice from the gardens below caught Nylana's attention. Recognizing it as Artryl's, she went to the balcony to listen; careful to remain hidden.

"Why do you stay?" asked Artryl.

"I swore and oath to my lady," replied Narúl.

"But, you are a slave," said Artryl.

"A man is only a slave if he chooses to be one. I swore an oath to protect the Lady Nylana. And to that I hold."

"But it was only a promise."

Narúl looked Artryl in the eyes when he responded. "Listen to me, boy. An oath is not to be sworn lightly. If a man loses everything, the only thing he has left is his word. Your word is your bond, and your honor. If you do not keep the oaths you swear, then you are nothing more than a traitor. I am bound to the Lady Nylana as her protector. And that I shall never break."

Artryl noticed Narúl's sword for the first time. He pulled it from its scabbard. Its silver blade glowed yellow in the late morning sun. Artryl twisted it in his hands before Narúl wrapped his hand around it. He placed the sword back in its sheath ignoring the boy's disappointed face.

"Do you know the art of the sword?" asked Narúl.

Artryl mumbled a weak reply. "No."

"First you must master your mind before you can master the sword," said Narúl.

"How do I do that?" asked Artryl.

Narúl pulled a book out from his pocket. He tossed it to Artryl who clumsily caught it.

"What is this?" asked Artryl.

"It is a book," replied Narúl, "Books contain ideas that can make one think. Do you know how to read?"

Artryl's dirty blond hair waved from side to side as he shook his head.

"That is something we shall remedy. You learn to read and study and I will teach you the sword."

A smile crossed the boy's smudged face. He hugged Narúl catching the burly man by surprise. "May I swear an oath like you did?"

"Oaths are not to be sworn lightly. I suggest you master yourself first."

"Narúl, does the Lady Nylana know how to use a sword?"

Narúl rubbed his chin, attempting to mask his growing impatience with the boy's questions. "The Lady Nylana has no use for one." She has me, he added silently to himself.

Chapter II
Dark Musings

Krispyn stared out the triangular window at the dark city below. Not even a moon shed any light upon the quiet night. The impending review by the council and the new dispute with Pras'quel weighed heavily upon the young king. He always relied on his advisor for comfort in times like these, but even now, Krispyn wished to be alone. But solitude would not be his this night.

"My king," said the king's advisor, Shelwyk, "The council's review weighs heavily on your mind."

"Of course it does," replied Krispyn. "Six years I have been king and now I must be judged by my performance. I could lose everything."

"The council could decide to grant the crown to your sister," said Shelwyk.

"Nylana has no desire for the throne," said Krispyn.

"Nevertheless, they could choose her. She is well known for her kind heart and generosity. People admire her for her commitment to justice and her sound mind."

"She would never accept it."

"Yet, she might," said Shelwyk. "The law is clear. If the heir to the throne dies before he can claim it, then the crown passes to the second male child. For a period of six years he is allowed to reign before the Council reviews his performance. If they approve then he, meaning you, can remain king. But if they disapprove, then the crown passes to the next eldest sibling.

"Nylana is your only sibling. But if there is no other, then the crown must remain with the present king. If Nylana were to—"

"What are you suggesting?" demanded Krispyn. "I know the law. Yet, Nylana has never indicated she wanted the throne. She is content to remain as she is."

"She did challenge you this morning." goaded Shelwyk.

"She has always voiced her opinions. But the people love her. They always have," said Krispyn, "They cheer whenever she rides out of the palace grounds. They thank her for her charity. They whisper whenever she gives her horse to a poor man and walks beside him. And they admire her for giving a small boy a home."

"The council admires her as well. And no doubt her episode in the market today will earn her their favor."

Krispyn pondered Shelwyk's statement. Silence ensued as thoughts of the past, the present, and the future percolated through his mind.

"I will hear no more of this," Krispyn said, "I will meet the council in three months' time. They will do as they will and I will accept their decision. For now I must address Pras'quel's grievances."

"Pras'quel insists that you send an envoy to them," said Shelwyk.

"And whom would I send?"

"Your sister could go."

"Nylana?"

"You said yourself that her selflessness is well-known. She befriends everyone and has a way with earning people's respect," said Shelwyk. "I am sure the King of Pras'quel would appreciate it if you sent your sister to meet with him instead of some lowly ambassador."

"You could be right. Sending her to meet with him could be the solution I have been looking for. I will speak with her in the morning. Thank you, Shelwyk."

"Always a pleasure, my lord." Shelwyk bowed out of the room, leaving Krispyn alone with his musings.

Nylana's footsteps echoed through the palace halls as she walked briskly to Krispyn's room. The messenger said it was urgent he see her. She wasted no time in opening the giant doors and entering the room. "You sent for me, brother."

"Nylana," said Krispyn rising from his desk. "Please, come in. As you know Pras'quel has refused to sign the treaty I sent. Instead they wish to renegotiate the terms. I haven't the time, or the desire to negotiate with them."

"We have been more than fair," said Nylana, "They have no reason for reneging on their promise."

"My thoughts exactly. I know that the king of Pras'quel will not meet with an ambassador, but he may meet with you."

"Me?"

"I cannot leave at the moment to go. There is much that must be done here. But you are in a good position to go in my stead," said Krispyn. "As my sister, he will speak with you."

"Krispyn, I really don't think—"

"I need someone I can trust to go. The treaty must be signed."

"Is there no other you can send?"

"No."

"Then I will go."

"Excellent," said Krispyn, "You will leave in two days."

As Nylana left, a dark, cloaked figure watched from behind a drapery. Perfect, he thought, it is all falling into place.

Chapter III
A voyage

Nylana gently brushed the brown leaves from the sarcophagus in the gentle light of the morning sun. The carved image of a beautiful woman decorated the top. Blue roses grew around the tomb. Their brilliant colors never dimmed from the changing weather. Not for five hundred years. Fallen leaves caressed the ground as an icy breeze warned of a change that was to come. Nylana admired the marble that made up the tomb. Undimmed by the passage of time, it shone brightly even in the twilight.

As was her custom, Nylana stood by the sarcophagus staring at it. No one understood her habit. The servants passed by silently, leaving the Lady Nylana alone. It was not their place to question. Some just shook their heads silently, figuring that their beloved lady was coming to terms with death's nature. Others thought that perhaps she fantasized about the queen of old.

Her cloak flapped around her, but Nylana felt nothing. Always romanticizing about the past, she felt at home here. No one understood. Nylana felt a connection between her and the woman entombed here; a bond that spanned beyond the reaches of time and space. She had memorized the words inscribed in stone to the point where she recalled them easily.

"I thought I would find you here."

Pulled from her reverie, Nylana turned and faced the palace wizard. "Petra," she said with a small smile. "You always know where to find me."

"Since the day you took your first steps, you have been coming here to seek solitude," Petra said.

"It is peaceful here."

"Tombs usually are."

Nylana sighed. "I feel as though I know her. Amborese, the peasant girl who became a queen."

"She may have had humble beginnings, but her heart was noble. She possessed the qualities of a leader. Something that many who come from rich surroundings lack," said the wizard.

"Surely, you do not suggest—"

"I do not speak of you, my lady. You have always given of yourself without any expectation of something in return. You have sought neither power, nor glory. But I fear that if you do not leave the safety of the shadows that something will change these lands forever."

"Petra," said Nylana, "My brother may have a strong desire to be king, but I stand by him. He is a good man."

"The council meets in a few months' time."

"I do not wish to be queen."

"And yet you fulfill the duties of one so well. I know about your planned trip to Pras'quel," said Petra.

"As I've said," repeated Nylana, "I've no desire for the throne."

"Neither did Amborese," replied Petra.

"Things were different then."

"Were they?"

"What do you suppose those words mean," asked Nylana, changing the subject.

Sighing, Petra allowed the change. "It is said that the wizard Zolo put them there. In fact, he stood right where you stand now."

"How would you," Nylana cut herself off.

"In the days before Queen Amborese's death, I had been named the palace wizard. Zolo disappeared soon after leaving this inscription. Some believe that it is a prophecy."

"And what do you believe?" asked Nylana.

"I have learned not to take the markings of old wizards lightly. Zolo was a wizard who knew much and said little."

"'When danger comes from within the sorceress will return,'" Nylana read aloud, "'Trust the woman with the rose; trust the man with the sword.' What sword?"

"The sword of Tesnayr."

"But it has been lost for centuries."

"True, but it could turn up. When Amborese found the sword it had been missing for over a thousand years."

"Meow."

Nylana and Petra looked up at the cat sitting quietly in the tree above them. It swung its tale back and forth in exasperation at going unnoticed for so long.

"Why do you keep that cat?" asked Petra.

"Magi has been with me since I was a child. I enjoy her company," replied Nylana. "Sometimes I feel as though she wants to tell me something."

"Twenty-five years is a long time for a cat to live. And yet, this one hasn't aged."

The cat jumped from the tree onto the tomb before landing softly on the cobblestone ground. As the feline padded towards them, a single rose fell from the vine and landed before Nylana's feet. Awed, she picked it up. "I do not believe a rose has ever fallen from this bush," she said.

The wizard stared at it rubbing his beard. A clouded expression covered his face. "That is because none ever has." The wind rustled through the trees swirling the leaves around them before falling silent. "The season is changing."

Nylana chuckled. "It always does at this time of year." She handed the rose to Petra.

The wizard folded it in her palm. "Keep it," he said, "It came to you."

"As you wish. Come, Magi." Nylana left the wizard alone with the cat close behind.

Petra stroked his white beard in meditation. He had never believed the prophecy on the tomb. Yet, certain things fell into place. Only once had he known a cat to be so loyal. That was five centuries ago.

"I guess as a wizard, I should have known better," he murmured to himself.

The cry of a great bird filled the air. Petra glanced at the tree next to him in time to see the brilliantly colored phoenix take to the air.

"The season is changing," he whispered to the world.

"When you can carry these buckets of water to the topmost part of the city and not tire, then you are ready to handle the sword," said Narúl.

Artryl wobbled under the weight of the water buckets that Narúl had placed on his shoulders. He did not complain as he ran off almost stumbling in an effort to keep the water from sloshing.

"Aren't you being a little hard on him?" asked Nylana as she approached.

"No more than I was with you," replied Narúl.

"I think you were harsher with me."

"Of course I was. You are a princess and a woman."

"And that makes all the difference?"

"As a lady of the court much will be asked of you," said Narúl, "And women are more able to carry heavy burdens."

"Men are weak?"

"Surprisingly so."

"Narúl, I leave tomorrow for Pras'quel. You will be staying here."

"My place is with you," protested Narúl.

Nylana struggled inwardly with the command she was giving her most faithful bodyguard. She always looked to Narúl for strength and guidance. And he was a friend.

"You must stay here. I have been instructed to go alone to Pras'quel without you. There will be other members of the court to accompany me, but my brother feels that to take a bodyguard might send the wrong message."

"I do not like this. As a member of the royal family you are allowed an armed escort."

"Pras'quel has promised to provide one. I do not like this any more than you, but we must have that treaty signed."

Nylana released an exasperated sigh. Soft fur brushed her ankle as a tannish-brown cat walked by chirruping. "Hello, Magi," Nylana greeted the cat.

It arched its back and purred even more loudly.

"Why do you dote on that cat?"

"Because she is special. And sometimes I think she knows things and listens to every word you say."

"It's just a cat. Unimportant at most," said Narúl.

On hearing Narúl's statement, the cat whacked him twice with her tail. Each smack stung slightly, but the man never flinched.

"I think she understands more than we know," said Nylana. "Narúl, I need you to stay here and look after things. Take care of Artryl. Besides, if anything happens I know you will come for me."

Narúl took a long, curved dagger from his belt and handed it to Nylana. "In case trouble arises," he said as she took it.

In that moment unspoken words of affection passed between them. Each knew how dear they were to the other. Nylana walked away to pack for her voyage.

Long ago when she was only four, Nylana had saved his life. From that moment on Narúl had vowed to serve as her protector. He loved her as though she were his own daughter. An ominous feeling rose within him as he suddenly felt that he would never see her again.

*   *   *

"My lady," said the captain of the ship as Nylana boarded. "My cabin has been made ready for your use."

"Thank you, captain," said Nylana. "Are you ready to leave?"

"We can leave now."

Nylana stepped aboard the ship taking a moment to become familiar with its rocking motion. She never did like sailing.

"Hoist the anchor," ordered the captain. "Ready the sails."

"Heading, captain?" asked a sailor.

"North," replied the captain.

Instantly, the metal chain ground against the wood as it was raised. The ship lurched. Wind filled the sails pushing the great boat forward in the direction the helmsman steered.

Nylana relished the wind in her face. Its crispness woke her senses. She admired the work of the men.

"Something wrong, my lady?" asked the captain with a note of concern.

"It's nothing," replied Nylana, "I just miss home already."

"You'll be back before you know it. This voyage isn't long. In two months' time you will be back in Norlyk."

"You're right. Thank you, captain."

"For now, enjoy the voyage and the freedom of the sea."

*   *   *

The cloaked figure stood in the shadows away from the torchlight. He kept his hood up covering his features.

"You're late," said a harsh voice. The barbaric man emanated a menacing presence. The spikes around his wrists spelled danger for any who angered him.

"Stahl," said the cloaked figure.

"What do you want?" asked Stahl.

"The king's sister travels to Pras'quel. I want your men to ensure that she does not return."

"And how am I to do that?"

"The king of Pras'quel has no love for women. He has no love for anyone," replied the shadowy figure, "Journeys are troublesome affairs. Sometimes, accidents happen."

"I tire of these games," said Stahl, "And how does this help my general?"

"Without his sister Krispyn will be weak. She is the real power behind his rule."

Stahl paced the ground. He hated this. Another request before his master achieved what he wanted. "You promised my general the whole of Tesnayr. What is this madness?"

The cloaked figure shot his arm out catching Stahl by the throat. "He will have what he wants so long as you do not test me."

Stahl gurgled as he was choked. The man released him. "Pras'quel you say."

"See to it she does not return."

"It will be done as you wish," said Stahl.

*   *   *

Nylana stood on the bow of the ship as it plowed through the open water. She closed her eyes soaking up what little warmth the sun had to offer on the cold morning. Droplets of water sprinkled her face as the ship bounced upon the waves and the wind whipped her royal robes around her. She'd never before been away from Norlyk as long as this. The past three weeks upon the water seemed like a life time to her.

Nylana gazed at the blue water. White crests of the waves indicated a strong current carried the ship. So empty. So vast. Nylana preferred her home, but she could see why a man would choose to spend a life at sea. It felt liberating.

A bird's cry caught her attention. Shielding her eyes from the sun, Nylana looked up. A bit far from land for a bird, she thought.

The bird flew high above the ship keeping pace with it. It seemed familiar to Nylana. It cried again. She knew she had seen it before. A strange feeling swept over her as she remembered the stories of old. Shaking her head, Nylana looked out at the open water once more. *Ridiculous.*

"My lady," said the captain, "We shall land at the port soon." He, too, looked at the strange bird. "An omen. That bird has followed this ship since we left Norlyk. For good or ill—I shall have one of my men shoot it."

"No," said Nylana. "Please don't. I do not think that the bird means any harm. We have had a gentle voyage."

"Birds never fly this far from land or for so long. Never before have I seen such a thing. I have carried your family on this ship for many years and not once did such a bird accompany us. This is your first time at sea?"

"Yes," said Nylana.

"Strange."

"Captain, what is so strange about it?"

"It almost seems as if that creature is following you. Pardon me, my lady." The captain left to tend his ship.

It hit her. She had seen that bird before. Since the day her brother had been crowned king, a bird landed upon the balcony of her chamber. This bird was no ordinary bird. It feathers shone brightly in the sun, in colors she had never before seen. It always stared at her. Studying her. She had seen it each day since.

"I shall ask the wizard about it upon my return," she promised herself.

Chapter IV
Pras'quel

Land approached.   Excitement filled Nylana as she stood on the topmost deck observing the men work while they steered the ship into port.

"Reef the sails," ordered the captain.   "Secure the lines!"

Men darted about rolling up the mainsail and hoisting lines. Nylana watched in awe finding the sailors' actions fascinating. Gradually, the ship turned to the right as it eased into the dock.

"Drop the port anchor!"

The men released the anchor chain dropping the anchor to the sandy bottom and hold the ship.

"Here," the captain tossed a line to a passing sailor, "Secure us to the dock."

The man caught the rope and scrambled to the pier fastening it tightly.

"Fetch the princess' belongings," ordered the captain.   He turned to Nylana with a broad smile.   "My lady, welcome to Pras'quel."

The captain led Nylana to the ramp that connected to the pier.   Gracefully, she stepped onto it maintaining her balance as best she could.   Willing her sea legs to grow accustomed to dry land, Nylana strolled down the wharf to a waiting area.

An elegant carriage pulled up stopping directly in front of her. The door opened.   Out stepped a man finely dressed in shimmering black robes bowing low before her.

"Lady Nylana, I am Welton, advisor to the king.   The king apologizes for not welcoming you personally, but alas, he had matters to attend.   Will you allow me to accompany you?"

"Thank you, Welton. Your company will be most appreciated," Nylana replied.

Welton flicked his hand. Instantly, two men snatched up her trunks and hoisted them onto the top of the carriage.

The snap of a whip caught Nylana's attention. She turned in its direction and watched as a group of ragged men in chains were shoved forward. Slaves, she thought. The whip cracked again. One man bore its wrath and crumpled in pain. Disgusted, Nylana bit her tongue to remain silent. Alone and on a mission, she could ill afford to anger anyone.

"Is something wrong, my lady?' Welton held the door to the carriage for her.

"Just the awe of a new place," said Nylana, trying her best to sound joyful. She motioned for those that accompanied her to fall in behind the carriage.

"Before you leave here, it will be as much your home as it is mine."

Welton helped Nylana into the carriage and climbed in behind. They sat opposite each other. With a snap of the reins, the carriage ambled away from the pier and to the road out of the port city heading for the castle.

The coach rocked side to side as it rolled along the bumpy road. Nylana passed the time by staring out the window. Much of the landscape reminded her of home, but without the magic; the flowers held no song and the trees glared at her.

Another whip startled her. They had come upon a group of people travelling by foot. *More slaves.* Nylana did her best to remain impassive as they passed groups of men, women, and children all chained together and forced to march barefoot. Hatred rose within her.

The wet eyes of a child stared hollowly at her. Moved, Nylana swallowed the lump in her throat forcing herself to control her emotions. One in particular drew her attention.

"That one," blurted Nylana, unable to contain herself, "He is an elf!"

Welton glanced out the window. "By Jove, you are right. He is an elf."

"I was not aware that elves lived in Pras'quel."

"They don't," said Welton, "But occasionally one thinks he can venture here. Vile creatures the lot of them. Always using their magic to influence people. Apparently, this one got caught. A life of servitude will benefit him."

"The elves are our allies in Tesnayr," said Nylana.

"My apologies, my lady. I forgot that they lived there and that you had to deal with such a disdainful race daily."

Nylana squeezed her hands until they turned white. She fought the urge to kick the man and knock his condescending tone out of him.

"Does such treatment bother you?" Welton asked, his face turning to concern.

Nylana eyed the man. Welton appeared genuinely troubled that what she witnessed on the road might have upset her sensibilities. No doubt he was to make certain I arrived in prime condition, she thought to herself. Not wanting to cause a diplomatic blunder, she decided to bury her feelings.

"It seems senseless to walk your slaves to their destination. They might die before they get there," Nylana said.

Welton beamed. "I like how your mind works. I shall bring this matter to the king."

Nylana smiled stoically at him still wrestling with the urge to kick him.

Late in the evening they pulled into the castle grounds. The long journey had tired Nylana and she looked forward to a hot meal and a warm bed that did not bounce with the motions of the sea. The carriage rolled through the open gate and into the courtyard in the waning light of the sun.

"We are here," said Welton. He opened the door and held his hand out for her.

Gracefully, Nylana took it allowing him to assist her as she stepped out of the carriage. She studied the black walls of the castle with specks of gold light in the window as a wave of homesickness wafted over her.

"Boy!"

A young lad of about ten years ran up to Welton.

"Take the princess to her chambers." Welton turned to Nylana. "I hope you will enjoy your stay with us, my lady."

"I wish to meet with your king as soon as possible."

"Indeed, my lady, but he is busy and unable to meet with you today. Tomorrow shall be soon enough. But you and your party are free to wander as you please. Think of this place as a home away from home."

"Thank you, sir." Nylana followed the young boy as he led her through the castle entrance and into a long corridor. The guards and maid whom had accompanied her trailed behind. They wound their way through the maze of dimly lit hallways. Nylana marveled at how the boy kept his bearings as she had already gotten confused.

"Here," said the boy, pointing to a door.

Nylana entered with her entourage. The dreary room did little to lift her spirits. It had been elegantly decorated, but the sparse light gave it a depressing atmosphere.

"There will be nothing else, thank you," Nylana dismissed the boy.

She removed her cloak and gloves with a frown not liking the situation. Not only had the king not greeted her, but now she had been shut away in a room and brushed aside.

*   *   *

Narúl gently untangled the book from Artryl's limp fingers as he admired the sleeping boy. Thirteen years old and so eager, he thought. In the weeks that Nylana had been gone, Narúl taught the boy how to read marveling at his ability to learn quickly.

Gingerly, Narúl tucked a blanket around Artryl. In the morning he would start his lessons. Narúl had managed to convince the drill master of the palace guard to allow Artryl to join.

Clacking heels on the stone courtyard outside pulled Narúl from his thoughts. He doused the lamp as he opened his door a crack. Krispyn hurried through the darkness being careful to avoid detection. *What is the king up to?*

Curious, Narúl slipped through the door and followed. He kept to the darkest shadows walking noiselessly with all the skill of his training. Though he knew the king could do as he pleased, Narúl thought it strange that Krispyn would be out at this hour without a guard. He peeked around a corner.

He watched as Krispyn ducked behind a wagon out of sight of the guards at the gate. Once past, he darted through the gates and into the city streets. Narúl started to follow.

"MEOW!"

Nylana's cat jumped off the rafters above Narúl, onto his shoulders before leaping to the ground and running away. Startled, Narúl lost sight of Krispyn. "Stupid cat."

Knowing he would never find the man, Narúl walked back to his quarters. Though he knew that it wasn't unusual for members of the royal family to sneak into the city without their escort, he thought Krispyn's actions strange. Krispyn had never shown any interest in the people before. Shrugging his shoulders, he chalked it up to being Nylana's influence winning out.

Narúl reentered his small room. One quick glance and a soft snore told him that Artryl still slept peacefully. Tired, Narúl sat in a chair and drifted off.

*   *   *

Bored, Nylana wandered through the garden at the castle. Dead plants greeted her everywhere. Frustration coursed through her veins. For days she had requested to see the king;

each request unheeded. All of her inquiries remained unanswered.

She strolled through the dismal orchard wondering where the gardener was. Dried flowers and rotting trees filled the area. She listened for the birds, but heard nothing; not even a cricket. Uneasiness welled within her.

Fed up, Nylana turned to march straight for the king's chambers running straight into Welton.

"My lady," he said in false greeting, "What a pleasure to see you."

"I found myself in need of some air," answered Nylana, masking her surprise at seeing Welton.

"Yes, well, I must insist that you stay inside."

"It was my understanding that I had free run of the castle."

"You do," said Welton, "But there is unrest in the kingdom and some fool might take a chance on your life. For your own protection, I must insist. I'm sure you understand."

"When will I be allowed to meet with the king?" asked Nylana, "The sooner we can conclude our business the sooner I can be on my way."

"Soon, my lady. But the king has found himself immersed in other unfortunate business. Believe me, your concerns are his top priority. Now, I must insist that you remain inside."

Welton waved his hand and two palace guards appeared. "Escort the princess back to her chambers. Ensure she arrives there safely."

Nylana smiled sweetly. "I understand completely. Thank you for your consideration." She allowed the men to take her back to what had now become her prison.

*   *   *

Narúl crept through the hall of the castle to the secluded area that the note had asked him to come. *Meet me at the west tower by nine.* Puzzled as to why someone would want to meet him there, he made certain to be on time.

Torches lit the way. No matter; Narúl knew his way through the palace of Norlyk well. He paused when he reached the meeting area. No one was there.

Disappointed, Narúl searched the area for signs that anyone had been there. *Could I be late?* He stood in a corner waiting for the mysterious note writer to show up. Nothing. Frustrated, Narúl prepared to leave when a voice stopped him.

"You're early."

"I prefer punctuality," said Narúl. "Why did you ask me here?"

"Because Nylana is in trouble and needs your help."

"How do you know this?"

"I know a lot of things," said the voice, "There isn't time to waste. Something lurks within the lands of Tesnayr and wishes to be rid of your lady. You must go to her in Pras'quel and see to it that she returns safely."

"I do not like taking secrets from some mysterious voice. Step into the light."

Slowly, a shadowy shape appeared in the torchlight. It sat on its haunches wrapping its tail around itself.

"Magi," said Narúl, recognizing Nylana's cat "Is this a joke?"

"Hardly," answered Magi. "Yes, I talk and have for some time. Explanations are best saved for later. There is a boat headed to Pras'quel soon. You must be on it."

"Do you know who is behind this plot to harm Nylana?"

"No, but someone in this palace wishes her dead. Now go."

"How do I know I can trust you?"

"Have I ever given you reason not to?" asked Magi.

"I will go as you ask," said Narúl, "But if you have lied to me, I will be back for your head."

"Fair enough," said Magi. The cat scurried away.

Narúl hurried down the stairs leading out of the tower. He made a quick stop in his room. Throwing a few necessary items in a bag, he dashed out the door and headed for the docks.

Narúl found the first available ship for Pras'quel and bartered passage. The captain of the ship agreed to let him work in exchange for his way across and he would have to sleep with the animals. Narúl didn't care. Only Nylana mattered. Narúl stepped on the plank before catching sight of a familiar shape.

"What are you doing here?" he demanded of Artryl.

Hesitantly, the boy stepped out of hiding. "I followed you."

"Go back to the castle."

"If Nylana is in trouble, I want to help."

"How did you—" Realizing that Artryl had managed to overhear his conversation with Magi dawned on him. Clearly, the boy was skilled at trailing others unnoticed. "Go back."

"But I can help," pleaded Artryl.

"You there!" A man rushed toward Narúl. "Take the boy back to the palace and see that he stays there."

The man grasped Artryl by the shoulder and steered him away from the docks. Disappointed, the boy allowed himself to be pulled away.

Shaking his head, Narúl boarded the ship hoping he wasn't too late to help Nylana.

Chapter V
The King of Pras'quel

Nylana paced her room furiously. More than a week had passed and still no audience with the king. She hated these games.

A rap at the door drew her attention. Hurriedly, Nylana opened it. Welton stood before her. "Well?"

"I am sorry, my lady, but the king is indisposed. He cannot meet with you today," said Welton.

"There is always some excuse. I have been here for eleven days. When will I meet with your king?"

"I'm sorry—"

"Sorry? You are always sorry," stormed Nylana, "First he was meeting with the lords of his council. Two days ago he left the palace. What is his excuse this time?"

"He has matters of state that are more pressing."

"I tire of this." Nylana marched into the corridor shoving Welton out of her way. With all of her spare time, she had learned the maze of hallways well and knew the way to the throne room.

"My lady, please," pleaded Welton as he chased her. "You cannot—"

"Oh, but I can. And I will," said Nylana, "It has become clear to me that you are merely here to waste my time."

Swiftly, she moved through the corridor with its few torches providing the only light, her skirts rustling behind her. She wound her way around corners and through open areas.

Finally, the door to the king's courtroom appeared. A lone guard stood there. Nylana marched up to him determined not to be turned away.

"Let me pass," she demanded.

"No one goes before the king without his authorization," said the guard. "Especially not a woman."

Nylana pushed the guard aside; the amount of force she used caught him by surprise. She heaved open the giant wooden doors and marched into the king's hall. Everyone within the room jumped to their feet. Murmurs filled the air and spread rapidly upon her intrusion. Holding her head high, Nylana strode down the aisle toward the king.

"What means this interruption?" demanded the king.

"I demand to speak with you," said Nylana.

"Have you no courtesy?" said the king.

"I am the Lady Nylana from Tesnayr on an envoy to meet with you. For eleven days you have kept me waiting. My inquiries have been left unanswered," said Nylana.

"The servants were instructed to meet your every wish."

"They followed their instructions well for they treated me with the same civility as their king." Nylana's words echoed around the room.

The king's face turned red at such insults, but he dared not lose his temper. Nylana was a representative from another country and custom had to be upheld. "Leave us." he told those within the chamber. "You are here, no doubt, because of the grain."

"For months you have withheld your grain from the lands of Tesnayr. We have sent you the livestock as agreed. Yet, you failed to keep your end of the bargain."

The king smiled at her. "I am changing the agreement. I demand that your king send us more of your livestock as well as a certain metal that you seem to have in abundance. I want five hundred crates of that iron, as you call it, and then you will have your grain."

"Unacceptable," said Nylana. "My people need that grain."

"Perhaps you should have the wizards in your land conjure it up," mocked the king. "My people did away with such riffraff long ago."

"You will get no iron from us."

"Then perhaps you should go home and tell your king to send someone better able to negotiate. That is, if he is still the king. A weak land you have, subjecting your kings to the whim of a council." The king's face coiled into a sneer.

"At least our kings are honorable. It is better than exalting a man who fails to keep his word," snapped Nylana.

The king shot to his feet. "You are free with your tongue. Women in my kingdom know their place. I'll not be talked to in such a manner."

"Indeed, your majesty," said Nylana, "I know the state of your people. I know that their farms have failed. Made barren by the early frost. Your people are starving. You need the harvests we provide. How long do you think your people will go hungry before they rebel? My people may need grain, but we can get it elsewhere.

"Perhaps we shall cancel our relations. I will go to a land with a more reputable king." Nylana inclined her head slightly and turned to leave.

"Wait! Perhaps some agreement can be met. You will get the grain that was promised," said the king.

"We shall agree in writing."

"In writing!"

Nylana waived one of her aides forward. He unfolded two pieces of parchment, with the contract she had drawn up, before the king.

"Apparently, verbal agreements are not binding enough. We will both sign and seal a written contract. I took the liberty of having one drawn up. What you see before you are two copies of the same pact. You will keep one here and I will take the other with me. As I understand it, you must abide by anything you sign and seal or your crown is forfeit."

The king glared at Nylana. He hated this woman who talked down to him. He wished he could make her a servant in the kitchens. There he would teach her some respect. His wish remained unspoken. The king snatched up a quill and dipped it in ink. Reluctantly, he signed both contracts and pressed his seal next to his signature.

Nylana's aide rolled up both pieces of parchment handing one to the king and the other to her. "I thank you. Good day, your highness," she said.

"My lady," the king said through gritted teeth.

Nylana left the king's court quickly making her way back to her rooms. She summoned one of her aides. "Take this," she said handing him the signed parchment, "Travel as a commoner and barter passage on a ship. Make your way straight to Norlyk and give this to King Krispyn. Make certain you are not seen leaving the palace or followed."

The aide bowed and left clutching the contract tightly.

"Emri," Nylana continued, "Pack our things. We leave tonight."

The maid bowed and set about her task.

"Sergeant." The well-armed man ran up to her, saluting. "Find us some horses, a carriage, anything so that we may leave hastily. We will leave by the side gate. And make certain you are not seen."

The sergeant darted off.

"What is it, my lady?" asked the maid.

"I believe we have overstayed our welcome," replied Nylana.

Chapter VI
From Princess to Slave

Stealthily, Nylana and her party moved through the castle carefully avoiding armed guards. Their light steps barely echoed on the ragged stone floor. Her skirts rustled as Nylana swept through the maze with her companions.

The sergeant stopped them. Peering around a corner, she noticed a man standing guard in one of the parlors. Cursing silently, Nylana knew they hadn't time to turn back. The sergeant tapped the point of his sword against the wall. The guard turned around. Curious, he stepped toward them. Quickly, the sergeant slammed the hilt of his sword into the man's head rendering him unconscious.

"Come on," he said.

Wasting no time, Nylana and her party hurried past into another corridor that led to the outside. They scurried through the hallway past paintings and tables. At last, cool air greeted them as they reached the exit.

The carriage awaited them as Nylana and her maid climbed inside. The sergeant shut the door and jumped into the driver's seat. The reins cracked as he whipped them and the horses sped off. Only their hooves and the wheels of the carriage penetrated the night's silence as they charged through the open gates.

The coach raced down the open road bouncing and jolting violently as it sped away in their desperate attempt to escape. Nylana held tightly to the sides of the interior to maintain her balance. Her maid's frightened expression prompted her to say something.

"We'll be alright. We'll make the boat."

Nylana had spoken too soon. Suddenly, the carriage screeched to a halt propelling her forward. Nylana bumped her head on the side of the coach as it skidded.

The door ripped open. "My lady, you need to leave!" The sergeant yanked her from the carriage. "Now, my lady!"

Whirling around, Nylana noticed a tree lying in the middle of the road. Ominous cries rose around her as men in tattered clothes burst from behind the trees.

"Run, my lady!"

Screams filled her ears as her maid was grabbed and thrust to the ground. The sergeant pulled out his sword blocking an attack.

Nylana ran. She darted into the forest delving deep inside. Hoisting her skirts, she ran as fast as she could over the uneven ground. Her breaths came in ragged gasps from the exertion. Crunching footsteps alerted her to her pursuers. A twig snagged her dress. Desperately, Nylana yanked it free ignoring the loud rip.

Aimlessly, she ran. She hoped her pursuers would eventually tire of the chase. Deep down, Nylana knew that she was the prize they were after. Her feet pounded the mushy earth as she fled.

Twigs snapped all around her. An arrow crashed in a tree next to her. Glancing at it for a second, Nylana noticed men approaching from the side. She veered to her left and then made a sharp turn to the right. Her movements bought her time, but did little to shake her attackers.

A great weight crashed into her. Nylana gasped loudly as the air was knocked from her lungs. She squirmed violently to get away, kicking and screaming. Leaves and brush flew everywhere from her desperate movements. Strong hands grabbed her arms wrenching them behind her back. Rope cut into her flesh as it was roughly wound around her wrists.

A moment of dizziness struck Nylana as a man hauled her to her feet.

"Let me go," she screamed.

"Why would I do that?" said a sneering voice. A tattooed man stepped into the moonlight. Nylana hated him immediately.

"Do you know who I am?" spat Nylana. "Men will be looking for me."

"I don't think so, princess," said the tattooed man. "The men on your ship met with an unfortunate demise. In fact, your ship is little more than ashes."

Nylana gaped at him in shock. She could not believe what she heard. "But surely the king—"

"The king has no liking for you and you did little to endear yourself to him. No, princess, I have been paid well to get rid of you, but I don't see why I can't make a little extra profit on the side." The man waved his hand. Instantly, someone shoved a gag in Nylana's mouth and carried her away.

They dragged her back to the carriage and the wreckage that remained there. Her maid's body lay in a crumpled heap on the ground. Another wagon stood nearby. Her captors shoved her into the dark interior. Before the door shut, Nylana glimpsed the body of the sergeant with a gaping wound in his chest. The sight of his hollow, sightless eyes forever seared into her mind.

The cold, rusty steel of the shackles cut deeply into her wrists. Nylana stood tall and proud despite the humiliation the guards attempted to impose on her and the other captives who were being auctioned off in the town square. Her fellow prisoners stared at the ground or their feet, afraid of inadvertently challenging their captors. The chain jerked and Nylana stepped forward to keep from being pulled over.

"100 gold coins. 100 gold coins," called the auctioneer. "Do I hear 200?"

"150," said a voice in the gathered crowd.

Disappointed the auctioneer continued his gambit in an attempt to garner more money. He ended up settling for 175 gold coins for the scrawny, old man that stood on the podium.

"Sold," he yelled.

A guard hauled the man away.

Her turn. Nylana found herself being pushed to the podium. The burly men put her roughly on the platform. Instead of hunching like the others, Nylana stood straight backed, squaring her shoulders, her chin level as she stared defiantly at the crowd. She challenged the prospective buyers to look her in the eyes. A stern expression steeled her face.

"100 gold coins for the lovely lady," the auctioneer began. "Look at her strong muscles and her curves. A beautiful specimen. Perfect for housework or more."

As though to emphasize his point, the auctioneer tore a sleeve off her dress and ripped her skirt to show off her legs and toned arms. Nylana whacked him on the head with her chains. The crowd roared with laughter. The auctioneer almost returned the favor but stopped at the last minute. A bruised slave brought less profit than an unmarked one.

"She has spirit," he said, joining in the laughter. "Perfect for you men out there."

"100 gold coins," said one bidder.

"200."

"250!"

"500!"

"850!"

"1,000 gold coins!"

The auctioneer nearly fainted. Clearly he was going to make a lot of money off of this one. "1,000 gold coins! 1,000 gold coins! Don't be shy. Any more bids?"

Before he could stop the bidding a deep, gruff voice cut into the excitement. "4,000 gold coins."

Nylana faced the newcomer. Richly dressed, the man commanded obedience. A long moustache snaked past his chin. "4,000 gold coins," he said again.

The auctioneer controlled his surprise. He glanced around to see if any would challenge the bid, but no one moved. "Sold," he called.

The guards snatched Nylana's arms. She shook their grasping hands off and proceeded to walk where the others who had been sold stood. Her erect posture announced that she was no slave. She went because she willed it. Her statement did not go unnoticed by the man who had just purchased her.

Within moments Nylana was thrust into a carriage. It meandered through the crowded city streets until it pulled up to a grand estate. Stone pillars lined the entrance. Perfectly trimmed topiaries dotted the driveway. Nylana eyed them callously as she passed them. She wondered if anyone would come for her.

With a lurch the carriage stopped. The door opened and once again rough hands yanked her pulling her into the harsh sunlight. Nylana tried to shake them off. She received a sore cheek for her efforts.

"Here she is," said the man holding her.

A servant rushed outside. He handed the man a bag of coins. The servant took Nylana's arm and led her inside the manor.

"Unhand me," spat Nylana.

"SHHH," said the servant. "Best keep your mouth shut, or we will both be punished."

"But I am no slave."

"Whatever you were before is gone," warned the servant, "This is your life now."

The servant steered her up marble steps and into a well-lit chamber where the man who purchased her waited. "The slave you bought from the market, my lord."

Nylana stood before the man that had purchased her. "My name is Lord Gorganof. You will be a slave in my household, especially to my wife. I try to treat my slaves fairly. Obey the house rules, do your tasks, and you can live a fairly comfortable life here. If not, you will be disciplined accordingly. Is that understood?"

"I am no one's slave," Nylana said, coldly.

Lord Gorganof arched an eyebrow at her tone of voice. Most slaves that came to him were overjoyed at the prospect of working and living in fine conditions. He treated his slaves better than most of his compatriots. Though they never lived in luxury, they usually had a hot meal and warm bed. But Gorganof was also a hard man. He did not tolerate disobedience and this woman openly challenged his authority. He would not risk such an act to encourage the others in his household.

"You are my slave," Lord Gorganof said. "And you will learn to call me master and my wife mistress. Take—."

"Lady Nylana." Nylana filled her name in for Lord Gorganof giving special emphasis to the word lady.

Lord Gorganof scrutinized her. The name seemed familiar but he shrugged it off. He cupped his hand around her chin digging his fingers into her delicate skin. She never flinched from the pain he caused her. "My, my," he said, "You do think highly of yourself. You will soon learn your place."

Lord Gorganof thrust her across the room. Nylana crashed into a vase breaking it into three pieces. She bit her tongue to hold back a moan.

"No meal for her," Lord Gorganof commanded the other servants. "Take her to the mistress of the house."

He exited the room while the overseers hauled Nylana to her feet. Help me, she thought to herself, somebody help me.

*   *   *

Artryl plopped an empty bag on his bunk. He shoved a shirt in there. Hastily, he pulled out a box of candies and went to place it in his bag. The shirt was gone. Dismissing it as his imagination, he shoved the box in the bag and reached for a canteen of water. When he turned back around the box had gone.

Artryl scratched his head and put the canteen in the bag. He darted to a chest and pulled out a cloak. Upon his return, he found Magi tugging at the canteen.

"Will you stop?" he yelled at the cat. In response, Magi pushed the entire bag off of the bunk.

"Hey!"

"Leave it," said Magi, stopping Artryl as he reached for his bag.

"You talk!"

"Genius," scoffed Magi. "Where do you think you're going?"

"There is a ship departing for Pras'quel in an hour. I was going to—"

"Follow Narúl? That is an excellent way to get skinned."

"I'm going anyway." Artryl reached for his bag, but Magi hopped on top of it and hissed at him. "Hey!"

"You're not going anywhere."

"But—"

"Narúl can find Nylana more easily without your help. Take my advice and stay put. Do well in your lessons and await Narúl's return." Magi darted off. "And don't even think about sneaking away. I'm watching you."

Disappointed, Artryl slumped on his bed with his arms crossed. He reached for his bag, but found it gone. *Darn cat.*

*   *   *

Lady Gorganof admired herself in her three full length mirrors as she twirled in front of them listening to her crisp dress whoosh with each spin. Though not an ugly woman, she possessed no divine beauty and had always been sensitive about her plumpness. She smiled as she fiddled with an extravagant necklace that covered her bare neck. Lady Gorganof loved her jewels and never let anyone touch them.

Nylana watched in disgust as Lady Gorganof stared vainly into the mirrors. Never in her life had she seen such a narcissistic woman. Even raised in the palace with multitudes of servants, she had never been so selfish, nor did Nylana ever treat the palace servants as slaves. They were free people who worked there because they wanted to. Sighing, she set down the silk pillow that she held in her hands.

"My perfume, Carla," said Lady Gorganof.

A timid woman, Carla scooped up a purple bottle and brought it over.

"Now, girl," yelled Lady Gorganof.

The outburst startled the young woman and she dropped the open bottle of perfume spilling it on Lady Gorganof's back.

Smack!

Lady Gorganof backhanded Carla knocking her to the carpeted floor. She cupped the red welt that formed struggling to hide the tears from the sting that gripped her cheek. Nylana watched the scene in horror. She had witnessed it before in the weeks she had been there, but such actions always sickened her.

"Stupid girl," said Lady Gorganof.

Carla cowered on the floor backing away from the wrath of her mistress. Lady Gorganof towered over her. She kicked her foot out bringing it hard into Carla's stomach. The girl's gasp filled the room. Once again Lady Gorganof brought her fist down upon Carla, but it stopped in mid strike.

Nylana held the lady's wrist in a vice like grip. She felt the tendons squish between her fingers. A deadly expression covered her features as she glared at Lady Gorganof. "Do not do that again," she said firmly.

Astonished, Lady Gorganof just stared at her new slave. She tried to pull her hand away, but to no avail. Fearful of having her wrist broken, Lady Gorganof relented in her struggle. "You will pay for this," she threatened.

Nylana's expression never relented. She held the lady's gaze. "Do what you will to me," she whispered just loud enough for all in the room to hear, "But touch that girl again and I swear on my dead brother's life that I will kill you."

"Not if you are dead."

Lady Gorganof's words failed to frighten Nylana and she felt idiotic soon after saying them. At that moment all Nylana had to do was squeeze and her wrist would snap. But that wasn't what scared her. The expression on Nylana's face unsettled her. It made Lady Gorganof shiver as Nylana's slight smile told her that this woman feared nothing and would fulfill her vow one way or another.

Without another word, Nylana released Lady Gorganof's wrist. The woman shrunk backward afraid of being caught by her again.

"Guards," called Lady Gorganof.

Two armed guards appeared immediately.

"Take her to the pit," she said pointing at Nylana.

The guards reached out to seize Nylana's arms. She dodged their grip, swung around, and flung one of the guards across the room. Everyone stood still; stunned by the display. The second guard pulled back his hand waiting for her to make the next move. Proudly, Nylana walked out the door allowing the remaining guard to lead her to her fate.

Lady Gorganof watched Nylana leave. That girl is dangerous, she thought. But she would enjoy breaking her.

*   *   *

Narúl hunched over the deck of the ship on his hands and knees as he scrubbed it clean. His raw hands stung each time he dipped the brush in the bucket of water. Ignoring his sore knees, he worked furiously to ensure that he earned his way across the ocean.

A favorable wind filled the sails giving Narúl the hope that they would reach Pras'quel within a few weeks. He hoped they made it in time for him to find Nylana.

"If all of the men worked the way you do I'd be out of a job," said the overseer as he observed the freshly cleaned deck.

"We wouldn't want that would we," said Narúl.

"You should take a break. You've been at this all morning."

"I will be finished soon enough," said Narúl as he continued scrubbing.

"As you wish." The overseer walked away to check on the rest of the crew.

Narúl momentarily paused wiping the sweat from his face as he looked out at the endless horizon of the sea. "I am coming for you, Nylana. Remain strong."

*   *   *

The pit was a two hundred foot deep hole in the ground on the outer edges of the Gorganof's manor. Sludge and garbage filled it. Any unfortunate enough to be tossed in there had no chance of climbing out. Only a platform lowered by rope served as an escape.

Cold and hungry, Nylana hunkered in the pit hugging her knees in an effort to keep warm. She scraped some garbage around her to form a blanket. Wrinkling her nose, Nylana tried to ignore the odor. The cold won out.

Rain pelted her. As the droplets formed on her skin, whatever warmth she had left. Nylana shifted as she sat in the oozing mud surround by waste. She just wanted to go home.

Laughter greeted her from above. Guards and servants routinely strolled by the pit to taunt the latest victim. Now they taunted her by throwing insults and bits of rotten fruit. A moldy tomato smacked her on the cheek filling her mouth with a foul taste.

Bastards, thought Nylana.

She wondered how long she had been stuck in this nightmare. By now her brother must have known she was missing. *We were paid to ensure that you never returned.* The words of the tattooed man echoed in Nylana's mind. Who wanted her out of the way and why? The jeering of the guards dissipated as they continued about their duties.

Nylana piled more garbage around her.   Despite its grotesqueness, it was her only salvation at the moment. Braving the slime and the smell, she nestled in it hoping that her time in the pit would soon be at an end.

Chapter VII
Missing

"My lord," said a messenger as he walked briskly into the throne room toward Krispyn. "The ship has not returned. There is no sign of Lady Nylana. The King of Pras'quel refuses any inquiry."

"How can this be?" demanded Krispyn. "Where is she? She was supposed to have returned by now."

"No one knows, sir," replied the messenger, "It is well-known that slavers attack carriages and kidnap those in them. Her carriage was found abandoned. Everyone was dead but her."

"I want her found."

"My lord, the chances of her being alive is very slim. Slaves do not live long in Pras'quel. And the chances of finding her are equally slim. Your sister is gone. I am sorry."

Krispyn squeezed the quill in his hand so tight that it snapped in half. "I promised her it would be a quick errand. That she would be home before she knew it. Now because of me she is likely dead."

"I am sorry, my lord. We all mourn for your loss. But she did manage to get the treaty signed. Another messenger arrived with this." The man handed Krispyn a folded piece of parchment. He took it, read it, and placed it on the table. "Small comfort," he muttered.

"Pardon?"

"Nothing. I shall have to make the dismal announcement soon. Make sure all the arrangements are made."

"Yes, my lord." The messenger turned and left.

Silently, a tannish-brown cat trailed behind.

*   *   *

Artryl parried his weapon attacking the mounted dummy profusely. He struck it clunking the wooden stake that held the dummy. Practicing every move that Narúl had taught him, Artryl marveled at how his muscles began to instinctively follow his movements.

"Artryl!" One of the other boys ran up to him. "What are you doing out here?"

"Practicing," answered Artryl as though it should have been obvious.

"Haven't you heard?" asked the boy.

Artryl stopped his practice session and stared at the other boy. "Heard what?"

"The princess' ship has gone missing."

"What? What does the king plan to do?"

The boy shrugged his shoulders. "Nothing I suppose. He has not issued any orders. Anyway, all studies have been suspended in memoriam of the princess. You should get back to the barracks before the sergeant notices you are missing."

The boy ran off. Artryl stood poised with his wooden sword hanging in midair. Princess Nylana missing, he thought to himself, and Narúl is searching for her alone.

*   *   *

Petra somberly looked out the frosted window at the city streets below as a throng of people slowly moved on past. They sang a melancholy dirge as they carried their candles. He choked back a tickle in the back of his throat before he allowed himself to weep.

A portrait of Nylana when she was only nine hung in the room. Staring at it, Petra allowed himself to remember a time when he pretended to pull a coin from her ear. He chuckled as he remembered her laughter. *So much pain for one small child.*

A note appeared by his hand. Cautiously, Petra opened it and read it.

Find the book with the phoenix. Libraries are a good place to start.

Petra furrowed his brow. *What nonsense*. He crumpled the note and started to toss it away, but stopped. Glancing at it again, he decided it best to keep it.

"I guess I have some business in the library," he muttered to himself.

Chapter VIII
Pursuit

Narúl sat at a table in an outdoor café sipping his drink as he watched the crowd. They disgusted him. The voice of the auctioneer selling new slaves to rich nobles droned in his ears.

"Sold!"

If he could get away with it, Narúl would burn the place to the ground, but he had a more important mission. At least two months had passed since he had set out to find Nylana; half of that time spent on a ship.

Narúl tapped his foot impatiently on the ground. *Where is he?* The man he had arranged to meet with was late. Narúl hated tardiness.

A group of giggling girls sauntered past. They pointed and stared at him with interest. No doubt they had never seen a man with such dark skin, or so heavily armed. He checked the placement of each of his weapons making certain that only his sword was visible, and even then not by much.

Something plopped on the table beside him. Instantly, Narúl snatched it up, tossed a coin on the counter for his drink, and left. Carefully, he opened the folded piece of paper. A symbol for the auctioneer was on it.

Narúl tossed the paper in a nearby fire before trotting over to where the sale of slaves took place. He feigned interest in the frightened woman standing on the plank.

"Nice day for a purchase," said a man.

Narúl glanced at him.

"Eyes forward," hissed the man. "I hear that you are looking for a particular slave."

"She isn't a slave."

"Here she is.   Not that it matters.   Foreign girl, beautiful, proud, dark hair. Does that meet your description?"

"Yes," whispered Narúl.

"200 coins," shouted a woman next to them in response to the auctioneer's babbling.

"There was someone matching that description about two months ago.   Definitely not from around here," said the mysterious man.

"Name?"

"Don't have one.   You have to realize that these slave auctions are always very crowded, frequented by almost the whole of Pras'quel. But I do know that the man who bought her paid 4,000 gold coins."

The thought of Nylana being bought like a common animal infuriated Narúl. He kept his temper in check. Losing it now would not aid his search for her.

"But at that amount, it means that only one of Pras'quel's richest and most influential could have bought her."

"Do you have a list of who those people are?"

"It numbers to nearly a hundred and no one knows who they all are."

Narúl clenched his fists. Everywhere he went either people had no idea what he referred to, or were too frightened to talk. He figured it was a bit of both. "Is there anything that you can give me?"

"It is rumored that the man who bought her lives on a manor just outside the city. But there are at least twenty of those and she may not be there anyway. Most of our nobles have four or five homes spread throughout the land. They travel to all of them throughout the year and take their servants with them; especially the more prized ones. Your lady falls into that category."

"Thank you."

"Here is a map of the country. I've marked where the main estates are around here, but I am afraid I do not know all of them. Good Luck." The man departed quickly disappearing in the crowd.

Narúl noticed soldiers marching past. Not wanting to attract attention, he pulled his cloak up and slipped away. He joined the rear of a group sauntering past before darting around a corner and into the alley beyond.

*   *   *

Nylana darted and swerved through the marketplace with her loaded basket of goods. Finally freed of the pit, it had taken her a few weeks to recover from the ordeal. Now, she was the errand girl. She glanced at the list that the head servant had given to her. Bread.

Quickly, Nylana headed in the direction of the baker. The Gorganofs always wanted fresh bread and they only accepted loaves from one particular baker.

A hand snatched a package from her basket. Instantly, Nylana grabbed it. She and the thief struggled a moment as each yanked on the package trying to get away with their prize. Finally, Nylana kicked the man in the shins forcing him to let go. She stuffed the bundle back into her basket and darted off before he could alert the authorities to a riotous slave. Even common criminals enjoyed more freedom than her.

The baker came into view and Nylana dashed across the muddy street and into the building.

"Well?" said the baker, rudely. After a quick glance at the bracelets on her arm, he knew what Nylana was. *Less than an insect.*

"I need a loaf of your finest bread for my master," she said.

Grunting, the baker walked to his storage bin and pulled out an already wrapped loaf.

"Not that one," said Nylana with an air of authority, "One fresh from your ovens."

"How dare you—"

"My master demands it," interrupted Nylana. "And if you insist on giving me the stale loaf in your hand, then you can tell Mr. Gorganof why his bread tastes like refuse."

"Why you insolent slave," spat the baker.

"I'll not be punished for your indiscretion."

The baker tossed the stale loaf back into the bin. He yanked one out of the oven, wrapped it, and tossed it casually into Nylana's basket. "Two silver coins," he said.

"It will be one coin as before," replied Nylana. She placed the single, silver coin on the counter and left. Just because the Gorganofs were allowed to treat her poorly, she refused to accept the same from others.

After the long walk from the market, Nylana finally reached the path to the manor. She hurried along trying her best to not spill the contents of her basket. Its heavy load made walking difficult.

Voices caught her attention. Nylana glanced over to see what the commotion was. The foreman threw an elderly man to the ground. She heard the sickening gasp as the foreman kicked the other in the stomach.

"You worthless, wretch," spat the foreman. "Sitting on the job! I'll teach you the meaning of hard work." The foreman lashed his whip across the one on the ground. "Get up! Get up, I said!" Another lash.

Nylana seized the salami in her basket and dropped her bundle running straight for the foreman. With one swift strike, she smacked the log of salami into the man's head.

"Stop it," she yelled, "Can't you see that he is barely able to stand? How can you expect him to work if you beat him?"

Nylana smacked the man again with her log of salami catching him off guard and forcing him to take two steps back.

Like a ferocious animal, she repeatedly pounded the foreman with the salami. Guards hurried to her, grasping her arms and yanking her off of her victim.

Slowly, the foreman wiped blood from the side of his head where Nylana had broken the skin. "You will regret this. Take her to the stocks and have her flogged. Maybe then you will learn your place." He backhanded her forcing her head back.

The guards dragged her to a remote area of the grounds filled with wooden stocks and chains. Her heart skipped several beats as the realization of her fate flooded her mind. *What have I done?* She pushed her feet into the soft ground in an effort to avoid her punishment. Mercilessly, the guards pulled harder on her arms nearly ripping her shoulders out of their sockets.

They threw her into the stocks shoving her wrists into chains. The clink of the lock frightened Nylana. She knew what came next. The guards ripped the back of her dress exposing the soft, pale flesh below it. Breathing heavily, Nylana desperately yanked on her bounds in a futile attempt to get free.

Crack!

Nylana screamed in pain as the lash slashed her back creating a long, red stipe stretching from her shoulder to her hip.

Crack!

Another stripe appeared on her back burning into her flesh stinging so immensely that tears welled in her eyes and streamed down her face. Nylana slumped. Another burning sensation hit her as the whip struck for a third time.

The foreman smirked menacingly as he watched her punishment, relishing each strike and each cry of agony. Onlookers gathered to watch the proceedings. Nylana easily told the slaves apart from the others; they turned away while the more richly dressed looked on with glee.

The minutes passed like hours as Nylana bore every strike of the lash. Her back resembled a bloody rag.

Immediately, men ran to her to free her from the chains.

"Leave her," yelled the foreman. "Let her stay there so that her punishment will sink in. Let this be a reminder of what happens to slaves who question their masters." He walked off.

Others trickled away attending to their duties since the entertainment had ended leaving Nylana alone with her agonizing back.

*   *   *

Lord Trisk strolled into the throne room of the palace of Norlyk. He hated being summoned like this, but the king was never easily refused. The gaiety that used to reside there had left the moment news of Nylana's disappearance had reached them.

"You summoned me, my lord," said Lord Trisk.

"Yes," replied Krispyn, "As you are aware, the treasury is depleted. In order to ensure the safety of the five lands, I am asking each of you to pay more in taxes. You have not only paid nothing, but have been most vocal in your refusal."

"No more than the other lords," said Lord Trisk.

"True, but you are here now."

"And why is it you have not summoned the other Lords?"

"I did," replied Krispyn, "But they have refused my summons. Only you have done the courtesy of coming here."

"And it would be best if you remember that. It is a courtesy. I'll not give you any more in taxes. This is the third time in three months that you have raised them. My people have little enough as it is."

"And how shall I protect the five lands if you all refuse to pay what is owed to the crown?"

"Your sister would never have—"

"My sister is dead," interrupted Krispyn, "It is time we accept that. I know that I was never your first choice for king, but I am all you've got."

"And what of the rumors about an army that moves through these lands unchecked? Unhindered? Have you bothered to investigate them?" demanded Lord Trisk.

"They are merely rumors," said Krispyn.

"Are they?" challenged Lord Trisk. "I have sent my men into the mountains of Belyndril. The charred ruins that are left indicate more than mere hearsay."

"Then I shall look into it," said Krispyn.

Lord Trisk eyed the king warily. "See to it that you do. And until this is dealt with, there will be no more funds from Belyndril. A treaty once governed these lands, but you seem to have forgotten all about it."

Lord Trisk swept out of the room leaving Krispyn alone in his anger.

"Why do they challenge me?" he asked himself.

*　　　　　*　　　　　*

Nylana leaned over the bar she was chained to barely able to hold her head up. Her bare back burned from the bloodied stripes across it. Not even the damp cold could numb the pain. Drizzling rain sprinkled her skin in an attempt to wash away the oozing blood. Nylana tried to ignore it. It hurt too deeply. The proud lady of Tesnayr had nothing left but the chains that held her. She wept inwardly; her tears ran dry as she wondered if she'd ever be free again.

Mud swallowed her knees as she sank further into the muck unable to stand. Her soaked and tangled hair fell limply around her face as she prayed for release. A sharp sting cut into her flesh as the lash struck her again. A guard leered over her. Despite the fact the she had already received her punishment; he felt she needed a little more. He wrenched her head back. Nylana's half closed eyes barely focused on him. The guard rammed his knee into her stomach before marching away.

People hurried past her without a glance or a word. If they felt pity they kept it to themselves. The lord of the manor had left her in the square as a warning to others. Nylana never heard their feet as they splashed through the mud quickly so as to not be forced to notice her.

A bird landed nearby. It was the phoenix. Peering up, Nylana stared at it.

"Why have you abandoned me?" Nylana whispered.

"Sometimes you have to fall so that you can rise," said the phoenix.

Nylana dropped her hear disappointed by its answer.

The bird flew away.

A gentle hand touched her forehead. Nylana couldn't even moan. "Drink this," said a soft voice as a cup was put to her lips. Nylana attempted to, but most of the liquid dribbled down her chin.

"You there! What do you think you're doing," yelled a harsh voice.

The woman dropped the cup and darted off leaving Nylana alone in the rain with her pain.

*   *   *

Darkness engulfed the manor of the Gorganofs as Narúl slipped over the high wall. One of the other nobles had informed him that the Gorganofs had a woman matching Nylana's description. He hugged the wall as a guard walked past. Quickly, he seized the man pinning him against the stone wall.

"Where is Lord Gorganof's chamber?" demanded Narúl.

"Up there," pointed the frightened guard.

Narúl knocked him unconscious and hid him behind some bushes. An ivory lattice stretched up to the window that led to Lord Gorganof's room. Quickly, Narúl climbed onto the trellis in the still night allowing the shadows to conceal him.

Once at the top, Narúl leaped onto the balcony and forced the doors open. He hurried inside where he waited. Voices sounded beyond the door to the corridor. It opened and in walked a man too finely dressed to be a servant.

Narúl burst from his place of hiding and snatched the man twisting him around until he had backed him against a dresser. Swiftly, Narúl clamped his hand over the man's mouth while placing a dagger at his throat.

"You have a slave that belongs to me," hissed Narúl, "Where is she?"

"I'll tell you nothing," spat the man.

"Tell me, or I'll cut you from ear to ear."

"Go right ahead," said the man, "You'll be doing me a favor."

Something was wrong. Narúl sensed it. Hands clasped him on the shoulders. In a short scuffle, two guards wrenched the weapon from Narúl and clapped him in irons.

Lord Gorganof stepped out of the shadows with a smug expression. "Did you think that I was unaware of your arrival?" He glanced at the man that Narúl had mistaken for him. "I had one of my servants dress as me when I first heard about a man who searched for one of my slaves. I don't know who you are or where you come from and I don't care. But sneaking into my house in the dead of night and trying to kill me—well that I do have a problem with. Take him away."

Narúl resisted the guards' restraints. A solid blow to the head caused him to go limp. Lord Gorganof watched coldly as his men dragged Narúl away and to the prison.

*   *   *

Petra rummaged through the books in the library, the light of the candle flickering with his movements. He had spent the last several weeks searching through the library looking for what the note had told him to find. Nothing. There were references to a journal of sorts with the emblem of the phoenix: Amborese's journal.

"Oh beautiful mead how I love you. You're all fizzy and bubbly in my tummy."

The strange singing distracted Petra's attention as it bounced off the walls. He thought he was alone. Carefully, Petra walked to the door and opened it slightly. No sign of anyone in the hallway.

The singing continued. Petra followed the tune to the end of the corridor where a few barrels of mead sat. On them lay an orange tabby cat with a mug of ale. The cat belched.

"Was that you singing?" asked Petra.

"It certainly wasn't the drink," said the cat. "Now be a good man and fill up my cup." The cat pushed the mug to the wizard.

"You are a talking cat."

"Whatever gave you that idea? I wasn't always a cat though," said the feline, "Once I was a boy. A human boy. Woke up one day to find myself changed into a cat. Never did figure out how it happened. Anyway, I ran away from home scared, fell into a vat of mead, and developed a liking for it since. Never do seem to get intoxicated though."

"Are you familiar with the books in the library?" asked Petra.

"I know where they are if that's what you mean."

"I am looking for a specific book. It has the emblem of the phoenix on it."

"I know that book." The cat's eyes lit up. "The king was in the library a few days ago looking for the same book. He never noticed me watching, but I remember where he put it."

"Will you get it for me?" asked Petra.

"I don't work for free."

"A barrel of ale awaits you if you do—"

"Tabs is the name," said the cat. "Well, I've changed my mind. Make it two barrels."

The cat hopped off the barrel he sat on and trotted to the library with Petra right behind him. Tabs jumped on some shelves. He hunkered down, positioned himself just right before leaping to another set of shelves. Upward, he went in a crisscross, his claws scraping on the wood with each landing. Once on the topmost shelf of the room, Tabs rifled through the books.

"Here it is," he called.

The cat grabbed it in his mouth and dropped it into Petra's open hands. With a few good leaps, he jumped from shelf to shelf until he reached the floor.

Cradling the book like a prized possession, Petra hurried to a table with a lamp. He opened it, being careful with the crinkled and discolored pages. Quickly, he scanned the entries looking for one in particular.

"You might try the end of the book," suggested Tabs. "That was where Krispyn spent most of his time."

Petra flipped to the last pages of the book. One entry stood out among the rest.

The sun is setting while I write this. My physician tells me that I should not be out of bed, but there is one thing I must do. My joints ache with the cold and illness nearly prevents me writing this last entry. Seventy years I have lived and I know that I haven't much time left. I shall die before the month ends.

But before I go, the sword that I have carried and has been my companion for so long must be hidden. I cannot pass it on. Such is the nature of owning the sword of Tesnayr. Just like he hid it over a thousand years ago, so too must I. Galin has vowed to assist me in this venture. It shall be in a place none will ever consider. And there it will stay until the sword chooses its third owner. I hope that when the time comes, he will be able to bear the burden handed him. Just as the sword chose me, it shall choose another when the lands of Tesnayr have most need of it. I pray that person has the strength to carry it.

I must go now. The light is fading and I tire easily these days. I leave Tesnayr a better place. I pray it continues. Now, I must say farewell. These are the last words of Amborese.

Creaking hinges kept him from reading further. Hurriedly, Petra blew out the lamp, closed the book, and hid behind some shelves. He watched as Krispyn stole into the library. Petra's brow furrowed at the king's stealthy movements. Krispyn went to where Tabs had gotten the book. He pulled a ladder over and hurried up it.

A series of curses escaped his mouth when he discovered the book missing. Petra glanced at the journal momentarily. Krispyn quickly descended the ladder and moved it back to where he had gotten it. He did a quick scan of the room before leaving.

"Now why does he want this book?" Petra asked himself. "Tabs, how do you feel about retiring to my chambers? It might be a safer place to examine the book further."

"Is there food and drink?"

"More than you can handle."

"Then I am your servant."

Petra headed to the door.

"Not that way," hissed Tabs. "I know a better way."

The cat scurried to a small opening barely big enough for Petra to squeeze through. The wizard followed the feline through the secret passage; his mind mulling on Krispyn's actions.

*   *   *

Days later Nylana awoke on her stomach in a soft bed, softer than she had been in in a long time. Her eyes fluttered open. Carla leaned over her placing a damp cloth on her wounds. Nylana shifted each time the cloth touched her sending shots of pain through her.

"I know it hurts," soothed Carla. "Just lie still." She placed another cool rag on Nylana's back. "Some of us have been talking about what you said earlier. Perhaps we can do something to end this."

"End what?"

"Our plight. Our lives as slaves. People were not meant to live like this and there are more slaves than there are nobles in Pras'quel. There must be something we can do."

"An uprising?" Nylana groaned as another cloth was placed on her back.

"Perhaps."

"No," said Nylana with finality, "Too much bloodshed. You were right before. There is nothing we can do except just accept this."

"You don't mean that," said Carla.

"Yes, I do," mumbled Nylana.

Chapter IX
Freed

The chains holding Narúl clanked with each movement he made as the guards brought him before the judge. He stood erect, his mouth clenched shut.

"Name?" said the judge.

Narúl said nothing.

"Very well," the judge continued in a drawn voice, "You have been charged with theft and the intent to harm one of our most respected men. How do you plead?"

Still, Narúl remained silent. He surveyed his surroundings noting where the guards stood and the exits.

The judge eyed Narúl for a moment. "You are hereby pronounced guilty and will be executed in the morning. Take him away."

Two guards clasped Narúl's arms and led him out of the courtroom.

"Next!" called the judge behind them.

Once in the hallway and away from the others, Narúl made his move. He wrapped the chain around one of the guard's neck choking him. Instantly, he swung the man around ramming him into the other guard. Narúl dropped the first man. He quickly snatched the sword from the other while bringing his elbow to the man's neck. Making certain the two guards had been subdued; Narúl took the keys and undid his chains.

He sped down the corridor and past the cells; his feet barely making a sound on the stone floor.

"Please," a prisoner's voice stopped Narúl. "Please, do not leave me here to rot like the others."

Narúl studied the man a moment before tossing him the keys.

"Thank you," said the man. "Hey! I know why you are here. There is a witch that lives east of here. Follow the main road. It will take you straight there. She can tell you what you need to know."

"Why are you telling me this?" asked Narúl.

"Let's just say, I no longer owe you one. But be careful to not insult her."

Narúl nodded at the man in gratitude before darting off. He snatched a cloak from the wall, wrapped it around himself, and bolted out the door where he mingled with the crowd and disappeared.

*   *   *

Nylana handled the tray of food with care as she carried it from the kitchen to the dining hall. Expertly, she steered her way through the mess of servants scurrying about to keep up with the guests' needs. The aromas of fine food tickled her nose causing her stomach to grumble; another reminder that she had not eaten since breakfast. Even that was a meager meal.

Though tempted to snitch a bit of the juicy, roast beef, Nylana contained herself. She knew what would become of her if she gave in to her impulse. Somehow, Mr. Gorganof always knew when a servant snitched from his plate of food.

Nylana placed the tray on the table between two disgustingly fat guests. Their fine clothes did little to mask their ugliness as each heaped a pile of the beef onto their gold plates. Nylana ignored their grotesqueness.

The clinking of a glass caught her attention. A guest was thirsty. Docilely, Nylana grabbed a pitcher of water and took the woman's glass. She filled it to the brim and carefully placed it back on the table. Any messes were automatically considered her fault.

"I must commend you, Gorganof, on how you manage to control your servants," said one man.

"It isn't that hard," replied Mr. Gorganof, "All one needs is a firm hand." He snatched Nylana's arm pulling her to him and nearly causing her to trip and fall. "Take her, for example. A feisty one when I bought her."

Nylana stared at the floor with her head bowed.

"Now she is as tame as any kitten," continued Mr. Gorganof. "She just needed a little discipline. The rod is a very effective tool in taming any slave."

"Some might disagree with you," said a man. "Kellig treats his slaves very differently. He feeds them well, gives them luxuries that most commoners do not get, so long as they earn them."

"I hear that he even gives his slaves a holiday every week," chimed a woman.

"Kellig is a fool," said Mr. Gorganof. "He spoils his servants and one day they will rise against him using his charity against him."

Nylana listened intently to the conversation. *So not all of them are scum.*

"My home in the country has need of a few slaves," said one of the grotesquely fat men. "I'd love to have that one." He pointed at Nylana. "I will pay you well for the privilege."

Mr. Gorganof stroked his chin. "That could be arranged. How many slaves will you need?"

"Three or four women."

Mr. Gorganof released Nylana's arm pushing her away. She darted out of the dining hall unnoticed. The conversation troubled her. She had a bad feeling about what Mr. Gorganof would decide.

*   *   *

Narúl moved briskly through the forest. His boots landed softly on the trail making no sound as he walked. The trail had grown cold and Narúl feared that if he did not find something soon, he would never find Nylana.

He strolled through the trees following the directions a peddler had given him. Somewhere near here the old lady's hut should be. Finally, he saw it. A small, one room hut lay just ahead nestled in a thick growth of trees and brush.

Carefully, Narúl approached, wary of a trap. He ducked behind a bush. For several minutes he watched the lone shack for any signs that he had been set up. No movement. Just smoke billowing form the chimney.

Narúl walked up to the door and knocked.

"Coming," said a crackly voice. The door creaked as it was pulled open. An old, wrinkled face peered out at him. "May I help you?"

"Are you the old lady of the woods?" asked Narúl.

"Well I'm old and I live here in the woods," replied the woman.

Narúl cleared his throat. "Some villagers told me that you know about a foreign woman sold as a slave a while back. I have a great need to find her."

The woman opened her door allowing Narúl to step inside. Its warmth nearly choked him as did the aroma of whatever she had cooking in the fire. She motioned for him to sit. He picked a pin cushion off of a rickety chair before settling himself down.

"Why do you wish to find her?" asked the woman.

"It is urgent," he said.

"They all say that."

"Please, it is imperative that I find this woman."

"Do you have something of hers?"

Narúl thought for a moment. He pulled a white handkerchief from his pocket as he remembered the day that Nylana had saved his life. Her father had just ordered his execution, but Nylana had thrown herself upon him. At only four years of age, she had demonstrated immense courage. Later that same day, she had used the same handkerchief to wipe the blood from his wounds. Narúl had kept it ever since.

"This," he said handing the cloth to the old woman.

The woman took it. She handled it a bit, sniffed it, and then put it to her forehead. Narúl watched with a doubtful expression. "She was sold to the Gorganofs," said the woman, "But isn't there now. Instead she is being sent to the home of another with other young ladies of her age. They travel the road through the forest not far from here. Head southeast. But you must hurry, or you will miss her."

Narúl took back the handkerchief. "Thank you."

He tossed a few coins into the woman's outstretched hand and left. Southeast, he thought to himself. He broke out in a run hoping that he would reach his destination and Nylana before anything else happened.

The old woman watched Narúl from the window. Slowly, she transformed into Quesha. "This was a nice home while it lasted."

A bird chirped beside her. Quesha looked over and smiled at the phoenix that had appeared on the windowsill. "I never asked you for your approval," said Quesha.

The phoenix cawed at her before flying away.

"I wonder who will find her first," muttered Quesha to herself.

*   *   *

The wagon rocked side to side as it rolled slowly down the uneven road. Nylana remained secluded in her corner ignoring everything. A part of her felt dead. She no longer cared much if she lived or died. Death would be more welcomed than a lifetime of slavery. The Princess of Tesnayr no longer existed.

Nylana stared blankly out the small opening in the side not registering the scenery that passed by. The trees were in full bloom. At one time she would have marveled at their beauty. But the sight did not delight her anymore. She shifted slightly to ease the cramp forming in her back. Absent mindedly, she reached back to touch the stripes on her back. The scabs had peeled away long ago, but with each one she knew that her will to fight had gone.

"Why do you not smile anymore?" Carla sat across from her with a couple other girls.

Nylana ignored the question. She had no desire to talk.

"Nylana," continued Carla, "What has happened to you? What have they taken from you? Why do you not fight anymore?"

"There is nothing left to fight for," replied Nylana, weakly.

"But you once said—"

"I was wrong!" Nylana swallowed back a lump in her throat. She suddenly regretted her outburst when Carla's face looked downcast. "Carla, we are slaves. That is all we'll ever be now. I thought once that a person could be free so long as he had the will to fight back, but I was wrong. I am tired of fighting."

"But you told me that you are only enslaved if your mind thinks you are enslaved," said Carla.

"Do you honestly believe that?"

"Yes, and you should too."

"Shh," said one of the other girls. "If they heard you talking like that, we'll all be punished."

"Carla, I know I said things in the past, but I was wrong," said Nylana.

"What have they taken from you, Nylana?"

"My spirit."

The wagon pitched and swayed as it continued onward. Nylana allowed it to lull her into a doze. She hoped the journey would end soon.

The wagon stopped. It lurched as the driver and his guard jumped down. Nylana looked around curiously. She, like the others, wondered why they had stopped. They hadn't reached the manor yet. Light spilled into the coach as the door was yanked open.

"Out. Now," ordered the driver. "I said get out!" He grabbed Carla by the arm and pulled her roughly out of the coach. The others followed in fear.

They lined up outside eyeing the men suspiciously. Other men stood nearby looking at them greedily. A sinking feeling filled Nylana. She did not like the look in their eyes.

"Here they are. Pay up," said the driver.

"Are you sure the master won't be angry about this?" asked the guard.

"He won't if he doesn't find out," said the driver. "No marks. Got it?"

"Got it," said one of the men. He reached for Carla and tossed a bag of coins to the driver. Carla tried to pull away but the man held on tighter. He hauled her away and behind the wagon. She screamed as the man threw her to the ground.

"I mean it about no marks!" yelled the driver.

Nylana listened to Carla scream as she fought the man who straddled her. The deadness inside of her faded away and was replaced by a low rage that rumbled and boiled within her. It started small, just a pin prick. With each passing second, her anger grew. A small amount of her began to care once more.

Ignoring the others around her, Nylana strode over to where Carla lay pinned. She seized the man by the collar and yanked him off of the woman throwing him against a tree. Carla stared at her a moment. Everyone gaped at her in disbelief.

The driver marched over to her raising his hand. Nylana's face stung as his fist struck her in the jaw. Gravel buried itself into her hands as she slammed into the rough ground spitting out blood. The cry of a bird distracted her. Nylana looked up in time to see it fly away. Her will to escape hit her with such a force that she decided now was the time.

Nylana noticed a branch. She snatched it and rammed it into the driver as her lunged for her. Nylana jumped to her feet and raced for the tree covered hill determined to be free one way or another.

"Run, Nylana! Run!" yelled Carla as Nylana disappeared.

Early morning dew still covered the ground as Galdin cleaned his face in the stream allowing the cold water to wash the sleep away. He dipped his hands back into the clear water and splashed more on his face.

Movement caught his eye. Grasping his sword, Galdin turned. A strange bird sat on a bush beside him. Its gold feathers shone brilliantly despite the sunless sky.

"Hello, there," said Galdin.

The bird cocked its head to one side as though it had understood.

"My name is Galdin."

The bird moved its head as if to say *I know who you are.*

Galdin began to feel as though this strange bird was studying him. He slowly got to his feet. Galdin and the bird stared at each other for several minutes before it jumped into the air causing the bush to shake violently. Now Galdin heard the voices. He tied his sword around his waist as he crept through the bushes and peered over the edge of the hill.

Five men surrounded four female slaves. One woman lay on the ground. One of the men lay unmoving as well. The others looked at the single woman standing alone after throwing a man into the trunk of a tree. Even Galdin couldn't believe it. One of the men marched up to her smacking her across the jaw sending her flying.

The woman gasped for air. She stretched her hand across the ground until she touched a fallen tree branch. She snatched it and smashed it into the man's head. Freed, the woman ran for the hills.

"After her," yelled one of the men as three followed her.

"Run, Nylana! Run!"

Breathing hard, the woman desperately clawed her way to the top of the hill. She tripped over her dress and stumbled.

"Do not let her escape!"

Frantically, she ran up the hill and sought shelter behind some bushes. A strange man met her. She stared at him. His hand grasped his sword. With regal eloquence, the woman stood straight and tall willing to accept her fate. "Kill me then. And get it over with," she said.

Galdin had no time to admire the woman's bravery. Three of the slave traders burst over the crest of the hill. Galdin knocked the woman down and blocked and attack by one of the men. He kicked another in the face. The first man charged again. Galdin sidestepped with ease. He cut off the head of the third man before plunging his sword into the second.

The first one charged again. Galdin braced for it. The attack never came as the man stopped suddenly and fell to the ground with an arrow sticking out of his back. Thirty yards away, stood a tall and beautiful woman with a bow. She quickly fired upon the remaining two traders on the bottom of the hill, catching them both in the neck. Her silver hair danced in the breeze.

Galdin walked over to the woman. She stared at him, expecting to meet the same end as the others. Slowly, he extended his hand to her. "I mean you no harm," he said. "My name is Galdin."

"Nylana."

Galdin helped her to her feet wrapping his cloak around her disheveled clothes. "Come. My camp is this way."

"The others," Nylana said remembering the wagon and where it headed, "We need to save them." She started to run off when a female voice stopped her.

"It's too late," said the new woman melting away from the trees. The pointed ears told Nylana that she was an elf. Her recognition did not go unnoticed by the new arrival. "The wagon is gone and so are its passengers."

"We can't just leave them to their fate," protested Nylana.

"You are safe," said Galdin, "You should be thankful for that." He steered her in the opposite direction toward his camp.

Smoldering coals rested in the ground with two packs nearby. Galdin motioned for Nylana to sit. Gladly, she placed herself near the coals and the little warmth they provided.

"You'd never know that spring was on the way," said the elf. "This damp chill is enough to depress anyone."

"Nylana, meet Trya," said Galdin introducing the two.

"Nylana? Named after the princess I'm sure," said Trya. Her eyes darted back and forth between Nylana and Galdin.

Nylana remained silent as she fidgeted under the elf's gaze. It was true that when she had been born and named, many mothers in the kingdom named their daughters Nylana in honor of the new princess. Nylana was happy to allow them to think that this was the case with her. *Do not tell them*. No one must know that she was the princess.

"Here," said Trya tossing her some garments, "These should fit you. You don't look like you weigh much."

Nylana took the bundle of clothing watching every move her two rescuers made.

"Galdin," said Trya, "Go fetch some firewood."

"We'll be leaving shortly," replied Galdin.

"I highly doubt that she wishes to change in your presence so make yourself scarce."

Grunting, Galdin disappeared into the trees. Nylana stared after him.

"I can assure you he is not watching," said Trya.

Nylana stood up and removed her disgusting dress. It was the same dress she had been captured in, though it didn't look it. Fingering the faint emblem on the gown, Nylana sadly tossed it aside.

Nylana glanced over at the elf as she changed from her rags and into more suitable clothing, using the belt to hold her tunic down. She had lost an incredible amount of weight during her months as a slave. She quickly yanked the sleeve over the birthmark on her wrist covering it; an act that did not go unnoticed by Trya's watchful gaze.

"So what possessed you to travel here from Tesnayr?" asked Trya.

"How—"

"I noticed your recognition of my race," replied Trya, "And no other land names its daughters Nylana."

"I was traveling on business," said Nylana. That much was true; she just wouldn't mention what kind of business. "While on my way back to the port city I was captured by slavers and sold at auction."

"Little surprise there," commented the elf. "Pras'quel has need of slaves and does not care where they come from or how they are obtained. What business brought you to Pras'quel?"

"Trade," replied Nylana.

"Don't find many female merchants," said the elf fingering Nylana's discarded garment, noting the faint emblem on the material. Trya tossed the dress onto the coals. It quickly caught fire, burning bright. She rose to her feet and whistled loudly. Immediately, Galdin trooped out of the trees.

"The wagon is long gone," he said, "There is little chance of catching them. We should make our way to the port and get out of here."

"That is at least a two week journey," said Trya. "You got the payment?"

"Yes."

Nylana listened to the exchange. Payment? Mercenaries, thought Nylana.

"Here," said Galdin handing Nylana a pack.

"Carry your own pack," scolded Trya, "She needs to get some meat on those bones before she can carry anything."

Galdin hefted his pack onto his shoulders. Together he and Trya walked off into the forest and toward the road leaving Nylana with little choice but to follow.

Chapter X
Through Pras'quel

The arduous trek through the woods strained Nylana's legs as she struggled to keep up. Easily tired and winded she needed constant assistance from either Galdin or Trya. Finally, Trya took both packs while Galdin carried Nylana on his shoulders. Though embarrassed by this, she accepted his help. Her strength had left her.

As darkness fell they stopped for the night building a small fire. "When was the last time you ate?" asked Trya.

"Two days ago," said Nylana.

The elf pursed her lips. She stalked off into the forest alone. In ten minutes she returned with a deer upon her shoulders. Nylana marveled at how quickly the elf had found game when she had seen none the entire day. With expert ease, Trya skinned it slicing off slabs of meat and placing it on the fire.

"Eat," said Trya handing Nylana a large piece of venison.

"I thought elves did not eat meat," said Nylana.

"We don't," replied Trya. "After spending many years with Galdin, I have come to understand that men have need of it and so I learned to hunt."

Nylana took the piece of meat. Gingerly, she broke off bits of the meat shoving them in her mouth. Despite not being seasoned, its juiciness made it taste delectable. Nylana finished it quickly helping herself to another piece of meat.

Trya watched her pleased that she had a hearty appetite. The elf dug through their pack and pulled out some dried fruit. "Here," she said handing it to Nylana, "Eat this as well."

After eating her fill, Nylana stretched out to sleep. She dropped off immediately.

Trya wrapped the remaining pieces of deer meat in leaves and shoved them into the packs. "We should take her with us," she said.

"But we have at least one more job to do," replied Galdin.

"The job can wait. Besides, I do not like our employer."

"But he has already paid us for it."

"I say we take it and leave. Consider it amends for neglecting to pay us last time," said Trya, "Things in Pras'quel are getting worse and I have no desire to stay here. Besides, we should get her home."

"Why do you care about her so much?"

"Why do you not?" Trya stared at Galdin studying every facial feature. She glanced at Nylana committing her features to memory.

"What is it?" asked Galdin.

"You two have the same nose and the same eyes," replied Trya.

"You know I have no siblings," said Galdin.

"None that you know of."

"What are you implying?"

"When I first met you and you told me that your mother had named you after the lost prince, I accepted that. But now a woman stumbles upon us who shares the name as the princess. A bit odd, don't you think?"

"Coincidence only," said Galdin.

"The elves do not believe in coincidence," said Trya.

"And I do not believe in some voice upon the wind. Come along now. It's time we both got some sleep."

Morning dawned crisp and clear. A bit of warmth filled the air; a reminder that spring was on the way. Trya handed everyone a bit of the leftover meat, which they ate while they walked.

The woods seemed unusually quiet that morning. Too quiet. Nylana glanced about her trying to decide if she could trust her two new companions or not. She trailed behind them taking up the rear and marveled at how silently the elf moved.

Trya stopped holding up her hand to signal the others to do the same. Staring straight ahead, the elf listened intently.

Suddenly, a man dropped from the branch of a tree landing directly in front of them. Others dropped from branches as well surrounding them, but staying concealed in the trees. Only their shapes were visible. Instantly, Trya pulled her bow apart revealing two swords holding both at the stranger's throat.

"Don't kill me," shouted the stranger. "Or my men will kill you."

"What do you want?" hissed Galdin.

"Your money. Anything of value that you have. Hand it over and my men will let you go unharmed."

"You mean your puppets," said Trya.

"Puppets? I have no puppets. My men are dangerous cutthroats."

Trya moved one of her knives to a rope strung up above them. She sliced it. A plopping sound filled the area as one of the puppets fell to the ground. Nylana walked over to it. She kicked the stuffed form. A quick inspection told her that Trya had been right. All of the shapes surrounding them were puppets attached to ropes and pulleys.

She walked back to the others and observed the puppets hanging among the trees. From a distance they did appear to be real men. "Ingenious," she commented.

"I thought so," said the stranger, "Now will you let me go?"

Slowly, Trya lowered her weapon. "Your name."

"Ryk the honorable thief. This forest is my home."

"There is nothing honorable about being a thief," said Galdin.

"There is nothing honorable about being a mercenary either," said Nylana.

Galdin glared at her. "So you just hang around in the trees waiting for someone to venture through here and use your puppets to rob them?" he redirected his attention to Ryk.

"Something like that," said Ryk. "It usually works. Though most that come through here are wealthy and too scared to fight back."

"We should go," said Trya, sheathing her long knives and putting her bow back together.

"Let me come with you," said Ryk chasing after them. "I can be your guide."

"And rob us while we sleep," replied Galdin, "No thanks."

"Hey, beautiful," said Ryk, noticing Nylana for the first time.

"Get lost," said Nylana.

"You should stay here with me."

Nylana turned toward Ryk. "What?"

"I am an unmarried man and you are a pretty lady. You should become my wife and together we will rid the forest of wealthy invaders."

Shocked by his forwardness, Nylana gaped at him a moment. She knew that her loss of weight and smudged face did little to help her beauty. Anger filled her as she thought about his words.

Smack!

"What was that for?" demanded Ryk touching the red mark Nylana had given him.

"Get away from me," spat Nylana.

"As long I have breath in my body and legs to walk with I will follow you all your days," said Ryk.

"Not if I cut them off," Galdin said.

Ryk stopped, considering his statement. "Good point. Well, my fair lady, I am afraid I must bid ye farewell." He hopped up the trunk of a tree disappearing in its branches. "But be assured that I will never wash this cheek again."

"Let's move," urged Galdin.

"Where to?" asked Nylana.

"We are headed to the port. Since you are obviously not from around here and an escaped slave you may come with us. After that you are on your own," answered Galdin.

"I need you to take me to Norlyk," said Nylana in an authoritative tone.

Trya looked at her sharply as she spoke.

"Norlyk?" said Galdin.

"I have need to get there," replied Nylana, "I know you are from the lands of Tesnayr. And you know where Norlyk rests."

"I am no one's guide," said Galdin.

"I don't need a guide merely a—"

"I am not your bodyguard either," interrupted Galdin.

"Look, I need your help. As an escaped slave they will be looking for a lone woman, but not for three travelers."

"No."

"I have money."

Galdin whirled around. He studied Nylana and the proud way she stood before him; like one used to having her will obeyed.

"How much?"

"As much as you require."

Galdin huffed. "That is a nice way of saying you have none."

"I am not lying. If you take me to Norlyk you will be well paid."

"Merchants do not make that amount of money."

"My family is wealthy," said Nylana running to keep up with Galdin. "You will get your money. I promise."

"Merchants aren't that wealthy."

"I told you that my family is."

"So all I have is your word that you have money and that I'll be paid. Not good enough."

"When I give my word I keep it," said Nylana, a stern expression covering her face.

"Perhaps we should take her," said Trya breaking her silence. She had patiently observed their exchange studying each of them. "She does not strike me as one who reneges on a promise. Besides we have need to go to Norlyk as well."

"Need?" said Galdin.

"We owe the blacksmith a debt. Or have you forgotten?"

"Very well," relented Galdin. "You will do as I say, when I say. Keep your head down and do not attract attention," he told Nylana, "If we get caught with you we are all dead."

Nylana nodded in agreement.

*   *   *

Narúl knelt on the ground as he studied the dead bodies. He ran his hand over the tracks in the road. *Something is wrong*. Narúl paced the ground taking in every detail of what had occurred. He noticed that the tracks continued down the road. Narúl forged onward hoping that he had made the correct assessment.

*   *   *

The sun rested high in the sky beating over them as they stumbled upon a village. Shouts and screams alerted them to trouble. Quickly, the three hunkered behind some brush and watched the proceedings. Nylana spotted Carla immediately. She jumped up to help. Galdin gripped her arm and yanked her back down motioning her to be silent. He peeked through the branches frowning.

"Come on," he said waving the others away. They made their way back through the trees away from the road and the village.

"Wait," called Nylana, "Where are you going?"

"Away from here," said Galdin.

"We have to help them."

"They are beyond our help. Those slavers have done their job."

"We can't just leave them to their fate," persisted Nylana.

"We cannot help them either," replied Galdin.

"You mean you won't help them," shouted Nylana. "Like any true mercenary you think of yourself."

"I saved you didn't I?"

"Why did you?" asked Nylana. "Why did you rescue me, but do nothing to help those people?"

"What would you have me do? There are three of us and twenty of them."

Nylana marched away heading straight for the village.

"Where are you going?" shouted Galdin.

"To help them. I may be one person, but there must be something I can do."

Trya followed after her.

"And where are you going?" Galdin asked her.

"With her."

Galdin stared after them in disbelief. *Out voted by two women.* Mentally, he scolded himself. He knew Trya had a plan. Grudgingly, he trailed after them hoping that this was not a suicide mission.

"Here," said Trya giving Nylana a sword. "You'll need this. Just swing it at anything that comes near you."

Nylana took the sword thanking the elf.

Trya moved silently on the edges of the chaos. Swiftly, she reached her target, a wagon loaded with barrels of ale. Taking a lit piece of wood, Trya placed it in the center of the wagon just so. Deftly, she jumped into the driver's seat and released the brake. With a push, the wagon rolled down the small incline picking up speed. Trya jumped off of it rolling on the ground and springing back to her feet with ease. The wagon careened through the village center to where the majority of the slavers were. It exploded the moment it reached its target.

Quickly, Trya plunged into the center of the slavers. She pulled her bow apart revealing the two swords. With expert ease, Trya swung her weapons at her quarry slicing and dicing without mercy. She brought the blades together forming a cross to block an attack. With a flick of her wrists she disarmed the man and plunged both blades into his chest.

Trya whirled around just as another attacked. Galdin appeared beside her. Together they distracted the slavers killing any in their way.

Seizing her chance, Nylana dashed to where people stood chained up. "Where are the keys?" she asked them.

They pointed to a man staring at her hungrily. He reached for her wrist. Nylana dodged his grasp and butted him with the hilt of her sword. Cradling his nose, the man glowered at her with hatred.

"If that is how you want it," he spat, pulling out his own weapon.

He lunged. Nylana brought her sword up blocking it before twisting and jamming her heel onto his foot. She whirled away only to spring back with a raised blade. The man parried her attack. Nylana countered with a fist to his already broken nose. Expertly, she ducked, twisted, pointing her sword upward and ramming it into the man. He stared at her in surprise.

"How does a slave—" he died before finishing his thought.

Nylana ripped the keys from his belt. The chained people gathered around her with their wrists outstretched desperate for her to free them. As quickly as she could, Nylana unlocked their shackles.

A blunt blow knocked her to the ground.

"You wretch," said a man with an eye patch. "I'll teach you to free my stock."

Without warning, a great shape slammed into the man knocking him onto the ground. They rolled in the mud before coming up. The new arrival charged butting the other with his head. They wrestled in the mud for several seconds until the man with the eye patch lay still. Nylana didn't believe who her rescuer was. Ryk.

"What are you—" she began.

"Hurry up and free them," Ryk interrupted, finding another set of keys.

Together they unbound the prisoners. As each person lost their chains, they plunged into the riot attacking the slavers with a vengeance. Slowly, the shouts and screams died as the slavers ended up on the ground. Only a few moments of silence passed.

"You brought them here," said a man charging after another that shrank away. "This is your fault." The man raised his fist, which held a knife.

Nylana flung her sword at the man. It stuck into the side of a building next to the man's head. He lowered his knife.

"What goes on here?" demanded Nylana. "Why do you wish to kill this man?"

"He brought those slave traders here. He is the reason they came rounding us up like cattle," spat the man.

Nylana eyed the one huddling against the building. "Is it true?"

"No," he said, "I did not bring them here. They must have been eyeing this place for a while."

Nylana took note of the man's rich clothes. He did not blend in with the villagers. "Put your weapon down," she told the one with the knife.

Reluctantly, he lowered it.

"What is your name?" Nylana demanded of the one in fine clothes.

The man glanced about him. Everyone stared at him. "I'd rather not say."

"Tell me, or I'll let them have you," said Nylana.

"Orrin," said the man, "Son of the king."

"The king's son," whispered one, "What are you doing here?"

"I was traveling through. Look, I did not bring the slavers here. They tried to chain me up as well."

"That's true enough," said Trya, "I watched them do it."

People backed away from her allowing her to move. They knew she was an elf, but were frightened to be seen with her.

"I think he speaks the truth," said Trya. "I watched as he tried to help another only to have chains wrapped around his wrists. These men," she gestured to the dead slave traders, "Do not care about whom they sell in the market."

"Why are you out here alone?" asked Nylana. "The son of the king usually has guards."

"My father insists that his kingdom is happy. He believes that the people live well and love him. But I have heard rumors to the contrary and wished to see the truth for myself. So, I ran away. For a month now I have traveled my father's kingdom in disguise."

"Your clothes give you away," said Nylana.

"Nobility have an easier time travelling through my father's kingdom, more so than peasants."

"They didn't care about your purse when they strung you up," said Galdin. "You should get a horse and get out of here."

"I am not my father," said Orrin.

"Really? Cowering here like a rabbit. Why didn't you tell them who you were? You could have stopped this from ever happening."

"It wouldn't have mattered," said Orrin, "Besides, I am one man. What good could I have possibly done?"

"It didn't stop her from charging in here like a lunatic," said Galdin, referring to Nylana.

"Enough," said Nylana. "Orrin, you should get back to your father before more trouble ensues. The rest of you: why do you cower here waiting to be taken? For years your families are kidnapped and forced into a life of servitude. Yet, you do nothing. Stand up for yourselves. No king has the right to force his people into slavery."

"And who will lead them?" asked Orrin.

"You," replied Nylana. "You claim to not be your father. Well prove it. One day you will be king. Convince your father to undo his harsh laws. If he will not listen, then let the people know that when you are crowned, you will treat them with respect.

"Allow them to live as free men. End slavery and punish the slave traders. End the harsh taxes. As prince of this realm you are endowed with the power to do all these things.

"And all of you: would you not follow a man that did all these things?"

Murmurings spread through the gathered crowd.

"We will gladly follow you," said one meek man in the crowd.

Taken aback, Nylana stared at the crowd who all seemed to be waiting for her to issue orders. "You should follow your prince," she said, "In the meantime, position guards on every entrance to the town. Train a militia so that when the slavers come again you will be better equipped to defend yourselves."

"But who will train us?" asked the same man.

Nylana glanced over the crowd. "Is there any among you who has spent time in the king's army?"

One hand went up.

"Come forward."

The lone man stepped forward with a bloodied axe in his hands.

"What is your name?"

"Lyle," said the man, "I spent five years in the king's service."

"He is a deserter," yelled someone within the crowd.

Nylana's piercing stare silenced him. "Is it true?" she asked Lyle.

"Yes, ma'am," answered the man, "I deserted because I do not agree with the king and his laws. I will not serve a man like that."

"You, Lyle, will train a group of men from this town to fight. You will teach them to be trained soldiers, capable of banding together for the defense of this village."

"Yes, ma'am," said Lyle.

"You are encouraging rebellion," hissed Orrin.

"Maybe a revolution is what these people need," snapped Nylana, "Look around you. Is this how men were meant to live?

If you are not your father, then prove to them that you are different. Prove to them that you are a man worth following.

"Grow a spine.   They need your leadership, not your indecision."

"How dare you," started Orrin.

Nylana punched him.   "That is for being a coward."   She smacked him a second time.   "And that is for doing nothing."

Containing his anger, Orrin ignored the sting of Nylana's fist. "I have never been struck by a slave."

"You still haven't," whispered Nylana as she stalked off.   "We have a long ways to go before we reach the port," she said to Galdin, "We should leave."

Galdin gawked at her.   *Who is she?*   Gradually, he and Trya followed after her.

"Nylana!"   Carla ran up to Nylana embracing her in a hug.   "I thought I'd never see you again."

Nylana hugged her friend back.   "What happened?   I thought all of you were heading to that man's estate."

"The axle broke on the wheel so they came here to get it fixed.   That was when the slavers attacked," replied Carla. "Where are you headed?"

"Home," said Nylana.   "Come with me."

"I can't," said Carla, "I have family north of here.   I wish to find them."

"Take care of yourself."

"Same to you."

The two women parted, each going their separate ways.

"You are gorgeous when you're angry," said Ryk with a twinkle in his eye.

Nylana pushed past him.

"I don't think she likes me," Ryk said.

"What are you doing here?" asked Galdin, annoyed.

"I followed you and good thing I did.   You needed my help."

"Get lost," growled Galdin.

"I am coming with you," countered Ryk. "My days as an honorable thief are at an end since you discovered my secret. So I shall accompany you wherever you go and find a new line of work."

"You mean setting up shop in a different kingdom where your name is not known," said Galdin.

"You think so little of me," said Ryk with mock hurt.

Galdin shoved Ryk out of the way.

"I would keep my distance," warned Trya as she strolled past.

Chapter XI
Questions

Nylana awoke suddenly. Unsure of what had awakened her, she got up. Still dark. Eyeing the sleeping bodies around her, Nylana moved away from the glowing embers of the fire. Carefully, she moved through the forest taking extra care to not make a sound. Her soft footfalls did little to detract from the chirping crickets and musical night bugs.

She touched the knife in her belt for reassurance. A rustling noise startled her. Instantly, Nylana hunkered behind some brush. She peered into the darkness, but could make out nothing.

Clanging metal told her that she and her companions had company. Curiosity got the better of her. She crawled along the forest floor towards it. Stomping feet told her that she was close.

Suddenly, a hand covered her mouth while another grabbed her around the waist yanking her aside and into a thicket. She started to scream, but stopped when she noticed a group of men dressed in furs and metal plow through the very area that she had been moments before.

"SHHH," whispered a male voice. A hand pointed to the group marching past.

"Move it," growled a gigantic man.

Nylana's eyes focused on the man's boots as they lay inches from her.

"Go on you lazy, maggots," growled the man again. He shoved a soldier that moved too slowly for his taste. "Get a move on!" shouted the man. "Vasagius wanted us there weeks ago."

"What is the hold up?" The second voice sounded inhuman.

Nylana looked up. It looked like a black beast with red, glowing eyes that pulled you in. Instantly, her will subsided as her arms and legs went limp. A hand covered her eyes. Just as quickly as she had succumbed she recovered her will and control over her movements.

"Don't look at them," hissed the male voice in her ear.

Nylana stared at the moldy leaves in front of her. *What was that thing?* Rocks crunched beneath the shifting feet in front of her.

"Nothing," said the fur covered man. "We are moving as fast as we can."

"Then I suggest you speed things up," said the creature. "Those boats will not wait forever." The creature stalked off to harass another bunch of men as they marched along.

"Get going, you swine," yelled the muscular man cracking his whip against the flesh of those before him.

Nylana watched, her heart pounding as the barbarian army marched past unaware of her presence. As the army vanished through the trees, the grip around her slackened. Immediately, Nylana whirled on the man placing her dagger by his throat.

The man put his hands up. "If I wanted to harm you, I would have already."

Slowly, Nylana recognized the man: Orrin. "Are you following me?"

"Hardly," answered Orrin, "I am headed in the same direction you are."

Nylana stared at him suspiciously. She jumped to her feet lowering the knife to her side, but maintaining the tight hold upon it. "What do you mean?"

"I need to get back to my father's palace before he notices that I have been gone too long. But lately, the slavers have shown little regard for nobility traveling through here. And they will think nothing of selling the prince into a life of servitude. You witnessed that today."

"So you want a bodyguard."

"I think it would be best if I travel with you," replied Orrin, "Besides, I know these parts and can be of some use."

"Who are those people marching through here?" demanded Nylana.

"I've no idea. Honestly," added Orrin when he saw Nylana's doubtful expression. "For months now these barbarians, as some call them, have moved through Pras'quel unchecked. Their leader paid my father well to garner passage through here. Thus far, they have no interest in this land or its people, but I believe that it is only a matter of time until they do."

"Have they set up camps here?"

"No. They have truly passed through. The eastern edge of Pras'quel is mountainous and borders the sea. They are truly traveling from one ocean to the next. Rumor has it that they are traveling to the lands of Tesnayr."

Nylana's head jerked up at the mention of her home. Thankful for the dark, she busied herself with cleaning her knife hoping that Orrin had not noticed her sudden interest. "Rumors. Who leads them?"

"No one knows. The man who negotiated passage with my father kept his face covered. He refused to let any see him and never gave a name."

"And he allowed this man to move his army through?"

"Gold speaks louder than anything in this kingdom."

"What was that creature," Nylana asked. Just the thought of those red eyes sent chills down her back.

"I do not know what they are called," said Orrin, "But no one cares for them. Any who look at them become helpless as an infant."

"Come along," said Nylana, "The others can decide what to do with you."

"For a slave, you issue orders with ease."

"I am no slave," said Nylana, "And if you call me that again, I'll see to it that you meet one of those red eyed creatures personally."

She led the way back to the camp. By the time they reached it, the sun poked over the horizon allowing dust particles to dance in its light.

"Where've you been?" demanded Galdin as he looked up from digging through his pack.

"Picking up more strays," replied Nylana.

Orrin stepped out from behind her and into view. "I am coming with you."

"Of course you are," scoffed Galdin, "What's another stray in a land of marauders and thieves?"

"I don't appreciate your tone," snarled Orrin.

"I don't care," replied Galdin. "Her I take because I must." He pointed at Nylana.

"What about him?" Orrin gestured toward Ryk.

Sighing loudly, Galdin's features became unreadable. "Tried getting rid of him, but he's worse than a cockroach."

"Such a statement is an insult to cockroaches," said Trya as she stamped out the last vestiges of the fire. She turned toward Orrin. "You are different from your father."

Orrin moved nervously under her sharp gaze.

"Perhaps you can come with us, for a time," said Trya.

Galdin glared at his friend wondering why she allowed this man to tag along. As always, when the elf chose to remain unreadable, no one discerned her intentions. He chucked a heavy pack at Orrin. "You can carry this. Give her a break," he said indicating Nylana.

For the first time, Orrin noticed the similarities between Nylana and Galdin. He stared at them in the morning light; a shadowed expression covered his face.

"What?" demanded Galdin.

"Nothing, it's just," began Orrin taking another glance at the two of them, "You two act as though you do not know each other."

"Because we do not," replied Galdin, "We did not meet until a few days ago."

"Forgive me, but are you sure you do not have the same— never mind. It's preposterous. But you two have the same nose and the same cheekbones." Orrin strapped the pack around his shoulders and took the lead.

Galdin stared after him. His eyes met Trya's and he knew that she had noticed the same. "You stay with me," he reached out and snatched Ryk by the collar of his shirt yanking him back.

"I was just," Ryk began taking a quick look at Nylana as she followed after the elf.

"I know what you were thinking," said Galdin. "You're staying by my side."

Disappointed, Ryk slumped his shoulders and fell in line beside Galdin.

The trek through the wilderness of Pras'quel proved long and arduous. To avoid detection, Orrin steered them away from villages and towns. The warm day reminded them that the weather would soon change.

"Harper's Point is where I will take you," said Orrin in answer to unspoken questions. "It is a way station for travelers. Many use it. That is where I will leave you."

"How far?" asked Galdin.

"Another day or two," said Orrin.

"But this is the wrong way," said Ryk. "The quickest way to Harper's Point is west."

"That goes straight through towns and villages," countered Orrin, "If you wish to avoid entanglements with other slavers, then we must take the way through the wilderness."

Orrin faced the others. "I am not leading you into any traps."

"And how do we know that that is the case?" asked Ryk.

"He speaks the truth," said Trya.

Trya always had the ability to determine if one spoke the truth or not. As an elf, she knew how to read men's hearts. Her word was enough for Galdin.

"Continue walking," he said. "Why do you help us? And why did you follow us?"

Orrin surveyed the landscape a moment before answering. "My father is not well," he said, "He hides it, but the physicians all believe that within the year he will be dead. You were right when you said that one day I would be king." Orrin turned to Nylana. "It will happen sooner than anticipated. No one else can sit on the throne. If I do not make it back to the castle safely, then there will be no one to ascend to the throne when he dies."

"So you help us because it is mutually beneficial to you," said Galdin. "Same old story."

"And are you any different than me?" Orrin whirled on Galdin.

"You use my knowledge to get through here. That is no different than me using you for protection. And do not take the air of honorability when we all know you only allow her to come along because she promised you wealth." Orrin glanced at Nylana.

"Why you—" began Galdin.

"You are a mercenary," said Orrin, "Nothing more. Do not chastise me when you have yet to criticize yourself."

Galdin pulled his fist back.

"Enough," interrupted Trya.

Galdin put his fist down.

"So you wandered your father's kingdom to learn more about its people," continued Trya, "Are you certain you were not running away?"

Orrin sighed. "A part of me wished to escape and considered the possibility. Pras'quel is dying. There are more slaves than slave owners. I wish to avoid an uprising. I wandered the kingdom to see if people would be open to the idea of abolishing slavery."

"It will be bloody no matter what you choose," said Nylana as Ryk helped her over an upturned tree.

"True," said Orrin, "But I learned that slavery is the least of our troubles. Those barbarians moving through here that you saw earlier; it has been going on for months."

"You said that they were merely passing through," said Nylana.

"And learning the layout of the land as they go," said Orrin, "When they finish with their current mission, what is to stop them from coming back here?"

Nylana hadn't thought of that. Tesnayr. *Why were they going to Tesnayr?*

"Enough talk," growled Galdin. "We have a lot of land to cover before nightfall."

*   *   *

Lord Stefon noticed smoke rising from within the mountains. With the few men by his side, he steered his horse towards it. It wasn't far. Within fifteen minutes they had arrived at the ruins of a small settlement.

Lord Stefon jumped off of his horse as he walked through the few homes that lay there. Smoke drifted past floating over blackened bodies. A child's doll rested by his foot. Somberly, he picked it up noting the torn stitching on it.

"How did this happen?" asked one of his men.

"How does any of this happen?" replied Lord Stefon.

A strange form caught his eye. He walked over to it using the toe of his boot to flip it over. Dead, red eyes stared back at him. Somewhere within his memory, Lord Stefon recalled stories about beasts with blood red eyes that forced one to lose their sense of self-will.

"My lord," called another of his men.

Lord Stefon ran over to him. Another body that did not belong lay on the ground. This one wore furs and an emblem he did not recognize.

"What does all this mean?" asked one soldier.

"It means that something is terribly wrong," said Lord Stefon, "Head back to the keep." He mounted his horse and they galloped away.

*   *   *

That night as they camped, Nylana stared into the flames of the fire thinking. Her mind traveled to Krispyn and to Narúl. Did they miss her? Hopefully, in a few months' time she would be home again in Norlyk. A part of her didn't want to go.

Absentmindedly, she hummed a tune that all children within the lands of Tesnayr learn. It was a song of sorrow and regret and of warning.

"What is that you are singing?" asked Ryk as he listened to the doleful melody.

"Nothing," said Nylana.

"It sounded lovely."

"You're just trying to get on my good side."

"Burnam's Song," muttered Galdin. He remembered it from his youth. "Every child where I am from knows it."

"Burnam?" said Ryk.

"It's about a man who made all the wrong choices in life and lives long enough to regret it," said Galdin as he fiddled with the spit over the fire.

"Sounds cheerful," said Orrin who had listened to the entire conversation.

"Sing it for me," Ryk said.

Nylana shook her head.

"Come on," goaded Ryk.

"All right," Nylana relented.

> Burnam is my name and here is my tale.
> I followed a man named Murnok.
> Vile, destruction lay on his trail.
>
> Power and prestige is what I sought
> And Murnok promised all I desired.
> So I did his bidding and all he taught.

I became a thief, cheat, murderer, and liar.
With each day I fell deeper into his web.
Until serving him was my deepest desire.

Though breathing, inside I was dead.
Left with a soul blackened and hollow,
I believed Murnok and all that he said.

Where he went I followed
Faithfully, and without question,
Never noticing what I sowed: sorrow.

I obeyed his command without hesitation
And fulfilled his grand plan
As all that he wanted came to fruition.

Word reached him of a woman
Claiming to be Tesnayr's heir.
A claim Murnok could not stand.

Murnok chose me; her death my task to bear.
I searched and searched until I found her.
I gained her trust and lured her into my snare.

She accepted my story; of that I was sure.
As I promised to be her guide
And led her in circles.

Whispering lies until she took my side
Then I tried to kill Amborese,
But over a cliff we fell and I almost died.

Why I lived, I'll never know in the least.
But my life changed that fateful day

Because on that day my former life ceased.

I returned to Murnok hoping that he may
Forgive my failure and take me back.
Instead he threw me aside and turned me away.

Shattered I didn't know how to act.
My faith in Murnok was no more.
So I searched for Amborese and followed her tracks.

Amborese forgave me offering me more
Than Murnok ever bestowed upon me.
But I refused her gracious offer.

I charted my course of melee
Distant and aimless I wandered,
Secured in my bundle of grief.

Do not follow my wretched path,
For I lived the life of a hermit,
Friendless, faithless, and utterly alone.

No one spoke after she had finished. They absorbed the words, except for Galdin who had wanted to leave the lands of Tesnayr behind.

*   *   *

Narúl crept through the small village keeping his cloak up, hiding his face. He listened to the people as they talked. Inwardly, he scolded himself for continuing after the wagon. He should have known that Nylana would have attempted an escape.

Voices drew his attention. Narúl moved closer to listen. He learned that Nylana was rescued by a man and a woman. No one in the village knew who they were. Two more joined their company.

"Do you know where they went?" asked Narúl from the shadows.

The man who had been talking assumed that one of his companions had asked the question. "West," he answered without a moment's hesitation.

Narúl peeled away from the shadows moving through the village. He walked carefully, blending in with the people so as not to attract attention. Once he reached the edges of the village, Narúl sprinted away heading westward.

*   *   *

"I recognize this landscape," said Ryk as they all trekked further into the wilderness of Pras'quel. "We shouldn't go this way."

"And what other way would you have us go?" asked Orrin.

"Turn back," said Ryk.

"What's going on here?" demanded Galdin.

"We should not go through here," said Ryk, "This place is—"

"Inhabited by terrible monsters and creatures of the underworld," interrupted Orrin. "Those are stories. Nothing more."

"How do you know?" asked Nylana. "How do you know that there isn't some truth to them?"

"Because the peasantry will believe anything. Their simplemindedness leaves them open to such nonsense," replied Orrin.

Nylana pushed past him with a sour look on her face.

The landscape quickly changed from lush trees and grass to sand, rocks, and no water. The aridness of the area sapped moisture from their skin. Giant rocks surrounded them as they walked across the barren landscape with puffs of dust following their every step.

"This is the wilderness?" asked Galdin. "How is it so different from the rest of Pras'quel?"

"Magic makes this place unique," replied Trya. "It was cursed long ago. Before Pras'quel ever existed."

"Impossible," said Orrin, "No sorcerers have ever lived here."

"They did before your ancestors eradicated them from the land," said Trya. "Long ago magic roamed freely in all corners of the earth. But no more. Now only a few vestiges of it remains; like this place."

"Utter nonsense," said Orrin. "There are stories about this place, but that is because it is unsettled. No one lives here so it is overrun with animals."

Galdin ran right into Ryk who had stopped walking and just stared at a boulder. "Get a move on."

"That rock," said Ryk, "I think it just winked at me."

Galdin looked at what Ryk pointed to. It was just an ordinary rock about waist high. "It's a rock."

"No. I'm telling you it winked at me," insisted Ryk.

Sighing heavily, Galdin turned and continued.

"Look, it moved," shouted Ryk.

"It's a stupid rock," said Galdin.

"It's blinking," said Nylana.

Galdin peered closer at the opaque boulder crusted over with dried clay. Ridiculous, he thought. He approached it until only inches remained between him and the ordinary boulder. Eyes appeared in the rock. Startled, Galdin jumped back. "What?"

The rock blinked.

"Impossible," whispered Galdin.

The sound of splitting trees filled the area as the rock transformed into an animal. A jagged tail unwound itself from around the boulder as a head and four legs popped out. Each foot resembled a hand with claws several inches long and webbing between the fingers. The dog sized creature eyed each of them with its four eyes making chirruping sounds.

"Nobody move," said Galdin.

"Well, hello there. My name is Ryk." Ryk stuck his hand out to the creature.

Galdin groaned.

The animal studied Ryk's hand a moment. Immediately, racking coughs shook its body until it spat out a giant glob of mucus coating Ryk in slime. It glanced at Galdin. With incredible speed the thing ran up to him and knocked him to the ground licking his face with excitement.

"Get off me," Galdin shoved the creature off of him. He wiped the slobber from his face trying his best not to vomit from the stench.

The creature's eyes welled up with tears. A baleful sound emanated from it as it howled in sorrow at being rejected.

"You hurt its feelings," said Nylana as she walked up to the strange creature.

"I wouldn't," began Orrin.

"What kind of monster are you?" Ryk scolded Galdin.

"One more word out of you and I'll see to it that you have nothing to complain about ever again," muttered Galdin to Ryk.

Nylana slowly approached the creature holding her hand out to it. The animal ceased its crying as it studied her outstretched hand. "Come on, boy," cooed Nylana.

It sniffed her hand. Suddenly, it rammed its head into it with such force that it nearly knocked her over.

"No," Nylana stopped the others from approaching.

Panting with excitement, the creature rubbed against her hand again. Nylana scratched its chin as it purred. It flopped on the ground rolling onto its back and placing its feet into the air. Laughing with delight, Nylana scratched its smooth belly with exuberance. The animal rolled and writhed on the gravel as it enjoyed every bit of it.

"He's harmless," said Nylana. "What should we name him?"

"No," said Galdin, "We have enough strays in this party."

"I say we call it Trog," said Ryk. "What?" he added at Galdin's menacing glare, "It's a cross between a turtle and a dog."

"What do you say, boy?" said Nylana to the newly named Trog.

Trog panted with excitement; its tongue hanging out.

"Then Trog it is."

The ground shook beneath their feet swaying for a few seconds before going still. Silence ensued. Instantly, Trog pulled his legs and head in turning back into a giant rock.

"What was that?" asked Ryk.

"Nothing," replied Orrin, "The ground always shakes in Pras'quel. You know that. Now, let's go. We only have a few hours of daylight left."

The air around them changed from dry to humid forming a sweltering environment. No sounds echoed around them. All had gone still.

"Where did those trees come from?" asked Ryk pointing behind them.

Tall, twisted trees with palm fronds and vines surrounded them forming a thick expanse that had not been there before.

"You worry too much," said Orrin as he turned and walked in the direction they had originally been headed.

"No, I'm telling you," Ryk chased after him, "Something is not right."

"You have nothing to worry about," said Orrin.

A low rumble moved beneath their feet.

"You just had to say that," grumbled Ryk.

Nylana stared at the strange trees. She had never seen any like them before with their broad, vivid emerald leaves and spiked trunks. "I think we should leave," she said. "Now."

Instantly, the trees jumped out of the ground as the branches and leaves twisted violently, winding themselves into arms and legs. Heads appeared on each of them with menacing eyes that took in everything.   A series of roars and screeches echoed around them pounding against their ears.

They raced across the sand away from the trees that now chased after them.   Their feet pounded the hard earth in their efforts to escape.

"Rocks that turn into dogs," shouted Ryk, "So why not trees that turn into monsters?"

"At least it can't get any worse," yelled Orrin.

As though it meant to taunt them, the sky darkened rapidly turning daylight into night.   Thunder rolled across the sky as lightening flashed around.   Rain drops pelted their exposed skin with vicious stings making it difficult to see where they went.

"You just had to say that," Ryk shouted at Orrin.

Nylana's scream stopped them.   A vine had wrapped itself around her ankle and dragged her across the newly soaked earth to an outstretched hand of one of the creatures.   She clawed at the ground, but to no avail.   Another vine wrapped around her mouth stifling her cries for help.

Galdin charged for her.   He dove to the ground and grabbed her hand pulling her toward him.   One of the tree monsters snapped a vine at him striking him in the stomach and sending him flying.   Pain coursed through his side as he rolled across the ground.   Ignoring it, he jumped to his feet and ran for Nylana again.

Desperately, Nylana scraped the ground with her hands trying to find anything to hold on to.   A loud growl filled the air as Trog appeared from nowhere latching his teeth around the vine on her ankle.   He tore at it ripping it to pieces.

Freed, Nylana ripped the vine from her mouth.   Together, she and Trog dashed for the others.   Nylana took out her knife. Facing a charging creature she threw it at the thing catching it in the eye.   Angered, it swiped at her with its green fist.   Trog pushed her out of the way before it could strike her again. Instantly, Trog picked her up in his mouth and tossed her onto his back darting away with Nylana clinging for dear life.

Something crashed beside her sending mud everywhere. Trog panted heavily as he ran. A vine shot out and caught the animal by his feet sending them sprawling in the mud.

One of the monsters headed straight for Nylana. She lay there helpless. Trog didn't move.

Before the thing reached her, Galdin jumped in its path swinging his sword upward and catching the creature in the mouth. He shoved it deep within the thing's head. It crumpled to the ground.

Nylana jumped to her feet, snatched the spare sword from Galdin's hip, and cut off a vine heading straight for her. "Trog," she shook the animal, but it didn't budge.

"Leave him," yelled Galdin as he snatched her arm and pushed her ahead.

"But—"

"You can't help him," shouted Galdin.

They ran as fast as they could across the expanse joining up with the others.

"Is there any way we can outrun them?" shouted Trya.

"Once we're to the other side we should be safe," replied Orrin.

"How do you know?" asked Ryk.

"Well, you haven't seen these things in Pras'quel have you? I think there is something that keeps them here."

"We'll never outrun them," said Ryk as his side began to ache.

"Well, it's not like it can get—," began Orrin.

"Don't say it!" yelled Ryk.

"—any worse."

Instantly, the creatures stopped chasing them. They all looked back curious as to why. With horror, they watched as the separate tree like creatures ran into each other wrapping around one another forming a single, gigantic beast that stood on four legs with razor sharp teeth. A spiked tail twisted behind it as gigantic wings spread across the ground.

"You just had to say it," scolded Ryk. "I told you not to! Why won't you listen to me?"

"I think it's worse," muttered Nylana.

"Run!" shouted Galdin.

The newly formed creature spread its wings releasing a huge cry that shook the entire earth. Each step it took caused the ground to quake beneath their feet.

It pounded the earth with its claws. Nylana and Galdin swerved barely missing the deadly blow. Several vines at once shot out from the thing's mouth for her. Nylana brought her sword up slicing all of them. She spun on her toes with ease dodging each vine that reached for her slicing and dicing as she went.

For a few moments, Galdin watched her in awe. He was brought from his wonderment as the giant creature swatted at him. Somersaulting out of the way he heard Ryk shout for his weapon. Galdin tossed his sword to the thief. Ryk caught it turned it around and stabbed the monster's hand as it slapped the ground.

Crying in agony, it knocked Ryk aside.

"Distract it!" shouted Trya.

Catching onto her plan, Orrin whistled at the creature. It snapped at him.

Seizing her chance, Trya took a running leap landing on the monster's neck. She held on tightly chopping at the vines that attacked her. Pulling a long knife from her belt, she jabbed it into the monster's neck. It reared up howling and thrashing its head from side to side.

Another vine charged for Trya. Waiting for just the right moment, the elf let go of the creature's neck, grabbed the vine and swung down to the ground releasing her hold, landing softly on her feet.

They all watched as the thing teetered on its feet and crashed into the mud splattering all of them.

"Are you alright?" asked Nylana as she helped Ryk to his feet.

"I'll be fine," he said, brushing himself off. "Where is that little friend of ours?"

Nylana's face fell.

"I'm sorry," said Ryk. "I kind of liked the little bugger."

"We need to leave," said Galdin after making certain the thing was dead. "I thought you said you didn't know how to use a sword."

"I said I had no use for one," replied Nylana, "I never said I didn't know how to use it." She handed her weapon back to Galdin.

"Just full of surprises, isn't she," Trya whispered in Galdin's ear as she passed by.

They soon crossed the remaining wilderness and crossed the boundary into more familiar territory. The trees looked as Nylana thought they should; no arms or legs.

"There is Harper's Point," Orrin pointed it out to them. "I told you the wilderness was the shortest way. We should be there by morning. From there you can take Caravan's Road to the port. It's only a day's journey."

"You seem distracted," commented Trya as she plopped more wood into the fire.

Galdin had chosen to be alone after they had set up camp for the night. Something about Nylana bothered him. "Why does she seem so familiar?"

"How do you mean?"

"From the moment I met her I've had this urge to protect her."

"It is natural for a brother to protect his sister," said Trya.

Galdin gaped at her.

"Surely, you've noticed the similarities. The same mannerisms. The same features. You even bear the same mark. I put it together long ago."

"Why didn't you tell me?" asked Galdin, rubbing his arm where the birthmark was.

"Would you have believed me?"

Galdin glanced away. No, he would not have believed her. But the more he thought about Trya's conclusions, the more he sided with them. But how could they be related? And why were they split up if they were? Galdin rose to leave. He needed to think.

"She's no slave," said Trya.

"How do you mean?"

"Her mannerisms. Her speech. Those I have seen before, but in the court of kings," said Trya. "That girl was raised in a palace."

"Are you certain?"

"No slave knows how to wield a sword like she did today. No slave speaks the way she does. And if she is your sister, what does that make you?"

"You know who she is."

"I have my suspicions," said Trya, "But I'll not voice them here."

"Why not? There is no one here but us and I have never betrayed you."

"It is not you I fear," said Trya, "The trees have ears. And who knows who may be watching. There is something wrong here, Galdin. Barbarians move through Pras'quel unchecked. Orcs that were believed destroyed a thousand years ago roam free once more. We've watched them many times. And she is here as a slave. I will wait until we are safe in the lands of Tesnayr. By then you will probably learn it for yourself."

Galdin snorted, irritated that his friend would not confide in him.

"Do not leave her side even for a moment," warned Trya. "She needs you."

Harper's point bustled with activity as they entered the city. People ignored them, consumed by their own errands. Nylana looked around at the buildings with their streams of brightly colored ribbons. A man bumped into her.

"Excuse me," she said.

The man continued on ignoring her.

"Welcome to Harper's Point," said Orrin. "Here is where I leave you. I suggest you go to the stables there and buy a horse. Those with horses are thought of as wealthy. People should leave you alone. Once you make it to the Port City, sell it and get on the first boat out of here."

"Such concern," mocked Galdin.

Orrin stepped closer to Galdin. "None of you belong here. Her especially." He pointed at Trya. "Yes, I noticed the ears. Good luck to all of you."

Orrin walked away disappearing into the crowded streets. They watched him go.

"How do we know he won't turn us in?" asked Ryk.

"He could have done that long ago," said Galdin. "Come on."

They followed Galdin to the stables that Orrin had indicated. They bartered for a horse and left, making certain their exchange was quick. Within the hour they set out for Port City.

Chapter XII
Passage to Tesnayr

"How much?" asked Galdin.

"100 gold coins for passage," replied Trya.

"We haven't enough," said Galdin. "If only we had managed to get more for the horse." An exasperated sigh escaped him. He eyed the people around them.

Ryk smiled deviously as a plan formed in his mind. He snatched a cloak from one of the nearby vendors and wrapped it around Nylana, ripping sections of it into jagged pieces. "Come with me," he said dragging her with him. "You two stay there," he told the others.

Ryk steered Nylana down the street to a merchant who was buying fruit. "Follow my lead," he whispered to Nylana, "Do not speak unless spoken to. Keep your head down and your face hidden."

The richly dressed merchant paid no attention to them as they walked past. Ryk stealthily snuck up to the merchant's stock of supplies. He snatched a crate of apples. Nylana opened her mouth to protest, but Ryk had shoved the apples in her hands and pushed her in front of the merchant.

"Why hello, my good sir," greeted Ryk silkily. "Might you be a merchant of the north?"

"I am," came the merchant's deep voice.

"Might I interest you in some of our apples? My wife and I have a small plot of land far from here, but the soil is rich. Here, judge for yourself," said Ryk.

Nylana placed the crate of apples in front of the merchant, biting her tongue to keep quiet.

"They have a good color," mused the merchant. He picked up a few apples inspecting their freshness. "Very similar to a bunch I purchased earlier this morning."

Sweat poured down Nylana's face. She was certain that their ruse would be discovered. Ryk continued unfazed. Clearly, he's done this before, she thought.

"They are crisp and sweet. Try one if you must," said Ryk.

"No. No, that will not be necessary," said the merchant. "I can see that they are good apples. How much do you want for them?"

"200 gold coins," said Ryk.

Nylana nearly dropped the crate.

"200! That is a steep price."

"It may seem so," said Ryk, "But we have traveled far and this has been the first good year in a long while."

The merchant stroked his curly beard. He eyed Nylana and the tattered cloak she wore. Her bony features poked through. "100 gold coins."

"175."

"125."

"150," countered Ryk.

The merchant fingered his purse. He had never paid so much for anything. But the apples were good and would sell well in his country. "150 it is," he said. He waved a servant over to take the crate from Nylana.

Ryk shook the merchant's hand and collected the money.

"A little extra for your wife. Buy her a new cloak," said the merchant giving Ryk a few extra coins.

"Thank you, my good sir," said Ryk, "Your kindness is most appreciated. Come, my darling."

Ryk wrapped his arm around Nylana's waist and led her back to where Galdin and Trya stood watching from a distance. Galdin bore a grave expression while Trya suppressed a smile.

"I shudder to think of what will happen when he finds out," said Nylana.

"Doesn't matter. We will be long gone," replied Ryk.

"Perhaps I should leave you behind."

"My lady, vengeance does not become you."

"How much did you get?" asked Galdin.

"150 gold coins. Enough to barter passage on the ship and a little extra for food," said Ryk.

Trya grabbed the coins from Ryk. "I'll take those," she said before he could protest.

The elf walked over to the ticket master, handed over the coins, and came back with four tickets. She gave one to each of them. "Let's move."

They walked up the plank to the ship with the crowd unaware that a cloaked figure watched them. He slipped in behind, following the line of people boarding the ship.

"Tickets," said the man standing guard at the top.

They handed over their tickets. The man waved them on board. Gradually, the four companions worked their way to a secluded area near the back of the boat to bunk down until the ship set sail.

"Hoist the sails," shouted the captain, checking the onboard sundial.

Crewmen scurried about carrying out his orders. Others brought up the anchor. As the activity continued, the ship lurched slightly moving slowly away from the dock and into the open water.

"Let's go below," said Galdin. "Remember, we wish to go unnoticed."

Nylana grunted. *Did he think they were idiots?* The last thing any of them wanted was to draw attention.

The cargo hold below deck reeked of unwashed passengers, urine and rotten food. Raucous laughter and flat music pounded their ears. Men dressed in dark leather passed the time by arm wrestling each other spilling half-full containers of mead. One man in front, and clearly the leader, pounded the table with his fist while talking with another.

Slowly, they wormed their way through the crowd toward a table that had some food and a barrel of mead. Nylana reached for a hard piece of flat bread.

"Hey pretty lady," said a man walking unstably on his feet. His stale breath told her that he had been drinking.

"Leave me alone," said Nylana.

"Oh, what are you going to do about it?" The man grabbed her wrist pulling her toward him.

Instantly, Nylana grabbed the man's hand wrenching his thumb back and freeing her wrist. She twisted his hand until something snapped.

"You wench," spat the man, "You broke my wrist."

"I told you to leave me be," said Nylana, coldly.

Another man lunged for her. Galdin snatched him from midair and slammed him against the wall. The music stopped. All eyes rested upon them as people drew near. So much for going unnoticed, thought Nylana.

The big man she had noticed earlier pushed his way through the crowd and to where they stood. "What goes on here?"

His gruff demeanor forced others to back away indicating that he was in charge.

"She broke my wrist," shouted the man that had accosted Nylana.

"I told him to leave me alone," said Nylana, "He refused."

"He was one of my best men," said the big man before her.

"We just want some food and quiet," said Nylana, "Why don't we part amicably."

"Not on my ship."

"This is not your ship," piped up Ryk.

"While I am here," said the man, "It is my ship. None of you will be granted food or drink on this voyage."

Galdin stepped forward with his hand on his sword. "You cannot keep us from eating."

The two closed the space between them. Reading their body language Nylana knew they were on the verge of fighting; something she did not want.

"How about a wager," she said.

"Wager?" Galdin and the burly man spoke at the same time.

"Yes," said Nylana. She pointed to a post on the far end with holes in it as though it had been used before as target practice. "You have knives. Let us use that wood over there. Whomever can line up three knives in a row in the top part of the board wins."

"And the wager?" asked the man.

"If you win, my companions and I will go to the boat deck and remain there the rest of the voyage. If we win, you and your associates will allow us food, drink, and leave us alone."

"Agreed," said the man. "Give the lady some knives."

"Now wait a minute," said Galdin, "You do not expect her to do it?"

"The woman and I will throw the knives. The wager was her idea."

Someone shoved three knives into Nylana's hands. The crowd parted, standing clear of the target. The burly man took his knives handling them expertly. He threw one. It flew through the air striking the top of the post. He threw the second and the third. Each knife lined up in a neat row in the top half of the vertical board. He turned to Nylana with a smug look on his face waving her forward.

"Your turn," he said.

Nylana took her position. From the jeers she received, she knew that no one expected her to make the target, convinced that she would fail. Nylana bounced the knife in her hand feeling its weight. Eyeing the target and calculating the force needed for the throw; she raised the dagger above her head and chucked it. In quick succession she threw the other two. Silence enveloped them. Each of her knives stuck in the handle of her opponent's blades.

The burly man gaped at her. "No one could ever do that."

"And yet I just did," said Nylana, "Now it is your turn to keep your end of the bargain."

"Never."

"Keep your part of the bargain, or let everyone here know that you are a man who breaks his word. How long do you think they will follow you after that?"

The man scanned the crowd as they eagerly watched him. Knowing he had been beaten, the man relented. "Give the lady and her friends some food and water."

"But she can't—" began one.

"I said give them food and water!" The husky man threw the other to the floor.

Gradually, the crowd thinned forming a path for the four companions to reach the area with the food and mead. They each took a plateful and settled in a secluded area of the boat.

*   *   *

Narúl strolled up to the ticket man on the dock. "Pardon me," he said warmly, "I am looking for a woman."

"The brothel is five buildings down that way," said the ticket master in a bored voice, turning away.

Not having time for such nonsense Narúl grabbed the man by the shoulders and held him out over the water. "I am looking for a specific woman," he said, "Just short of my height, foreign accent, and dark hair."

"That description fits many women around here," said the man struggling to get free.

"She is from Tesnayr."

The man's eyes opened wide as he remembered something. "There was a woman matching the description who boarded a ship headed for Tesnayr. But she did not travel alone."

"Who was she with?"

"Two men and a woman. The second woman seemed strange, rather tall for a woman and she kept her cloak up."

"The ship, where is it?"

"It set sail yesterday."

Frustrated, Narúl almost released his grip on the ticket master.

"But there is another headed to Tesnayr today. It leaves in five minutes. But you'll need a ticket to get aboard."

"Then give me one," hissed Narúl holding the man farther out over the water.

"Here! Here!" The ticket master held out a ticket to Narúl.

Narúl snatched it. He tossed the man aside and darted toward the ship barely making it aboard before it departed. Just missed her, he thought. He hoped he found her in time.

*   *   *

A cloaked figure crept along the boat deck of the ship as it rocked in the sea. He found the captain waiting for him. "Well," he said.

"She is aboard," said the captain, nervously.

"Good," hissed the cloaked figure. "I want you to ensure that she does not reach her destination."

"But she travels with companions."

"Then get rid of them all," snapped the cloaked figure. He tired of people's unwillingness to do what was necessary.

"Well, I could—"

"You could what?" Out stepped the man that Nylana had bested with knives. "Who are you, stranger?" he demanded of the cloaked figure.

"No one of consequence," the figure replied with an oily tone.

The muscular man glared at the shadowy figure displeased at the way the stranger kept his cloak closed and his face hidden. "Captain, I'm sure you have duties to attend."

The captain scurried away.

The man turned back to the cloaked figure. He disliked the woman he spoke of, but he hated this man even more. "This is my ship. You will leave that party alone. If anything happens to them, I'll know who to come looking for." He pushed his way past the cloaked figure. The burly man hated those who worked in secret; he always thought that one should openly confront their quarry, not plot in the safety of shadows.

Miffed, the cloaked figure stared after the husky man that had ended his plotting. No matter, he thought. He may not be able to accomplish his end aboard the ship, but there was always the dock.

*   *   *

"Why will they not listen to me?" demanded Krispyn of Petra.

"Perhaps it is the manner in which you ask them," answered the wizard. "The lords of Tesnayr are proud men and they each govern a sovereign land. Or have you forgotten that the King of Tesnayr is not an overlord who must always have his will obeyed, but a man who is to protect the five lands and keep them united?"

"I am aware of that."

"Are you? You demand the presence of the five lords, but what concessions have you made? My king, you have treated them like children, not men."

Krispyn turned to Petra. "What would you have me do?"

"Go to each of them. Your sister would have visited each of their realms and talked with them. Treat them with respect and they will be more open to your suggestions."

Krispyn listened to Petra's words. "I know that neither you nor the council ever liked my being crowned king. You all would have preferred my sister on the throne."

"What we wanted is of little consequence," said Petra, "The laws stated that you were to be crowned. And now that Nylana has gone missing, what difference does the rest make?"

"What indeed?" Krispyn stood in silence as he thought about his options. "I will take your advice into account. Thank you, Petra."

*   *   *

The ship pitched forward as a loud bang sounded against the side of the hull as a wave slammed into it waking Nylana. Thunder echoed all around the ship booming against the wood. She shook the others awake.

"What's wrong?" asked Ryk.

Another loud crack of thunder answered his question.

"Hurricane!"

Instantly, everyone jumped from their sleep and rushed about in a panic. A crewman ran into the cargo hold. "I need all able bodied men on the boat deck! If you can move and lift things, go above. Now!"

Nylana followed everyone out. Pushed and shoved about, she rushed to the boat deck only to be stopped by the massiveness of the storm. Lightning streaked the black sky giving life to the terrible storm that bore down upon them. The wind whipped around her knocking her off balance. Barely able to stand upright, she brought her arm up to protect her face from the pelting rain.

"Take this," said a crewman shoving rope into her hands. "Tie it around here. Tie it tight."

She took the rope obeying the command. Nylana hoped that she tied it well enough.

"Take down the sails," yelled the captain.

Men rushed about slipping on the wet deck. One sail was quickly brought down. Another refused to budge.

"Captain, the sail is caught!"

"Get a man up there to cut it loose," ordered the captain.

Galdin jumped onto the main rig and hoisted himself up. He knew where it had snagged. More lightning flashed. He held tightly to the soaked wood as his feet fought for a place to rest. He climbed upward ignoring the gales that tried to knock him down.

"Galdin!" yelled Nylana.

He didn't hear her over the roar of the storm.

"Secure the lines," the first mate screamed at Nylana. She immediately set about her task ignoring Galdin's efforts to reach the top of the sail. Her frozen hands refused to grasp the soggy rope in her attempts to tie a knot. The ship pitched again as a wave slammed into it forcing Nylana to hang on to a bar as her feet slid on the ice like surface of the deck.

Gradually, Galdin climbed upward. The blinding rain made the process difficult. His hand slipped. Swinging precariously as he held on with his other, Galdin reached up grabbing hold of the mast. Almost there, he thought. He lifted himself up higher. Finally reaching where the canvas had snagged, Galdin secured himself before pulling out his knife. He sawed at the material, his knife moving back and forth as he cut it loose.

The ship lurched again. Galdin dropped his knife and clung to the mast as his body flailed in the wind. Cursing, he grasped the sail and yanked hoping that he had cut it enough to be able to rip it free. Galdin pulled again. Lightning struck the surface of the ocean sending shocks of electricity everywhere. More thunder roared around him deafening him.

"Come on," shouted Galdin at the sail.

Finally, it pulled free.

"It's loose!"

Immediately, men at the bottom worked the lines tying down the canvas. Galdin slid down the pole. When he reached the bottom he found his knife sticking straight up stuck in a loose plank. He snatched it.

Suddenly, the wind stopped as the rain turned to a slow drizzle. Everyone looked about them wondering if the storm had ceased. No one moved.

"Is it over?" asked a young man of about eighteen.

"No," said Trya as she studied the night sky, "It is the eye of the storm. The calm before hell breaks free."

"What are you all standing there for?" roared the captain, "Tie yourselves down. Now! Secure the lines. Batten the hatches. It ain't over yet!"

Nylana looked about her confused like the rest of them. How could the storm end so suddenly? More lightning flashed in the sky revealing the mass of swirling clouds above. In that split second she realized that Trya was right. It hadn't ended.

Thunder boomed above them as streaks of lightning lit up the sky in a flurry of bursts. The ship lurched to the side.

"Tidal wave!"

Nylana turned in the direction of the sound. In the bits of lightning she saw a huge wall of water heading straight for them.

"Hang on!"

The wave crashed into the ship covering them and drowning everything. Men washed overboard as the boat was tossed about.

Nylana clung to a rail holding tightly. She never noticed the dark shape approaching her; reaching for her. Massive hands grabbed her pulling her free of the wood. Desperately, Nylana flung herself back to the bar she had been holding onto. The cloaked figure held tightly to her preventing her from finding safety. With a strength she had never known, the figure tossed her aside towards the edge of the ship.

The ship lurched again as another wave tore into it. Splintering wood filled the air as a rigging crashed into the deck of the boat. Knocked off balance, Nylana slid straight for the side of the ship. Her hands latched onto a loose rope. "Help me," she said to the cloaked figure.

A black boot reared up and smashed into her face forcing her to let go, tumbling into the treacherous water below.

"Nylana!" Galdin turned in time to see her disappear. He rushed to the side of the ship leaning far over. "Nylana!"

"You can't save her," said the first mate as he gripped Galdin's arm preventing him from jumping overboard. "No one can survive the water in this."

Galdin shook the man off. Again, he was prevented from jumping in as Trya put her arm out stopping him. She tied a rope around her waist handing the other end to Galdin. "Hold this."

Expertly, the elf leapt off the side of the ship and into the water below.

She plowed through the waves swimming straight for Nylana who splashed about in a vain attempt to keep her head above the surface. Moving with great speed and agility, Trya reached Nylana and grabbed on. Coughing, Nylana spat out the salty liquid as it choked her.

"Stop moving," ordered Trya.

Nylana obeyed.

Trya grasped the girl's shoulders holding her above the water. "Can you swim?"

"No," coughed Nylana.

"We'll have to remedy that."

Trya held on tightly with one arm while using the other to steer them back to the ship. Waves tossed them about. The rope pulled taut as those onboard yanked them toward the ship. Gradually, they drew nearer.

"Hold on to me," said Trya as her grip slipped.

Nylana clutched the elf tightly afraid of the water and of the storm.

Slowly, those on board heaved the two out of the raging water. Hands grabbed them hauling them onto the deck.

More thunder sounded, but it resembled a dull roar instead of the explosion it had been before.

"Are you alright?" asked Ryk as he wrapped a blanket around Nylana.

"I'll be fine," said Nylana. "Thank you," she said, turning to Trya.

Trya just clapped Nylana on the shoulder and rose to her feet.

"Get her below deck," said Galdin to Ryk.

"The storm seems to be dissipating," said the captain. "Everyone, except the crew, below deck."

*   *   *

Magi watched from her perch as Krispyn scribbled on a piece of parchment. Her glowing eyes barely visible to any who might have known she was there. She noted the stern expression on the king's face.

"Messenger," said Krispyn as he sealed the note, "See to it that this is delivered by tomorrow."

"Yes, my king," replied the messenger.

"And summon Shelwyk."

"Shelwyk is gone, my lord."

"Gone? Where?"

The messenger quivered under Krispyn's penetrating glare. "I do not know, sir. I only know that he has not been seen for many weeks now. I shall inform him of your wishes the moment he returns."

"Very well. Off you go."

The messenger darted out of the room.

Shelwyk gone, thought Magi. She knew it was not uncommon for the king's advisor to occasionally travel away from Norlyk, but she thought it odd that he would leave when strange folk moved about the five lands. Magi hopped off her perch and scurried into a small hole in the wall used by both mice and her. Perhaps she could learn for whom the king's message was intended.

Chapter XIII
Home

Nylana moved down the plank with the mass of people leaving the ship glad to have finally reached her homeland. She allowed herself to be pushed and shoved doing her best to ignore those that bumped her with their bundles. She winced as a heavy boot stomped on her toes once again. Desperately, Nylana tried to see over the crowd to make certain that she had not lost the others. They were ahead of her. At the risk of being rude, Nylana shoved her way down the plank to the port.

A sharp sting struck her right hand as she reached the bottom. She glanced about her, but with the massive crowd surrounding her she never noticed the hooded figure that darted away. Nylana inspected the back of her hand. A small prick mark lay in the center. Ignoring it, she ran to catch up with her companions.

"There you are," said Galdin as she approached. "Quickly, we need to leave."

"This isn't Norlyk," said Nylana looking around.

"That is because we are in the port near Drynelle," replied Galdin.

"Drynelle? Why are we in Drynelle?"

"Because that is where the ship was headed," said Galdin, "Does it matter? We are in Tesnayr. We'll be in Norlyk in a few days, but first we go west."

"West? Where are you headed? Norlyk is south," said Nylana.

"There is someone I need to see first."

Reluctantly, Nylana ceased her protest.

The hot sun beat down on Nylana as she walked on the dirt road weaving from side to side. She felt very warm; the wound on her hand burned. It had turned a bright shade of red, yet still she refused to tell the others. *I need to rest.* She lagged behind the others who talked merrily amongst themselves unaware of her predicament.

Her feet flopped uncontrollably on the dirt with each step she took as waves of dizziness swept over her. Her graceful movements had disappeared as she used what strength she had to keep going. "Might we stop to rest?"

"The river is just ahead," replied Galdin. Nylana's constant insistence that they should pause annoyed him. Soon they would be across the river and to his mother's home. Only then would they stop.

The sounds of water reached their ears informing them that they had reached the river. Galdin scanned the bank.

"This is a good place to cross," he said, "It is shallow here."

Galdin waded into the strong current of the river followed closely by the others. His home lay just on the other side.

Slowly, Nylana approached the stream. She felt lightheaded as she attempted to focus on the river. She stepped into the water. Its cold temperature felt good against her skin, but she remained uneasy about crossing. "Galdin, please, I don't think I can cross."

"We're almost there. Stop complaining." Trya's touch on his arm seized Galdin's attention. Behind him, Nylana was nowhere to be found. The current carried her unconscious body downstream.

Instantly, Galdin dove into the water and swam with the current after her. Once within reach, he snatched her cloak and pulled her to him as he made for the riverbank. Galdin carried the unconscious Nylana ashore, her skin burning against his own. Suddenly, he felt guilty for being short tempered with her.

"Quickly, to the cottage," ordered Galdin.

They burst through the cottage door startling Galdin's mother. "Galdin, what—"

"Mother, quick," interrupted Galdin, "She's ill."

Instantly, his mother jumped up and led him to the bedroom. "I'll go fetch some water," she said as he laid Nylana on the bed.

Trya felt Nylana's forehead. "She burns with fever. Get these wet clothes off her."

Galdin did as ordered. He removed Nylana's soggy outfit. Upon seeing the stripe marks on her back his brow creased in anger. Trya laid a hand on his. Later, her expression said. Galdin's mother rushed in with a bowl of cool water and some cloth. She soaked the cloth and put it on Nylana's forehead.

Then, the elf noticed it. She snatched Nylana's hand studying the mark. "She's been poisoned. Do you have any herbs?" asked Trya.

Galdin's mother nodded and led the elf to her herb collection, handing the soaked cloth to her son. He continued mopping Nylana's brow as she fidgeted from her fever. *Poisoned? Who would poison her? She is just a merchant's daughter.*

Nylana shook violently from chills while sweat formed on her face. Galdin wrapped a soft blanket around her.

Trya marched in with a cup of tea. "Get her to drink this. It should slow the poison."

"Should? Do we not have an antidote?"

"I would need to know what she was poisoned with," said Trya. "There is little we can do, but hope that this slows it enough for her to overcome it on her own."

Galdin lifted the unconscious Nylana, tipping the cup to her lips. He managed to get about half of the liquid in her mouth while the rest pooled on the bed.

Later that night, Galdin sat up with Nylana. He perched himself in a chair watching her as she slept fitfully. The color in her cheeks had changed to an ashen look; the look of death.

Worry creased his brow. He did not know why, but he felt strongly about the need for her to recover.

Galdin's mother walked in. "How is she?"

"The same," said Galdin.

His mother shifted the blanket tucking it neatly around Nylana. Gingerly, she felt the woman's forehead. Still hot. Frowning, the elderly woman turned toward Galdin. "There is something I must tell you."

"Can it not wait?" Galdin was not in the mood for secrets.

"No, it cannot," said his mother, "Come with me."

Grudgingly, Galdin followed his mother into the other room. She reached down a box from a high shelf. Slowly, the woman opened it pulling out a baby's blanket. "This is yours," she said.

"I know that."

"Take it." She handed the blanket to Galdin. He took it turning it over in his hands wondering what was in his mother's mind. Finally, he saw it: the crest of the lands of Tesnayr. "Why is—"

"You are not the son of a shoemaker," said his mother. "Strictly speaking you are not my son. I found you in the river long ago and took you in. I knew by that emblem that you were the son of the queen, but with the rebellion it was unsafe to return you. So I took you in and raised you as my son.

"When the rebellion ended and things returned to normal, I knew I had to return you, but I couldn't. By then I had grown too attached and looked upon you as my own. So I kept you and allowed the queen to believe that her son had died.

"I can only imagine the pain I put her through for my own selfishness."

"Why are you telling me this?"

"Because it is the truth. The truth that I should have told you long ago. Now I am afraid it is too late. The queen married, had another son, and now he is the king. But you were the first born son. You are the rightful heir."

"Why didn't you ever tell me?" asked Galdin, still trying to take it all in.

"Because I wanted to protect you," said his mother. "I had hoped that I would never have to tell you. You are my son. I love you, Galdin. But now I have the Princess of Tesnayr in my bed; ill from some unknown source. She is your sister and when you came here with her, I knew I had to tell you the truth. It is time that you know.

"Things are changing in the lands of Tesnayr. They need you. They need her."

"You should never have lied to me," said Galdin slamming the blanket on a table. He stormed out of the cabin and into the night.

"Galdin, please," pleaded his mother.

For the next two days, Nylana lay in the bed growing worse. Her fever continued to rise until her skin became too hot to touch. She shook from chills as the sheets became soaked with her sweat.

The others watched helplessly knowing that there was nothing they could do for her. They could only sit and wait.

"Galdin!" Trya ran out to him as he came back with a goose for supper. "She is worse."

Galdin dropped the fowl and rushed into the cabin. He tore into the room where his mother sat with Nylana dabbing the girl's head with a damp cloth. Coughing fits racked Nylana's body. He knelt by her bedside in emotional agony at what he saw. Don't die, he silently pleaded,.

Gently, he took his sister's hand in his own. "You cannot die," he whispered, "The world needs you."

A sharp intake of breath moved Nylana's body followed by the slow hiss of air as stillness settled on the room. Galdin placed his hand over Nylana's mouth.

Nothing.

He took out a dagger and placed it by her lips hoping to see the faint fog appear from her breath.

Nothing.

Nylana had died.

His mother pulled the blanket over Nylana's head. Ryk stood in the doorway, an angry expression covering his face.

"Trya," said Galdin's mother, "There are some flowers blooming just outside the door. Pick some of those to prepare her body with."

The elf left the room keeping her face impassive.

"I am sorry, Galdin," his mother said. "Can you ever forgive me?"

Galdin wrapped his mother in a hug. "There is nothing to forgive. You took me in when I had nowhere to go and raised me. No matter my parentage, you will always be my mother."

"You should have had more time to know your sister."

"At least I got to meet her. She is in every way, a noble lady." Galdin left the room to find a shovel. It may seem cold, but he knew that the grave would not dig itself and it wouldn't be long before Nylana's body began to rot.

Chapter XIV
A Noble Lady

Morning dawned on a solemn group of people as they gathered around a freshly dug grave and a body lay before it. Galdin's mother and Trya had done a splendid job in preparing the body for burial. Nylana looked every bit like the noble woman she was. Flowers dotted her golden brown hair. Galdin's mother had placed red powder on Nylana's cheeks to make them glow. She appeared as beautiful in death as she was in life.

The wind brushed past them as though to offer its condolences. Suddenly, the world seemed a sadder place.

"We are gathered here today," said Galdin's mother, "To say farewell to a woman beloved by her people. The lands of Tesnayr will never be the same without her love and grace. Farewell, my lady."

Ryk placed a bouquet of flowers in Nylana's hands. Tears dotted his cheeks. He said nothing.

"She was far braver than I," said Galdin, "I only wish I had treated her with more kindness."

"I'm sure she knows," said Trya. "Pig-headed the both of you. The elves will mourn this day."

A baleful scream filled the air. A lone man with black skin ran up to them in frenzy. Galdin prepared to defend them all when the stranger halted before Nylana's lifeless body. He dropped to his knees.

Leaning over Nylana's still form, the man cried out in anguish. "I have failed you, my lady. It should be me laying there not you."

The black man plucked a flower from the bouquet Ryk had placed in her cold hands. Gingerly, he stuck it in her hair removing stray strands from her face. "Curse you voice on the wind," shouted the man, "I prayed that you'd lead me to her while she lived. But you brought me to her grave. Curse you all."

Galdin and the others stood still watching him. Clearly, this man knew Nylana. None wanted to disturb him unsure of what he might do considering his outburst upon seeing her.

The soft cry of a bird distracted them. A brilliant bird of gold and red swooped low and landed near Nylana's head. Galdin moved to chase the animal away. Recognizing the phoenix, Trya grabbed his arm holding him back.

The black man looked into the phoenix's sad eyes.

"You curse what you do not understand," the bird said.

Gracefully, the phoenix bent low over Nylana. A tear escaped its eye as it placed its head upon her chest. Gradually, a glow of gold and white light emanated from it. It grew in intensity enveloping all of them. Slowly, the light died until only the sun warmed them.

The phoenix had gone. A blue rose rested in its place. A sharp intake of breath alerted everyone that Nylana lived. Her eyes fluttered open focusing on the black man kneeling beside her. Slowly, she lifted a hand to his cheek. "Narúl," she whispered, "I knew you'd find me."

Elated, Narúl took her hand kissing it. "My lady, you live. Forgive me. I should never have let you go to Pras'quel alone. If I had accompanied you—"

"It would have made little difference. You would have died like the others."

Narúl helped Nylana sit up. He had her lean on his shoulder as he helped her stand. The others gathered around them in excitement at the miracle they had witnessed. Slowly, they led her into the cabin so that she could rest. Only Trya remained outside.

She stared at where the phoenix had been. Suddenly, the world felt different. It felt more barren than before. There was only one phoenix in the world and it had given its life so that a woman might live. Now its magic had gone, and so had life itself. But only Trya noticed it.

At dawn the next morning they left Galdin's mother for Norlyk. Despite attempts to make her rest, Nylana insisted on returning home. "I am fine," she had told Narúl during one of his protests. "It is time I return home."

"And what of this man," Narúl gestured to Galdin. "I do not trust him."

"But I do. And if it wasn't for any of them, I would have died in Pras'quel."

Nylana walked over to Galdin's mother. "Thank you for your kindness."

"You are most welcome," replied the old woman.

"I will return as soon as I am able," said Galdin as he bade farewell to his mother.

"You'll not return," said his mother. "Oh, do not look at me like that. There is a change within the air. Take care of her, Galdin. She needs you."

"I will return."

His mother smiled at him giving him a gentle kiss on the cheek. "My door is always open."

All of their farewells said, they traveled down the road that led straight to Norlyk. Galdin's mother watched them leave. A horrible cough sounded as she brought a handkerchief to her mouth. As she pulled it away, a spot of blood rested in the center. Carefully, the woman folded it and put it away.

Galdin turned around and waved at her. She returned the wave with a broad grin. "Farewell, my son. Take care of yourself."

Chapter XV
Norlyk

The palace spires shone brilliantly in the sunlight as they approached Norlyk. Warmth filled Nylana as she looked upon it, glad to be home.

The smells of the various vendors cooking meats and vegetables overpowered her nose. Nylana took it all in enjoying every minute of it. The clanging of cast iron pots overflowing with the special of the day caused her stomach to growl.

"Free soup," yelled one man in an attempt to draw customers in.

Galdin shook his head pushing everyone forward. "Here we are," he said as they came upon a small shop. He steered Nylana inside.

"May I help you?" asked the owner.

"Sheldon," said Galdin.

"Galdin! Trya!" Sheldon gave them both hugs greeting them warmly; clearly excited to see them. "How long has it been?"

"Too long," said Galdin. He placed a pouch of coins on the counter.

"Now, you know you didn't have to," said Sheldon taking the money.

"We owed you for the items we borrowed," said Galdin. "How is business?"

"Oh, can't complain. Things haven't been going well here. There are grumblings of conflict between the five lands."

"They always grumble," said Trya, "But it will subside in time."

"I do not think so," said Sheldon. "King Krispyn has not handled things at all well. And with the Lady Nylana dead, I fear that there will be no calming them."

"Dead?" Nylana stepped out of the shadows where she had been standing with Narúl and Ryk.

"Yes. She disappeared over half a year ago. The King of Pras'quel sent his condolences, but—" Sheldon noticed Nylana for the first time. "My lady, forgive me—I—I didn't mean—"

"Calm down," said Nylana. "You had no reason to know I was here."

"Why this is a cause for celebration. We must tell everyone."

"I do not wish my presence to be known yet," said Nylana. "It is best if I speak with my brother first."

"As you wish, my lady," said Sheldon. He started to kneel before her, but Nylana caught his arm and gently pulled him back to his feet.

"We must go," said Trya. "As always, Sheldon, it was a pleasure."

They left the tiny shop stepping out onto the busy street. Nylana kept her hood up to avoid being recognized. Though many merchants continued business as usual, things seemed different.

"Stop," said a guard as they approached the palace gate. "Only those with express invitations are allowed in."

"Invitation?" said Trya, "The palace is always open to visitors."

"Not anymore," said the guard, "And shouldn't you have left with your own kind."

"My own kind?" Trya's testiness showed in her voice.

Nylana listened, curious as to why the rules had been changed. "Let them through," she said, authoritatively.

"On whose orders?" challenged the guard.

"On my orders," said Nylana as she lowered the hood of her cloak, "Or have you forgotten who I am, sergeant?"

The guard gaped at her not believing his eyes. "Princess? Is it you?"

"Yes, it is me. Now let us pass."

"But I have orders from King Krispyn," said the guard.

"And those orders are being rescinded," said Nylana, "Now let my friends and I through."

Narúl grasped the blade of his knife prepared to fight if necessary. He sensed a change in the atmosphere since the day he had left.

"Ye...Yes, my lady," stammered the guard. "We will provide you with an escort."

"No escort will be necessary," said Nylana, "Where is my brother?"

"In the council chambers," answered the guard, "He called a meeting."

"Thank you. Now open the gates," ordered Nylana, "The palace has always been a place where people could come and go freely and that is to remain. The rest of you come with me."

Nylana marched across the courtyard toward the castle entrance with her friends in tow. She held her head high allowing all eyes to notice her presence.

Unbeknownst to all of them, Magi watched from above waving her tail happily. Her lady had returned.

Nylana burst through the giant doors of the council chamber allowing their squeals to announce her presence. "I leave for half a year and already the five lands have plunged into war. How is this possible when we have had five hundred years of peace?"

Everyone stared at her as though they saw a ghost. "My lady?"

"Nylana!" Krispyn jumped from his chair and hugged his sister. For a moment, Galdin thought he saw a look of disappointment and anger, but it disappeared so quickly that he passed it off as his imagination.

"Brother," greeted Nylana. "It has been too long. Now what goes on here? And why were the castle gates barred?"

"For safety, of course," soothed Krispyn. "After we received news that you had died, I feared for the safety of everyone."

"I appreciate your concern, but I am not dead and you needn't worry. Now what goes on here?"

Nylana's new authoritative attitude caught the council by surprise; very different from her previous and more malleable manner.

"My lady," said one of the council members, "You seem changed."

"Six months of forced labor will do that," said Nylana, "I apologize for my abrupt manner, but it seems that I have returned home to a land that is much changed."

"It is nothing that cannot be solved," said Krispyn, "We were discussing my coronation. As I am—was the only heir we thought that by making my kingship formal it would quell the disputes."

"But now the council can conduct its normal review process of your reign," said an older member, "Now that the princess has returned."

Once again, Galdin thought he saw a glimmer of anger on Krispyn's face.

"I am afraid things are a bit more complicated than that," said Nylana. She reached out and pulled Galdin towards her. "Meet Galdin, my brother."

Silence ensued.

"Your brother?" asked the same elderly council member, "You mean, you've made him an honorary member of your family?"

"No," said Nylana, "I mean that he is my brother. The prince that was lost nearly twenty-five years ago."

A clatter echoed throughout the room as a cup hit the floor and an orange tabby cat scurried away.

"He does bear a resemblance," said one. "And who is the elf?"

"A friend," answered Nylana, "And she will be treated with the respect that is due."

"Yes, my lady."

"Fetch the wizard," ordered Krispyn. "He will know if this man is an imposter or not."

Though infuriated by Krispyn's words, Nylana maintained her composure. Petra would discern the truth.

Moments later the wizard entered the room striding briskly to Nylana and enveloping her in a giant hug. She returned the embrace thrilled at seeing him again.

"Petra," said Krispyn, "This man claims to be the lost prince of Tesnayr. Though I do not doubt you, sister, he could be anyone."

Intrigued, Petra eyed Galdin who moved uncomfortably under the wizard's gaze. *Same basic facial features. Same mannerisms.* Petra reached out and snatched Galdin's arm noting the mark on it. He reached for Nylana's and the mark she bore. A smile crept across his face as he placed the two together and the marks formed a bird.

"It is he. It is Galdin the Prince of Tesnayr, true heir to the throne."

Galdin opened his mouth to protest, but Trya touched his arm lightly, warning him to remain silent.

"Then we shall have a feast," exclaimed the members of the council, "To celebrate the return of our lady and of the lost prince."

"Why this changes everything," said another council member, "Galdin here, by law, is the rightful heir. We must talk about succession there isn't any time to waste."

"Later," said a third member, "Tonight we celebrate. Tomorrow we will discuss what the law says about these things."

"Krispyn," whispered Nylana, "Why do you look so disheartened?"

"It is nothing," replied Krispyn as he hugged his sister, "It's just a moment ago you were dead and now you are here while they discuss the line of succession. It is just overwhelming."

"Do not worry about it. In the end it does not matter who is crowned so long as the lands of Tesnayr remain safe and prosperous. Besides, you will always be my little brother."

"It warms my heart to see you again," said Petra pulling Nylana away from everyone, "What happened?"

"Later," said Nylana. "For now, see to it that Galdin, Ryk, and Trya are taken care of while I go and rest."

Nylana wandered among the tombs of past kings and queens of Tesnayr. She studied each of them; their structures and art. She fiddled with the blue rose allowing the silky petals to brush between her fingers. Thoughts plagued her mind. She had died, yet remembered nothing of it. Now she stood among the living. *How is it possible?*

"I thought I'd find you here."

Nylana turned toward Petra who had come up behind her.

"Is something on your mind?"

"A great many things," said Nylana.

She moved the rose to her pocket, but Petra stopped her. Taking it, the wizard studied it. A clouded expression covered his features as his bushy brows scrunched together.

"So, it is true," he said. "I thought I felt a change in the air."

"Change? What do you mean?"

"A week ago I felt something different. It is difficult to explain, but those with magic sense when the balance of the earth has been upset. Magic has died. It is dwindling. The earth is more barren than it was. It is void of light."

Nylana shook her head in frustration. She hated it when the wizard talked like this. "Petra, you're not making any sense."

"That is because you are not listening." He handed Nylana her rose. "What do you feel?"

"Confused."

"Not emotion. Sensation."

Nylana fingered the blue rose. Its brilliance shocked her.
Most flowers would have wilted by now, but this one still looked
as though it was still attached to its stem.

Her fingers tingled as a warm sensation moved through them
and up her arm; a pleasant feeling. Music entered her ears. She
never remembered hearing it before. She heard the chirping of
the birds, but not as most people heard them. They sounded
sadder as though a deep sorrow had entered their hearts. Even
the wind wept and cried. But amongst all that sorrow rested a
glimmer of hope.

"I don't understand," said Nylana.

"Only one other ever had a flower such as that," said Petra,
"And she died five hundred years ago. The phoenix spared her
life as well, but there was a difference. There were two in her
day, so when one died the other lived on and the earth remained
as it was.

"There was no other phoenix to replace the one that died for
you."

"Petra, you're not making any sense."

"I am an old man, Nylana. In all my years I have learned a
few things about the world. There is a magic in this world that
enables grass to grow and crops to ripen. It is what gives the
wind life and the power to spread it across the land. But it is
there no longer. It died when the phoenix died. You feel it too,
even if you do not realize it."

Frowning, Nylana finally understood what the wizard meant.
The plants seemed wilted as though they were dying. Emptiness
prevailed. "Trya said something similar as well."

"The elves have always been connected with the land. She
would feel it. I have something that might be of interest to you."

Nylana trailed after the wizard, curiosity guiding her
movements.

From dark shadows eyes watched as the wizard left with the princess. *So she survived the poison*, thought the cloaked figure. No matter; he had the ear of the king. All proceeded according to plan and soon the lands of Tesnayr would have bigger problems.

A tail brushed his leg. "Stupid cat," spat the stranger as he kicked the animal that roamed the palace grounds. The cat screeched and darted off disappearing around a corner. The man stalked back to the celebrations. A man in his position could not remain absent for long or questions would arise.

Peeking around the corner, the cat wrinkled her whiskers watching the mysterious man walk away. Her eyes studied him memorizing what details the cloak did not hide. Unnoticed, Magi padded across the stone courtyard after Nylana and Petra.

Galdin stared at the finger food on the banquet table trying to decide if he dared eat it. He pulled on the collar of his tunic. It itched and scratched. Wishing he could leave and go back to the wild, Galdin snatched a chicken leg and walked away staying on the sidelines.

The constant chattering of the court annoyed him. He missed the simplicity of his life before he met Nylana. He wanted to leave.

Galdin put his food down and marched out of the chamber and to the room where he had been placed as a guest. Quickly, he changed from the formal clothes he wore to his usual fare. Swiftly and noiselessly, Galdin packed his bag with food and water making certain he had enough to last a few days.

He scribbled a note for Trya telling her where to meet him figuring that he could leave it in her room before he left.

"Leaving?"

Galdin whirled around. "Trya! How did you—"

"I noticed you had left the festivities and figured I would find you here." She strolled elegantly into the room allowing the dress that the servants had gotten for her to flow behind her in waves. "You never did care for such elaborate settings."

"I've done what I promised," replied Galdin, "The princess Nylana is back home safely. It is time for us to leave. We can slip out unnoticed."

"A coward's way," scolded Trya.

"I am no coward."

"Not on the battlefield. But here you shrink away like a child afraid of being caught stealing sweets from the kitchens."

"I don't belong here."

"But you do," said Trya, "The prince of the five lands; the first born son belongs here in Norlyk."

"I have no place here. Krispyn is the king and he has Nylana to guide him. I need to get out of here." He shoved more items into his pack.

"You fear responsibility too much," said Trya.

"No more than you."

"The life we've led the past seven years has been a good one. But selling our services for the highest bidder cannot continue. We are mercenaries, Galdin, loyal to no one. Such a life always leads to a dismal end.

"I left Belarnia because I feared what would be asked of me if I had stayed. I left for the same reasons you are fleeing now. Do not make the same mistake."

"I do not want to be king," sighed Galdin.

"Perhaps, but why not let them decide?"

"And allow others to dictate my life?"

"There is a difference between accepting responsibility and allowing yourself to be ruled by it. Before you knew who you were, you could roam the wilds without a care. But now that you know the truth, to abandon it is cowardice."

Trya snatched the bag from Galdin and tossed it aside. "Stay. For once in your life do not run away."

Galdin sat on the bed staring at the flame of a candle. He remembered the day he had left home. It had been his fifteenth birthday and his mother had arranged for him to be apprenticed to a tanner. Fearing his life would be over, he left. Soon afterwards, he met a stranger, a lone warrior. Together they traveled the lands while he learned the man's trade. And so began Galdin's life as a mercenary. Such a life suited a man afraid of staying in one place for long.

"Why did you save her?"

"I don't know. I saw her running that day, fleeing from those men. On any other day I would have ignored it, but I could not ignore this. I can't explain it."

"And why did you stay with her? Why bring her here? You haven't asked for the money that was promised."

"It doesn't mean anything now," replied Galdin.

"Because it is natural for a brother to save his sister. You may not have known then, but something within you did. There is a change in the wind, Galdin. Something is coming. Something dark, and elusive."

"I hate it when you speak like that," said Galdin.

"It's there," replied Trya, "All that is needed from you is a decision. Will you stay and help Nylana, or will you run and hide as you've always done?"

"Help Nylana?"

"You can be certain that whatever happens, Nylana will not flee from it." The elf walked out.

Galdin gripped his sword. Grimacing, he untied it from around his waist and tossed it aside. Shamed into staying.

Nylana read the passages in the book that Petra had given her listening intently to what he said about the phoenix and how it brought life to the world.

"But, Petra, does it really matter?"

"It does," insisted Petra. "The phoenix has always been a symbol of great hope. Without it people will lose faith."

"Most think that it is merely a myth. Very few believe in magic these days."

"And yet you hold proof that it isn't a myth." Petra pointed to the blue rose in Nylana's hands. "It is up to you to restore it. The phoenix can be brought back."

"How can I possibly restore what has been lost?"

Frustrated, Petra rubbed his temples.

"Tears of healing," muttered Nylana, "My tears do not do that."

"What was that song that your mother sang when your father died?"

"Nylee y'lee nisele'han," whispered Nylana, tears welled in her eyes as she remembered the day they buried her father and mourned the loss of Galdin.

Petra brought a knife to his hand cutting it deep as red blood spilled onto the desk.

"What are you doing?" cried Nylana in horror.

Ignoring her outburst, the wizard wiped a tear from her face and rubbed it onto his bleeding hand. He held it up to her. Awestruck, Nylana watched as the cut healed itself.

"What more do you need in the way of proof?" asked Petra.

"You want me to travel the five lands searching for this magical thing that will resurrect the phoenix? Petra, this is madness. I don't even know where to look. I don't think I can."

"Tap, tap go my feet."

Petra and Nylana looked up as Tabs entered the room. The cat paced around to the song he sang.

"Crisscross." Tabs crossed his front paws and then uncrossed them. "Come on you two. Join in."

"Who—What—" began Nylana.

"Meet Tabs, the talking cat who never stops singing," said Petra.

"Cats really do talk?"

"I just wish I knew how to get him to quit talking," mumbled Petra.

"I am a talking cat that sings. Oh, give me a drink and I'll do a beat," sang Tabs.

A finch landed just outside the window and pecked at a flower. Tabs licked his lips as he watched it greedily.

"Oh, sweet bird of music, how I wish you were in my tummy," sang Tabs. He continued after receiving a piercing glare from Petra. "Perhaps I should refrain from that prospect as the wizard would get all grumpy."

Nylana chuckled at the orange tabby's performance. "You have a most wonderful singing voice, my dear cat."

Nylana noticed the serious expression on Petra's face. "I'll think about it. After tomorrow's council I'll let you know what I've decided."

"Very well," said Petra, "Perhaps I should not have burdened you with this just now."

"Good night, Petra. You have always been a good friend." Nylana rose, scratched Tabs' ears. She suddenly felt very weary.

Chapter XVI
A Lost Relic

Vasagius strolled through the village reveling in the wails of broken hearted mothers as they cradled their freshly murdered children. A sardonic grin crept across his face when he noticed a young man weeping over the body of his new bride. Tendrils of smoke stretched from the fires his men started. Breathing deeply, Vasagius relished it. He enjoyed these moments.

King Tesnayr, he thought, if only he could see this now. A crying child caught his attention. He strolled over to the boy and knelt down.

"Hello," said Vasagius, pretending to be concerned.

"I can't find my mommy," sniffed the boy.

"No? Here," Vasagius held out his hand.

The boy took it while wiping away his tears with the back of his hand. Together they walked among the carnage searching for the boy's parents.

"Jimmy!"

A woman broke away from a small group running for the boy. She slid across the rough ground as she fell to her knees and hugged him tightly.

"Jimmy."

The two cried as the woman planted kisses all over her son's face.

Vasagius enjoyed every minute. "Where is your husband?" he asked in mock concern.

Shakily, the woman pointed to a man. Instantly, two of Vasagius' men grabbed him and dragged him over to their general. They forced him to his knees. With a mixture of hatred and fear, the man stared defiantly into the barbarian leader's eyes.

"You love your wife," said Vasagius.

The man glanced at the woman with the boy.

"Of course you do," continued Vasagius, "And you love your son as well. Tell me, with whom could you live without?"

"No," breathed the man as the realization of Vasagius' words dawned on him. "Please, don't."

Smirking, Vasagius circled the man. He loved it when they begged. It made it more satisfying. He gripped the woman's hair jerking her away from the boy. "Answer me! The boy or your wife."

"I beg of you," pleaded the man, "Leave them be. They are innocent."

"There are no innocents." He ripped out his knife and slashed it across the woman's throat enjoying every second as she clutched the wound gasping for air. He walked over to the boy. Wide eyed, the boy stared at Vasagius. Any other man would have been moved. His meaty hand grabbed the child by the chin holding him before his father.

"Why?" asked the man through tears.

"Why not?" Vasagius broke the boy's neck and dumped the body before the man. Slowly, he leaned down so he could whisper in the grieving man's ear. "I want the last thing you see to be the corpses of your family."

Vasagius stood up straight eyeing the work of his men. "Though, I can be merciful."

Suddenly, he whirled around jabbing his knife into the man's lower back. As the man lay dying, Vasagius casually wiped his weapon clean; the man's last sight being that of a man that enjoyed death.

"So weak," mumbled Vasagius to himself as he watched people attempt to flee. "Burn it all. Leave none alive."

*   *   *

"We are glad to have you returned to us safely, my lady," said Byron, the ambassador from Hemíl. "As always, we appreciate your input on the council's decision."

"Thank you, Byron," said Nylana.

"The council's decision concerning Krispyn is meaningless as the true heir of Tesnayr has returned," said the wizard.

"What do you mean?" asked Byron.

"Nylana's first brother, Galdin, has returned. By law he is the rightful heir to the throne and Krispyn must step aside."

"Step aside? Have my years as king meant nothing?" demanded Krispyn. "I have given much to the lands of Tesnayr and you are going to throw me aside with the scraps?"

"Krispyn we do not mean—"

"Mean what? To toss me aside? This man only just arrived and already you are willing to hand him the throne. Where was he when Tesnayr needed him most?"

"He only just learned the truth," said Nylana, "We all have only just learned of his survival. And he did save me from a life of slavery."

"For which I will always be grateful," said Krispyn, "But how do you know he is your lost brother?"

"He bears the mark," said the wizard. "It is him."

"The mark? Next you will be telling us that the sorceress has returned," mocked Felize.

"Sorceress?" asked Galdin.

"There is a story," began Nylana, "That at a time when Tesnayr is in grave danger, Quesha, the sorceress will return for the last time."

"Foolishness, really," added Krispyn.

"Is that so?" said a silky voice, "Of course, you would know all about it wouldn't you?" Appearing from a far corner within the court was a tall, elegant woman. "Allow me to introduce myself. I am Quesha du'Adieu and I have returned."

Everyone stared at the stranger. She approached Galdin with a gracefulness none could ever hope to possess. "Heir you may be," she whispered to him, "But you will never sit on the throne."

"I don't understand," said Galdin.

"Oh, take it if it is offered." Her breath moistened Galdin's ear. "But remember this: only the one with the sword, the phoenix, and the horn can command the throne."

"Do you know whom that will be?" asked Galdin.

"I know not," replied Quesha. "But this I do know." At that instant Quesha repeated the lines of a child's song that all within the five lands knew well.

> When darkness looms
> And all is gloom
> Two will rise
> Bearing the mark combined.
>
> One, the phoenix dwells within
> And hope he shall restore.
> A gift he needs from its glen
> And a tear from old lore
> And one item more
>
> The other, harsh punishment will he bear.
> To keep alive a people's soul, he must spare
> Them sorrow's pain and betrayal's snare.

"We all know that children's rhyme. What is this all about?" demanded Byron.

"No man in this room will sit upon the throne of Tesnayr," said Quesha.

"Are you really the sorceress?" asked Nylana, doubtfully.

Quesha eyed Nylana for a long moment. "What do you believe?"

"But Tesnayr is not in any grave danger," said Nylana.

"It is in more peril than you realize. Than all of you realize," Quesha said.

"Enough of this," yelled Krispyn. "Sorceress or not, we have other matters to discuss. I am not comfortable handing the throne to a man who has never concerned himself with the affairs of Tesnayr until now."

"It is not your decision," said Petra.

"Krispyn," soothed Nylana as she stepped behind the throne her brother sat upon, "As always you are eager to prove yourself. You will be given what you are owed, but first you must learn to govern wisely."

"As always, sister, you are right," said Krispyn.

"However, I must agree that to hand the throne to Galdin indefinitely is not wise. Perhaps he should be given a test to prove himself, and then the council may choose the one they feel is best suited to be king," said Nylana to the court.

"My lady, once again you have proven your wisdom," said Felize. "As the representative of MurDair, we will abide by this decision. What say you, Galdin? Do you wish to prove yourself?"

Galdin remained silent. He had no wish to be king and wanted to leave. But something Quesha told him stilled his tongue. He looked at his sister. Her pleading eyes made the choice for him.

"Yes," he said.

Nylana patted Krispyn on the shoulder in loving reassurance. As she stepped out from behind the throne, she tripped. Before losing her balance completely, she reached out and clutched the side of the throne. A deafening clatter filled the room as a sword fell onto the marble floor for all to see. Everyone stared at it in astonishment not believing what it was.

Krispyn reached down. The moment he touched it a sizzling zap struck him leaving a burn mark on his hand. He yanked it back in pain.

Concerned, both Nylana and Galdin picked up the sword. A warmth flowed through them as they wrapped their fingers around the hilt. The blade glowed brightly revealing the symbols upon it, especially that of the phoenix.

"Take it," said Galdin, releasing his hold on the blade. "It was you who found it."

"It cannot be," said Felize.

"That sword was lost," breathed Byron in disbelief.

The wizard strode over and inspected the weapon. He turned it over in his hands studying it closely. Gingerly, he handed it back to Nylana. "There is no denying it," he said, "The sword of Tesnayr has been found. And clearly, it has chosen its master. Or masters." Petra glanced in Galdin's direction.

"How interesting," said Quesha with a smile. "How very interesting."

"I'm sorry," said Nylana, "But what is so interesting?"

"The sword has chosen both of you," replied Quesha.

"My Lord Krispyn," shouted a messenger as he darted into the courtroom out of breath. "My Lord Krispyn, Belyndril burns!"

"What?" Krispyn jumped from his chair. "How is this possible?"

"I do not know, my lord," said the messenger, "But the western edge of Belyndril is in flames."

"Sorceress," Krispyn turned toward Quesha only to find a vacant area.

"What are we to do?" asked a member of the council.

"I shall send someone to Belyndril. To observe what has happened there. Shelwyk."

"Yes, my king." Shelwyk stepped forward in his usual attire of black clothing.

"Find a man to travel to Belyndril."

"No need," said Nylana, "I will go."

"But you've only just returned," said Krispyn.

"I know, but it would be best if it were me. You are needed here."

"But, Nylana, surely another can go in your place," said Krispyn.

"No," said Nylana, forcefully, "I will go. Narúl will be with me so there is no need to worry about my welfare."

"Very well," conceded Krispyn, "If you insist. But, be careful."

Nylana smiled at her brother and left. Petra chased after her. "My lady," he stopped her. "You mustn't go chasing shadows. You are needed here. You need to find—"

"I am sorry, Petra," said Nylana, "But I cannot do what you want me to. I must go to Belyndril. And I need you to stay here as my eyes and ears."

"Nylana, please," begged Petra, "There is more to this than a band of barbarians invading from the north. I feel it."

"I cannot spend my time searching for some lost relic that may not even exist."

"Nylana—"

"I'm sorry." Nylana touched Petra's cheek before marching away to her chambers. She had much planning to do.

*   *   *

Orrin leaned on the balcony in the moonlight. He sighed heavily. His father had died the previous week and he was the newly crowned King of Pras'quel. So much to do, he thought to himself, so many wrongs to right.

His mind momentarily lingered on the band of people he had traveled with a month before. I wonder what's happened to them, he thought, did they make it home safely?

He felt something in the palm of his hand. Carefully, he unfolded the bit of paper. *How did this get here?* Orrin read the note before scrunching it up and tossing it into the fire.

"Pity you do not like my note," said a sly voice.

Orrin whirled around coming face to face with Quesha. "Who are you? How did you get in here?"

"I might have come through that open window. Or perhaps the door. And there is always the chimney."

Orrin stared at her.

"How I got in is unimportant. What is important is that you follow the instructions in that note and do not detour from them.

"The lands of Tesnayr are about to face their greatest test and they will need you before the end. If you wish to preserve your treaty with them I suggest you heed my warning."

"Perhaps I should kill you where you stand," threatened Orrin.

"If you like." Quesha vanished before his eyes.

Orrin turned in circles searching for her.

"But I doubt you will succeed," whispered Quesha into Orrin's ear.

"What is your purpose in all this?" asked Orrin.

"Long ago I was charged with the protection of the lands of Tesnayr. That is my purpose." Quesha reappeared and placed her hand over Orrin's before turning to leave. "Heed the instructions I have given you. Follow them exactly, or Pras'quel will diminish." Quesha had gone.

Carefully, Orrin opened his hand to find the same piece of paper with the same bit of writing on it. He folded it neatly before placing it in his pocket. "Guard!"

A man entered the chamber.

"Summon the generals and their troops. Tell them to assemble on the transport ships. We leave for Tesnayr in the morning."

Chapter XVII
Leaving Norlyk

Galdin stood in the window staring out at the gloomy dusk settling over Norlyk. He remembered the city. He recalled coming here with his mother one day as a child to assist her in selling her quilts.

How the city has changed, he thought to himself. It seemed less robust. The five lands had changed. He noticed it upon his return from Pras'quel. Never before had he cared. *Why do I care now?*

One answer: Nylana.

Her insistence that he claim his birthright forced him to stay in the city. Her insistence that he remain forced him to see the five lands in a new light. Nylana's love for her people gnawed at him.

A drizzling rain beat against the window lulling him with a soft tapping on the glass. Movement below caught his attention. Galdin peered more closely and noticed Trya strolling to the stables. *What was she up to?* He did not remember the elf telling him about her intentions to accompany Nylana.

He felt the urge to rush to the courtyard to learn what his friend was up to. Galdin reached for his cloak to find it missing.

"Going somewhere?" said a silky voice.

Galdin whipped around.

Quesha stood erect in the room facing him; his cloak in her hands. "I thought you had decided to leave Norlyk. Then you decided to remain and not accompany your sister to Belyndril. Now it appears that you have changed your mind once again."

"What business is it of yours?" spat Galdin, annoyed.

"None really," replied Quesha, "But then again, it is my business."

"I don't see how."

"The lands of Tesnayr are my business. You are the crown prince; the first born son. So that makes you my business."

"What do you want?"

"The real question, Galdin, is: What do you want? You have spent your life as a mercenary. Always selling your services to the highest bidder. It worked for a time. Until now.

"But life has a way of dealing out indecision. One day you are working for a wealthy lord of Pras'quel and the next you free a slave girl owned by the same lord. A girl who turns out to be your sister. Oh, and what a twist that she is the Princess of Tesnayr. Why did you rescue her that day?"

Galdin thought for a moment. He hadn't truly thought about it since. "I don't know really. I just felt I had to."

"Had to?"

"Look, if that stupid phoenix hadn't shown up I never would have noticed her."

"The phoenix," whispered Quesha as she meandered through the room, "How very interesting. Such coincidence."

"What is your interest in all this?" demanded Galdin.

"I am asked that question every time I appear. Amborese asked me that once. Do you know what I told her?"

"What?"

"The same thing I tell everyone: I have my reasons."

"You and your games. Tell me why you have come or get out."

"You are much like Tesnayr," said Quesha, "He never liked my mistress when she appeared to him. Very well. I am here to prevent you from making a grave mistake."

"And what mistake might that be?"

"The mistake of doing nothing," said Quesha. "You have always been satisfied to watch the world do away with itself. But now you have a responsibility. What will you do with it?"

"I'll not discuss this with you."

"One day, Galdin, you will have to make a choice. You must decide what sort of man you wish to be." Quesha peeked out the window. "Oh, your friend Trya has three horses saddled and ready. My guess is that not a one of them is for you."

Galdin eyed the sorceress. He disliked her immensely. He glanced out the window hurt that Trya had not told him she was leaving. Or had she and he hadn't listened?

"It eats away at you doesn't it?" said Quesha, watching him, "That conflict within. You wish to continue as you always have. It's familiar. It's easier. But something deep inside picks at you, and reminds you that you are more than what you have become. Urging you to leap forward and do the unexpected. If you are not careful, it will destroy you."

"What should I do?"

"Only you can decide that," said Quesha as she stepped away. "Though, Nylana is still in her room packing. It will take her at least an hour to finish as a few of her things have mysteriously disappeared. That gives you enough time to make your way to the stables and saddle a horse."

"But barely enough to pack myself."

"You think so?" Quesha tossed a heavy bag to Galdin. He caught it marveling at its weight. "I took the liberty of packing for you. Hope you don't mind."

Galdin strapped the bag to his shoulders. "I am not fit for the throne."

Quesha smiled one of her all-knowing smiles. "You, Galdin, are far more worthy of the throne than others. You are heir to a throne that you will never sit upon. But there are other ways to save the five lands."

Galdin stared at Quesha a moment before moving towards the door.

"Galdin," said Quesha, "You might want this. It's a little wet outside." The sorceress threw him his cloak.

Nylana placed the last bits of wrapped food into her pack. After learning of Belyndril's demise, she decided to leave immediately. Petra had tried to talk her out of it. She refused to listen. Something had changed in the lands of Tesnayr.

In the early hours of the morning, she met Narúl at the stables. "I believe we will not be going alone," he said.

Nylana charged inside to find Galdin and Trya waiting with four saddled horses. "What's this?"

"We are coming with you," said Galdin.

"You need to stay here. As the possible heir to the throne, you should remain and—"

"As the possible heir to the throne it is my duty to learn what ails the land. And as I have not been recompensed for returning you safely, I figure that means you are still my charge."

"But—" began Nylana.

"We are wasting time," finished Galdin.

Relenting, Nylana mounted her horse. "Fine. But it is my command we will obey. Understood?"

"I would never dream of arguing with you," said Galdin.

They rode outside to find Ryk seated upon a horse waiting impatiently.

"What's this?" asked Nylana.

"Did you think that I would allow you to go so easily?" replied Ryk. "I love you, my lady, and wish to marry you."

Aggravated, Nylana steered her horse past him mumbling under her breath.

Galdin, rode up to Ryk and smacked him on the back of the head.

"Hey!" said Ryk. "I thought it was a good proposal."

"The only way you will marry Nylana is if I don't kill you first," whispered Narúl to Ryk.

"You're joking, right?" said Ryk as he followed the others. "You wouldn't really kill me, would you?"

Narúl and the others remained silent as they left the palace grounds.

Above them, Artryl leaned over the stone wall as he watched them leave. He rushed to the barracks where the other boys slept. Without wasting any time, Artryl tossed a bag onto his bed and shoved items into it. He wrapped a cloak around his shoulders before dashing to the stables. This time, no one was going to stop him.

By midafternoon the rain had stopped and the sun poked through the clouds drying everything. The light reflected off of the few drops left behind creating miniature rainbows. The plains sparkled brilliantly from the moisture that remained on the grass.

"What do you keep looking at?" Galdin demanded of Ryk who had spent the last five minutes glancing behind them.

"Nothing—it's just—"

"Just what?"

"I think that rock is moving," said Ryk, "I mean, it seems to be following us."

Everyone looked where Ryk pointed. None of them noticed anything.

"I'm telling you," insisted Ryk, "That rock is following us."

"Are you certain?" asked Nylana.

"You believe him?" said Galdin.

"Well, yes," replied Nylana, "The last time he saw a rock move it turned out to be—"

At that instant the rock that Ryk had been watching unfolded.

"Trog," exclaimed Nylana.

"It can't be," said Galdin.

"But it is him," said Nylana as Trog rolled on his back wagging his tail.

"Impossible," said Ryk, "The only way that thing could cross the ocean is if he can...fly."

A pair of wings peeled away from Trog's back as he stretched them out for all to see. He flapped them wildly tipping over from the exertion.

"You mean to tell me he followed us here?" said Galdin.

"He must have," said Nylana.

Trog noticed Galdin. Instantly, the animal leapt at the man knocking him off his horse. Galdin landed with a thump on his back as Trog stood on his chest licking his face until slime covered it.

"I think he followed you," said Trya.

"That is just disgusting," said a muffled voice from Nylana's saddlebag.

Nylana lifted the flap revealing a cat. "Magi!"

"Yes, it's me."

"You—you talk!"

"Of course I talk," said Magi, "Always have. I just never had a reason to reveal it until now. Now let's get going. We're wasting valuable time. And get rid of that thing." Magi pointed her tail at Trog whose face fell as he slumped to the ground.

"How many more are we going to attract on this trip?" demanded Galdin as he wiped the slobber off his face.

"I don't think you'll find anyone else," said a voice from his saddlebag.

Galdin peeked inside. Tabs' head popped up as he blinked in the sunlight.

"Hello everyone," said Tabs, "That was a wonderful nap. Everyone should take naps. I'm famished. What's to," Tabs noticed his surroundings for the first time, "eat? Where are we?"

"In the Azul Plains, you idiot," said Magi. "What are you doing here?"

"Don't know," replied Tabs, "Last thing I remember was looking for a nice place to curl up."

"And you chose my bag?" asked Galdin.

"It was comfy," said Tabs. "Well, you can just take me back to the palace and I'll be on my way."

Growing tired of the delay, Nylana jumped back on her horse. "We've wasted enough time. Come on. The quicker we reach

Belyndril, the quicker we can solve the problem of the barbarians."

"Belyndril?" said Tabs, "I don't want to—"

"Too bad," said Nylana, "Next time, be more careful about where you choose to sleep."

"Is she always like this?" said Tabs as Narúl passed by.

"Yes," answered Narúl.

Chapter XVIII
Fruitful Encounter

Vasagius looked out across the vast expanse before him with a satisfied smile. He spotted La'nar in the distance. The sorcerer's magic had allowed him to move his army unnoticed, even if it did mean putting up with the red eyed beasts. There were only a hundred of them, but they scared his men. Instead of dwelling on what he didn't like, Vasagius focused on what he wanted.

"What are you thinking, general?" asked Stahl.

"That this shall soon be mine."

*　　　　　*　　　　　*

Galdin looked up, pleased that they had finally entered the lower hills of the Ársa Mountains. The grassy plains become a rocky exterior with sharp gravel that cut through their boots. Whatever color the earth had to offer disappeared the further they traveled.

As the sun rose higher in the sky, they paused for a short break. Silence ensued as they ate a meager meal. Too quiet for Galdin's liking. He glanced around surveying the rocks and dusty hills. No birds. No bugs. Not even a breeze.

The hair prickled on the back of his neck as he pondered it. There should be some sounds. He placed his jerky back in his pack as he continued to survey the area.

Ryk noticed his movements and did the same. "What's the matter?" he asked.

"Nothing," answered Galdin, "Continue eating. I want to reach the mountains themselves before nightfall."

Ryk didn't answer.

Knowing this was unusual for the man, Galdin glanced at him. "What is it?"

"Nothing," said Ryk, shakily as he stared at a gigantic boulder that formed a smooth oval shape.

"Please do not tell me that the rock is moving," breathed Galdin. "Every time you see a rock move something happens." He stole a quick glance at Trog who gnawed happily on a stick.

"It looks like it's breathing," muttered Ryk.

By this time, the others had stopped nibbling on their food and looked at what Ryk pointed at. Galdin took a step closer. The boulder rose slightly, similar to an animal's body when it inhales. He jumped back. Frowning, Galdin knew Ryk had not imagined anything; he just seemed adept at noticing what they happily ignored.

"Everyone back away. Slowly," said Galdin.

Their feet shuffled on the ground as they backed up, gradually turning to head in another direction. Instantly, a massive, scaly tail rose from the ground and slammed into the dirt beside them cutting off their escape. They charged in another direction. Again the tail crashed into the ground stopping them.

"Dragon!" yelled Trya.

The earth shook as the boulder transformed into a dragon. The head swiveled around exposing razor sharp teeth covered in dark stains. Yellow eyes watched callously as they tried to flee.

"This way," yelled Galdin thinking he had found an escape route.

The others ran for it. With lightening quick reflexes, the dragon jumped in front of them cutting them off. Saliva dripped from its fangs as it growled and looked at them hungrily. The group backed away unsure of what to do. The rotting stench of the dragon's breath caused them to recoil with nausea. The dragon noticed Trog who cowered behind a lone, leafless bush. It dove for the frightened animal.

Nylana noticed the movement. "No you don't," she said as she pulled out her sword and smacked the dragon on the nose with the flat of the blade. A loud pop echoed around them. The dragon recoiled in shock. "You leave him alone," shouted Nylana, her face flushed in anger.

"Who dares speak to me with such insolence?" demanded the dragon.

"Nylana, Princess of the five lands of Tesnayr." Nylana held her weapon tightly ready to defend herself if necessary.

"Your name means nothing to me," said the dragon.

"It doesn't matter," said Nylana, "I will strike you again if you touch him."

Taken aback by her defensive and aggressive stance, the others gawked at her. Narúl moved closer to Nylana unsheathing his own weapon. "As will I," he said.

The dragon eyed them both. Quickly, it lashed out grasping the sword in its teeth only to receive an electric shock. Stunned, the dragon dropped the blade shaking its head. It roared and licked its lips to ease the searing pain.

Cautiously, Nylana picked up her sword. Though she had no idea of what had just happened, she resumed her stance ready to defend Trog and the rest of them.

"What is that menace?" demanded the dragon.

"My sword," said Nylana.

"Lies," spat the dragon, "That is no sword. No blade does what that just did. My lip will hurt for a week. Let me see it."

Thinking this a great way to buy time, Nylana held up her weapon so that the dragon could study it. While she did so, Galdin looked around for any possible chance of escape. He found none.

"That blade, where did you get it?" said the dragon.

"Uh—it just appeared one day," answered Nylana. She did not know how to explain it.

"Appeared?"

"Yes," said Galdin, stepping forward, "We were all there. It seems to be a magical sword."

"Magical barely describes it," said the dragon, "You do not know the value of what she carries." The beast turned back to Nylana, "You may carry Tesnayr's sword but you do not command me."

Nylana stared at the dragon confused. "Command?"

"The horn of Selexia," said Trya, "Amborese severed its power."

"She released the dragons from service to Tesnayr's heirs," said the dragon.

"And so you thank her by making meals of us?" demanded Nylana.

Galdin debated inwardly with himself about smacking his sister for her authoritative tone. Taking such a stance when a dragon can easily eat them all in one bite was not ideal. "Nylana," he whispered out of the side of his mouth.

"Food is scarce," the dragon continued ignoring Nylana's outburst, "And I must eat."

"You will have to find food elsewhere," said Nylana not knowing where this new attitude came from. The sword in her hand glowed brightly surrounding her with gold light. "We have business in Belyndril. You will let us pass safely."

"Nylana," Galdin's voice took on a more insistent tone. *Is she crazy?*

The others gaped at her.

"You are a bossy one," said the dragon. "I will silence you—"

"If you must," Nylana's tone changed. "But I would know your name first."

"Uriel."

"I was going to ask a favor but you probably couldn't do it anyway," said Nylana as she casually studied her fingernails.

The others stared at her wondering what she was doing.

"Do what?" asked the dragon, intrigued.

"Well, if you wish to eat us that is fine, but we need to get to Belyndril. I just thought you could carry us there so that we may complete our errand first. But you look so tired I wouldn't want to impose. We will just be going."

Nylana turned and started to walk away. She had gotten a few feet when—

WHAM!

The dragon slammed its tail into the dirt inches from Nylana sending pebbles and grit everywhere. The others ducked to avoid most of it.

"You dare insult me?" snarled the dragon, whiffs of smoke escaping his nostrils.

"Merely a concern," replied Nylana, innocently.

The dragon reared up on his hind legs spreading his massive, leathery wings to reveal his entire size. "I may be old, but I am not embolic. I can get you—all of you—to Belyndril. Unharmed even."

"I wouldn't want to impose," said Nylana, "You can go ahead and eat us if you must."

"Are you insane?" Ryk said to her, "I don't want to be dragon food."

Nylana stomped hard on his foot to shut him up. "I know how difficult such a journey is for a dragon of your years."

The dragon's nostrils flared as his eyes formed slits. "On my back, all of you."

"I really—" began Ryk.

"Now!"

Heeding the dragon's command, they all scrambled onto his back placing themselves between the ridged backbones. The dragon spread his wings wide flapping them as dust swirled in circles. Gradually, Uriel ascended into the sky until the mountains looked like tiny specks beneath them.

"Don't you ever do that again," scolded Galdin in Nylana's ear.

She smiled inwardly at managing to shave weeks off of their journey to Belyndril and avoiding the treachery of the Ársa

Mountains. Though, she was uncertain as to what they would do when they landed.

Chapter XIX
The Fall of La'nar

Uriel landed safely outside the city of La'nar. His passengers gladly set foot back upon solid ground. Each of them eyed the dragon warily unsure of what to do.

"Now I shall claim my payment," said Uriel.

"Not yet," Nylana stopped him, "First, we must speak with Lord Trisk. Only then, may you claim your prize."

Uriel brought his face close to Nylana's studying her. Smoke escaped his nostrils as he snorted. "You are a feisty one. Very well. Since we had an agreement, I will be back for you all when your task is finished."

"We thank you," said Nylana.

"And do not attempt to flee," warned Uriel, "I will find you."

"Another kindness," said Nylana.

"Try not to get yourselves killed before I return." Uriel spread his wings and took off.

Everyone released a huge sigh of relief after the dragon's departure.

"What do you propose we do after you have spoken with Lord Trisk?" asked Ryk. "How far do you think we'll get with that dragon on our tail?"

"Honestly?" replied Nylana, "I didn't think we'd get this far."

Nylana strode off taking the lead to La'nar, which lay just below them. The others followed after her amazed at their luck, but worried about their future.

When they reached the gates, Nylana announced herself. Immediately, guards appeared to escort her and her companions to the castle. She looked around at the city and its sculptures.

Trimmed vines stretched up the ivory walls forming illustrations. The peacefulness of the place awed her as she considered the dangers that had brought her here.

"Lord Trisk is expecting you," said a messenger when they entered the castle.

Nylana entered the courtroom chamber of the palace of La'nar with her entourage of Galdin, Ryk, Trya, and Narúl. The two cats and Trog seemed to have disappeared.

"Lady Nylana," greeted Lord Trisk, "As always it is a pleasure to have you here."

"Lord Trisk," replied Nylana, taking his hand. "I am certain you know why I have come."

"Yes, but first, you must be tired from your journey. Let me get you refreshments and perhaps a chance to rest?"

"We haven't time. I came the moment I heard of the invasion of Belyndril."

Lord Trisk's face fell. "Should not your brother have come?"

"He is busy at the moment, but I am here and so is Galdin, my brother."

Lord Trisk did a double take. "Your—I do not understand."

"The Lost Prince," said Nylana.

Understanding dawned on Lord Trisk as he realized who Galdin was. "My Lord Galdin," Lord Trisk took his hand, "It is an honor to meet you. After all this time, you have returned."

Unsure of what to say, Galdin clasped Lord Trisk's hand and smiled.

"Who are these invaders?" asked Nylana.

Lord Trisk directed her to a map. "We do not know for certain. They have a base of operations here." He pointed at the map. "All my scouts are able to gather is that they came from the north; from across the sea. They have not plundered anything. They simply burn as they go."

"Raiders who take no treasure," said Galdin, "That is odd."

"Odd indeed," said Lord Trisk. "They seem intent on destroying the land for no reason except their own. Each day they head further south making their way here to La'nar. I think they are headed to MurDair next."

"Who leads them?" asked Galdin.

"No one knows," replied Lord Trisk. "It is rumored that they are led by a man dressed in black. A man who refuses to reveal his face. Yet, they also seem to be led by a man named Vasagius."

Nylana pursed her lips. She knew the name well. It belonged to the man that murdered her father and caused Galdin to be lost all those years. "So he has returned."

Galdin listened to the exchange. He knew the name as well. Everyone in the five lands did.

"I am afraid so, my lady," said Lord Trisk.

"What are we to do?" asked Nylana.

"I had hoped King Krispyn would have come. It is his doing that they are here. His new laws and taxes have weakened the five lands of Tesnayr. He sits on his throne doing nothing while people fall into squalor." Lord Trisk noticed the look on Nylana's face and stopped himself. "I am sorry for my outburst, my lady."

Nylana said nothing. She knew that there was some truth to what Lord Trisk had said.

"But people are desperate for relief and will turn anywhere, including aiding these barbarians."

"Have they given out food and aid to any who will join their cause?" asked Galdin.

"Yes," replied Lord Trisk, "And are gathering a huge following. For the price of a loaf of bread a man will sell himself and his family.

"My forces are depleted. I am afraid there is little I can do on my own and no one has answered my calls for help."

"No one?" Nylana's stunned voiced echoed through the chamber. "Do the alliances mean nothing? Does no one honor the treaty signed nearly fifteen hundred years ago?"

"I am afraid, my lady, the lands are divided once more," said Lord Trisk, "Your brother has seen to that."

"What do you mean?"

"He called on the dwarves in MurDair to send more of the treasures they find in the earth to Norlyk. He claimed that they do not contribute enough and that the other lands have been forced to make up the difference."

"That is an excellent way to cause discord," said Trya.

"Yes, it is," agreed Lord Trisk. "I am sorry, my lady, but things in Tesnayr have changed and your brother is a fool."

Nylana controlled her emotions. She loved Krispyn dearly. She helped raise him. But deep down she knew that he was not fit for the throne. "I am sure that he will come to reason."

"As always, my lady, your presence brings it," said Lord Trisk.

"Thank you, Lord Trisk. But right now we have a battle to prepare for. If we can keep the barbarian hoard contained, we should be able to minimize the damage they do. Galdin, as newly appointed general, what would you suggest?"

Not questioning Nylana's statement, Galdin stepped forward to the map noting the markings on it. Though not liking the way Nylana threw everything into his lap, he contained himself, studying the map and formulating a plan. "We should—"

An explosion roared outside as something barreled into the gates of the city.

They rushed to the outside balcony to see what had happened. The barbarians had arrived, ready for war.

An explosion rocked the walls of the castle as a boulder slammed into the watch tower. Rubble pounded the roof. Another boulder slammed into the castle. Bits of the ceiling crashed around them.

"Take me to the gates," said Galdin.

Lord Trisk motioned for one of his men to obey Galdin's request.

"My lady," Lord Trisk turned to Nylana, "We should get you out of here."

"No," said Nylana. "I'm not going anywhere."

"You cannot stay here."

"I'll not leave. What message would that send to your men if I flee like a coward?"

Galdin grabbed Ryk and shoved him to Nylana's side. "You stay here with her. If anything happens to her, I'll have your head."

Ryk touched his throat for a moment as he nodded.

"And you," Galdin turned to Nylana, "Stay here and do not do anything stupid. Trya, Narúl, with me."

Galdin raced to the front gates where the battle raged; Lord Trisk close behind. Nylana watched him disappear, disappointment on her face. She hated being left behind. Her mind raced trying to think of the weaknesses of La'nar. The sewers. They are always overlooked.

Nylana ran from the room.

"Nylana," shouted Ryk as he chased after her. "You're not to—"

She smacked her hand over his mouth. "Shh."

The clanging of spurs and heavy boots echoed just around a corner. Nylana and Ryk watched as a barbarian walked through the hallway searching for something.

How did he get in here, thought Nylana, they only just started the attack.

She pulled Ryk into the shadows as she observed the slow movement of the barbarian. He moved purposefully with his weapon raised. Nylana motioned for Ryk to go in the opposite direction hoping they wouldn't be spotted.

Just as she turned the man saw her. His weapon crashed into the wall above her barely missing her head. Bits of stone rained around her. She dodged just in time. Nylana whirled around in time to duck as the man released another blow. Ryk jumped on the man grabbing his arm. They wrestled as Ryk tried to pry the weapon out of the attacker's hand.

Nylana's hand went to her sword. She didn't know what made her do it. Power sizzled up her arm as she grasped the hilt. Knowing what to do, Nylana pulled out her sword and brought it down upon the barbarian's weapon slicing it in half. The sword glowed brightly. Staring at her in disbelief, the barbarian swung at her. Nylana dodged, twisting her body so that she could launch another attack. She jammed her sword into the man's belly.

Stunned, Ryk stood still staring at her. "Where'd you learn to do that?"

"I've always known the use of a blade," said Nylana.

"No, that was different," said Ryk. "You fought as though you were in some kind of rage."

A noise startled them.

"We should leave." Nylana sheathed her weapon and ran from the room. Ryk quickly stripped the weapons from the corpse and darted after her.

As they charged through the corridors of the castle two doors tore themselves from their hinges sprouting arms and legs. They rushed for both Ryk and Nylana swinging wildly.

"Look out!" yelled Ryk as he pushed Nylana out of the way of one of the creatures. "What is happening? Is the furniture coming alive?"

Unaware that outside the gates a sorcerer muttered spells to bring inanimate objects to life, Ryk snatched a spear from the wall and swung it at one of the creatures. The thing caught the spear and wrenched it from Ryk's hands.

A chandelier fell from the ceiling slipping over the thing's head and pinning its arms to its side. Nylana burst from the sides leaping off a table and bringing her sword down upon the creature killing it.

The second creature headed for them. "Attack from behind," said Nylana as she darted off forcing the thing to follow her.

Ryk seized a sword that had been displayed on the stone wall. While Nylana taunted the monster, he attacked. At the same instant, Nylana charged from the front. They reached the creature at the same time plowing their weapons into it. Wrathful cries reverberated around them as the roars of the creature echoed off the walls. Nylana brought back her sword. With renewed strength, she hacked at the head of the wooden creature until it rolled across the floor.

"Come on," ordered Nylana as she ran out a nearby door and to the outside world.

Raucous noise drummed against Galdin's ears as he reached the gates. The hinges rattled violently as those on the other side slammed a battering ram into them. He ran up some steps to the top of the wall so that he could see the field which was covered with armed men, catapults, fires, and other creatures he did not recognize.

"What news?" he asked the nearest soldier.

"They outnumber us twenty to one," said the soldier, "We don't know where they came from. They just appeared."

"Appeared?"

"Yes, sir," said the soldier, "It's as though something cloaked their movements until they were on our doorstep."

The gates shook again.

Galdin noticed barrels of oil lining the wall. "Take those barrels and load them into the catapults."

"Sir?"

"Do it!"

The soldier ran off to carry out the orders. Men grabbed the barrels of oil rolling them to the catapults lining the wall, loading them. Upon Galdin's orders, they fired sending the containers over the wall.

"Archers," yelled Galdin.

Archers raised their bows and fired flaming arrows at the oil drums. Instantly, the sky lit up as the barrels burst into flame spreading burning oil onto the barbarians below. Screams rose from the field as men ran in every direction to escape the fiery rain.

"Ladders!" shouted Trya as one attached itself to the wall before her. She braced herself awaiting the first person to climb over. As the head of a man dressed in fur with a horned helmet appeared, she brought her blade down lopping off his head. With a harsh kick, Trya sent the ladder and its occupants back to the ground.

An arrow whizzed past her head. Another ladder appeared. Quickly, Trya ran to it, pushing with all her might away from the castle exterior. Trya brought her bow before her. Aiming carefully, she fired arrow after arrow at the mass of barbarians below. Their numbers continued to swarm as they stormed the gate with a battering ram.

Narúl noticed one of the savages heading for the elf. Quickly, he slammed his arm into the man's throat and knocked him to the ground. In a fluid movement, Narúl whipped around catching another with his sword before tossing the body of a third over the wall. More scrambled over the wall as more ladders appeared.

Air shot from Narúl's lungs as a great force slammed into his back sending him flying forward. He crashed into the walkway along the top of the outer wall rolling over the edge and landing on the ground below.

Thud!

Six giant feet with the sharpest of nails loomed before him. Looking up, Narúl found himself staring into the orange eyes of a creature he had never seen before. Its snout was only inches from him smothering him in its foul breath as rows of teeth poked through its lips. An ominous growl filled his ears.

Narúl backed away slowly feeling for his sword. Inch by inch the monster mimicked his movements. A glint of steel caught Narúl's attention: his sword! As though it read his mind, the six legged creature jumped over him landing on the weapon; daring him to reach for it.

Holding his stance, Narúl whipped out the knives from his belt and jumped at the creature plunging both into its head. He stabbed repeatedly releasing a strangled battle cry. Blood spurted all over him as he hacked at the creature's head. As the body grew lax, Narúl stopped; watching coldly as it collapsed.

He marched to his sword. Seizing his blade he turned to face the battle at hand. A low groan caught his attention. Warily, Narúl turned around. The body of the monster stirred as it slowly rose to its feet. Without warning, the thing's tail jabbed at Narúl.

Arms seized him throwing him to the ground. With a quick glance at his savior, Narúl watched as Galdin slashed at the lashing tail. He brought his sword up just as the tail headed for him. Narúl watched as the end of it sailed through the air smacking an invader in the head.

"Get back!" shouted Galdin.

The headless creature wobbled on its feet as it thrashed about. Gradually, two round heads formed where the first had once been. They grew in size until they were twice the size of Galdin and Narúl combined.

Galdin ducked as one of the heads snapped at him. The second reached for him as he rolled across the ground. Charging into the fray Narúl lunged for it swinging wildly. His steel blade sliced through the soft flesh of the creature's neck. Narúl jumped at the second one lopping it off with ease.

"No!" shouted Galdin.

Realizing his mistake too late, Narúl watched as four heads appeared where two had been. All four lunged for him. Narúl barely escaped them as he leapt out of the way.

Galdin rushed for the creature's body. Before he could strike its middle, a great spike shot out. Startled, Galdin jumped back. Spikes appeared all over the things body as it whirled on him.

Seeing their plight, Trya darted to where rows and rows of oil drums sat unattended. She seized men along the way forcing them to follow her.

"Take these and surround the creature," she ordered.

Two at a time the soldiers rolled the barrels over to where the strange beast battled with Galdin and Narúl. They formed a circle around the trio.

"Dump them," said Trya.

The soldiers tipped the barrels over spilling their contents. Black liquid splashed all around the creature until it stomped and stamped in it.

"Galdin! Narúl! Get out of there!"

Galdin snatched Narúl's arms and pulled him away from the fight just as Trya flung a torch upon the oil. Flames roared to life smothering the strange monster. Anguished squeals of pain shrieked through the night as it squirmed in the inferno. Its six feet slipped and pounded the earth in an effort to escape. Gradually, the creature ceased moving until nothing remained but a burnt carcass.

Nylana's muscles strained as she struggled to maneuver an oil drum to the sewer opening. A second pair of hands appeared as Ryk showed up. "Grab a torch," he said.

Nylana obeyed. She spotted a burning piece of wood and grabbed it while Ryk pushed the barrel to where she directed. Once finished, he heaved the metal plate away from the sewer exposing the darkness beneath. Eyes looked up at him in surprise. Nylana had been right.

Ryk knocked the barrel over allowing the oil within to pour into the confines of the sewer. Taking one last look at the barbarians within, Nylana tossed the torch into the hole. Screams burst forth as fire engulfed all those inside.

In an effort to block the sound, Ryk plopped the metal plate back over the opening sealing it. He grabbed Nylana's shoulder as she stood transfixed. "Come on," he said.

Eight small paws dashed across the courtyard of the castle as two cats raced through it. Tabs and Magi squirted through the chaos heading for the side entrance. Afraid that the barbarians might have discovered it, Magi had convinced Tabs to come with her to check on it.

Heavy feet of fighting soldiers crashed around them. Magi noticed one soldier of Belyndril struggling against an invader twice his size. She motioned for Tabs to follow as she spotted something above the man's head.

Together the two cats scurried up a post and across one of the rafters. They trotted along to where the loose board lay. Together, Tabs and Magi jumped on it forcing it down until it smacked the barbarian in the head. Stunned, the man never noticed as the two cats climbed down his back lading gracefully in the soft dirt. Seizing his chance, the Belyndril soldier killed the man unaware that two cats had saved his life.

Magi spotted a hole in the stone wall. "Wait," she hissed at Tabs.

The cat stared out the hole spotting a man with a metal plate over one eye directing the invading forces. She watched for several seconds. Slowly, the realization that they had lost dawned on her.

"Let's move," said Tabs.

"Forget the side entrance," said Magi, "They have already broken through it. We need to find the others."

Magi darted off. Slightly confused, Tabs followed after her trusting her judgment.

"Reinforce the gate," ordered Lord Trisk as it rattled violently on its hinges.

A deafening thud sounded on the other side as the front gate shook menacingly. The metal chains on the door rattled with each hit of the battering ram.

Men carrying large planks appeared. They hauled them to the door placing them crosswise hoping that it would secure the gates. A soft clinking caught Lord Trisk's attention. He picked up a metal rod recognizing it as one of the hinges. His heart sank.

BOOM!

Splintered wood zigzagged across the wooden gates.

BOOM!

More cracks appeared.

"Fall back!" yelled Lord Trisk. "Retreat to the second level!"

Men rushed from the confines of the entrance heading for the stairs that led to the topmost level of the city. Lord Trisk led his men away urging them onward. He watched as they raced to safety.

A loud crash echoed around him as the gate doors burst open, being ripped from their hinges. Savage looking men poured into the city slaughtering any in their way.

"Find the princess," shouted one of the barbarians. "She is here somewhere. Find her and bring her to Lord Vasagius."

"My lady," breathed Lord Trisk as he realized exactly what the assault had been about. Shoving men out of his way he dashed for the upper level of the city where he had left Nylana.

The roar of an explosion forced him from his feet propelling him through the air. Sharp pain racked his body when he slammed into the concrete. Dazed, Lord Trisk looked at what was left of the upper level of the city as more enflamed boulders bombarded it. Men scrambled in fear trying to escape the onslaught.

Another explosion snatched Lord Trisk's attention. One of the outer walls of the city caved in as it crumbled to dust. A flood of barbarians spewed forth spreading throughout the city. Any in their path met a dismal fate.

"Nylana," breathed Lord Trisk.

He shot to his feet forcing his way through the mayhem as he headed for where Nylana last was; focused only on reaching her before the enemy took her prisoner.

Not far from Lord Trisk, Narúl and Galdin heard the explosion. They watched as La'nar fell to the barbarian invaders. Knowing there was nothing left to do; Galdin grabbed Trya and pushed her away from the fight. "We need to find Nylana and Ryk," said Galdin.

"I will check the king's court," said Narúl, "You look for her here."

"Here? She should be—"

"You do not know her as I do," replied Narúl. "Do you know the place where the rocks are red?"

"Yes," said Galdin, knowing exactly what Narúl meant.

"We will meet there."

"Narúl," called Galdin as the man headed off, "Good luck."

Nylana touched her lip as blood dripped from it. A man bent over her sneering. Suddenly, power surged up her arm as the sword glowed brightly. Of its own accord, Nylana's arm jerked upward catching the man in the face. Shock filled his features as he tipped over.

Hands grabbed her from behind as a second barbarian grabbed her. Her body jerked and swayed as Ryk tore the man from her. He jammed his fist into the savage's face before thrusting him backward.

"Come on," said Ryk as he hauled Nylana to her feet.

He pulled her through the melee of fighting men. Heart racing, Nylana held fast to Ryk's hand allowing him to dictate her movements.

Ryk shouldered someone out of their way. The movement knocked her off balance, but Ryk immediately steadied her. "I've got you," he said.

Nylana staggered slightly as Ryk yanked her along. He pushed and shoved her through the mass of people. Haphazardly, they ran across the courtyard until they crashed into Galdin and Trya.

"Nylana," Galdin said in surprise.

Nylana didn't hear him. Her eyes rested upon Lord Trisk pinned between two of the invaders. Once again her arm acted on its own as the sword of Tesnayr dictated her movements. Raising it behind her head, Nylana flung the sword. It flew over the fighting mass until it struck its target.

Startled, Lord Trisk stared at the protruding sword for several moments before regaining his senses. The thrust of a knife at his throat forced him from his trance. He blocked the blade with the steel bracelet around his wrist. Slamming his foot into the back of his opponent's knee, Lord Trisk wrenched the man's head back snapping his neck.

Nylana and the others appeared before him. "Lord Trisk," she said as she reclaimed her sword, "They have broken all of our defenses."

"The city is lost," replied Lord Trisk, "You must leave now. This way."

A man jumped from above. Suddenly, Trog appeared. He rammed his front paws into the barbarian's chest forcing him to the ground. Trog looked at Galdin with a pleased expression.

"Good boy," said Galdin.

"Now," urged Lord Trisk as he shoved Nylana to the side.

Magi and Tabs approached just as Lord Trisk led everyone away. They turned sharply and ran hard to catch up.

From a distance, Narúl stood with his back to a wall. The savage before him smirked enjoying the bloodbath. Movement caught Narúl's eye. He looked up in time to watch as Galdin and Nylana disappeared around a corner. Pleased, that his lady would be safe, Narúl lurched toward the man before him. He stopped short. The man jerked to the side thinking that Narúl would strike there, but he had been tricked. With fluid movement, Narúl charged from the other direction stabbing the man in the side.

He leaped away noticing a rope just above his head leading up to the city's aqueduct. Snatching it from the air, Narúl pulled himself up away from the battle. His muscles gleamed in the firelight with each movement.

Tumbling over the side of the aqueduct, Narúl splashed into the water as it flowed red with blood. The current carried him out of the city. Narúl noticed a gap ahead of him. Bracing himself, he shot from the channel of water over the outer wall and into a tangle of weeds.

Swiftly, Narúl regained his balance as he jumped to his feet. He took one last glance at the city before dashing into the dark and wilderness beyond.

Panting, Nylana and the others ran through the city and the chaos that reigned within. Lord Trisk pushed them along down alleyways and away from the worst of the fight. Her knee stung as she fell scraping the skin. Lord Trisk heaved her up.

"Go!"

Nylana ran, ignoring the yells and the screams. The others followed close behind. A horned man charged them. Instantly, Galdin jumped between her and her attacker. He brought his sword up blocking the attacker's blade. In a fluid movement, Galdin ripped the enemy's weapon from him and plunged it into his chest.

"Come on," urged Lord Trisk. "That wall there."

He pointed to a metal gate in the northern wall of the city. It looked as though it led nowhere. Hurriedly, Lord Trisk felt around the gate for a lever. He pulled it. Suddenly, the metal grate swung upward as a hole materialized in what appeared to be a solid wall. He shoved Nylana through.

"No, I can't run like this," she protested.

"You don't have a choice," yelled Lord Trisk over the battle noise, "I'll not let those savages get their hands on you. Now go! GO!"

Ryk grabbed Nylana and yanked her through the hole and into a small tunnel. Trya and the cats followed with Galdin and Trog making up the rear.

An explosion sounded behind them. A wave of barbarian soldiers came straight for them. An arrow struck Lord Trisk in the shoulder. He slumped slightly as blood poured from the wound.

"Come with us," yelled Galdin.

"No," shouted Lord Trisk, "I have to close it from this side. Get away from here. Make for the hills and don't let them get her."

Lord Trisk pushed Galdin into the hole and yanked the lever again closing the grate and making the wall solid once more. He took his sword and broke the lever off. Determined, Lord Trisk turned around and faced the barbarians heading straight for him ready to meet his end. At least they wouldn't be followed.

Galdin paused by the sealed doorway wishing a silent farewell to Lord Trisk. Fortifying himself, he ran after the others. Water splashed with each step he took. The narrowness of the short tunnel funneled the sounds of the battle to them. Nylana slipped and fell into the muck. Galdin reached out for her at the same time as Ryk. They locked eyes a moment as they helped her up.

Trya held up her hand forcing everyone to stop. She listened intently searching for signs of immediate danger. "Let's go," she waved them onward.

They hurried away from the opening of the tunnel and for the trees. War raged around them, but no one noticed their escape.

"This way," said Magi as she scurried up a hill. "Quickly."

They followed the cat as fast as they could through the brush. Nylana ignored the wayward branches that snagged her clothing and tugged at her hair. Ryk helped her when she tripped over an upturned rock. Horns echoed around them. Nylana paused to look at what took place below them.

"Keep going," ordered Galdin. He pushed her onward in the darkness. Galdin turned momentarily to make certain no one followed. Nothing.

Huffing, they raced up the hill ignoring the battle below them. Twigs snapped beneath their feet with each movement they made. Trya put her arm out stopping them. She stared down at the battle and the screams of frightened people as armed savages swept through the city slaughtering them. For the first time, Galdin saw emotion etched on the elf's face.

Nylana stood poised on the small rise silhouetted in the light of the burning flames that consumed the city of La'nar. Tales of an earlier battle filtered through her mind. This was the resolve of the invaders. The dark shape on a horse caught her eye. Evil emanated from the lone figure. She felt it as she looked into his eyes; the only feature exposed on his face.

"Nylana," said Ryk, reaching out for her.

"Lord Trisk. Did he make it?" She looked at all of them pausing on Galdin.

The downhearted look on Galdin's face answered her question.

Nylana turned back to the inferno. Despair won that night. Belyndril was lost. Even the breeze released a woeful melody. For the first time, Nylana craned her neck and listened understanding what Trya heard.

An echo of the last cry of the phoenix pulled her back to reality. With sudden clarity, Nylana understood why Petra wanted her to search for the mythical object. It wasn't just an object, but hope. A hope only she could restore.

"Once the flames subside, they'll come for us," said Galdin. "We should put as much distance between them as possible."

"You head to MurDair," said Nylana to Galdin. "There is something I must do. Something I must do alone."

She checked the items attached to her belt making certain that the canteen was full. "Go," she said wrapping her cloak around her, "I'll meet up with you when I can. If I don't come by the next full moon, convince Lord Belznyc to accompany you back to Norlyk."

"Where are you going?" Galdin grabbed her arm forcing her to face him.

"It is best that you do not know," answered Nylana.

"No," said Galdin holding tightly to her arm. "I won't let you go. I don't care what it is you think you need to do. You are not going."

"I have to," said Nylana. "I know now what I must do. And I'm going alone."

"Are you insane?" Galdin stared at her in disbelief. "Those barbarians are all over the five lands. They are looking for you. You'll be killed. You'll be going to your death."

"Yes, death is certain!" Nylana yanked her arm from Galdin's grip. "We all die sometime, Galdin. What matters is how we meet that end. What matters is what we do before reach it."

"Is that what you believe?" challenged Galdin. "That you must sacrifice yourself?"

"Yes," answered Nylana, "These are my people. I am the Princess of Tesnayr. If I do not stand up for them, who will? I will gladly die for them if it will save them from this horror. What do you believe in, Galdin? What are you willing to die for?"

"Where are you going?" Galdin asked again, more quietly.

"To find hope."

Book Two
Shrouded Mist

Masks and illusions surround us
Guiding our will with little to trust,
But their unending maze
Of lies and lust.

Our footsteps buried in a haze
Of vapors and mist. Gaze
Upon the veiled path
Illuminated only by torch's blaze.

Why suffer a shadow's wrath?
What did we commit to hath
Warranted the cloaked puppeteer's
Strings forging our path.

Fog of deception, let us be.
Undo thy shroud of mystery.
Let in the light so that we may see
And forge our own Destiny.

Chapter I
Search

The sun bore down upon Trya and Nylana as they trudged through the lower part of the mountains. Galdin had reluctantly agreed to let Nylana go on this mission of hers. She thought back to the conversation they had had that night as La'nar burned.

"You cannot go alone," said Galdin. "You have to take someone with you."

"I will go with her," Ryk had readily volunteered.

Nylana chuckled to herself as she remembered the look on her brother's face. "Trya, you will go with Nylana. In one month's time we will meet you in MurDair."

"But," Nylana had tried to protest.

"One month. That is how long it will take us to reach it. That is how much time you have to find this thing of yours."

They parted that night against Galdin's better judgment. Nylana felt a bit guilty for forcing him into this situation.

She glanced over at Trya as the elf walked tirelessly over the rough terrain. *How does she do it?* Nylana always marveled at how elves never tired. Or rather, they never displayed fatigue.

"Do you know where you are headed?" asked Trya.

"Yes," lied Nylana.

"How much farther?"

Guiltily, Nylana looked at Trya. "Far."

Trya stopped, facing Nylana. "You have no idea, do you?"

"No," answered Nylana, "I do and I don't. I know that what I must find is in this region but I do not know its exact location. I do not even know what it is exactly."

"What did the wizard tell you?"

"Not much. He said for me to listen. To feel. Listen to the wind. That was what happened that night we fled La'nar. I heard the wind and suddenly everything made sense, but now I cannot hear it anymore."

Trya nodded her head understanding what Nylana meant. She placed her weapons on the ground. "Come here."

Nylana moved closer to the elf.

"Take my hand."

Unsure of herself, Nylana placed her hand in Trya's amazed at its softness.

"Do you feel that?"

Nylana paused. A tingling sensation moved through her, different from the sword, and yet very invigorating. The wind sounded different. It sounded mournful as though it sang of terrible death. Even the trees and flowers joined in the sorrowful melody.

"Do you feel it now?"

"Yes," said Nylana.

"We elves feel this all the time. We hear the wind. We hear the birds; not the chirping that you normally hear, but their actual voices. We feel the grass and the trees and everything around us. To us it is alive."

"Then why do you sound sad?"

"Since the day the phoenix gave you new life, the world has sung this song. Listen."

Nylana strained her ears to hear it, but nothing came to her.

"Not with your ears," said Trya.

Confused, Nylana listened again. How was one to hear without their ears? She heard the wind. She heard the rustling of leaves. Absently, she touched the blue rose in her pocket. A song played in her mind. She heard the music, but not with her ears; inwardly.

Ni'lee y'lee ni se le'han.

Aghast, Nylana let go of Trya's hand. How could it be? She heard the words from the song her mother sang when they buried her father. A song she had sung to Krispyn when they were children and he felt afraid. The very song that burned within her heart.

"You heard it, didn't you?" asked Trya.

"Yes," breathed Nylana, "But how?"

"It is an ancient melody."

"My mother sang that when I was a child. How is this possible?"

Trya strolled over and leisurely gathered her weapons, considering how to explain this to Nylana. "The words in your mother's song are ancient words. The fairies believe that they are the first words, or belong to the first language spoken in the land. Some believe that they are the words spoken by the voice on the wind when evil entered the world."

"But that is all—"

"Myth? Well, most things are. And yet you sing them. Have you noticed anything different since the day you died and came back?"

Nylana thought about it but kept silent, afraid of what the answer would be. She had noticed some changes. The flowers were not as vibrant as before and did not stand as proud. The grass, once emerald, had browned, yet it was spring. The trees seemed worn, tired. "The land is dying."

"Yes," said Trya, "I've felt it since that day. And you have too. But the land is not just physically dying. That is merely a symptom for what has actually been lost.

"People seem disheartened. You've noticed it. They no longer dream. They no longer look forward to the future. Despair fills their hearts."

"Invasion by a bunch of savages will do that," said Nylana.

"That is not the reason and you know it," scolded Trya.

Taken aback by the elf's harsh tone, Nylana kept her next remark to herself. "What has been lost?"

"You do not know? You told Galdin that that was what you intended to find. Though, you may discover that you needn't look so far."

"I just wish I knew how to find it," said Nylana as her shoulders slumped.

"You will. Learn to listen. Hear what the wind tells you. Remember the melody."

Trya bent down and picked up a handful of grass. She released them above her head studying their movement in the breeze.

"We should find some shelter," she said, "A storm is brewing."

Nylana looked up at the calm and sunny sky. Storm, she thought, it looks so calm.

Rain pelted the already soaked earth as Nylana and Trya huddled together under a makeshift roof of leaves. It kept the worst of the water off of them, but did little to keep them from getting soaked. Misery etched their faces as they stared at the soggy expanse.

Nylana wished they could have a fire, but the rain made any chance of one impossible. Thunder rolled across the sky as the rain picked up. Rivers of water flowed past them carrying bits of debris and mud.

"You know there is a nice dry cave nearby in case you are interested," said a snide voice.

They turned to find Magi standing on a rock with her tail whipping about. How she managed to remain dry in this weather was anyone's guess.

"Or you two can continue to sit here and die of the cold."

"Show us the cave," said Trya.

Magi bounded off. Nylana and Trya jogged after the cat. The dreary landscape made it difficult to see the feline, whose fur coat blended in nicely. Eventually, the opening of a cave came into view. They ran to it scrambling over saturated logs and squishy mounds of grass welcoming the dryness that the cave offered.

Once inside, Nylana peeled off her cloak and wrung the water out of it. She looked at Magi who sat upright with a pleased expression. "What are you doing here?"

"I followed you," replied the cat. "And, no, Galdin does not know."

"Why didn't you let us know earlier?" asked Nylana.

"I didn't feel like it." Magi hopped to the middle of the cave. "A fire would be nice."

"Is that a demand or a request?" asked Trya.

"A little bit of both," said Magi.

Grinning slightly, Trya dug through the debris in the cave looking for dried bits of wood she could use. After stumbling upon a small pile, she built a neat mound and lit it. "There is your fire."

Magi stretched in front of it. "About time."

Nylana hung her cloak by the flames so it could dry. "Trya, how did you and Galdin meet?"

"It was seven years ago," replied Trya, "He saved my life."

"But you are so much older than him and yet you two act like you've been traveling together for centuries."

"It is true that I am two hundred of your years," said Trya, "But I am young for an elf. In Belarnia, I was being trained to be part of the Elven Council, but I ran away. The thought of spending my days listening to the Elven Lords complain about their trifles horrified me.

"I wanted to be free. So I fled Belarnia with little thought as to what I would do afterward. One day, I was captured by a band of thieves. They had tied me up and threatened to kill me.

"Out of nowhere, this young lad sprang from the trees and attacked the bandits. He fought with a ferocity I had never seen before. Once he had disarmed the leader, I expected him to kill the man. Galdin didn't. He lowered his sword and let the man and his band go.

"Then, he untied me. He never asked for anything in return. Instead, he tossed me a bag of coins so that I could make my way back to Belarnia."

"And you have traveled with him ever since," said Nylana.

"Yes," replied Trya, "Galdin, may be a mercenary, but there is far more to him than that. At eighteen, he possessed a wisdom that few achieve in eighty years."

Nylana lowered her head feeling guilty for scolding him the night La'nar burned.

"Do not feel guilty for your words to him," said Trya, knowing what lay in Nylana's heart. "For a while now he has needed some guidance. For months I thought I was the one to provide it to him. Now I realize that he really needed you."

"If only Vasagius had not attacked Norlyk twenty-five years ago. If only he had not murdered my father. Galdin would have grown up in the palace like the prince that he is."

"True. But then he would not have been in Pras'quel to rescue you," said Trya. "Do not second guess yourself, and then ponder over those guesses as well. Such a path only leads to misery."

Trya looked out at the darkening sky. "You should get some sleep. The cat, there, seems to have the right idea."

Nylana glanced at Magi who lay curled up by the fire. Soft snores escaped her. "She has such sweet snores."

"I don't snore," huffed Magi.

Chapter II
To MurDair

Narúl waited for them just like he had said he would. Galdin approached the muscular, black man unsure of how to tell him that Nylana did not come with him.

"Galdin," greeted Narúl. "Where is Nylana?"

"She's not here," said Galdin as he moved past Narúl.

"Not here? Where is she?"

Galdin kept walking.

"Tell me!" Narúl grabbed Galdin and whirled him around. "Where is she?"

Galdin ran his fingers through his hair. "I do not know." He held his hand up before Narúl could protest. "I told her not to go, but she was so insistent. She said she had to go searching for this mystical item."

"And you let her go? Alone?" Narúl grabbed Galdin and slammed him against a tree anger etched on his face. "You let her go while this land is crawling with invaders?"

"It's not as though I had a choice," said Galdin. "Would you have been able to convince her to stay?"

Narúl released Galdin. "No. She's so stubborn."

"Besides," said Galdin, "She isn't alone. Trya went with her."

"And Magi," said Tabs, poking his head out of Galdin's pack.

"What?" asked Galdin.

"Well, she must have," answered Tabs, "I haven't seen her for a few days now. Now you want to talk about stubborn. She's a case in point."

"Let's go," said Galdin, with Trog on his heels. "In one month's time we will meet her in MurDair. In the meantime, I'd like to find a safe place to camp for the night."

"I know of a place," said Tabs, jumping with excitement. "There was a time when I knew this area quite well. There should be an abandoned cottage not far from here."

"Are you sure?" asked Galdin.

"Yes," answered Tabs," Cross this creek and turn left. Then it is just a few miles until the cottage. Follow me."

Not knowing what else to do, Galdin followed the orange tabby through some brush and across the narrow creek. Tabs hummed merrily to himself; a tune none of them recognized.

"How much further?" asked Galdin as they walked.

"Not far," replied Tabs, "It should be—Oh parsnips."

Galdin stopped cold. Trog had disappeared. He and the others looked about them as they realized that they had wandered into a group of armed barbarians who looked upon them as fresh meat.

"Tabs," whispered Galdin, "I thought you said you knew where you were going?"

"I did," said Tabs, "It might have been my other left."

"Cursed feline, you led us into a trap!" roared Galdin.

"I didn't mean too!"

"If I didn't know better I'd say you did it on purpose," yelled Galdin.

"Well maybe I did," snapped Tabs. "You never do show me any respect. You even scared Trog away."

"Because you haven't earned it!"

Amidst all this the barbarians stared at the arguing pair unsure of what to do. They had never seen a talking cat before, nor had they expected to have intruders. One grabbed his weapon.

"Well what are you going to do about it?" Tabs challenged Galdin.

"This."   Galdin chucked his knife at the nearest barbarian striking him in the throat.

Tabs launched himself at another crouched low to the ground. His hind claws tore into the man's flesh. The man threw the cat off of him. Spitting at his quarry, Tabs jumped at the man again sinking his fangs into the man's throat. Tabs kept his jaw clamped shut until the man ceased moving.

Narúl pulled out his curved blade. He lopped off the head of a charging barbarian while quickly spinning on the balls of his feet to block an attack by another. Sparks flew from their blades as they locked. Quickly, Narúl punched the man in the throat, unlocked their weapons, and plunged his blade into soft flesh.

He tossed the dead barbarian's sword to Ryk who caught it in time to stop another who charged him. Using the movements Narúl had taught him earlier, Ryk brought his sword up blocking an attack while simultaneously ramming his boot into his attacker's knee, breaking it.

The fight continued for a few moments longer. Galdin, Narúl, and Ryk suddenly found themselves unable to move as they stared into red, lidless eyes. Their body refused to obey their commands. Paralyzed, they stood victim to the barbarians.

Two black shapes hurled themselves into the red eyed monster. The moment the beast fell, the others regained control of their limbs. As the fog in their mind cleared, they rushed the creature to kill it, but Trog and the newly arrived stranger had already beaten them to it.

"This way, quick," said the figure.

"Artryl? What are you doing here?" demanded Narúl.

"No time," answered the boy.

More barbarians sprang from nowhere and seized Galdin. He struggled to shake them off as hands ripped his weapon from him. Narúl turned to help.

"No!" shouted Galdin. "Just go!"

Narúl shoved Ryk through the foliage and to safety. They followed Artryl as he led them to a rocky outcrop where they hid until the barbarians below left. Guiltily, Narúl watched as they led Galdin away.

"Tabs," said Narúl, "Follow them."

The cat scurried away.

"And you," Narúl turned to Artryl, "Better start explaining your presence here."

Chapter III
Imprisoned

The key clanked in the lock as the door opened and Galdin was thrust inside. The guard slammed the door shut allowing it to bang loudly as he locked it once more. Sighing, Galdin glanced around stopping when his eyes fell upon a teenage girl.

She wore a simple dress and stared back at him with the same amount of interest. "So I suppose we are to be cellmates."

"What are you doing here?" The question came out ruder than Galdin had meant it to be.

"I woke up one day wondering what it would be like to be imprisoned by a bunch of ruthless barbarians. So here I am."

Not liking the sarcasm, Galdin meandered over to the slit in the wall and peered through it. From what he saw, he deduced that he was in the mountains.

"It won't work."

Galdin faced the girl.

"You're thinking about escaping, but it won't work. Well, your way won't."

"Do you have a name?" asked Galdin.

"Tami."

"I am not content to stay here," said Galdin as he studied the interior of the cell.

"Neither am I," answered Tami, "But we are in the lower part of the Ársa Mountains, near the Perili. We also happen to be in an abandoned fort built into the cliff face of the mountain. The only known way out is through the front gate."

The girl's superior attitude annoyed Galdin. "I'll not be taking advice from a seventeen year old girl."

"Nineteen," huffed Tami, placing her hands on her hips. "I am more than just a girl, you arrogant miscreant."

Galdin chuckled softly to himself as he admired her spunkiness.

The hinges on the door squealed as it opened. A single man dressed in armor and furs entered. Tattoos ran up and down both his arms. A metal plate covered his left eye as a scar ran from the forehead and past the plate down his left cheek. A caved in section dotted his cheek where a chunk of flesh had obviously been torn out. "Name?"

Galdin eyed the man.

The man snapped his fingers and a second soldier walked in seizing Tami, pinning her arms behind her back.

"Tell me your name," said the man with the patch, "Or I will kill her."

"Go ahead," answered Galdin, "She means nothing to me."

"Such the gentleman," quipped Tami.

The man in charge eyed Galdin with his one good eye. A smirk crossed his features. "I believe you." He waved his hand and the man holding onto Tami released her.

Pulling out a crooked dagger, the man with the patch held it dangerously close to Galdin's face. "What if I take your eye, the way your father took mine." He ripped off the metal plate revealing the empty socket.

It was then Galdin realized that the man who stood before him was Vasagius; the one who rebelled and was defeated. Galdin kept his features stony, refusing to reveal anything. "If you know who my father is, then you already know my name."

Vasagius smiled. "I can see that no matter what I do to you, you will never talk. You do not fear torture or death. But what if I threaten someone close to you? Say, your sister? The fair lady of Tesnayr. She will not be so fair when I am through with her."

Galdin lunged at Vasagius knocking him into the wall. He punched the man repeatedly until he fell to the ground. Instantly, Galdin whirled onto the second man jamming his fingers into the man's throat just as Tami knocked him over the head with the chamber pot.

"Quick!" Galdin ran out of the cell and stopped cold. His mind willed his muscles to move, but they refused to obey as he stared into the eyes of a red eyed orc. Perspiration dotted his brow as he struggled to turn away.

"You did not think I would come into your cell unprepared," said Vasagius, rubbing his head. "Enough."

The red eyed orc turned away releasing Galdin. Faint of breath, Galdin allowed himself to be dragged back into the cell with Tami.

Tami scooped up a chipped cup and held it under a crack in the ceiling where water dripped from. When it filled, she handed it to Galdin. "Here."

"What was that thing?"

"The most evil of orcs," replied Tami. "They once numbered by the hundreds, but Tesnayr hunted them down during his reign and they were never seen again. How they are here is a mystery. And why they obey Vasagius is an even greater puzzle."

"The sorcerer," breathed Galdin.

"What?"

"When La'nar was attacked a sorcerer helped the barbarians," said Galdin.

"Then that explains it," Tami said.

"But who is working for whom?"

                    *   *   *

The hot sun beat down upon the motley quintet as they trekked through the lower hills of the Perili Mountains. Trog sniffed the ground swinging his head side to side as he sought out Galdin.

"Are we sure we're going in the right direction?" asked Ryk. "The tracks ended over two days ago."

Narúl wiped the sweat from his face. He hated this part of the mountain range. The lower hills of the Perili Mountains were always humid this time of year. "Quit complaining," he said. "That beast probably knows where we are better than we do."

"Well, if that cat hadn't lost Galdin's trail, we wouldn't need this thing," muttered Ryk.

Tabs repaid Ryk's comments by pricking the man's ankle with his claws. He hadn't meant to lose the group that had taken Galdin.

"Ouch!" Frustrated, Ryk walked up to Trog who panted happily. "Look you stupid beast, we need to find Galdin and we need to find him now. Now take us to him." He waved his arms. "Go on."

"That's not how you talk to him," said Artryl. The boy moved beside Trog and petted the animal's head. "Do we have anything of Galdin's?"

Narúl searched his things and found a canteen that had been on Galdin's belt, tossing it to the boy.

Artryl caught it and held it out to Trog who sniffed it. "We need you to find the man to whom this belonged."

Trog's nostrils flared as he sniffed the canteen rapidly taking in every scent. Immediately, he sped off leaving a trail of dust.

"He knows where Galdin is," said Artryl, "Come on!"

Narúl and Ryk followed after the boy and the animal. They ran down the dusty pathway in the crevice of the mountains. Not daring to stop, they ignored the cramp in their side as Trog continued to run ahead. Occasionally, Trog paused, stared at them with impatience, and took off again.

"I hope he knows where he's going," said Ryk.

Narúl remained silent not wanting to speak while jogging. Pacing himself, he ran at a steady pace managing to keep up with the strange animal that had followed Galdin from Pras'quel.

Trog stopped. They had come to the edge of a cliff overlooking a deep canyon. To the right rested the Ársa Mountains themselves towering over the whole of Tesnayr. To the left lay the Perili Mountains which included the ledge they stood upon. And nestled just above the gorge and diagonally from them was an old fort.

Narúl studied the structure. He recognized it. It had been in use during the days of King Arylllian, Nylana's grandfather. But for the last twenty years it had been abandoned. He pulled a looking glass from his bag. Narúl frowned as he focused it. Guards patrolled the perimeter. Of course, thought Narúl, why leave such a well-defended place unused?

"Tabs," said Narúl.

The cat bounded up with excitement.

"See if you can sneak in there. I want you to scout out the place. Learn the number of guards, weaknesses. Then report back here."

The orange tabby waved his tail in a sort of salute before running off, blending in with the landscape.

"How are we going to get him out of there?" asked Ryk. "There are only two of us capable of fighting."

Narúl flipped the looking glass closed. "I'll make certain the boy protects you."

*   *   *

"I know a way out of here," said Tami.

Galdin's ears perked up at her statement, but she read his doubtful expression. "Really?"

"I do. I can open that door." Tami walked over to the bars and muttered a spell. Nothing happened.

"Well?"

She gave him a piercing glare before turning back to the bars. The guard leaned back in his chair ignoring her. "Oh, guard," she called.

He turned around.

"Hey, handsome."

Intrigued, the guard walked over to her his keys jingling loudly as they bounced up and down on his belt. A toothless grin spread across his face indicating his interest in her.

"Come a little closer," cooed Tami, "Don't be shy."

The guard leaned in eager for what she had to offer.

Unexpectedly, Tami reached through the bars, grabbed the guard by the shirt, and smashed his face into the metal bars. He slumped to the floor unconscious. Quickly, Tami snatched the keys waving them before Galdin. "Will this do?"

Galdin took the keys. He unlocked the door and waved Tami through. They charged up the steps and to the outside, their feet making soft plops. Guards patrolled the outer perimeter.

"Quickly," Galdin pushed Tami through a doorway before anyone noticed them.

"What are we doing here?" demanded Tami. "The escape route is that way."

"We won't get very far without weapons." Galdin snatched a sword and knives and anything else he could carry.

Footsteps sounded outside. They paused listening intently. Sighing with relief as the footsteps moved away, Galdin peeked out the door and shoved Tami through. Quickly, they darted along the wall sticking to shadows so as not to be noticed.

"Which way?" asked Galdin.

"Through here," Tami pointed to a grate.

Galdin removed it, allowed Tami through and replaced it after he crawled into the sewer. The stench overwhelmed his nostrils as he fought a gag reflex.

"Hurry," urged Tami.

Brown muck covered him as he crawled on his hands and knees following Tami who moved with ease, unbothered by the smell. Slipping in the slime, Galdin lost his balance and fell into it with a loud splash. The sewage covered him entirely clinging to his clothes. Galdin wiped his face willing himself to not vomit. Rotted carrots floated past him as he continued to creep through the dross toward the spillway. The closer they got, the louder the constant roar of the falling water became.

"The river is down there," said Tami. "But if we jump the cliff, the fall could kill us. We need to climb up there."

Galdin studied the cliff face. Movement caught his eye. Men ran along the edge shouting erratically. As Galdin listened to them he knew that their absence had been discovered. "Can you swim?"

"Yes, I can swim but—"

Galdin pushed her over the edge and into the raging river below. An arrow struck near his head. Glancing at the one who had fired, he leapt off the cliff.

The water stung the moment he crashed into it, piercing his skin like a thousand sewing needles. Allowing the current to carry him, Galdin held onto his breath. When his lungs burned for release, he propelled himself to the surface and swam for the riverbank.

"You crazy son of a—"

"I just saved your life," interrupted Galdin.

"We could have been killed!" shouted Tami, flinging her fists as droplets of water flew in every direction.

"But we weren't." Galdin checked his weapons. "If we had tried your way, we would have been killed. They had already noticed our absence."

"Where are you going?" asked Tami as Galdin turned to leave.

"To find my friends."

"I'm coming with you." She skipped a moment to catch up.

"No."

"Why not? I just saved your life."

"I think it was I who saved you." Galdin marched away.

"You'll never get out of here," warned Tami. "This part of the Ársa Mountains is a labyrinth. Many travelers have gotten lost in these parts."

Grudgingly, Galdin turned around. He did not like where this conversation was headed. "And do you know these parts?"

"Quite well."

"I set a fast pace," said Galdin, "Keep up or get left behind."

"And how will you navigate without me?"

"Keep up."

Chapter IV
A Dragon's Request

Petra perused through the library searching for anything that might tell him more about the mysterious item he had sent Nylana to find. Inwardly, he worried that he had sent her on a fool's quest. He had found various pieces of previous kings' journals, but wished Tabs was there. He wondered where that cat had gone.

Footsteps echoing in the lonely corridor attracted his attention. Carefully, Petra crept over to the door opening it slightly. Shelwyk hurried past glancing over his shoulder every so often. Curious, Petra slipped through the door. Sticking to the sides of the wall and its shadows, the wizard trailed Shelwyk. He ducked behind a suit of armor when Shelwyk turned around suddenly. The man's eyes flickered back and forth as he studied the hallway behind him. Once Shelwyk looked away, Petra crept out of the shadows and continued his pursuit.

The wizard did not like Shelwyk's secretive manner. In truth, he never liked the man. He followed Shelwyk through the corridor taking extra care to make no sounds. *Where is he going?* He could think of no reason for the man to be in this part of the palace.

The hallway forked. Shelwyk paused. Instantly, Petra dashed behind a marbled statue. A tapping noise forced him to look around taking his focus from the man he followed. When Petra turned back, Shelwyk had gone.

"Hiding among relics?" Quesha materialized from the shadows staring straight at Petra. "You should be careful, lest you become a relic yourself."

"It's you," hissed Petra.

"Yes, it is me," purred Quesha.

"Why don't you haunt someone else?"

"Such animosity."

"You made me lose Shelwyk. Now I'll never know where he's gone."

"Pity," mocked Quesha.

Petra whirled on her. "You know where he's gone."

"I know many things," replied Quesha. "It is my curse from long ago."

"Do not play games with me," snarled Petra.

"You are very much like your old teacher, Zolo," Quesha danced around the wizard. "No one ever trusts a sorceress."

"And for good reason."

"Have I given you reason to doubt me?"

"Your habits make trusting you difficult."

"Perhaps," replied Quesha. "I will not tell you what you wish to know."

"Such information could save many innocents," said Petra.

"Or harm many more."

Petra opened his mouth to speak, but Quesha cut him off.

"You would never believe me if I just told you. This is one thing you must discover on your own."

Angered, Petra stormed back to the library.

"Why do you spend your time among books when you are needed in the world?" Quesha chased after him.

"One can learn things from books," Petra replied.

"They can learn the same things out in the word. Zolo knew that well."

"Zolo is no longer here."

"True. He has gone to where we all must one day." Quesha blocked the entrance to the library preventing Petra from going through. "I have come to give you a message. Leave the castle before it is too late. And when you do, you might want to know these words." The sorceress handed him a slip of parchment with four words written on it.

"What's this?"

"A teleportation spell."

"Giving away one of your secrets?"

Quesha smiled mysteriously. "This one will prove useful for Nylana."

Though distrustful of the sorceress, Petra pocketed the slip of paper. He knew the stories about Quesha well. Her warnings were never to be taken lightly. "Why is it you never speak plainly?"

"If I did, would you listen?"

"Why did you return to the lands of Tesnayr?" asked Petra.

"I knew I must," replied Quesha, "When I left all those years ago, I knew that one day I would have to return. My last bit of penance."

"You've aged since then."

"So have you. Our song is ending, Petra. Magic is dwindling. I know you've felt it. The fairies left long ago and many of the Elves have also fled. The dwarves' number lessens by the day. The world has changed and will continue to change."

"Quesha," Petra stopped the sorceress as she turned to leave, "You take care of yourself."

"I always do. Heed my words, young wizard. This time I leave the five lands never to return."

Petra watched as the sorceress vanished before him. He looked at the spell she had given him pondering the wisdom of using it. Teleportation was something few possessors of magic ever did. He pocketed the spell and went back to his research.

*   *   *

Nylana studied at the stone bridge in the middle of the valley; wondering why it was there. Something in the old tales made it seem familiar. Then, she remembered: the troll in the tale of

Amborese. This was the bridge that Amborese herself had encountered.

Moss covered the structure attempting to force it back into the ground and wipe it from memory. Nylana approached the solid bridge marveling at its construction and the markings upon it. She reached out and touched it with her hands wondering if Amborese had done the same. The troll was nowhere to be found. Many said that he disappeared and was never seen again.

"The bridge of legend," said Trya as she walked up from behind.

"Why is it here?" asked Nylana.

"Because some crazy old troll decided to build it," answered Magi. "Strange creatures trolls. But Zorlik was stranger than most. He abandoned the other trolls and chose to live here under the stars. I guess he got bored and built this."

Nylana examined the markings. "What do these mean?"

"These are ancient runes. Dwarfish runes—Odd." Trya leaned closer clearing away the moss.

"Odd? Why odd?" asked Nylana.

"Trolls never put dwarfish runes on their work. To combine their writing with a troll's structure would create—" Trya never finished her statement.

"Look," exclaimed Nylana, "This writing seems to depict the rebellion that resulted in my father's death."

"Nylana," Magi pointed her to something on the wall. As they all watched, Nylana's face appeared on the wall with the burning of La'nar.

"This bridge keeps a record of everything that has happened," whispered Trya.

"This is the result of the combined magic of dwarves and trolls." A dragon's tail appeared from above as Uriel landed above them and lazily stretched out on the bridge.

Everyone jumped back ready to run, even though such actions were useless against a dragon.

"How is it you arrived without our knowledge?" asked Nylana.

"Dragons can be stealthy if we wish," replied Uriel.

"What do you want?" demanded Nylana.

"I have come to claim my prize.   We had a bargain remember? I take you to Belyndril after which I eat you and your friends." Uriel looked around. "Seems my snack has diminished in size."

"How about a new bargain?" said Nylana.

"You're a bold one," growled the dragon. "Oh, very well. Answer my riddle correctly and I will let you live."

"Agreed," said Nylana.

"What touches the sky, but not the heavens? Is crowned in snow year round, but is king to none but its own kind. Treacherous, yet loyal."

Nylana pursed her lips. She hated riddles. They were never her strong suit. Silently she repeated the riddle to herself hoping the answer would appear. Nothing.

"The Ársa Mountain," replied Trya with confidence.

"Wrong," said Uriel.

"On the contrary," Trya stepped forward, "I am correct. It is the Ársa Mountain. The tallest mountain in the range. The one from whom the others are named."

"Alright, so you are correct, but I shall eat you all anyway. It was for her to answer," Uriel pointed at Nylana.

"You never specified that," challenged Trya. "Now let us go, or let it be known that dragons are an untrustworthy lot who make false promises while finding ways to betray others."

Smoke billowed from Uriel's nostrils. "Fine," he snorted, "You will all come with me."

"But you promised to let us live," protested Magi.

"I did," said Uriel, "But I never specified the manner in which you would be allowed to live." The dragon sneered at Trya.

"No," said Nylana with authority. "You will release us, or eat us. But we'll not be your slaves."

Uriel put his face directly in front of Nylana's boring into her eyes and noting the fire within them. "I couldn't eat you even if I wanted to. And if I eat your friends I will make a dangerous enemy of you. There is something that lives within you. Something which died not long ago, but the world needs."

"What do you really want from us?" asked Nylana, more gently.

"The trolls have stolen the last of the dragon eggs. Our only female laid it a month ago. It is the last hope for my kind. My race is dying."

"Dying?" said Magi.

"Yes," answered Uriel. "Once we numbered more than the stars, but now we are but a few. We need that egg. I could never go into their underground realm, but you three could slip in unnoticed."

"And where are the trolls?" asked Nylana.

"In the foothills of the mountains," replied the dragon.

"Why didn't you come to us while we were still there?" demanded Magi.

"Because it would not have been as interesting," replied Uriel.

"Very well," said Nylana, "We will retrieve this egg. You will take us to where the trolls are. Once we give you the egg, you will bring us here to this exact spot. And if at any time in the future should I need your assistance, you will come when I call."

The dragon glared at Nylana. "Agreed."

Uriel crouched on the ground so that they could climb aboard. Trya scooped up Magi as she mounted the dragon with Nylana seated directly behind her. With momentous force, the dragon beat his wings sending dust everywhere as he made for the sky and carried them back to the foothills of the Perili Mountains.

Uriel landed gently on the ground before a small opening within the side of the hill. "Through there is the way to the troll realm," said the dragon. "I will be awaiting your return."

They scrambled off the dragon's back and stared at the small opening. Uriel looked at them expectantly.

Leading the way, Nylana crawled through the tiny opening and into the dark interior. "Remember our bargain," she said.

Trya followed with Magi just hopping through the entrance. It took a few moments for their eyes to adjust to the change in light.

"We need a torch," said Nylana.

In answer to her wish a lit tree branch shot through the opening landing by her feet. She picked it up.

"You have two days," Uriel's voice echoed around them, "If you have not retrieved the egg by then, you will be dead."

"I thought you said you weren't going to kill us," said Magi.

"I won't have to," answered Uriel, "The trolls will do it for me."

Nylana led the way holding the torch high to light the path. Echoes flittered around them as their boots touched the stone floor, much to Nylana's ire. Water trickled down the walls as yellow fungus inched up them covering them in yellow goo.

They steadied themselves as they walked down a steep incline. Silence surrounded them. The path snaked its way through the caverns deep under the mountains changing from narrow to wide with sharp drop offs.

"How far?" asked Magi.

"Uriel never said," replied Nylana. "Magi, what happened to the five lands after I left for Pras'quel?"

Magi swished her tail as she walked.

"Magi?"

"Your brother, Krispyn, has let the kingdom fall in disarray."

Nylana turned toward Magi. "What do you mean?"

"Krispyn raised taxes on all five lands. He gave no reason for it other than that money was needed for the coffers."

Nylana frowned. She saw no reason for this because after 500 years of peace the treasury overflowed with revenue.

"He has emptied the treasury to fund lavish parties that only the nobility attend. He did start an assistance program for the poor and downtrodden of society. Bread is handed out in his name. He said that he started it in your memory. Something you proposed yourself."

"Why that's not true at all," exclaimed Nylana, "I had proposed a home for orphans, but not what you described."

"Ironic isn't it," said Trya as she walked silently, "The very people receiving the bread from Krispyn are paying for it themselves. I am certain that the lords of the five lands have increased the taxes they already impose just to cover what they now owe the king."

"Belyndril and MurDair have been especially vocal against Krispyn's new edicts. Hemíl is expected to join them. They especially dislike the edict demanding that they decrease the size of their armies."

"At a time when we are being invaded, that makes no sense," said Nylana.

"Your brother has no interest in the invasion," said Magi. "The attack on La'nar was not the first. There have been others across the land. All reports went unheeded."

"But surely—"

"Nylana," said Magi, "Everyone knows that you were the one governing the five lands, not Krispyn. For seventy years I have been in that palace at Norlyk and never have I seen such an inept man on the throne."

Nylana remained silent. She wanted to respond to Magi's statement, but deep down she knew the truth of the cat's sentiments. Whenever Krispyn made a decision that benefited all, she had been the one who first suggested it. It was always her who tempered his ambitions.

"It should be you on the throne," said Magi.

"I do not want it," snapped Nylana.

"You may yet end up with it," said Trya. "The council clearly does not want Krispyn as their king."

"Then it will go to Galdin," said Nylana, "He is the rightful heir."

"A mercenary," scoffed Magi.

Nylana turned on her. "I'll not hear another word said against my brothers. Krispyn is no leader. I know that. But he isn't a bad man. And Galdin may have been a mercenary, but he has a kindness to him. I know he has a good heart."

"How do you know?" asked Trya, respectfully.

"He saved a slave from a terrible fate. A true mercenary would have looked the other way."

"Silence! Both of you," hissed Magi. The urgency in her voice forced them to pause. Cautiously, Magi sniffed the air; her whiskers wrinkled with each breath.

"What is it?" whispered Trya.

"Drulocs," said Magi.

An ominous growl sounded behind them. Slowly, they turned coming face to face with the snarling face of a druloc. The animal lunged at them barely missing them as Trya shoved both Magi and Nylana out of the way. Its claws scraped the solid ground as it skidded to a halt before turning and lunging again. It slapped the ground with its front paw snarling venomously as it dove for them again, spreading its bat like wings.

Nylana pulled out her sword swinging it upward cutting off one wing of the druloc. The beast slammed into the sharp, rock wall.

"Run!" Nylana yelled as three more drulocs appeared.

Instantly, the trio sped through the narrow cavern delving further into the deepening darkness. Heavy breathing echoed as the drulocs chased them. Ignoring all ounces of sanity, Nylana charged ahead coming upon a wide expanse. She stopped suddenly and forced herself to fall backward before she tumbled over the edge.

"I don't think our situation has improved," said Magi looking back at the drulocs that were close behind.

Trya picked up the cat, ran, and jumped over the space landing agilely on the other side. Nylana followed. She gasped from her hard landing.

The drulocs spread their wings and sailed over to the other side. One plowed into Nylana snatching her cloak and yanking her to the ground. It tore viciously at her as she tried to free herself.

Trya pulled her bow apart revealing the two swords. She threw one at the druloc. Roars of pain pounded their ears as the beast cried in agony from being struck in the eye. Seizing her chance, Nylana plunged her own weapon into the druloc. She yanked Trya's weapon from the beast's corpse and tossed it to the elf who caught it with ease.

The remaining two drulocs thumped on the rocky ground as they landed. Saliva dripped from their jaws as they bared their fangs crouching low for the attack. Trya and Nylana backed away with their weapons before them.

"This way," called Magi.

A druloc that they hadn't been aware of attacked from above landing on Nylana. Pain coursed through her arm as its curved claw ripped her flesh. In an instant, Trya jumped on its back plunging both her blades into the thing's neck. It squealed, swinging its head back and forth violently, but the elf hung on. She twisted her knives allowing them to cut deeper into the creature. Slowly, its movements died.

Trya jumped off the druloc's back. She pulled Nylana to her feet and shoved her towards a small opening where Magi stood. "In. Quick!"

Nylana crawled through the opening and into a small space.

"This way," said Magi as she pranced ahead. "Follow me."

Maneuvering her hands and knees so she could worm her way through the cramped tunnel, Nylana followed the cat's urgings.

Trya followed close behind. With the movements of a contortionist, the elf turned herself around to stab at the drulocs attempting to follow. Their razor claws tore at the tiny opening; jaws snapping. The elf jabbed her sword into the mouth of one causing it to recoil and yelp.

A lone howl echoed through the underground. The drulocs bounded away seemingly drawn to it.

Wasting no time, Trya turned back around and followed Nylana and Magi.

Sticks protruded from the walls catching them in the face. Snap! A twig broke in half as it caught Nylana in the face. Gently, she touched where it had drawn blood. Ignoring the sting, Nylana moved onward on her belly, inching her way through the mud.

Squishing sounds followed each time she placed a hand in the sludge. Breathing heavily, Nylana continued crawling through the cramped tunnel. Damp air stuck to her lungs.

Finally, they reached the end. Another small hole led to freedom, poised above them. Magi leaped through the opening with ease. "Come on," she said.

Grimacing, Nylana reached up twisting from side to side to get her shoulders through. A loud rip told her that she would need a new shirt.

Trya slipped out of the hole with ease; barely a speck of mud dotted her. She brushed herself off, surveyed the area, and set her mouth in a thin line. "This is a good place to rest."

"What if more of those things come for us?" asked Nylana.

Magi sniffed the air. She pointed her nose upward taking several whiffs before flopping on the ground with a lazy posture. "They are not here."

Noting the blood on Nylana's sleeve, Trya pulled some cloth from her bag. "Here, let me treat your arm."

For the first time, Nylana realized she had been cut. She gave her arm to Trya's waiting hand. Carefully, the elf rolled the sleeve up. Puzzled, she flipped Nylana's arm studying it. No mark lay upon it.

"I thought you had been scratched," said Trya.

Nylana jerked her arm away and looked at it. "I was." She brushed the smooth skin, yet she remembered feeling the claw of the druloc. "I don't understand."

Trya grabbed Nylana's face and studied it. Where the sticks in the tunnel had scratched her, only smooth skin remained. "I think I do." The elf pulled out a small dagger and swiped the edge of the blade across Nylana's arm.

"Ouch!" exclaimed Nylana. "What'd you—"

In answer, Trya held Nylana's arm up. They watched as the freshly made cut disappeared being replaced by smooth skin. "I think more happened when the phoenix healed you than we realized."

"I don't get it," whispered Nylana, "Even Queen Amborese did not have this ability."

"No," replied Trya, "Small cuts healed, but even she was not immune to mortal wounds. I suggest you sleep. We will leave in a few hours."

The elf took a stance nearby for first watch. She watched as Nylana stretched out with Magi and fell asleep. Tiredness plagued her, but Trya refused to pay any attention to it. She nestled against the wall vainly forcing her heavy eyelids to stay up.

Meow!

Trya startled awake at Magi's insistent meow.

"For an elf," said Magi, "You fall asleep easily."

"I was not sleeping," insisted Trya, though she knew she had dozed off.

"Don't worry. I won't tell anyone."

Trya glanced at Nylana who lay sleeping in a lone corner. "How long have you been with the family?" asked Trya.

Magi sat on her haunches wrapping her tail around her paws. "For over seventy years I have been at the palace in Norlyk. I watched the royal family in the shadows, but one day I decided to leave my solitude."

"What changed your mind?"

Magi glanced at Nylana. "She did."

Trya's inquisitive look told the cat to continue.

"When Nylana was only four years, a man was brought before her father. He had been sentenced to execution. But before the guards dragged him away, she rushed past everyone within the court and flung herself upon the man.

"I had never seen a more determined person in all my life. For whatever reason, Nylana stood before her father begging for this man's life. Moved by her words and boldness, the king relented. He gave the man a conditional pardon: protect the princess from all harm or his life would be forfeit."

"What was the man's name?" asked Trya.

"You do not know? His name is Narúl."

Narúl. Of course, thought Trya.

"I remember watching that incident. From that day forth, Nylana endeared herself to more than just the king. That was when I made my presence known. One morning the princess awoke to find me on her bed and I became the palace cat. Sadly, a year after that Vasagius attacked Norlyk and killed the king."

Trya mused over Magi's story. She remembered the news of the uprising and the death of the king. The mourners of the king and the Lost Prince. Even the elves held a memorial for them.

"I shall never forget the day of the burial," continued Magi, "Two tombs: the king's and the one meant for Galdin. A lone woman, weeping as she sang farewell and a little girl, standing proud—not a tear on her cheek.

"If only we had known that Galdin had lived. How different things would be."

"We can never dwell on what might have been," said Trya, "Just be satisfied that Galdin has returned."

"Very interesting, how that happened."

Stretching, Trya moseyed over to the sleeping Nylana. "Time to go," she said as she shook the woman awake.

Yawning, Nylana sat up. "What time is it?"

"Hard to say in the underground," replied Trya.

"Thank you, for letting me sleep." Nylana scooped up her knapsack fastening it tightly around her shoulders.

The trek through the underground was long and uneventful. No sounds except for the clacking of their boots as they walked along the hard stone. The narrow path had many drop-offs which forced them to hug the wall.

No sign of drulocs or trolls. Nylana wondered if they traveled in the right direction.

"They live far beneath the surface of the earth," said Trya when Nylana voiced her concern, "The deeper we go, the sooner we shall find them."

"This darkness is coarsening my fur," complained Magi to no one in particular.

Nylana glanced at blackened areas on the tunnel walls pondering what they were and how they got there. Gingerly, she touched one stunned by its smoothness. Without warning, little specks of light dotted the black spots in the cavern. They flickered momentarily before disappearing.

"Night stones," said Trya. "Some use them as a lantern." The elf popped one off of the wall and gently blew on it bringing it to life. She held it out to Nylana who took it gratefully. "They grow down here much like the plants of the earth grow above."

Time bypassed them the deeper they went. Without the sun as guidance, they had no idea how long they had been underground.

"I hope we find it soon," whispered Nylana.

No sooner had she said that, than Trya put her arm out to stop her.

An abyss delving endlessly into the earth opened before them as they slowly realized that they had stepped onto a veranda; one carved by hand tools. Nylana caressed the railing in front of her marveling at the intricate details in the carving.

"I thought trolls were unfriendly creatures," she said.

"They are best left alone," replied Trya, "But for a race that hates others, they are marvelous builders."

"Ironic," said Magi.

"Most things in life are," replied Trya. "Come, I see the egg."

Always aware of their surroundings, they found some stairs to a lower level. Tipping her head back, Nylana looked up at the ceiling above, but she only saw columns stretching beyond the limits of her vision.

No plants grew, but carved, rock topiaries speckled the place. Nylana touched one. It felt as though it had branches and leaves; it felt lifelike.

"Quickly," urged Trya.

Suppressing her desire to look at everything, Nylana followed after the elf with Magi padding beside her. They found more stairs leading to the center of the surrounding buildings.

All the while Nylana felt that something was not right. *Where are the trolls? If this was their city, they should be here.* She glanced around her. Silence loomed. No sign of life.

They found a narrow walkway that led to the center crevice with the lone egg.

"Let's get the egg and get out of here," said Magi.

Nylana touched the egg's black shell in wonderment as the smooth exterior showed her reflection. "How are we to carry this?" she asked, "It is twice the size of us."

Trya studied the egg. "We shall find a way."

A malevolent laugh boomed around them bouncing off the underground buildings. The laughter grew in volume as armed trolls materialized around them, stepping out of the darkness. Spears and axes pointed at their throats.

"Drop your weapons," said one troll as he stepped forward.

They obeyed.

"You are, no doubt, wondering how we knew you were coming."

The troll walked around them, towering over them. His roughhewn clothes reeked of refuse. What trolls carved into beauty was overshadowed by their rough mannerisms and lack of hygiene.

"Our soothsayer foresaw your coming."

A sightless troll stepped forward leaning on a walking stick. "You should let them go, Crolyk."

"Silence!" Crolyk glared at the soothsayer.

"I warned you of their coming, but I also warned you to let them pass unharmed."

"Quiet!"

"If you do not let them leave with what they came for, you will meet a power even greater than yours."

"I said silence!" Crolyk punched the soothsayer in the face knocking him backward. "You will speak when I say."

"Let us go," shouted Nylana. "Let us have the egg that you have stolen and we will leave peaceably."

Crolyk glared at Nylana. "So you dare come into our realm to steal our prize?"

"Steal?" snapped Nylana. "Who committed the first theft? That egg belongs with the dragons and yet it is here in your underground realm. I come to return it to the dragons."

"Arrogant human," snarled Crolyk. He backhanded Nylana reveling in the force of his blow as her head whipped to the side. A cut appeared on Nylana's cheek spilling drops of blood. Just as quickly, it healed.

Crolyk snatched her chin forcing her head upward so he could look at it. "You do not bleed."

He backhanded her again. Just like before, the mark disappeared. "What magic is this?" He raised his fist for a third time and swung with brute force, but a slender hand stopped him as Trya took hold of his meaty wrist.

"That is enough," said the elf, her eyes full of menace.

Despite being twice her size, Crolyk backed down freeing his wrist from the elf's viselike grip. "Very well. Perhaps this will be better."

Crolyk walked up to the dragon egg with his poleaxe. He heaved it high above his head before letting it swing and crash into the egg.

"No!" screamed Nylana.

Crolyk hit it again. A sickening crack filled the cavern as the egg split, bursting open. A writhing figure oozed out of the confines of the shell squirming on the rocky ground before going limp. Silky white slime covered the baby dragon's still form.

"You bastard!" Nylana struggled against the troll holding her. She kicked and squirmed as the surrounding trolls laughed relishing her anguish.

"You can take that back to the dragons," scoffed Crolyk.

The troll holding Nylana released her as she ran to the dead, infant dragon and cradled it in her arms. None paid any heed to her. None, except an elf and a cat.

Gradually, the mood within the cavern changed. A golden glow emanated from Nylana; dim at first, but growing in intensity with each passing second. Tendrils of gold and silver light stretched from Nylana shooting about the underground realm leaving glittering marks upon the moldy walls. The trolls' laughter dwindled into silence.

Crolyk stared at Nylana stepping closer. "What the—"

Slowly, Nylana rose to her feet and faced the trolls. The gentle woman of before had been replaced with eyes of fire and tears of ice as her entire body glowed. Nylana ripped out her sword and smacked Crolyk across the face with the flat of the blade knocking him to the ground.

"Where did you get that blade?" demanded Crolyk as he eyed the sword of Tesnayr.

"As it was given to High King Tesnayr," Nylana's voice thundered in the cavern with a deep, bass tone, "As it was given to Queen Amborese, so it has been given to me. I, Nylana, Princess of the Five Lands of Tesnayr bear the sword of Tesnayr.

"You in your foolish revelry have murdered an innocent. As such, suffer my wrath."

Nylana pointed her sword upward as light spilled from its markings to the farthest reaches of the cave; streaks of golden white light shot from it with an ear splitting crack. It struck a stalactite severing it from the roof of the cave. Crumbling, the massive rock crashed to the floor sending bits of stone in every direction.

"Tell me why I should not punish you all for this transgression?" shouted Nylana as she pointed her weapon at the nearest troll who quaked before her.

"Nylana!" Magi appeared from the blackness poised on a ledge; her cat eyes staring straight into Nylana's.

Gradually, Nylana lowered her weapon. At that instant she understood two basic truths about the phoenix: it possessed a terrible wrath tempered by mercy and love.

Nylana turned to Crolyk. "You who would bring death to this realm will suffer the same fate, but not by my hand. You who bring death, bear witness as I bring forth life."

Gently, Nylana knelt beside the lifeless dragon. She caressed its silky skin as light flowed from her fingers and surrounded the beast's body. A soft growl filled the area as the small beast took a deep breath. With each breath it took, the light surrounding Nylana dissipated until they were all plunged back into the dimness of the underground realm.

The dragon lifted its head peering into Nylana's now compassionate eyes as the fire within them had gone. The animal shook itself. With each movement, its gray skin sloughed off to reveal shimmering gold scales that glittered. The gentle creature nuzzled into Nylana's arms as she cradled it.

"You shall be called Mishkunn for you were born of mercy," said Nylana.

The dragon nodded at its name, accepting it.

"We are leaving," said Nylana to Trya and Magi as she stood up holding the dragon.

*   *   *

Somewhere deep in the Perili Mountains Tami woke with a start.

"What is it?" asked Galdin.

"I felt a tremendous amount of magic," replied Tami, "As though the phoenix had returned."

"Impossible," said Galdin, "I watched it die."

"I don't know how," said Tami, "Look at the trees and the flowers. They seem more alive."

Galdin glanced about him. What had been dry sand only hours before had become overgrown with emerald grass. Flowers of every variety and color dotted the newly formed meadow as the withered tree straightened growing luscious leaves. It was as though the land spawned new life as he watched.

"This land was barren," Galdin said in disbelief.

Tami brushed her hand through the silky grass. "Not anymore."

*   *   *

Scraping and scratching snatched Uriel's attention as he waited patiently outside the tunnel. With remarkable grace, the dragon faced the opening into the side of the mountain waiting for the noise maker to appear.

Out popped a cat.

Uriel relaxed knowing that directly behind the cat was an elf and a woman; and hopefully the egg. His eyes grew wide as he saw the infant, gold dragon in Nylana's arms.

"What is this?" asked the dragon.

"The egg hatched," answered Magi as though it should have been obvious.

"Hatched?"

"Yes, that sort of thing does happen," replied Magi.

"Do not get coy with me," warned Uriel.

"Enough," Nylana's voice silenced them. "Uriel, great dragon, we have done what you asked. Here is the product of the egg. I believe the trolls will leave your nest alone from now on."

"How did they manage it, anyway?" asked Trya, "The Fiery Caves are not easily climbed."

"Trolls are adept at forming rock to fit their purposes," said Uriel, "And time has a way of eroding many things."

The infant dragon screeched. Softening his demeanor slightly, Uriel spoke, "Very well Princess of Tesnayr. As you and your friends have kept your part of the bargain, I shall keep mine."

Uriel lowered himself, while gently picking up the infant dragon in his jaws. Nylana, Trya, and Magi climbed aboard. Spreading his massive wings, Uriel rose into the sky becoming little more than a speck. Wind rushed over them as they hung on. Nylana marveled at the landscape below.

Six gigantic, snowcapped mountains divided the five lands, clustered together and surrounded by smaller, lesser ones. In the sky, she appreciated the new view of her home. Never before had Nylana travelled far from the confines of the palace of Norlyk. Inhaling deeply, she relished the newfound freedom and excitement.

Uriel dipped to the right slightly. Reveling in the freshness of the cold of the higher altitude, Nylana's stomach lurched slightly as Uriel dipped lower in the sky.

"We're already here?" she yelled over the howl of the wind.

With a soft thump, the dragon landed and crouched low so that his passengers could disembark.

"The Changing Woods," said Trya, "I thought we were farther north when we came out of the mountain."

"We were," answered Uriel, "But with the girl on my back, I feel renewed strength, allowing me to go farther and faster than I thought possible.

"I thought you would prefer landing here as you once said that you had need of this place."

"Thank you, Uriel," said Nylana.

"Farewell, human. You'll pardon me if I say that I hope we never meet again."

"Remember our bargain," said Nylana, "When I call, you must come."

Snorting, the dragon dropped an item on the ground by Nylana's feet. "In that case you will need this."

"Selexia's Horn," exclaimed Nylana, "I thought it had been lost."

"It always finds its way to an heir of Tesnayr," said Uriel, "Though Queen Amborese freed the dragons, the horn still possesses the magic to summon us. Though being freed we do not have to heed its call."

"You best be careful with that," said Magi, "Anyone could use it."

"Stupid cat," puffed Uriel, "It only works for an heir of Tesnayr. And you best hope that only I answer its call."

Uriel scooped up the gold dragon and disappeared into the sky, leaving them alone with their quest.

Chapter V
On the Run

Vapors of moist air puffed before them as both Tami and Galdin ran through the small canyon trails that wormed their way through the mountains. Spindly brush snatched their clothes attempting to halt them. Sharp rock cut through their shoes as they pounded the earth with their feet.

With burning lungs they dashed onward as their pursuers closed in. Both knew that the barbarians would chase them, but neither expected the speed with which they were found. Thunder loomed behind them as their pursuers closed in.

They turned a corner hoping to shake their enemy. Galdin seized Tami and pulled her close, away from the sunlight and into shadow. They hunkered in the small hollow as the barbarians charged past with their armor and swords clanking loudly. Like statues they stood watching with wide eyes as the army passed. One man near the end stopped to fasten a strap on his boot. The moment he turned his head, Galdin knew they had been spotted.

In a flash, Galdin shoved Tami to the side and plunged his sword into the back of the barbarian's neck. A quick glance told him the others hadn't noticed. He seized Tami and dragged her along backtracking the way they had come. They ran back through the maze hoping that no one followed.

They raced back to where the channel began. Glancing all around, Galdin kept his eyes peeled for more of the invaders.

"Wait," said Tami, "Where are we going?"

"Away from here and them," replied Galdin.

"But this is the wrong way," said Tami. "I told you, these channels are the only way through these lower hills."

"We'll have to find another way," said Galdin.

Tami scanned the rock walls surrounding them. "I guess we could climb."

"What?"

She pointed upward. "This looks like a good spot."

Tami grabbed protruding rocks and hoisted herself up placing her feet carefully on the sides of the earthen wall. With measured skill, she reached up for another handhold. Bit by bit, she scaled the wall going upward toward the cleft above her.

Galdin followed. He placed his hands and feet exactly where Tami had earlier. With great effort he slowly moved up following the young woman knowing there was nowhere else for them to go. Sweat covered his hands causing them to slip as he tried to grab the wall. Hanging on, he reached again grasping the rough surface tightly.

Hugging the canyon wall, both Tami and Galdin inched upward to the ledge. Tami reached it first. She heaved herself onto the flat surface of the mesa followed closely by Galdin.

"There they are," said Tami pointing at the black mass moving through the channels of the mountain.

"And how are we to get out of here?" asked Galdin.

"With this," Tami pointed at a thin rock line bridging the crevices spread throughout the lower part of the mountains. "These things are all over. We can trek through the mountains above while they look for us down there. Just don't look down."

Tami stepped onto the rock delicately crossing it with grace. Following suit, Galdin walked across. Pebbles clacked below with each step he took.

*   *   *

Krispyn stood alone in the torchlight. He knew that the council watched him carefully and his handling of the barbarian invasion, but he had other matters on his mind. The careful footsteps of a wizard approached from behind.

"Why do you walk so silently?" asked Krispyn.

"I did not wish to disturb you," answered Petra.

"And yet you are here. What news do you bring?"

"La'nar has fallen and Lord Trisk is believed to be among the dead."

"And Nylana?" Krispyn faced Petra, his face concealed by dancing shadows.

"No word about her," answered Petra, "She most likely made it out alive."

"What makes you say that?"

"Until I know for certain that she is otherwise, I'd rather believe that she still lives," said Petra.

"Thank you, Petra, for telling me. As always your council proves most comforting." Krispyn left with the solemn posture of one wanting to be alone.

*   *   *

Narúl and the others followed after Trog hoping they went in the right direction. The commotion at the fort had told them that Galdin had escaped. Right before they planned to go in, the gates opened and barbarian soldiers trooped out. From the shouts and yells, Narúl knew that Galdin had escaped. He decided they would trail behind the force sent to recapture him. After the first two days, Narúl thought it best to cease following the barbarian force, knowing that Galdin would not remain on the main trails. Once again, they relied on Trog to find their friend before the others did.

"I want to know why you left Norlyk," Narúl said to Artryl as they walked.

"I wanted to help," said Artryl, sheepishly.

"I told you to stay put," scolded Narúl, "This is no place for a child."

"I'm not a child! I am thirteen."

"And with much to learn," said Narúl.

"I can help," pleaded Artryl.

"Once we find Galdin, you are going back."

"No."

"Do not test me."

"I will not go back," said Artryl, "You need me."

Narúl's face twitched from anger. The boy's obstinence wore on him. "These lands are overrun by these savages. For your own safety, you must return."

"You need me."

"We shall see," said Narúl.

They came to dead end and stared at the wall of rock.

"Where would he have gone?" asked Tabs. "He could not have climbed this."

Trog pranced around sniffing the ground and the wall. He sat back on his haunches looking up with his tongue lolling out of his mouth.

"What if they did?" said Ryk. "Galdin might have climbed up there to get away."

"It is too steep," said Narúl.

"Trog seems to think that he went that way," countered Ryk.

"Artryl, what are you doing?" Narúl looked at the boy who had started climbing the rock wall to the ledge at the top.

"If they did go this way," said Artryl as he climbed, "There is only one way to find out."

"Get down from there," commanded Narúl. "You are not climbing up there alone."

Instantly, Trog grabbed Artryl by the shoulders and swooped him up into the air placing the boy gently on the top of the ledge. The animal licked Artryl's face before dashing back to the canyon floor where the others waited.

"I see tracks," shouted Artryl, "Galdin did go this way and he wasn't alone."

"Stay put while we—"

Narúl's words were cut short as Trog snatched him and carried him to where Artryl was. In a matter of minutes the strange creature carried Ryk and Tabs there as well. Trog lay splayed on the ground panting heavily when he had finished.

Narúl looked around. He studied the tracks in the dried mud noting the cross bridges made of rock. "Galdin did come this way and with another. They must have climbed up here to escape their pursuers. The tracks head that way. They must be using these bridges to get through the foothills."

"The barbarians could be using them too," said Ryk.

"I do not think so," said Narúl, "There are no tracks. They may not know about these bridges. Even I did not know of them. Somehow, Galdin discovered them."

"We should leave," said Ryk.

Narúl glanced at Artryl who comforted the worn out Trog. He looked at the low hanging sun in the sky. "We should rest here tonight. It will be dark within the hour."

Ryk nodded. He gathered some sticks and dried grass to start a fire. Soon after he had pulled out his flint to light it Narúl stopped him.

"No fire. Remember, we are not alone in these mountains."

"It is going to get cold up here," said Ryk.

Narúl noted how Artryl and Trog slept close together. The animal purred lightly as it snored. "We shall keep warm by huddling together."

Ryk put his flint away and settled beside Trog. "Do you mind if we cuddle?" he teased the animal.

Trog replied by smacking Ryk with his tail.

"I'll take that as a no."

*   *   *

Stahl paced the ground while anxiously waiting for a visit from the cloaked stranger who had a habit of showing up unannounced. He did not know why Vasagius insisted on doing this man's bidding. Deep down, Stahl felt that his general would be better off without the stranger. The man gave him the shivers.   A sorcerer, thought Stahl, and sorcerers cannot be trusted.   That must be why Vasagius does the man's bidding, Stahl told himself.

"Something unnerves you," said a coarse voice.

Stahl whipped around. "On the contrary, my lord."

"What news?"

This was the moment Stahl wanted to avoid. "The prisoner escaped," said Stahl.

"And the woman?" asked the stranger, his voice cold and hard.

Stahl choked back a croak. "She is gone too."

"Fools!" The cloaked figure backhanded Stahl forcing him to take a step back. "How could you lose them?"

"Their escape was quite unexpected, my lord," said Stahl.

"Escapes always are.   I want them found," shouted the cloaked stranger.

"They will be," answered Stahl.

"And where is Vasagius?" demanded the stranger.

"He sends his apologies for not meeting with you," said Stahl, "But he is busy."

"When I arrive I expect to meet with him not his lap dog. How did they escape?"

"Does it matter? They will be found."

"Oh, I have no doubt of that," said the cloaked figure. He whistled. Suddenly a niht'anda crashed into Stahl sweeping him into its claws holding him high in the air. "This is Graf. He will help you find them."

Stahl stared at the hideous creature. He had never seen a niht'anda before and thought them mere tales told by parents to scare their children. "I do not think—"

"I did not ask you to think," sneered the cloaked figure, "It is done."

Disturbed, Stahl stalked off to report to Vasagius.

"Go with him, Graf," said the figure to the niht'anda, "Find them and bring them to me."

Graf, nuzzled against the cloaked figure releasing a snort before bounding off after Stahl.

The cloaked man glanced around at the servants that darted to and fro. He watched with boredom as they accepted their servitude to the barbarian horde, and later to him and his master. They disgusted him. Sheep, he thought, meant to be ruled.

One woman in particular caught his attention. She carried a water jug, but her movements did not match the rest; she seemed too erect in her posture. He trailed behind her as she maneuvered her way through the crowd seemingly unaware of his presence.

The woman weaved her way around people going behind buildings and down an alleyway. She walked casually as though nothing was amiss. The cloaked figure followed as the woman turned a corner. He quickened his pace to catch up rounding the same corner before she could turn down another street.

"Halt!" he called.

The woman ignored him.

"I said stop!"

The woman stopped, still hugging her water jug.

Carefully, the cloaked figure confronted the woman stepping in front of her. She kept her face down and her hood up. Unlike the others, she did not quake from fear; instead she remained perfectly still and calm. Cautiously, the man lifted the hood off of the woman's face letting it fall until it draped her shoulders. The face was old, but young at the same time. Bits of silver and black hair fell from the tied bun delicately framing her chin.

"Quesha," said the cloaked figure, "I should have known."

"So you know of me," said Quesha with a smile.

"Everyone knows of you. What are you doing here?"

Quesha grinned broadly in the serene way of hers. "I should think you could figure that out." She placed her water jug on the ground.

"Do not toy with me."

"It is not I who is toying with the world. Oh, don't worry. I will not reveal your secret. You who are closest to the king."

"Whatever information you managed to glean from here will be of no use to you," snarled the cloaked man.

"I did not come for information," said Quesha.

"Really? Maybe it is just as well. I have heard that your influence on this world has waned. That you are a shadow of what you used to be."

"Do not be so certain of that," warned Quesha; her voice remained soft, but her features had hardened.

"No one has the power to stop me," said the man, "Magic is gone from this world. That fool of a princess and her brother can try all they want but nothing will stop me."

"I was hoping for something more original," said Quesha as she brushed the man's chin with her finger. "I have heard many say the same and they all met the same fate."

"I am not them."

"Oh very well, be boring." Quesha moved away a few paces. "There is one more powerful than you."

"You will never live to tell them who I am," said the man.

"Oh, I have no intention of revealing your secret," said Quesha. "They will learn it soon enough."

"Then leave empty-handed."

"I will leave, but not empty-handed." Quesha held up her hand revealing a small blue orb within her palm.

The cloaked figure checked his pocket finding it empty.

"I told you I did not come for information."

"You will die, you witch!" The sorcerer held his hands before him shooting out streaks of black lightning at Quesha. A great blast of light and thunder followed. When all had quieted, nothing remained but a single cloak on the ground where Quesha had stood.

"You will not be rid of me so easily," Quesha's voice echoed around him.

Thunder rolled through the hills as the mysterious sorcerer shouted curses to the night sky.

Chapter VI
The Feather

Nylana stared at the mass of trees before them. She had never been to the Changing Woods before but remembered the tales. A place where the landscape always changed. A wolf howled in the distance. Instinctively, Nylana turned around to make certain there were none behind her, but animals seemed to avoid this area. She glanced back at the forest only to find that it had changed. Trees huddled together in clumps with vines wrapped around their massive trunks. Boulders formed a jumbled mess.

"Where did the path go?" asked Nylana.

"Welcome to the Changing Woods," Trya replied.

"I don't like this place," snapped Magi.

"You don't have to come," said Nylana as she walked toward the only opening. She climbed on a boulder that stood four feet high scratching her hand on the sharp edges as she hoisted herself up. Trya glided over the rocks with ease. Nylana watched enviously as the elf jumped atop one and gently landed on the other side with grace. She flopped on the ground landing roughly on her rump.

"If you were a cat," gloated Magi as she floated to the top of a boulder and leapt to the other side, "You would have more grace."

Glaring at the cat, Nylana picked herself up and dusted off her rear. "Wiseacre."

"SHHH," said Trya, "Listen."

Nylana strained her ears to hear what the elf did, but nothing came to her. "I don't hear anything."

"Exactly," said Trya, "It's quiet."

A string of cursing escaped Magi as the cat voiced language that Nylana didn't know the animal knew. "Stupid root appeared from nowhere."

"Let's go," said Nylana as she led the way.

"Do you even know where you are going?" asked Magi as she plucked a sticky substance from her fur.

"Lead the way," said Nylana.

"What?"

"Go on. Take us through here."

Scowling, Magi marched ahead of Nylana and Trya. "Fine." She stalked off stiff legged through the thick foliage with the others close behind, smirking.

"Let the cat go first," Magi muttered to herself, "Let the cat be the one to get into trouble."

Wind rushed over the forest knocking Trya and Nylana over. It howled with intense ferocity that leaves and twigs swirled around them, stinging them. Just as suddenly, instant calm settled among them as though nothing had happened.

The scenery had changed once again. Sticks for trees stuck out of the ground as rays of sunlight reached them. The once thick canopy of leaves had evaporated.

"Wow," whispered Magi as she looked up at the sky. "The sky, it's so blue."

"Actually it's purple," said Nylana.

Trya glanced up and smiled. To her the sky looked orange. Such was the nature of the Changing Woods.

Nylana looked at the sky once more. It had turned a vivid shade of emerald. "Does nothing stay the same in this place? It always changes."

"Hence why it's called the Changing Woods," quipped Magi, "I should think the name was self-explanatory."

A mist settled over them as they walked. Thick and heavy, it blocked all visibility. Nylana's head smarted as she walked right into a tree. She rubbed the throbbing bump on her forehead silently cursing the fact that a tree had appeared from nowhere.

"Are you alright?" said Trya as she held her hand out to help Nylana up.

"Yes. Only my pride's a bit hurt."

"This forest is old," said Trya. "Very ancient."

"Why is it everything in here changes?" asked Nylana.

"No one knows the real reason. The ancient scrolls say that this forest was once the home of an ancient being, but no one knows his name."

Just then Nylana heard the cry of the phoenix. It came from a great distance, but to her it seemed as though it was nearby. "Did you hear that?" she asked.

"Hear what?" replied Trya.

"The phoenix."

Trya and Magi looked at Nylana as though she had lost her mind.

"Nylana," said Trya, tentatively, "The phoenix is dead."

"No, it isn't. I heard it. Just now!"

Trya looked upon Nylana with pity.

Nylana wanted to smack that look right off of the elf's face, but restrained herself. "I'm telling you I heard it."

Frustrated at their lack of belief, Nylana marched away. She stomped through the woods allowing her boots to noisily crunch twigs and leaves without any regard that someone might be watching her movements. She heard it again: the clear cry of the phoenix. *Why does no one else hear it?*

She darted in the direction of the sound. Humming to herself as she went, Nylana ignored the other two and continued her trek. Nothing else mattered. She didn't know why, but Nylana felt herself being led. She had to find it. Purposefully, Nylana tramped through the Changing Woods ignoring the landscape as it transformed around her. She knew it was here. What she searched for. What she had to find.

"Nylana!"

Trya's voice barely registered as Nylana charged through the woods following what only she heard. Another cry. Nylana veered to the left. She continued running even as an immense fog settled over the landscape.

"Nylana!"

Ignoring their pleas, Nylana kept running. It was here. She knew it was. The cold wetness of the fog barely fazed her. Plowing through the brush, Nylana tore herself free from the snags of sharp branches and rocks. She jumped over exposed roots. Nothing was going to stop her.

Her lungs burned for air as she ran. She was close. She didn't know how she knew, but she felt it.

"Nylana! Stop!"

No, thought Nylana, I can't stop.

She charged through the woods until—

SMACK!

Nylana slammed into a solid rock wall. It stretched over two hundred feet high and its smooth side told her that climbing it would be impossible. "Blast it," screamed Nylana feeling cheated.

"You stupid, girl," scolded Trya. "You never run away like that in these woods."

"It's here," said Nylana, "I know it is. Why does it taunt me like this?"

Leaves gently fell around her. Nylana caught one in her palm. She studied the purple leaf. Intrigued, she looked up as a cloud of leaves fell delicately around her forming a rainbow of colors. Even Trya seemed amazed at the sight. Never had she experienced such a place.

A round of cursing filled the air. "Magi, I will take a bar of soap and—" Nylana never finished her statement as the ground fell out from beneath her feet and the landscape changed once again. Suddenly, she and Trya plunged into a mud hole. Slime oozed into her boots and places she didn't want to think about.

"I blame you for this," said Magi to Nylana.

"Can you touch the bottom?" Nylana asked Trya as she realized with horror that she was sinking.

"No," replied the elf, calmly.

Nylana noticed Magi struggling profusely to get out of the mud. She grabbed the cat and chucked her to the side where solid ground was.

"Feed me that vine," said Trya to Magi.

The mud laden cat picked the slimy vine in her teeth. Carefully, she slid it into the mud feeding the line until Trya managed to grab it. "Give me your hand," she yelled to Nylana.

Nylana reached out for the elf, but their fingers barely touched. "I can't reach," coughed Nylana as mud slipped into her mouth choking her.

Trya tied the vine around her waist. She treaded over to Nylana. Her efforts proved useless as she sunk lower with each movement she made. "Nylana," she yelled as mud crept up around the woman's neck.

"Just go," choked Nylana. "Save yourselves!"

A hand reached out to her from above. Nylana glanced up into the face of a middle aged Byleon as he hung from a tree branch. "Take it," he said in a deep voice.

Mustering her strength, Nylana shot her hand out of the sticky mud and grasped the one above her.

The Byleon clicked something which set a pulley system in motion pulling them into the air. A great sucking sound filled the area as Nylana was hoisted out of the mud hole and into safety. Trya wasted no time pulling herself to safety with the vine she held in her hands.

Nylana breathed a sigh of relief when her feet touched solid ground once again. She tried wiping the worst of the muck off of her, but her efforts made it worse. "Thank you—"

"Valn," said the Byleon.

"How did you find us?" asked Nylana.

"Your cat's cursing carries," said Valn.

Magi glared at the Byleon. She swatted him with her slime covered tail leaving a nice stripe on his leg. "Perhaps you could take us to a place where we might wash up."

The Byleon pulled a flask from his pocket and dumped the contents on Magi. "Better?"

The cat scowled at him even more infuriated than before.

"This way," said Valn. "My home lies deep in the forest far away from intruders."

They followed Valn as he led the way through the woods not noticing as surroundings changed. He never wavered from the path he charted or questioned his location within the Changing Woods. Soon they arrived at a small hut with smoke coming from the chimney.

He led them into the inviting interior and showed them where they could bathe. Nylana thankfully cleaned the mud off and wrapped up in some blankets that Valn had given her and Trya while he cleaned their clothes.

"They should be dry within an hour," he told them as he hung them by the fire.

"Do you live here alone?" asked Trya.

"For the most part," replied Valn, "My grandson pops in every so often, but not often enough."

"How do you know your way through these woods?" asked Nylana.

"It's not so hard when you know the landscape," said Valn. "There are certain parts of this area that never change. Once you learn those, navigating the Changing Woods is quite simple."

"How did you know we were there?" asked Nylana.

"I just did," replied Valn.

Magi snorted as she groomed herself by the fireplace.

"Very well. I happened to be out walking like I always do and heard the commotion. I had always hoped to meet outsiders like my great-great-great-great grandfather did."

"What was his name?" asked Trya.

"Philip."

Magi stopped her grooming. "Not the same Philip that Queen Amborese knew!"

"The very same," said Valn. "It is not a common name among Byleons. Though there are few of us left. After Clymorus was destroyed, most of my kin left the five lands. Some remained and with the help of Philip we moved away from our more primitive ways and began to resemble the Byleons of old."

"How old is your race?" asked Nylana, curious.

"We are as old as this land. According to legend Byleons lived in a great kingdom far across the vast ocean. But the land died and they were forced to leave. Near the end of King Tesnayr's reign, they came here seeking refuge. He granted it to them and they settled here."

"Why do I feel that this is all connected?" breathed Nylana.

"Because it is all connected." Valn put a bowl of stew in front of her. He handed one to Trya and Magi as well. "Too bad the land is dying."

"What do you mean?"

"Do you not feel it? I am sure the elf does."

Trya said nothing.

Nylana thought about what the elf had told her in the mountains. The earth, the wind, everything seemed different since the day the phoenix had saved her life. She didn't know why.

"All this means is that the phoenix has died," said Valn.

"What makes you say that?" asked Magi.

"It was the phoenix that brought bounty to the land. But the flowers wilt, the wind weeps—"

"And the trees moan," finished Trya.

"It is not dead," said Nylana.

"If that is so, then it has left us," said Valn. "Maybe we brought it upon ourselves always thinking that we own the world."

"The phoenix has not left," anger filled Nylana's voice. She didn't know why it did, but when Valn looked at her he saw fire in her eyes: the flames of the phoenix.

Harsh winds roared around the hut beating against the sides rattling the window and the door. The fierceness of the outside world caused all of them to shiver. The roar pounded against their ears until nothing else filled them and then—silence.

Nylana dropped her spoon and ran to the door tearing it open. Before her lay a meadow of many colors. The grass melted from one color to the next forming a rainbow of orange, red, yellow, purple, blue, and pink with gold specks glittering in the sunlight. A soft melody filled the air.

Ni'lee y'lee.

"The meadow of rainbows," whispered Trya as she looked out upon the multicolored grassy expanse. "I have heard stories of this place, but never believed—"

Nylana took off running across the meadow relishing in the glee of exercise.

"Not again," grumbled Magi as the others followed, "Someone ought to put a leash on that girl."

She knew where she had to go. Allowing the forest to guide her, Nylana raced across the expanse becoming a small black dot among bright colors in the setting sun. She ran until she came upon a lone Ash tree in the middle of the grassy plain. She did not remember it being there before, but paused before it knowing that in the Changing Woods things sometimes just appeared.

Nylana noticed a hole in the tree. She shoved her hand in there pulling out a simple, ornate box. She showed it to the others when they arrived.

"Interesting," said Valn as he took it. He tried opening it but the lid held shut. "Won't open."

Trya took the small box and picked at the lid. No matter how hard she tried, it never opened. "There is no keyhole."

"And yet it requires a key," said a mysterious voice. Quesha materialized before them sauntering up in her usual manner allowing her gown to sway with every movement of her hips. Silver hair trailed behind her in the wind. "But you are not the key."

"What do you mean?" asked Valn.

"Why don't you speak plainly so we all can understand you?" said Nylana, irritated.

"This place is amazing, isn't it?" Quesha turned to Nylana. "I've known of it, but have never stood in it before now. The wizard Max was here once, long ago. My mistress wanted to come, but he would not allow it. I can see why."

Nylana eyed the sorceress. She wanted to yell at her for speaking in riddles, but remained silent.

"Take the box and you will know what I mean," said Quesha.

Nylana grabbed the box from Trya. "It's just an ordinary box." She flicked the latch with her fingernail and it popped open. Inside rested a single gold feather. Nylana held it up allowing the last rays of the orange sun to shine upon it. It glittered in her hand. "I don't understand."

"The feather of the phoenix," Quesha's voice echoed around them, "The feather of legend. You set out to find hope, Nylana, and you have found it."

"What am I to do with this?" Nylana whirled around, but Quesha had gone. The others stared at her in confusion.

"Strange ones, sorceresses," griped Valn. "They always speak nonsense. Looks as though you found yourself a useless feather. Come along. It's getting dark."

"Useless and well hidden. Strange, don't you think?" Trya smiled at Nylana.

Nylana tucked the feather in her pocket with the rose that already resided there. Confused, she decided to push it all out of her mind as she followed the Byleon to his hut. Maybe in the morning things would be clearer.

Chapter VII
South

"My liege," Stahl entered the chamber where Vasagius stood staring out the window at the grounds below.

"What news?"

"We have failed to find them."

Vasagius faced his second in command. He noted the red mark on the man's face where the cloaked figure had struck him. "It appears you have found something else instead. And what of our friend?"

"He is angry that we lost the prisoners," said Stahl, "We are to allow his pet to find them."

"That disgusting creature in the courtyard below?"

"Yes, my lord."

Vasagius paced the room. "I tire of that sorcerer. I tire of his orders. Every day the deal changes."

"What would you have us do, my lord?" asked Stahl.

"I came back here to claim what was mine," said Vasagius, "This land is mine. I think it is time I renegotiate our terms." Vasagius strode from the room. "Use that thing to find those two. I want them back in their cell by morning."

Stahl saluted his commander's back. Summoning his courage, he marched down to the courtyard, and to the niht'anda.

*   *   *

"How did you learn your way through these woods?" asked Nylana as Valn led them through the Changing Woods.

"It isn't that difficult," answered Valn.

"Says the Byleon who has spent his entire life in this forest," mocked Magi.

"You have a point, my dear, little feline," said Valn. "I have lived here all my life. Spend enough time in the Changing Woods and you learn her secrets."

"But this forest changes constantly," said Nylana.

"Yes, it does," said Valn, "But even here a few things remain constant. Watch that rock there."

Nylana and Trya both turned to where Valn pointed. They watched the rock intently; their eyes never leaving it. A howling breeze wafted over them as mist settled around them.

"Keep your eyes fixed upon that rock," repeated Valn.

Peering through the mist, Nylana squinted to make certain she never lost sight of it. Slowly, the mist dissipated leaving the landscape crisp and clear.

"Notice anything?" asked Valn.

"The rock is still there," exclaimed Nylana, "But everything else around it has changed."

"Exactly! Everything changes in this forest, except for that rock. But that rock is not the only constant in these woods. There are other things that do not change. Learn where those are and you will never be lost."

"How did you learn it?" asked Magi.

"As you have pointed out before, I have spent an entire lifetime in this place."

They continued their trek through the woods. Nylana and Trya looked upon it with a new set of eyes always searching for the things that remained constant. When Nylana thought she had found a landmark she would point it out to Valn. He either congratulated her or told her to try again. After several hours, Nylana started to get the hang of navigating the Changing Woods; no more would she fear that place.

"Ah, freedom at last," breathed Valn as they exited the trees and entered a meadow. The Byleon took a deep breath relishing the scent of the spring air that brought warmth and yet held a chill. "You wished to head for MurDair?"

"Yes," said Nylana. "We need to get there before the next full moon.

"That should be simple enough," said Valn, "Assuming we do not run into trouble."

"That is assuming a lot," quipped Magi.

*   *   *

Artryl widened his stance as he held his sword before him. He parried an attack by Narúl with ease. Narúl lunged again. Artryl jumped back swinging his sword to the left not realizing that he had been tricked. Suddenly, Narúl changed his attack forcing Artryl to lose his balance and fall over.

"Never assume that you know your opponent's movements," said Narúl. "You must learn to read him, to be able to anticipate his next attack."

Artryl hauled himself back to his feet. He repositioned himself with his sword held before him.

Narúl attacked. Artryl easily sidestepped clipping Narúl's sword with his own. He whirled back around and smacked Narúl on the back with the flat of his blade. Unexpectedly, Narúl reached back and grabbed Artryl by his collar, pulling him to his front.

"No fair," said Artryl.

Narúl knocked the boy's weapon from his hands before ruffling his mop of hair. "On the battlefield, your opponent will never fight fairly."

Out of nowhere, Trog leapt at Narúl snatching his sword in his mouth. The animal whipped back around pointing the sharp end of the blade at Narúl daring him to fight.

"I think Trog has got something there," laughed Ryk.

"Here, Trog," Artryl held his hand out to the beast.   Trog moved over to him nuzzling in his cloak as the boy took the sword and handed it back to Narúl.

"I think that is enough swordplay for today," said Narúl with an amused smile.

Tabs popped out of the bushes out of breath. "We need to leave! Now!"

"What's the matter?" asked Narúl.

"The invaders have set a niht'anda on Galdin's trail."

They hastily snatched their belongings and put out the fire before running after Tabs.

*   *   *

Tami glanced over at Galdin's sleeping form. The steady rise and fall of his chest indicated that he slept soundly. Hastily, she got up and walked a little ways away keeping Galdin in sight. For the last few nights she had been practicing teleportation; something her mother had tried to teach her before she died.

Tami listened to the night sounds making certain that no one watched her.   Softly, she muttered the spell her mother had taught her.

Nothing happened.

Frustrated, Tami tried again saying the words in a harsh whisper. The ground vibrated around her as a breeze swept up. She felt the pull of the spell, but still she remained where she was.

Determined to get it right, Tami uttered the words once more. A gust of wind whipped around her as a mini cyclone surrounded her. Feeling the full effect of the magic she had summoned, Tami laughed to herself in satisfaction. Suddenly she disappeared from her spot and reappeared a few feet away.

Tami looked around elated that she had finally managed to get the spell to work. Something laying on the ground from where she had been caught her attention.   Carefully, Tami picked it up. It was her ear.

Frowning, she remembered her mother warning her about things like that happening when one isn't experienced at teleporting. Tami snapped her ear back in place. Galdin groaned from where he slept as he shifted position. Tami rushed back to where he was and laid back down in her spot hoping that he hadn't noticed her absence.

Galdin relaxed into more steady breathing. Satisfied, Tami closed her eyes hoping to get some sleep before dawn.

＊   ＊   ＊

Screams pierced Nylana's ears as she watched the barbarian savages thrash their whips at a group of frightened people forcing them into a single line.

"Come on, scum!" A well-armed barbarian cracked his whip as he shoved a child into the line and started them marching.

Nylana started to rise, but Valn's hand stopped her.   "Do nothing."

"But I can't just stay here while they hurt those people," hissed Nylana.

"You must," said Valn, "They have the upper hand right now. You must wait until the opportune time."

"But—"

"He is right," said Trya, cutting Nylana off. "There is nothing we can do now, but we can follow them. Then, perhaps while they sleep we can free those people."

"What if they take them to a well-armed facility?" asked Nylana.

"I do not think they will," said Trya, "See how many men there are? This looks more like a rounding up party. They will probably head to the next town for more before they head back to their main camp. But this move disturbs me."

"Why is that?" asked Nylana.

"Before, when we reached these places they were completely destroyed. Nothing was taken," answered Trya. "Something has changed."

Nylana watched the proceedings. The elf was right; something had changed Nylana realized as she watched the savages loot the town.

The whips and shouts filled the air as the barbarians led their new horde of slaves away. Wagons followed behind overflowing with treasures.

"Let's move," yelled the one in charge.

Nylana studied everything waiting for her window of opportunity. Valn spotted it before her.

"Look, there," said Valn, "That man that lags behind. There is our opportunity. Though how are we going to reach him without raising the alarm?"

"Leave it to the cat," said Magi as she bounded away.

Expertly, the cat crept through the destruction left behind making no sound. She stalked up to her prey while he paid more heed to his bag of loot than what followed behind him. Darting past, Magi swept under a wagon and waited.

Suddenly, she jumped from the ground to the man's chest knocking him down. Startled, the man dropped everything as he slammed into the hard earth. "What—"

"Silence," hissed Magi as she placed her claws on the man's neck. "Where are you taking them?"

"What?" The confused man still had not grasped the fact that the cat could talk.

"Fear me, human," said Magi, "Where are you taking those people?"

"I do not fear strays," scoffed the man, thinking that Magi was alone.

"Then fear me," said Nylana as she appeared from the shadows and placed the point of her sword at the man's throat, the blade glowing.

Scuffling seized their attention as another barbarian they had not seen charged Nylana. Instantly, Trya appeared with her swords. She caught the man's sword arm, breaking it. In a flurry of movement she flipped him up and over letting him crash into the dirt before plunging both her blades into him. After making certain he was dead, the elf snapped her two swords together allowing them to reform into a bow.

"I will not ask again," said Magi.

"Please, don't kill me," pleaded the man, "They are taking them to a place twenty miles from here. But they will have to stop and rest at some point before they get there."

"What do you want with them?" demanded Nylana.

"People are worth a lot of money as slaves."

"You never rounded them up before," said Trya.

"Yes, but it's all changed. Vasagius has decided that there is more profit in it," replied the man.

"Vasagius," whispered Nylana. She remembered the name, and the man.

"Please," pleaded the man, "I told you what you wanted to know."

Nylana looked upon him with disgust. "Release him, Magi."

The cat jumped off the man and sat by Valn's feet.

"Take his weapons," said Nylana.

Valn stripped the barbarian of his weapons.

"You are not going to kill me?" asked the man.

"No," said Nylana with coldness in her voice, "I will not. But the wolves might."

A lonely howl filled the air.

"Come," said Nylana, "We haven't much time."

                    *   *   *

Snorts puffed dust from the ground as Graf burrowed his nose into the dirt searching for Galdin's scent. *The two morsels headed south*, he thought. Taking another big whiff, the niht'anda dashed off crashing through the trees and underbrush; not caring about the sounds he made. All that mattered to him was pleasing his master.

*   *   *

Two days of following the barbarians paid off when they stopped to camp. Many of their "prizes" had collapsed from exhaustion. In an effort to ensure that they still lived when sold, the barbarians threw food at them and told them to eat.

Nylana, Trya, Magi, and Valn followed at a distance careful not to alert their quarry to their presence. They hunkered behind some brush and abandoned logs observing the barbarians that sat around a fire drinking and laughing while those chained together fought over scraps of bread.

"Where are they taking them?" asked Valn.

"Probably to one of the western ports," said Nylana. "We use them to send trade ships to the Islands of Monmor. But they do not buy slaves."

"Your ships are not the only ones that make port in our harbors," reminded Trya, "We need to free those people before they reach the forests on the western edge."

Nylana agreed. "Any ideas?"

Magi slipped off the log. "Once again, the cat must come to the rescue. You three wait over there while I get the keys." She scurried through underbrush toward the firelight.

Cautiously, Magi padded into the camp; her fur blending with the ground. She moved toward the imprisoned people keeping far away from their feet and the light. Jingling caught her attention. Magi's head whipped to the side where she spotted the man with the keys. *Perfect.*

The cat crept up to the man with the key ring around his belt. He moved suddenly guffawing with laughter which caused Magi to hunker down and glance about her for reassurance that her presence had gone unnoticed. The man sat back down.

Carefully, Magi undid the fastener that held the keys. She slipped them off the man's belt and skittered away with them in her mouth.

"Psst!" said the cat as she reached Nylana and the others.

"What took you so long?" asked Nylana.

"I stopped for tea," quipped the cat.

Nylana glared at Magi for her sarcastic remark as she took the keys.

"You know where the prisoners are," said Magi, "I will cause a disturbance on the far end of the camp. Unchain them quickly and get out." The cat darted off.

Nylana motioned for the others to follow her. She handed a key to Trya and another to Valn hoping that they all would undo the chains.

A loud crash echoed around them as flames appeared in the distance. Jumping to their feet, the barbarians ran for the fire yelling and screaming. The dark shape of a cat scurried away from the flames as men gathered around.

"Let's go," said Nylana.

They ran for the prisoners. Fearful eyes turned to them as they ran up with the keys.

"SHH," said Valn to a woman before she could speak. He undid the chains around her wrists and ankles. He ran to another and undid her shackles as well.

Nylana and Trya both undid the chains around the limbs of men, women, and children. They moved quickly and quietly, silencing any who started to speak.

Shouts rang out from the far end of the encampment. Not wasting time, Nylana undid more chains. "Make for the hills," she told those who had just been freed.

With speed, the three undid the shackles of all who had been captured by the barbarians. Those recently freed ran away to where Nylana instructed them. One man tripped over a bucket in his effort to get away. The noise drew the attention of one of the barbarian soldiers.

"Go, all of you!" yelled Valn. He undid another's restraints.

The guard ran for them yelling at his comrades. "The prisoners are escaping!"

Trya tossed her key to Valn and reached for her bow. She tapped it on her knee pulling it apart and freeing the two blades within. Rising with grace, the elf ran for the barbarians that charged them.

She ducked, attacked, swerved, and brought one sword up stabbing a man in the chest while simultaneously plunging her other blade into his back. Without missing a beat, Trya freed her weapons and blocked another attack. She performed a backflip allowing her feet to strike an opponent in the chin. When she landed, Trya crouched low while spinning with her arms outstretched; her weapons merely an extension of her hands. No enemy got close enough to strike a blow.

Suddenly, Trya stopped twirling, jumped up with her arms forming an x before her. As she fell back to the earth, she uncrossed her blades and hacked any in their way; her movements graceful, resembling a dance.

Heart racing, Nylana undid the chains of others. Her hands shook as she tried to work quickly.

The screeching of a cat filled the air as Magi leapt onto a man closing in on Nylana. The savage roared in pain as he threw the cat off. He charged Nylana again. Magi jumped from the ground to his head clawing at his face. Angrily, the man thrust the cat off of him throwing the animal into the side of a wagon. Blood poured from above his eye and nose as he glared at Nylana.

Hurriedly, she undid a small child's shackles and handed the girl the keys. "Undo the rest."

Nylana pulled out her sword. She raised the blade in time to block an attack by the man. He charged her. Nylana side-stepped his blow and held her blade horizontally to block further attacks. The blade glowed a tremendous shade of gold in the darkness as the firelight reflected off of it.

Suddenly, Nylana's mind filled with the knowledge of generations of swordsmen. She disengaged their weapons, pointed hers downward while jabbing her elbow into the man's mouth. While he staggered back, she flipped her weapon upward and plunged it deep within his chest.

Someone grabbed her from behind wrapping his arms around her neck. Panicking slightly, she tried to break away, but his grip tightened. A force knocked her off balance as her attacker's head was ripped back and his throat slashed. Blood covered her shoulders as she freed herself from the dead man's grip. Trya stood behind her with bloodied weapons.

Nylana stared at Trya a moment. The elf spoke no words as her expression said it all. Nylana recalled Narúl's words to her mind: "Always be mindful of what's behind you."

Nylana nodded her head in appreciation. Movement caught her eye. She noticed a dark shape heading straight for Valn. "Valn!"

Instantly, Trya whirled around and flung one of her swords at Valn's would be assassin. It struck the man in the middle of his back; he sank to the ground. Valn never noticed the commotion as he relentlessly continued freeing the last of the refugees.

Two more headed for Valn. Trya ran after them covering the distance in seconds. She slid on her knees across the ground under their weapons before jumping back to her feet. She seized the weapon arm of one, plunging her own into his neck.

With a flurry of movement, Trya swung the dead weight into the other allowing it to take the full impact of his charge. She swept the feet of the second man out from under him, dropped to the ground and seized the sword she had flung earlier and brought it up in time to block a strike by the man she had just knocked down. She swept his attempt at her life away and slashed at his throat.

Trya grabbed Valn and ran back to Nylana. More barbarians headed for them; they had underestimated their numbers.

"We cannot defeat them all," said Nylana.

Lightning flashed in the sky and a low rumble rolled above them. Trya noticed Nylana's glowing sword. Remembering the old tales she said, "Use your sword."

"What?" asked Nylana, confused.

"Point it to the sky," said Trya.

Trusting the elf, Nylana thrust her blade toward the sky holding its point high above her head. "Help us," she whispered.

A tremendous crack broke through the sounds of the men racing toward them as a bolt of lightning shot from the clouds to her sword, lighting up the entire area. The barbarians shielded themselves from this burst of power. When they looked up, the others had gone.

Nylana ran hard with Trya and Valn close behind. She had no idea when the elf grabbed her and forced her to move; she only knew that they had to run. The still form of Magi stopped her. Quickly, she scooped up the cat and disappeared into the darkness with the others.

Chapter VIII
Solemn Pursuits

The newly freed refugees waited upon the hill where Nylana had instructed them to flee to earlier. They gathered around her wanting answers for why their homes had been destroyed. Answers she could not give. She looked at the forlorn faces around her. What now, she thought to herself.

"Who are those people?" one woman asked.

"Invaders from the north," replied Nylana.

"But why have they come?" asked the woman.

"Does it matter?" replied Trya. "They are here. That is all that is important."

"What did I tell you?" said a man, "Those above you care nothing for you. They sit on their manors surrounded by luxuries while we perish. We should abolish these distinctions that separate us."

"And how exactly would that have saved you from the immediate problem of the invaders?" asked Magi with disdain in her voice.

"Perhaps if we were not all consumed by our own interests we would have seen them coming." said the same man. "The king grows fat while we suffer here. And where is he? Where is his army?"

"I am here," said Nylana, the fire returning to her eyes. "My brother has sent me to help you. We—" Nylana indicated her, Trya, and Valn, "—have freed you from your imprisonment. And yet you blame those above you for your ills. Have you sought the means to protect yourselves?"

The faces around her looked downcast.

"You are a princess," said the same man, "Born and raised in the luxuries of a palace. What do you know of suffering?"

Nylana looked the man squarely in the eyes. "Much," she said; her voice deadly.

"Why should we go with you?" demanded the man.

Nylana refused to answer him. She surveyed the faces around her growing impatient with them. "I am heading to MurDair. Any of you who wish to join me, feel free to do so. Otherwise, remain here. The choice is yours."

Nylana walked away. She did not look behind no longer caring about who chose to follow her. Trya, Valn, and Magi trailed behind not giving a moment's thought for those they just rescued.

Gradually, the newly freed refugees fell in line behind Nylana, including the man who had challenged her earlier. None wanted to be left on their own to face their captors.

*   *   *

Krispyn sat on his throne with two walnuts in his hand. He listened as Shelwyk recited reports from messengers. He scrunched his hand cracking the nuts within it. "In addition to La'nar, entire towns and villages have also been destroyed," finished Shelwyk.

"How can this be?" asked Krispyn.

"The barbarian invaders were well-armed and prepared for these attacks. They have been planning it for months," replied Shelwyk.

"The fortress of La'nar is well protected. Such an attack would require inside knowledge, would it not?"

"Yes, it would appear so, my lord."

"And my sister?" asked Krispyn.

"She seems to have disappeared along with Galdin," answered Shelwyk.

Krispyn's face remained impassive. He flung the walnuts away. "And no one knows her whereabouts?"

"I'm sorry, my lord," answered Shelwyk.

"This is the second time I have lost my sister. Do not make it a third."

"Yes, my king," said Shelwyk, "I will send a search party for her."

"No," said Krispyn, "If she were dead we would know it. If the invaders had captured her they would have sent for ransom. My sister still lives and I've no doubt that she will come to us."

"You can presume, my lord, that the barbarian invaders will be heading here next," said Shelwyk.

"What makes you so certain?" asked Krispyn.

"They have burned much of Belyndril and will have ravaged MurDair shortly. Once that is done, they will have little choice but to cross the mountains."

"Which will make Hemíl the next target," said Krispyn, "Send reinforcements there."

"My lord?"

"I will not have it so easily taken," said Krispyn, "You have your orders."

"Yes, my king." Shelwyk saluted and left the chamber.

"And, Shelwyk," said Krispyn, "Where were you the last few days?"

"My lord?"

"For the last several months you seem to disappear completely for days at a time."

"My apologies, my lord," said Shelwyk, "My mother is ailing and I try to visit as often as I can."

"I shall have her brought to the palace then."

"No need, my king. The slightest upset could end her."

"Very well. See to it that you inform me of your absences before you take them."

"Yes, my lord."

Shelwyk hurried out of the room unaware that he walked right past Petra, who remained concealed in the shadows.

*   *   *

The snarling and growling of the creature caused their pulse to quicken. Dirt crunched as the animal placed its massive claw on the ground sniffing the air.

They huddled behind rocks to stay out of sight, but nothing could mask their scent. Its breath came in snorts as its nose ran across the ground hunting for the odor of its prey.

Artryl moved from his hiding place and climbed on the rocks for a better look.

"Artryl," hissed Narúl, "Get back here."

The boy ignored the man as he scrambled up the rocks and peeked over them. The strange creature scoured the ground sniffing and snorting as it went. Artryl studied it, recognizing it from his books.

Artryl slipped. Pebbles clacked as they rolled down away from the boy. The creature's head popped up abruptly. It stared at Artryl. Suddenly, the thing rushed toward the boy pinning him against the ground. Its mucus encrusted nose brushed over Artryl as it breathed deeply memorizing his scent. Artryl squirmed, but to no avail.

Narúl moved to help the boy, but Ryk caught his arm. "Let me go," said Narúl.

"No, look," said Ryk pointing at the creature as it breathed on Artryl.

The thing snorted, blowing bits of mucus onto Artryl; the chain around its neck clinking. It snapped its jaws shut and darted off leaving them alone in the wilderness.

"What was that?" asked Ryk.

"Niht'anda," said Artryl as he brushed himself off, "But I thought they were extinct. No one has seen one in over 500 years."

"Its behavior is odd," said Narúl.

"I don't think it is wild," said Artryl, "It had a collar. But I have never known one to have been domesticated."

"It didn't seem very tame to me," said Ryk. "But it does seem to be searching for something."

"How do you mean?" asked Narúl.

"It could have killed the boy here, but didn't," Ryk said, "That means it is meant to find—"

"Galdin," interrupted Narúl.

"How can you be sure?" asked Ryk.

"Who else could it be?" replied Narúl.

"Nylana," Ryk replied.

"Unlikely," said Narúl.

"We should follow it," said Artryl. "Tabs, you can follow it more closely than us. I want you to stay close, but not too close. The rest of us will keep a greater distance."

"And how are we going to know when we have found him?" asked Ryk.

"Trog," replied Artryl, "Trog will let us know when we have found Galdin and perhaps we can still get to him before that thing does."

"I don't like the idea of following that thing," said Ryk, turning toward Narúl.

"But at least we'll know where it is," said Artryl.

Narúl rubbed his chin a moment pondering over the boy's words. "We will chase after it for a few days, after which we will work our way around it as we try to beat it toward Galdin. Tabs, do as the boy says, but do not get too close and be mindful of where we are."

The cat bounded off without protest.

"I still do not like this idea," Ryk said.

"You don't have to like it," replied Narúl.

Chapter IX
Burned to the Ground

Nylana and those with her moved cautiously into the forest that belonged to the unicorns. She knew they were close to MurDair and hoped to find sanctuary and rest. The line of people behind her crept slowly with effort; listless as though they spent their last energy just to put one foot in front of the other. She felt worn as well and looked forward to recuperation.

Nylana glanced at Trya. The elf walked erect and purposefully as though the last seven days of marching meant nothing to her. *How does she do it?* Nylana always marveled at how the elves could go for weeks without any signs of fatigue. Her rubbery legs protested each movement she took. "We'll be there soon," Nylana told herself, "Soon we can rest."

As though knowing her innermost thoughts, a piece of ash fell from the sky landing gracefully on her shoulder. Nylana picked it up with her fingers and studied it. She looked up. Above them all floated bits of ash swaying in the breeze. Smoke reached her nostrils and the sound of burning flames permeated her ears.

Fearing what atrocity lay ahead; Nylana took off dashing through the trees and the thickets that snatched at her.

"My lady!" yelled Valn.

She ignored the Byleon's pleas. Panting uncontrollably, Nylana tore through the woods. She had to see for herself; assure herself that her intuition was not correct. Ignoring the pain in her side, Nylana continued, leaving the others behind.

The smoke thickened. The roar of a massive wildfire deafened her. Unconcerned about her safety, Nylana ignored every warning signal in her mind.

She stopped.

Before her lay the remains of a meadow hidden deep within the forest. Soot rained upon her as flakes of burnt ash settled around her. Charred remains were all that was left of the grass. Vast blackness blocking the sun made a hole that trees once filled. Intense sadness filled the atmosphere as an anguished wail whirled around her. It took several moments for Nylana to realize that the scream came from her.

"NOOO!"

Nylana sank into the blackened earth allowing it to cover her calves. She remained on her knees while the others caught up to her, placing themselves around her; each with horror painted on their faces.

Amidst the destruction lay the silver bodies of unicorns with blood pouring from terrible wounds. Scattered were the remains—engulfed by the wrath of destruction. No birds sang. No insects buzzed. Even the wind had stilled. The home of the unicorns was no more.

A gentle hand rested on Nylana's right shoulder. She looked up into Trya's soft eyes.

"I am sorry," said the elf.

"Sorry," said Nylana, "Is that all you can say?"

"There is nothing more that can be said." Trya glanced out at the devastation and Nylana inwardly scolded herself as she watched a single tear make its way down the elf's cheek.

The slight rise and fall of a unicorn's chest caught Nylana's attention. She jumped to her feet and ran to the beast falling back onto her knees as she cradled the unicorn's head.

"Lie still," whispered Nylana.

"They came like thieves," wheezed the unicorn. "Vulgar monsters with weapons and fire."

"Do you know why they attacked you?"

"Why does anyone do this? We unicorns have done nothing, and for that we are slaughtered." The unicorn coughed violently.

Tears welled in Nylana's eyes and fell to the scorched earth. "Please, do not die. Live. I want you to live."

The unicorn looked directly into Nylana's eyes, focusing. "The princess Nylana. I remember your mother that day. I remember you—just a foal. Sing me the song."

Memories flooded Nylana's mind as she was taken back the day her father was buried. Her mother stood in front of the tomb and sang the saddest melody she had ever heard; a melody she often sang to Krispyn when they were children. She remembered the unicorns that came to offer their condolences.

Ni'lee y'lee—

Sobs racked Nylana's body as she found herself unable to continue. The moist and heavy breath of the unicorn ceased. She knew that the magnificent creature had died.

Rage boiled within Nylana. "Curse you! All of you!" she screamed at the sky. "I—"

A paw touched her thigh. Nylana lowered her eyes and looked deeply into Magi's amber eyes. She felt her rage ebb under Magi's steady gaze.

$*$ $*$ $*$

Somewhere in a valley just outside the lower hills of the mountains walked Galdin and Tami. A sudden anguish struck him as his arm burned. Gasping from shock he stopped, clutching it. Galdin looked at his arm. The mark that had always been there glowed a soft gold.

Images flooded Galdin's mind. His head filled with the scenes of death and destruction as barbarian forces slaughtered the unicorns. The screams echoed in his head as though he were there. Flaming torches littered the ground as trees burst into flame and helpless unicorn younglings squealed in fright as the fires consumed them.

"Galdin," said Tami as she bent over him, "Galdin, what's wrong?"

"I—I feel a terrible pain—sadness and fear all wrapped in anger. Something terrible has happened. My sister is in pain."

Nylana's anguished screams filled Galdin's ears. He knew she was there.

"Nylana!"

"Galdin," Tami shook him.

"Nylana needs me. Is there a faster way to MurDair?"

"No," answered Tami, "This is the only way. There is no other."

"Let's go," Galdin shook the girl off of him and marched away.

"Galdin!" Tami ran after him. "Stop! We have been traveling for days without rest. We need to stop."

"I cannot rest," Galdin whirled upon Tami. After several moments he regained control over his emotions. "I'm sorry. I watched my sister almost die once. I'll not lose her again. She is suffering. I can feel it and I must get to her quickly."

Tami placed her hand on Galdin's shoulder. "I am sorry for your sister. You will find her."

Galdin allowed Tami's smile to warm him.

"We have a few hours left of daylight," said Tami, "Let's make the most of it."

*   *   *

"Nylana!"

Galdin's voice stopped Nylana cold. She heard it clearly a moment before.

"Galdin?"

Nothing.

"Galdin," Nylana called a bit louder.

The refugees had gathered around her. They looked at her as though she had contracted a momentary bout of insanity.

"He is not here," said Magi.

"But I heard him. I heard his voice just now." Nylana's arm burned. She ripped her sleeve up and stared at the mark on her arm as it, too, glowed.

Instantly, Trya's hand covered the mark. "We should bury the dead and move on."

Slowly, Nylana stood up. She squared her shoulders and choked back her tears. "We need sage and mint," she said to those around her. "Gather what you can, so that we may send the unicorns to their new life."

People dispersed as ordered, walking away in groups of two or three.

"Do you think any of them made it?" asked Nylana.

"A few may have escaped to the hills," said Valn.

"I hope so," whispered Nylana.

No one noticed the few blades of green grass and flowers that spawned to life where Nylana had wept; too consumed by the tragedy of the unicorns.

Chapter X
Reunited

Galdin wiped the sweat from his neck as he took the lead. Tami wavered on her feet a bit from the intense heat of the midday sun.

"Here," said Galdin, handing her his canteen with the last of their water.

Tami popped off the cork taking a small sip. "We should conserve our water."

"Just drink it," said Galdin, "We'll find more."

"I'm not so sure. I thought we would have reached the river by now, but it's as if it's eluding us."

"Rivers don't move," said Galdin.

Tami laughed. "Have you ever been to the Changing Woods?"

Galdin hadn't and he had no desire to ever enter that place. He took off his vest and stuffed it in his pack. The unusual heat drained his strength. They were still in the lower hills of the mountains, having traveled south down them to avoid the barbarian army. Never had they been this warm and certainly not this early in the year.

"What drives you so?" asked Tami.

Galdin stared at her as her question caught him by surprise. "I'm not sure what you mean."

"Don't play coy with me," chided Tami, "You know perfectly well what I mean. Why are you so intent to reach MurDair before the next full moon? And what does that man from the prison want with you?"

"What did he want with you?"

Tami looked at her feet. "I was caught practicing magic. Apparently the barbarians do not like those who practice magic."

"They like them well enough to use them," said Galdin, "There are rumors of a sorcerer helping them. Perhaps they thought to use you as well."

"You still have not answered my question."

"My sister heads to MurDair as we speak. We were forced to split up and I am to meet her there by the next full moon. If I fail to show, she will continue without me."

"Continue where?" asked Tami, her curiosity piqued.

"None of your concern," answered Galdin. "When we reach the fairies' home, I am leaving you there."

"They do not live there anymore," said Tami.

Galdin faced her. That was news to him. The fairies had always lived in the northern part of MurDair. "Where did they go?"

"No one knows for certain," answered Tami, "I searched for them after my parents died. But all I found was an empty place with only one fairy. She told me that the queen had ordered them to leave the lands of Tesnayr before the darkness came. She said that I should do the same."

"Where is she?"

"I never saw her after that," Tami said, "But the fairies are here no more. In a way, I am the last of their kind and yet I am only half a fairy."

"Is there any place you can go?"

"With you," said Tami.

"No."

"Why not?"

"You are just a child—"

"I'm nineteen!"

"And still too young for the horrors of war. These barbarians are not here for child's play. They plan to conquer. And whether King Krispyn likes it or not, he will have to mount a defense against them. War is coming and it is no place for you."

"Says you," spat Tami, "Do you think you are the only one who knows what lies ahead? I have seen the same destruction you have. My family is gone. I have nowhere else to go and I am not going to sit around and wait for them to come for me again. I am going with you; with or without your permission. Besides, you need me."

"Need you?"

"I got us out of that prison."

"Not quite."

"It was I who led us through the labyrinth of the Perili Mountains," Tami's voice rose in intensity.

"Keep it down," cautioned Galdin.

"What?" Tami had noticed the expression on Galdin's face change.

"I think that rock over there moved," said Galdin, now feeling what Ryk had all that time ago.

"Don't be silly," scoffed Tami.

Galdin pulled out his sword and motioned for Tami to step behind him. Eyes popped open in the rock as a tongue stuck out. Without warning, it turned into Trog who leapt across the open space and landed squarely on Galdin's chest slobbering all over his face.

"Trog," coughed Galdin, "Get off." He shoved the animal away, saliva dripping from his chin as he sat up.

"He's cute," commented Tami, scratching Trog's chin as he chirruped with joy.

"Wait a minute," said Galdin as a thought entered his mind, "If he is here, where is—"

Trog growled menacingly causing both Tami and Galdin to look about them.

A dark, massive shape crashed through the trees and swiped at Tami knocking her through the air. She slammed into the trunk of a tree and lay motionless.

"Tami!"

Galdin jumped out of the way of the creature's claws as it swung at him. He faced the niht'anda noting the chain around its neck. It glared at Galdin snarling and exposing its rotted teeth. The thing lunged for him. Instantly, Trog knocked Galdin to the ground before quickly turning and lunging for the niht'anda. The creature blocked Trog's attack and flung the animal to the side as though he weighed nothing.

It leered over Galdin. He brought up his sword and swiped at the niht'anda's claw while rolling away. Quickly, he leapt to his feet and faced the solitary creature. The niht'anda rushed toward him ripping up dirt and plants as it went. Galdin jumped out of the way twisting around to strike at the creature's face. As he did so, something struck his wrist forcing him to drop his weapon. Defenseless, Galdin crouched low on the ground waiting for the creature's next attack.

A streak of orange fur shot from the thicket landing on the niht'anda's face screeching and clawing at it. At the same instant, three men burst from the trees armed and ready to face the niht'anda. One tossed Galdin a sword.

The boy with them clanged two pots together to cause a raucous noise as he danced around taunting the creature. The niht'anda kept its eyes on the boy seemingly confused by his antics.

"Don't just stand there," yelled the boy.

Within seconds Galdin realized that he knew two of the three people: Ryk and Narúl. Ryk charged the niht'anda catching it in the armpit. The thing roared in anger as it swatted at him. Barely dodging the blow, Ryk dove to the ground and scurried beneath the creature's belly toward the other side.

Galdin and Narúl charged the niht'anda together each swinging their weapons. The niht'anda whirled around to face them, its tail slashing toward Artryl who ducked just in time. Galdin fell to his back on the ground holding his weapon pointed up so that it stabbed the claw that reached for him. The creature yanked it back just as Narúl slashed at the thing's throat causing black blood to cover them.

"You have to strike the small of its back," yelled Artryl.

"Spear," shouted Ryk.

Narúl tossed Ryk a spear just as the man leapt for the niht'anda's back grasping one of the protruding spikes. The creature thrashed around to shake Ryk off. Trog snatched the chain around the niht'anda's neck forcing the creature to hunker on the ground. Using this advantage, Ryk raised the spear and plunged it in the exact spot that Artryl had pointed to. The niht'anda jerked and went limp.

Galdin ran to Tami who had begun to move. "Are you alright?"

"I'll be fine," said Tami, "What was that thing?"

"A niht'anda," said Artryl.

"Artryl," came Narúl's voice, "What were you thinking doing that?"

"Distracting it," replied Artryl, "And it worked."

Galdin looked around at all of them. "It appears you found me after all."

"Not that you made it easy," said Tabs. "We had to follow this thing—" he pointed at the dead niht'anda, "—to find you."

"We should leave," said Narúl as he cleaned his blade, "This thing is obviously someone's pet. And I have no desire to meet the owner."

"We are heading south," said Galdin, "We still have a ways to go before MurDair and now we will have to take an alternate route because of this thing. Those who controlled it can't be far."

Tami hopped from one foot to the other. "I know how we can get there."

"How?" asked Artryl.

"Teleportation," exclaimed Tami.

"No one can teleport," said Narúl.

"I can," said Tami jumping up and down with excitement.

"If you can why didn't you mention this earlier?" demanded Galdin.

"Because I wasn't very good at it then, but I've been practicing every night while you slept," replied Tami. "It's easy!"

The others just stared at her with doubtful expressions.

"I'll prove it to you," said Tami, "Fairies do this all the time. How do you think we are able to travel so far?"

"But you're just half a fairy," said Galdin.

Tami glared at him. She muttered words in the ancient language of the fairies. Swirls of light circled around her increasing in speed until it all stopped releasing a loud pop.

"Where'd she go?" asked Ryk.

They all looked around, but found no one. The rustling of a bush caught their attention as Tami spilled out from behind it landing on her behind. She lifted up her right leg which missed its foot.

"Blast it," she muttered, "I always seem to forget that last part. Have you guys seen my foot?"

"Foot?" said Galdin.

"Yes, my foot," said Tami, "Tends to happen sometimes. It's around here somewhere, just find it."

They searched for Tami's missing foot. Narúl, who rarely cracked a smile, laughed uncontrollably. Galdin's toes brushed something. Reaching down, he picked up Tami's detached foot which was still nestled in its shoe.

"That's it," exclaimed Tami, "Toss it here."

With a disgusted look on his face, Galdin threw the foot to Tami who caught it with both hands. Tabs placed both his paws over his mouth in a vain attempt to control his laughter.

"There's this bit at the end of the spell that I keep forgetting to say," Tami rammed her foot back onto her leg. It snapped into place. "Ah, there. Much better."

She stood up and placed her weight onto her foot rocking back and forth testing it. "Anyway, as you saw the spell works."

"If you don't mind losing a foot," chortled Tabs waving his tail back and forth.

"Doesn't that hurt?" asked Ryk.

Tami glanced at her foot for a moment. "No, not really. After a while you get used to it. Just pop it back in place and off you go."

Narúl snorted as more laughter squeaked out.

"You can get us there?" asked Galdin.

"Oh, yes, I can," said Tami, "Just everyone hold hands."

The others looked to one another.

"Come on. Don't be shy," Tami waved them together. "Now, how did that go? Oh, yes, that's right. Hold on really tight and don't lose anything."

Artryl rolled his eyes at that last comment.

Tami muttered words in the ancient language of the fairies; which had not been heard for many centuries. Wind swirled around them picking up sticks and leaves from the ground. Faster and faster it blew until they were in the midst of a mini cyclone. With a loud—pop!—they had gone.

Frigid winds beat against them as snow whirled around and they appeared from thin air. The thin atmosphere immediately took a toll on their lungs.

"This doesn't look like MurDair," yelled Galdin over the wailing wind.

"I think something went wrong," Tami said.

"Went wrong?" blurted out Ryk, "Of course something went wrong! We're on the top of a mountain!"

"I have icicles in my fur," shivered Tabs. "Look!" He lifted his tail as chunks of ice hung from it.

Narúl lifted the feline from the semisolid snow and cradled him in his arms as Trog nestled close to his leg.

"Th—thank you," stuttered Tabs.

Trog whined.

"Just let me think," said Tami. She mumbled to herself as she tried to remember the words that had brought them there. Ice pellets pricked their skin as the wind beat against them.

"We haven't much time before we freeze to death," said Galdin.

"I think I got it," said Tami, "Everyone hold hands again."

They all took one another's hand.

"Kali'mar sayd nokta," Tam yelled.

A loud crack echoed as they left the snow covered mountain.

A sonic boom echoed through the trees as a rag tag group of people and animals appeared from nowhere. They collapsed to the ground from exhaustion relieved to be away from the storm that raged in the mountains.

"I'm alive," yelled Tabs with exuberation as he kissed the soft grass.

Galdin chuckled to himself at the cat's antics. Suddenly, he found himself looking into the red eyes of a Nŏk'ta. All his will left him and the others.

Tami managed to wiggle her fingers as she willed herself to move. Slowly, she inched her hand away from her side. A deep growl resonated near her as Trog scrunched his features into a snarl. The Nŏk'ta ignored him. Crouching low, Trog lunged for the creature clamping his jaws around its throat.

Freed, Tami dropped to the ground and snatched a fallen branch, bringing it up in time to clonk a second Nŏk'ta in the head. Two more stepped into the sunlight.

"Help me," Tami said to nothing in particular.

A nearby bush wiggled. It sprang from the ground sprouting feet and arms. Its leaves and branches twisted around one another forming a head and a body. The bush stomped across the ground toward the two Nŏk'ta sweeping them up in its hands and banged the two creatures together until they went limp. The bush creature noticed Narúl with his sword. It sprang for the man.

Instantly, Tami threw herself in front of Narúl throwing up her arms. "No!"

The bush thing stared at her with confusion.

"He is my friend," said Tami.

The bush creature stepped back.

"Are there anymore of those things?" asked Tami.

"No," said Galdin.

"Thank you," Tami said to the bush creature, "We don't need you anymore."

The bush thing bowed to Tami and walked back to where it had been. Snapping and creaking filled the air as it unwound itself, shrunk in size, and turned back into a normal shrub.

"How did you do that?" asked Ryk, "And what was that thing?"

Tami fiddled with her red curls trying to avoid answering the question.

"Tami," Ryk insisted.

"I don't know," she blurted out. "I've no idea what happened. Ever since I was a little girl, I've been able to get plants to do my bidding—to a point.

"My mother was a fairy. She took my father as a mate, something that is practically unheard of among the fairies. When I was born, she left the fairies and she and my father moved to a small village. We were happy, but I have never been accepted among people. They are always suspicious of fairies and hate Halflings most of all.

"Does that answer your question?" Tami spat at Ryk before marching away in a fury, emotions reeling within her.

Galdin smacked Ryk atop the head giving him a scolding look. Tami had told him before that she was half fairy, but he never realized that such a fact held terrible memories.

Narúl picked a violet lily from the ground and handed it to Tami who tried to wipe the tears from her face. "Half fairy, half human. My people called your kind la'kofka. It means, gifted one. They believe that to meet one such as you is an honor."

Tami took the lily and smiled. "I wish everyone could be as enlightened as your people."

"Do not make such foolhardy sentiments," warned Narúl, "They were the very ones that sold me as a slave."

"How did you end up here?" asked Tami.

"My new master came here. When I tried to escape he died along with two others. So I was brought before the king as a murderer for which the penalty is death. The Princess Nylana convinced her father to spare me that day."

"That is why you serve her," said Tami.

Galdin stood in the distance with the others listening intently. He had never understood the relationship between his sister and Narúl; he only knew of the man's fierce loyalty to her. *This explains everything.*

"Part of it," said Narúl, "She was but a small child then. But she showed great courage that day. Her act did more than just spare me from execution; she showed me a better way to live."

"I'm hungry," Tabs blurted out.

Artryl stifled a giggle as the cat's comment broke the tension.

"I can sing it if you like," said Tabs as he looked at all the stares pointed his way. "My tummy growls from—MEORR!"

Ryk had lightly kicked the cat to shut him up. "I suggest we get out of here before more of those things show up."

"Agreed," said Galdin, "We still have a ways to go before we reach the northern border of MurDair. I only hope we reach it before Nylana does."

"We can tele—" began Tami.

"No," said Galdin as he started off before Artryl stopped him.

"Not that way," said the boy, "I know a better way. It is shorter and safer. And we might be able to find lodging."

"Lead the way," said Galdin.

By sunset they had come upon the abandoned cabin that Artryl led them to. The rusty hinges squeaked as they opened the unlocked door. Narúl set up a fire in the fireplace while

Galdin trapped small game. They ate a meager meal in silence, satisfying their stomachs.

Galdin had the most difficult time eating. He set his plate to the side only to hear it rattle as Tabs snatched a tidbit. Quickly, Galdin picked it up and glared at the innocent looking cat. His plate jostled again as Trog grabbed a piece of meat. Instantly, Galdin held it up high over his head. "Now listen you two. This is my supper."

Trog whined and Tabs purred as each looked at him with wide, hopeful expressions.

Finding it difficult to refuse them, Galdin placed his plate on the floor. "Oh, have at it. I wasn't hungry anyway."

"We will leave before dawn," said Narúl when they had finished eating, "I will take first watch." He glanced at Tami who had already fallen asleep on the lopsided cot. Taking note of her shivering, Narúl snatched Ryk's coat and wrapped it around her.

"Just help yourself," Ryk commented.

"You should sleep too," he said to Artryl.

"I'm not at all tired," yawned Artryl. "I can stand watch with you."

Narúl pointed to a small pile of hay in answer. "Take this," he handed the boy his cloak. "The night's chill does not affect me."

"But you'll—"

"Take it," Narúl insisted.

Artryl obeyed, stretching out on the hay with Narúl's cloak and falling asleep instantly.

"What is your interest in my sister?" Galdin asked once he was certain Tami and Artryl slept soundly.

Ryk glanced at both Galdin and Narúl as they awaited his answer. "Can we not discuss this while he cleans his fingernails with a knife?" Ryk pointed in Narúl's direction.

"Answer me honestly," said Galdin.

"I don't know if I can put it into words," answered Ryk. "From the moment I first saw her, I knew she was the one I wished to marry."

Narúl snorted.

"No, truly, I mean it," Ryk insisted.

"You say that because she is the Princess of Tesnayr," said Narúl.

"I did not know that at the time," said Ryk. "And after I learned of her true identity, it did not matter. I don't care whether she lives in a palace or a small cottage. I only care about her."

"Is that why you followed after us when we left Norlyk?" Galdin asked.

"Partly," said Ryk, "When I heard her speaking of leaving for Belyndril, I knew I had to come. Her cares are my cares."

"You don't even know her," said Narúl.

"No?" said Ryk, "I know that she cares deeply for the safety and security of the five lands of Tesnayr. I know that she will give anything to save them from this barbarian invasion. I know the respect she has for you, Narúl. The love she has for Krispyn. And I know the pain she carries for losing you Galdin; I see it in her eyes each time she looks at you. Are you certain that it is I who does not know her?

"And what of you, Galdin. Why is it you followed her to Belyndril?"

Galdin looked out the grimy window at the almost full moon. *Why did I follow her?* "I'm not sure I can answer that." He eyed both Ryk and Narúl. "You better get out there," he said to Narúl.

Narúl's mouth formed a thin line as he stepped out the door and took first watch.

Both Ryk and Galdin gave each other a passing glance as Ryk settled in a far corner. Galdin peered over at Tabs who lay curled by the fire; his ears pointed in their direction.

"I know you're not sleeping," Galdin said to the cat.

Immediately, a series of snores escaped the feline as he twitched his tail.

*   *   *

The open valleys of MurDair provided little cover from possible attacks. Nylana and Trya kept a wary eye on their surroundings hoping that they could get through without any mishap. Sparse trees dotted the landscape reminding them that they would reenter the woods again sometime.

Nylana halted everyone. They had reached the meeting place, but there was no sign of Galdin or the others.

"What is it?" asked Valn.

"He is not here," replied Nylana, "Galdin should have been here."

A rustling noise sounded next to them. Instantly, Trya crouched in a defensive stance; her bow ready to fire.

Tami popped from behind some bushes. "Oh my," she threw her hands up.

"Don't shoot," said Galdin as he appeared between Tami and Trya.

Trya lowered her bow; a smile crept across her face. "Galdin, it is good to see you."

Elf and man embraced each other for a moment glad to be reunited. Narúl and Ryk walked out followed by Artryl and Trog. Immediately, Nylana ran up to Narúl and gave him a giant hug overjoyed at seeing him again. She even embraced Ryk for a moment much to his surprise, and pleasure. Galdin coughed loudly to break them apart.

"Artryl?" said Nylana when she noticed the boy, "What are you doing here?"

"The boy has a head of stone," said Narúl in response.

Tabs spilled from behind a rock rolling across the ground ignoring everyone. "United we are. Together again," sang the cat.

"Trya," said Nylana, "You and Narúl find some food. We will rest here tonight. In the morning we shall take these people to a small town just outside the dwarf city of D'aar. They should be safe there."

Trya bowed and led Narúl away to a place she had noticed earlier would be good for game.

"Nylana," Galdin motioned for Nylana to follow him. "Who are these people?" he asked when they were out of earshot.

"Trya and I freed them from a group of invaders. Their home is destroyed but I know a place where they will be safe. I am taking them there. Afterward, we will head to D'aar."

"But we haven't time for any detours. The barbarians are moving quickly led by Vasagius."

Nylana's face twitched in anger. "Vasagius," she hissed.

"Yes, and he is wasting no time in conquering the land. His men burn as they go destroying everything and leaving no survivors, except for ones they wish to sell."

"Then that's all the more reason to take these people to safety. The place we are going is well protected," said Nylana.

"There is no time," hissed Galdin. "You said yourself that reaching Lord Belznyc was of utmost importance. We've wasted enough time allowing you to search for that thing."

Nylana's face hardened. "It wasn't a waste," she said, her voice cold, "I found it." Delicately, Nylana pulled out the gold feather. Galdin took it holding it in the fading light awed by its brilliance.

"What is it for?" he asked.

"I do not know, yet," said Nylana, "But I do know that I made a promise to these people and will not abandon it."

"They can protect themselves," said Galdin, "We have more important matters—"

Nylana punched him with a force that knocked him off his feet. "You sound like that heartless mercenary I found a while ago. If that is who you are then you are no better than Vasagius."

"Why do you care so much?"

"Why do you not care?" Nylana started to walk away before rounding on Galdin again, "I am the Lady Nylana, Princess of Tesnayr. It is my duty and responsibility to protect these people from invading savages. Until there is peace again they will be unable to protect themselves. And if you wish to remain as Prince of Tesnayr, then you better learn that for yourself!

"I have made my decision. In the morning we take them to the town, then, we go to D'aar. If that displeases you, then leave."

Nylana stormed away. Galdin watched her go, his mind whirling with conflicting emotions. He did not wish to abandon his sister, but still found it difficult to care for a people he hardly knew. "Yet, why do I stay?" he asked himself.

Galdin trailed after Nylana watching her as she soothed a pair of frightened boys who had lost their parents. The ragged group of forlorn faces stared at him as he walked among them. Despair mixed with fear, filled their eyes

Leaves scraped the ground brushing over the tops of his boots as the wind blew around him. Only he seemed to be aware of it. The mark on his arm glowed slightly.

"Help her bring hope," whispered a masculine voice that only he heard.

Galdin whipped around turning in circles; searching for the source of the voice. People moved about their business setting up places to sleep and eat.

"Galdin," said Trya as she returned.

"Did you hear that?" asked Galdin.

"Hear what?"

"The wind—it spoke."

"I may make an elf out of you, yet," said Trya, "Come along. You can help me prepare supper."

A weight suddenly clung to Galdin's calf when he tried to move. He looked down to find a girl of about six clinging to him. She stared at him with saucer like eyes. Unable to ignore her pleading look, Galdin unwrapped her from around his leg and knelt down so that he was eye level with her.

"I can't find papa," she cried.

Heart melting, Galdin placed her on his knee and wiped the tear from her cheek. "Where did you see him last?"

"Home," said the girl.

"You will be home in the morning."

"But that isn't home," said the girl shaking her head. "I live further south. Mommy and I were visiting her brother when those men came."

"Where is your mother?" asked Galdin.

The girl looked at her feet.

"Your uncle?"

She continued staring at her feet.

Realizing that the child was alone, Galdin carried her with him to the fire that had been started. "Do you know where your papa lives?"

Eagerly, the girl nodded her head grinning broadly. "I can take you there."

"Then once we take these people home, we will find your papa."

The girl hugged his neck and burrowed her head into his shoulder. "Do you have a name?" he asked the girl.

"Mira," came her quiet reply.

Galdin noticed Ryk staring at him. He glared at him to remain silent.

"Softy," mumbled Magi as she sat beside him. "I knew that tough exterior of yours was just an act."

"I think the cat talks too much," said Galdin.

Purring filled the space beside him as Magi closed her eyes.

By late afternoon that next day they entered a small town. Tears of joy were shared as those originally from there reunited with loved ones. Others just stood awkwardly unsure of what to do. This wasn't their home, but they had nowhere else to go.

"Silence! Silence," said the leader of the town as he approached Nylana. "What is all this?"

"My good sir," said Nylana inclining her head towards him, "These people are refugees and need a place to stay until the barbarian invaders have been eliminated from our land."

"But we can barely feed ourselves," said the man.

"Can you not find a way?" asked Nylana.

The man glanced at the pitiful faces before him.

"Your town is well protected," continued Nylana, "There is nowhere else for them to go."

Suddenly, the man realized to whom he spoke. "My lady, forgive me. I did not realize."

"Can you take them in or not?" asked Nylana.

"Yes, yes. We will find a way." The man motioned for the people to come into the town and find a place to rest. "As always, my lady, you are most welcome here. Will you not rest?"

Nylana shook her head. "My apologies, but no. We must reach D'aar and if we leave now we can be there before nightfall. Your kindness shall be repaid."

"Thank you, my lady," said the man.

Nylana turned. Trya noticed Galdin still holding Mira. "Galdin?" questioned the elf.

"Her home lies just a little south of D'aar. It will not be too much out of our way to take her there."

Nylana studied Galdin a moment before continuing on.

"Did I miss something?" asked Ryk noting the exchange.

Artryl laughed as he walked by. "You did."

Chapter XI
A Meeting with Lord Belznyc

"So how are we to get in?" asked Ryk as he looked around at what he thought was supposed to be the city of D'aar, "This doesn't look like a city."

"It's underground," said Nylana.

"But where is the opening?" demanded Ryk.

"Here," Nylana pointed at the arch standing in the middle of nowhere.

"So how do you make the opening appear?" said Ryk, "Knock?"

"Do you always ask so many questions?" snapped Galdin.

"I was just wondering," mumbled Ryk.

Nylana did not know how to open the doorway to the dwarf city. She did not know the words. Those were only handed down to dwarves. She studied the arch pondering what to do.

"I thought you knew the way in," said Tami.

"Normally," said Nylana, "When I met with the dwarves one was here to greet me, or they traveled to Norlyk." Thinking about Ryk's words, Nylana figured she had nothing to lose by knocking. She raised her fist and rapped on the structure as loud as she could.

The ground rumbled beneath her feet as it shook. Nylana stepped away from the opening that appeared in the ground forming into a stairwell, amazed that Ryk's suggestion proved useful.

"It worked," said Ryk with disbelief.

Nylana cautiously entered the underground opening with the others close behind. "Be on your guard," she said, "The dwarves do not like it when strangers discover their secrets."

Narúl lit a torch and walked beside Nylana. Ryk grabbed another torch and stepped beside Nylana as well only to be seized by Galdin and pushed to the back.

"Nice try," said Artryl as he passed by.

The darkened tunnel made their way difficult despite the torches that Narúl and Ryk carried. Nylana noted the decay and erosion from neglect. She hoped that the center of the city would be far better maintained. Soft echoes of their steps surrounded them as they moved quickly hoping that their journey would not be in vain. Artryl patted Trog on the head to quiet him as he whined.

"Whoa," said Ryk when they reached the end of the passageway. It opened into a vast expanse of courtyards with roaring fires and stone buildings connected by aqueducts.

"That is—" began Ryk.

"—magnificent," finished Galdin. He gawked at the underground city. Plants made from precious gems dotted the courtyard they entered as they trekked across the black marble. Immediately, dwarves armed with weapons surrounded them stopping their advance.

Nylana raised her hand. "We come peaceably."

"Give us your weapons," said one of the dwarves.

"No," said Galdin.

"Galdin—" began Nylana.

Galdin cut her off. "We will not relinquish our weapons," he said, "We come in peace and wish only to speak with Lord Belznyc."

"No one speaks to Lord Belznyc unless they first relinquish their swords," said the same dwarf.

"Do you insist that the Lady Nylana give up her armed guard just to speak with Lord Belznyc?" continued Galdin.

The dwarf lowered his axe slightly. "Lady Nylana?" He looked at her more closely as if seeing her for the first time. "Forgive me, my lady. I did not recognize you."

"Will you take us to Lord Belznyc?" asked Nylana.

"Yes, but I must ask that they remain here," said the dwarf.

"No," said Nylana, "As you have been informed this is my escort and in the current climate I will go nowhere without them. Either you bring us all to Lord Belznyc or none of us. You may keep your weapons pointed at us if that makes you more comfortable."

The dwarf signaled his unit. With uniform precision the other dwarves fell around them ready to escort them to the meeting chamber of the city. They followed the lead dwarf up a flight of marble stairs that reflected the torchlight wonderfully. Nylana strode tall and proud while Galdin, Trya, and Narúl kept a ready hand on their weapons; each not liking the dwarves over-excited manner.

Swiftly, they marched through the city and to the palace court. They passed through corridors with gems lining the walls as the dwarf led them to the chamber doors which opened upon their arrival. Lord Belznyc awaited them with an irate expression on his face.

"My lady," said Lord Belznyc, "You should not be here. There is little left of MurDair."

"Is this the way you greet guests?" replied Nylana, "Is this how you treat the Princess of Tesnayr?"

"My apologies," said Lord Belznyc, but his tone conveyed anything but penance. "Why have you come?"

"I had to come," said Nylana, "I need you and your forces."

"I'll not give my forces to your brother," said Lord Belznyc.

"Belznyc," said Nylana, "Why such sentiment?"

"Because of your absence I will allow your question," a hardened expression crossed Lord Belznyc's face. "Your brother has decreed that MurDair has not paid their share of the taxes and therefore increased our burden tenfold. He has also forbidden us from having a standing army for which to defend ourselves. We have always provided dwarves to be part of the army of Tesnayr, but as was set down by Queen Amborese, the five lands are allowed their own forces as well. Your brother has forbidden such a notion thus violating our laws."

Galdin stepped forward. Dwarves pointed their axes at him as a warning. "I would appreciate it if you did not say 'your brother', my lord, as I am also her brother."

"The lady Nylana has only one brother," said Belznyc, "I do not know your name. Who are you to speak to me?"

"He is my brother," said Nylana, her voice turned to stone. "He is Galdin."

Belznyc's features changed as he realized his rudeness. "My Lady, why did you not announce him?"

"For reasons that are my own," replied Nylana, "This is Galdin, the Lost Prince and my brother."

"When—how did you find him?"

"By a happy circumstance while I was away. I did not believe it at first, but he is Prince Galdin."

"Yes, of course," said Lord Belznyc seeing the resemblance between them for the first time, "You are most welcome and will be given the courtesy that is due."

Galdin nodded his head in appreciation.

"My Lord Belznyc," said Nylana, "I have come because barbarian invaders have overrun Belyndril. I have reason to believe that they will come either here or go straight to Hemíl."

"What makes you so certain?" asked the dwarf.

"Because that is what I would do," said Nylana.

"As would I," said Galdin.

"You both have keen military minds," said Lord Belznyc, "But I refuse to trust your—Krispyn."

"Lord Belznyc," said Galdin, "As Lord of MurDair, you are charged with protecting your people from these invaders just as we are charged with protecting the whole of Tesnayr from them. We need your help."

"I still refuse to serve Krispyn," said Belznyc, "It is because of him that these invaders are in our lands in the first place. There were warnings, but Krispyn ignored them."

"Then that is his mistake. Nylana is here to remedy that," said Galdin.

Nylana recognized a note of concern in Galdin's voice, as though the mercenary he had been had gone.

"I still—"

"Have I ever given you reason not to trust me?" said Nylana as Belznyc wavered.

"No, my lady, you have not."

"Then trust me now."

"I am sorry, my lady, but my answer is no," said Belznyc. "It is time for MurDair took after her own interests."

"At the expense of others?" said Nylana.

"I am sorry, my lady."

"Very well," said Nylana, "I will not force your hand. We will leave for Hemíl then."

"Surely you can stay for something to eat and some rest," pleaded Belznyc.

"We will stay until morning, but cannot remain beyond that." said Nylana, "The invaders are moving fast. They always seem to be one step ahead of us."

"As you wish," said Belznyc.

"Narúl," said Nylana, "You and Tami travel ahead to Hemíl and tell Lord Stefon that we're coming. You can travel faster alone. Artryl, I need you to carry a message to Krispyn. You will be my personal envoy. You'll have to—"

"Trog can take me," said Artryl, beaming.

Nylana smiled. "Very well. You and Trog will go. Travel as quickly as you can." Nylana took some parchment from Belznyc's scribe, scribbled a quick note, and sealed it with her seal. She then handed it to Artryl. He took it as though it were the most valuable bit of treasure.

"Get some food and then be off," said Nylana.

Artryl grinned and ran out the room with Trog close behind.

"And we will be traveling by another route," said Galdin.

"Yes," said Nylana, "Separately, we might attract less attention."

"And I suppose he is going with us?" said Galdin pointing at Ryk.

"Yes," replied Nylana. "Don't look so disheartened."

"Very well," said Galdin, "But we must head south first. There is a little village that Mira needs to return to."

Nylana glanced at the girl that clung to Ryk. "Are you starting to care?"

Galdin gave her a piercing look before walking off.

Lord Belznyc led them to the dining hall where rows of tables laden with all kinds of meat. The dwarf lord pulled a chair out for Nylana while another held one out for Tami. They took their seats while the others sat across from them. Even Magi and Tabs were awarded a place of honor.

The aroma of cooked meat reminded their stomachs that they had not eaten for nearly a day. Servants placed goblets of wine before the guests. Nylana took a delicate sip of the sweet nectar while Galdin dug into a slab of meat that had been placed before him.

Light conversation accompanied the meal as none wished to discuss politics. The clinking of glasses and plates gave a feeling of gaiety in a troubled time. Lord Belznyc could not refrain from one question. "How do you plan to cross the mountains?"

"Gangas Pass is not far from here." Nylana remembered that though Queen Amborese had sealed it, her grandfather had dug it open, but few ever ventured there.

"But that place is full of thieves and bandits. Knot's Pass would be safer."

"And it is far to the north of here," replied Nylana.

"Then how will you ever reach Hemíl in time?" asked Lord Belznyc.

"I guess she will have to use dragons," said Galdin.

"Dragons? You jest." Lord Belznyc looked at him with amusement.

"No, I do not," said Galdin.

"Nylana has managed to gain the trust of a dragon," said Trya with admiration.

Lord Belznyc placed his wine on the table. "I see."

"But we may not need dragons, after all," said Galdin, "There are many hidden trails that cross the mountains. I will guide us through one of them."

When they had finished, Lord Belznyc showed them where they could rest. Each was given their own room.

"Thank you for your hospitality," said Nylana to Lord Belznyc.

The dwarf took her hands giving her a warm smile. "You are always welcomed within these halls. Rest well, my lady."

The dwarf walked away as the others entered their room.

"I should stay by your side," said Narúl to Nylana.

"You have always been there to protect me, Narúl. But now is the time for me to protect myself. I need you to go to Hemíl and tell Lord Stefon of Vasagius' return. They must hold until help arrive. I will meet you there"

"I do not like this idea."

"You can travel must faster without the rest of us."

"And the girl?" asked Narúl.

"Tami can be of some use with her knowledge of fairy magic."

"Perhaps, but she has no control over it."

"She will learn control. She can help you if you run into any of the Nôk'ta. Take care of yourself."

Narúl clasped Nylana on the shoulder before walking off. He waved at Tami motioning for her to follow him.

A feeling of dread filled Nylana's stomach.

"Something on your mind, my lady?" said Valn as he walked up to her.

"Just the feeling that I might never see them again," said Nylana.

"You mustn't think that way," soothed Valn, "I am certain you will."

"Thank you, Valn," said Nylana, "Better get some sleep. We have an early start in the morning."

The scraping of the whetstone against the steel blade of his sword echoed off of the stone walls. Galdin sat alone sharpening his blade. Tiny footsteps caught his attention. Pausing, he turned around. Mira stood behind the door peeking at him.

"Come inside," said Galdin.

Slowly, the girl crept into the room before running and jumping in Galdin's lap. He hugged the girl as she wept into his shirt.

"What is it?" asked Galdin.

Mira looked at him with wet, wide eyes. "I miss my mommy. And I don't want those men to come back."

"There, there." Galdin hugged the girl calming her. "Would you like to hear a song?"

Mira nodded.

Rocking the child gently, Galdin sang a lullaby from his youth; one his mother sung to him whenever he feared the night.

> Sach le ge-lan, mac wehyn
> Fear not my child.
> This storm shall pass.
> Terrible and reviled
> It will not last.
> Now, dry those tears.
> Give me a smile.
> Despite its long years
> Dawn will light the isle.
> Sac le ge-lan, mac wehyn

Mira fell asleep in Galdin's arms. Gently, he placed her on the bed and covered her with a blanket; beginning to understand why Nylana acted the way she did.

"Sleep, little one. You will be home tomorrow."

From the shadows just outside the door sat Magi. Her glowing eyes barely gave away her presence. She swished her tail grinning to herself.

Chapter XII
Mira's Home

Mira smiled broadly as they approached her village. Her little feet scuffled across the dirt path as she ran for her home. People going about their business paused to see who raced toward them.

"Mira!" cried a man as he charged for the girl.

"Papa!" Mira ran into the man's outstretched arms.

"Mira." The man hugged the girl tightly.

Nylana and Galdin grinned at each other as they walked up to the man.

"They saved me," said Mira pointing at Galdin and Nylana.

"I cannot thank you enough," said the man. "My name is Clovis. Please, stay and share a meal with me."

"We can't," said Galdin. "We must be on our way."

"Please," said Clovis, "I insist."

"Seeing you two united is thanks enough," said Galdin.

"Very well," said Clovis, "Then let me get supplies for you for your journey."

Before Galdin could protest, Clovis had called people over to gather water and food for them. Within minutes bags of supplies were shoved into Galdin's hands.

Magi meowed impatiently. Mira swooped down and hugged the cat tightly squeezing out a screech. Instantly, Tabs laughed uncontrollably earning him a glare from Magi. Within seconds, Mira squeezed him too.

"Serves you right," said Magi as she stalked off.

Within the hour they had continued their journey leaving the little village behind and Mira. Galdin's gait had an extra bounce to it indicating the euphoria he felt inside.

*   *   *

Lord Belznyc stormed through the door to his quarters. He halted midstride at what greeted him. Instead of his room, he stood in the midst of a battlefield surrounded by the corpses of dwarves. Fires burned everywhere filling the area with smoke as behind him stood the archway leading into D'arr.

Horror struck, Lord Belznyc spun on his heels looking all about him. The scene vanished as his room filled the area once more.

"This is what will happen if you refuse Nylana's request." Quesha materialized from the shadows as she stepped into the firelight. Strands of graying hair framed her features.

"Who are you?" demanded Lord Belznyc. "How did you get in here?"

"Doors cannot keep me out," said Quesha.

"What do you want?"

"To give you a warning," said Quesha, "Heed Nylana's request or suffer death."

"You do not frighten me," said Lord Belznyc.

"No? Then fear the wrath of Vasagius, for he will stop at nothing until all are dead. Fear the wrath of the phoenix who will demand an explanation for your actions."

"The phoenix is gone."

"I would not be so certain of that." Quesha picked up a small object bearing the crest of MurDair. She tossed it to Lord Belznyc who caught it. "If you cherish MurDair, head for the Black Mountains. This is your only warning." Quesha disappeared.

Lord Belznyc stared at the place where she had been, fiddling with the thing she had given him.

Chapter XIII
Galdin's Death

They trudged along a rocky trail in the light of the low hanging sun as they neared where they hoped to make camp for the night.   Nylana tripped over an upturned rock losing her balance. Ryk caught her and steadied her. Nylana looked into his eyes as though noticing him for the first time.

"Watch your step," said Ryk.

Nylana smiled slightly.

The sound of Galdin clearing his throat broke up the moment. Hastily, Ryk put Nylana back on her feet and walked away.

Eerie silence surrounded them.   Magi's fur stood on end; something bothered her. She felt a presence as though they were not alone.

The cat's slowed paced caught Nylana's attention. "What is it?"

"Something is wrong," said Magi.

"I feel it too," said Tabs.

"I don't hear anything," said Galdin.

Trya paused and listened to the silence as she scanned the surrounding area. She didn't pick anything up, but even she began to feel uneasy. "I think it would be best if we leave this place immediately."

As a measure of caution, Trya took her bow and broke it in half revealing the two swords within. She held it protectively ready for whatever might attack them.

Goose pimples dotted Nylana's skin as she sensed the same uneasiness that the others experienced. Slowly, she moved forward. The soft whiz of an arrow filled the air. Trya shoved

Nylana to the ground out of the way of the arrow. The elf whirled around bringing her swords up before her and blocking an attacking barbarian as he released a yell of triumph. She wrenched his weapon from him before slicing off his head. Another appeared from the shadows. Trya twisted around and brought her left arm up dodging his blow while simultaneously using her right arm to stab the man in the stomach.

"It's a trap!" yelled the elf.

Galdin dodged an oncoming spear. He picked it up and thrust it into the man that charged him. Swiftly, he freed his weapon and allowed the clang of metal to fill the silence as he blocked an attack. Galdin rammed his heel into the knee of his opponent using the opportunity to plunge his sword into the now crippled man's chest.

Screeching cats drowned out all other noise as both Magi and Tabs jumped on a barbarian aiming an arrow for Trya. The man dropped his bow loosing the arrow straight into the sky. He kicked at the two cats in an effort to get rid of them. Tabs and Magi darted away while Nylana rammed her blade into him.

"We need to get out of here," she yelled.

Valn noticed a savage heading straight for Nylana. He ran for the man falling onto his side and tripping the man. Wasting no time, the Byleon seized the man's weapon and finished him.

He surveyed the scene. "This way," he said.

Ryk brought his sword blocking a charging barbarian. The force of the attack knocked him off balance. He braced himself, unlocked their swords and plunged his into the barbarian's chest.

Another barbarian struck Ryk in the back with a blunt object forcing the air out of his lungs. Ryk whirled around; his sword clashing with the barbarian's. Another man attacked from the side striking Ryk on the head and forcing him to drop to his knees. Dazed, Ryk dropped his weapon. Two pairs of hands grabbed him by the shoulders and dragged him away.

Galdin watched the melee unfold as savages sprang from the trees. He noticed one with a bow aiming directly for Nylana who battled another barbarian. Knowing what he had to do, Galdin charged for her. He dashed across the soggy grass desperate to reach his sister in time.

He stole a glance at the one with the bow. Dread filled him as he watched the man pull the string back taking careful aim. *No!* Galdin pushed himself to go faster reaching Nylana just as the man released the arrow.

Nylana braced herself for her opponent's attack. A force striking her from behind made her crash onto the hard, rocky ground. She rolled before jumping up in time to block an attack from another barbarian. Their swords clashed in the fading sunlight. She knocked the sword out of the man's hand before jamming her foot into his knee. The cracking bones sent a sickening feeling through her.

A horn sounded in the distance. The attackers dispersed and fled. Nylana braced herself, poised for another strike. It never came. The enemy disappeared faster than they had arrived. Sheathing her sword, she glanced to where she had been shoved moments before.

Galdin lay there. Blood spilled from the arrow protruding from his back. A second wound covered his chest. He had saved her from certain death.

Nylana dropped everything and ran to him. "No. No-No-No-No," she cried in anguish as she gently lifted his head.

Trya knelt by Nylana's side. She put a hand softly on Galdin's shoulder. "Rest easy," she said.

Galdin gasped for air, his breaths becoming shorter with each one. "Trya, protect...Nylan...a."

"I will," Trya promised.

Galdin's head fell to the side as the last of his life hissed from his mouth.

"Galdin!" screamed Nylana. "You can't die!" She clung to his lifeless body. "This cannot happen again."

"Nylana," whispered Trya.

Nylana paid no attention. Her heart ached uncontrollably. Consumed by her pain, she never noticed the single tear that fell from Trya's eyes, escaping the elf's tranquility. "Leave me!"

Trya stood silent refusing Nylana's request.

"I can heal him." A spark shone in Nylana's eyes. "I can heal Galdin." She placed her hands on his chest and closed her eyes willing the magic of the phoenix within her to revive her brother. Nothing happened. "Why does he remain dead?"

Footsteps crept from behind. Both Nylana and Trya turned at the sound. The sorceress stood before them. She had aged since Nylana last saw her. Her once black hair now shone gray. Her face, once young, now bore the lines of an old woman.

"I had warned you this would happen," said Quesha.

"Have you come to gloat?" snapped Nylana.

An expression of pity crossed Quesha's face. She understood Nylana's pain. "That is not why I have come."

"Then what do you want of me?" asked Nylana. "Why can I not heal him?"

"Because he is your brother and the only true reason you wish him alive is for your own gain, not his."

"Why does that matter?"

"It always matters," said Quesha, "What is in your heart—your true reason for doing something always matters. Sometimes we do not realize why we really want something, but the magic of the phoenix within you knows. Even it cannot always overturn death."

"But it brought me back," said Nylana.

"Yes, it did, because it knew the world still needed you and its will matched an even greater will."

"Do not speak to me about that voice on the wind," snapped Nylana.

"Its will is greatest of all and you know it," said the sorceress.

"What do you want of me?" said Nylana, her voice sounding defeated.

"There is a way to save him," said Quesha.

"He is dead," said Trya in a flat tone. "He is beyond saving."

"His spirit is trapped in the land of the dead. I can take one of you there. But we must hurry, while there is still time," said Quesha.

"It is forbidden to enter the realm of the dead. To meddle with life and death is considered a grave offense," said Trya.

"Nevertheless, you must decide," said Quesha, "But know this: only one may go and there is no return."

Trya glanced at Nylana. She sensed the girl considered Quesha's offer. "My lady, no."

"It is me that should be dead," said Nylana. "Galdin has sacrificed much for me. It is because of me that he is dead. I should be laying here, not him. Twice I've lost him. I'll not lose the only chance I have of saving him."

"There is a reason why no one ventures into the realm of the dead. Even the fairies, with all of their power, feared that place," pleaded Trya.

"Sometimes, it is necessary to go where others fear to tread," said Nylana.

"Nylana, there are horrors there that you cannot imagine."

"I am not frightened. The lands of Tesnayr need him, Trya." Nylana turned to Quesha. "I will go with you."

Quesha nodded her head. The sorceress circled her hand in the air, muttering an incantation. Black smoke filled the area.

"What is separated let there be a hole to let the living into death's kingdom."

The smoke grew and grew until it covered all of them before settling into one space shaped like a doorway.

"Come, time is short," Quesha beckoned to Nylana as she stepped through, disappearing into the darkness beyond.

"See you on the other side," said Nylana. She strengthened her resolve and stepped toward the doorway.

In a flash, Trya seized Nylana's arms and pinned them behind her back. "I am sorry," she whispered in Nylana's ear.

Trya flung Nylana to the ground. The girl tripped over Galdin's body and landed face down.

Nylana scrambled to her knees and faced the elf. "What are you doing?" she cried.

Trya stood her ground. The door to the dead began to shrink. "I cannot let you go," she said. "Tesnayr may need Galdin, but it needs you even more."

The elf removed the silver bracelet from her arm and tossed it to Nylana. "Tell Galdin, that I love him."

Trya leaped through the doorway and disappeared into the land of the dead. The black smoke vanished. Alone, Nylana wept in the dark next to a lifeless body.

Magi padded up to Nylana wrapping her tail around her paws.

"Where are the others?" asked Nylana.

"The savages have taken Ryk and Valn has disappeared. But Tabs is here."

Wind swept by Nylana. She looked up gradually as tears streamed down her reddened cheeks. Darkness encroached upon her.

"Please help him," pleaded Nylana to the night sky; her voice cracked as she spoke.

The wind brushed her again as though it attempted to wipe the tears from her face.

Ni'lee y'lee.

"I hate you!" Nylana's harsh words echoed through the night as she cursed seeming nothingness. "Why? Why did you take him from me?"

Racking sobs shook her body as she leaned over Galdin's still form. She never noticed when Magi crept away and disappeared; consumed by her grief. Silence enveloped her. No crickets chirped. No howls from the wolves. Nothing.

As dawn approached, the sun caressed a lone woman mourning the loss of her brother and only the softest melody could be heard.

Ni'lee y'lee.

Book Three
Sorrow's Triumph

Mournful victory of shouts and cheers;
Oblivious to one man's sneer;
Of the traitor in their midst.

She learns Truth's dark secret
Of betrayal and all it begets.
And the sting of Sorrow's Triumph.

Chapter I
The Realm of the Dead

The swollen bruise on Lord Trisk's cheek throbbed as he lay on the rough fibers of the rug in Vasagius' tent. Breathing shallowly, he ignored the pain in his body as he willed his mind elsewhere. Calloused hands seized his arms yanking him to his knees. His head flopped to the side as he wished for unconsciousness.

Fingers grabbed his hair jerking his head back so that he looked into the malicious face of Vasagius. Lord Trisk kept his face impassive refusing to reveal anything to this traitor.

"Lord Trisk," sneered Vasagius, "You didn't think I was going to let you die so easily did you?"

Lord Trisk remained silent.

"You were very vocal about my little rebellion making known how you thought I deserved death for trying to kill the royal family."

"You murdered the king and then hunted his wife and child down with impunity," spat Lord Trisk.

"It is time for the line of Tesnayr to come to an end," said Vasagius.

"With murder?"

"How do you think King Tesnayr achieved the throne?"

"He did not murder innocent people."

"No one's innocent."

"What do you want from me?" demanded Lord Trisk.

Vasagius smiled malevolently. "I'm glad you asked. Tell me about Galdin."

                    *   *   *

Trya stood in the darkness with Quesha as the portal sealed behind her. Straightening her shoulders, the elf walked onward refusing to second guess her decision. She had a job to do.

Crunch.

Trya bent down and touched what her boot had broken: white bits of bones and shells. She studied it frowning.

"Don't believe your senses," said Quesha. "This place is filled with the nightmares of others."

"So all souls are doomed to an eternity of misery?"

"No," replied Quesha, "Some do move on to a place of eternal joy. But as most people are miserable in life, they remain so even in death."

"So there is no hope?"

"There was while the phoenix lived." Quesha eyed Trya momentarily. "Come. Newly arrived souls are always on the farthest end of this place. Galdin shall be there."

The darkness of the realm of the dead closed on them permeating their mood. Carefully, Trya moved onward not liking the fact that she walked on old bones. Imagined or not, it seemed real enough. Eerie howls echoed around them. Their incessant noise sent chills down Trya's back forcing her to pause momentarily.

"Skulogs," said Quesha, "Guardians of this world."

Trya kept her face impassive. She remembered the legends about giant hounds that protected the realm of the dead from those who didn't belong. According to the same tales, these Skulogs kept the souls there in line. "I thought they were just stories."

"You'll find that here, those stories come to life."

The path narrowed into a tunnel. Trya bumped her head. Rubbing the sore spot, she bent low to walk through whereas Quesha stood erect. Dripping water echoed hollowly around them. Instead of bringing peace, it fed their anxiety. More howls sounded.

"They're getting closer," commented Trya.

"They caught our scent."

Trya tripped. She threw her hands out to catch herself. Instead they slipped on the slimy walls causing her to crash into the ground. She sank into oozing glop. Curious, Trya scooped some of it into her hand studying it.

The muck moved. Instantaneously, it turned into tiny insects and worms crawling up the elf's arms and legs. Trya jumped to her feet smacking them off of her. Tendrils escaped the wall wrapping around her neck. Choking, Trya yanked on the vine. A blast of light struck the thing that squeezed her forcing it to shrink back melting into the dark wall before disappearing. The black insects became the floor once more.

Still smacking her legs Trya eventually calmed herself. "What were those?"

"There are many horrors in this world. I suggest we move quickly to avoid more entanglements."

"More?"

"There are dark souls here. They feast off of the living as we do not belong."

More howls echoed around them.

Trya began to second guess her decision to come. An image of Galdin lying cold and dead on the grass fueled her resolve to continue. "Let's go. The sooner we find his spirit, the sooner this will be over."

Quesha walked onward taking the lead. Despite her added years, the sorceress moved briskly with determination. No warmth remained in that place; just the cold of loneliness. Fear flowed freely in the underworld.

"Why are you doing this?" asked the elf.

"I have my reasons," replied Quesha.

"You always have your reasons," said Trya, "I remember the stories about the help you provided Amborese, or even Tesnayr himself. In fact, whenever you do show up, there is trouble and not once do you give a valid explanation for doing what you do. What concern is Galdin to you?"

"Much."

Trya stopped. "Tell me. No riddles. No more mystery."

Frustrated, Quesha faced the elf. She had hoped to get through this without having to divulge information. "Without Galdin, the world will perish."

"Not another one of your 'the fate of the world depends on this'."

"But it does," said Quesha, "I don't expect you or anyone else to believe that one man could be so pivotal that his death would destroy us all. But that is the case with Galdin. The fate of Tesnayr relies on it."

"Really? You said yourself that he would never sit upon the throne even though he is the first born son."

"That is true."

"Well then—I assumed—"

"Only fools make false assumptions and you do not strike me as a fool, Trya. Do you honestly think that the only way he could bring peace to the five lands is by assuming the throne?"

"Then how?"

"He will save someone's life. It is that person who will bring peace."

"He's already done that."

"So you assume. The stone has shown me much, but not everything. What is left to do will come later."

"The future is not set," said Trya.

"No, but the danger still remains. By that alone I know that he has yet to fulfill what the stone has shown. Because when he saves that individual's life, the threat that currently plagues the lands of Tesnayr will be eradicated."

Soft steps filled their ears as Trya walked onward in silence pondering what Quesha had said. "The stone of Elya was destroyed long ago. How could you have learned all this?"

"You think I came by these revelations recently. I had the stone for a thousand years before Amborese destroyed it. Everything I know was revealed before then. Why do you think I returned to the lands of Tesnayr when I did?"

"So you knew of this threat."

"Yes."

"And you never bothered to warn anyone?"

"Would you have listened? Would anyone?"

Tyra's silence confirmed Quesha's suspicion.

"The threat had to arrive before anyone heeded my words and even then none of you listened."

"You still never answered my question: what is Galdin to you? Why do you care about the fate of Tesnayr?"

Quesha eyed the elf a moment debating her answer. "I learned the terrible lesson of what occurs when you do not care about what happens in this world. When you do nothing. I'll not make that mistake again."

"Changing death isn't the best way to go about it," commented Trya.

"And yet you are here."

Trya pursed her lips. She hated this entire affair, but Nylana's pleading tugged her heart and her emotions. "You do realize that even if we succeed in finding Galdin, neither of us will be granted peace. We will be cursed to spend eternity in this place."

"I knew the cost when I came. And so did you. Come what may, I'll not stand idly by while the lands of Tesnayr slip into darkness once again. I will gladly suffer the torments of this place if it means the five lands endure a while longer."

Trya stared into the sorceress' eyes. She read the truth within them.

More howls resonated around them filling them with anxiety. They were close. Too close.

"We've lingered long enough," said Quesha. "We must find Galdin before they find us."

They left the tunnel and entered a vast expanse that spread far beyond what the darkness allowed them to see. A starless sky bore down upon them. Trya knew it was not a real sky, just a trick of the place they were in. Green and purple mist floated up from the ground enveloping them. Trya coughed.

"Poisonous gas," said Quesha, "Do not breathe it in."

Quesha hurried away. Trya followed close behind. Her boots pounded the ground that had now turned solid. Covering her mouth and nose, she tried to not inhale the deadly fumes. She coughed as some of the gas leaked through her fingers. Tendrils of the mist wrapped around Trya's wrists and burning pain flared up her arms as she yanked away. Blisters dotted the skin where the mist had touched her.

"Do not let it grab you!"

Quesha's warning came too late. More tendrils from the mist shot toward them. Trya tripped as something snatched her ankle. Kicking, she shook it off jumping to her feet and running hard.

"This way," said Quesha heading for a black, metal door.

Trya had no idea where the door had come from, but she heeded the sorceress' orders.

Quesha placed her hand on the steel door. Its cold exterior consumed her hand sending a tingling sensation up her arm. Slowly, the grinding of gears filled their ears as the door opened, lifting just enough to allow them entrance.

"This is the place of souls," said Quesha as she motioned the elf through. "Galdin's spirit will be here. But be careful. The guards will not let him leave and if they find us, then we will become trapped in this desolate place."

Eerie silence engulfed them as they tiptoed through the dark expanse unsure of what to expect. Trya practically choked on the lack of air movement. No breeze. No wind. The stifling interior made breathing nearly impossible. Cautiously, the elf pulled out her bow, ready to fight should anything chance upon them. All was quiet; too quiet.

"Follow my every step," said Quesha pointing to a barely visible path before them. "If you stray even a little, they will be upon us."

Quesha placed her feet directly in front of the other creeping along the narrow rocks. Trya followed exactly. Thankful that elves were imbued with an excellent sense of balance, she hopped from rock to rock with ease. This is almost too easy, she thought.

As though the underworld had heard her, a long, menacing growl echoed around them. Trya stopped.

"They are quick," muttered Quesha. "Run!"

Trya's long legs stretched across the expanse as she dashed across the rocks to the other side. The growls grew louder as more joined in. Shapes rose from the ground around them. With horror, Trya realized that these shapes were the very rocks that she stood upon, except they took on a more humanoid appearance.

Long, gangly arms reached for her with bony fingers dripping in a sticky substance. Gnarled heads protruded from the shapes that stumbled for her. Their non-existent eyes unnerved Trya as she ran for the place Quesha indicated.

"Head for that opening," shouted Quesha.

Trya sped for it, but with each step she took, the opening seemed to move away. Nails raked against her skin as the claw like hands grabbed for her. She shook one off.

Trya's foot slipped as the rock she jumped for moved, transforming into one of the creatures. Crashing onto the remaining jagged rocks, the elf's back stung as bits of skin were scraped off. Instantly, the creatures were upon her. They jumped on her covering her body. Desperately, Trya threw them off, but to no avail as the swarming black mass of demons snaked for her.

She ripped her bow apart exposing the two swords. Trya jabbed one of the creatures in the face. Screaming in agony the thing backed away. Trya stabbed another. It too wailed in pain.

Suddenly, Trya realized that these things could not stand the touch of an elven blade. Wildly, she swung her weapons in every direction forming a circle above her. The dark creatures backed away as the sharp steel scraped their rubbery hides.

Trya jumped to her feet. She leapt from rock to rock desperately trying to maintain her balance as they wobbled beneath her.

"Keep going!" yelled Quesha.

Trya didn't need to be told. A boulder shifted below her. She pierced it with her sword causing it to shrivel into a gnarled mass that burst when she leapt off of it. Black ooze covered her. Agony seized her as the sludge burned her skin causing it to peel off in flakes. Screaming in pain, Trya tumbled over.

A hand seized her. Strong arms pulled her up to safety pushing her and guiding her to the other side. Barely conscious, Trya allowed whomever it was to direct her movements.

"Adon nai. Adon nai."

The chanting continued until the pain subsided, becoming a dull, but constant throbbing.

"Do not let their filth touch you," warned Quesha. Black goo covered her as well, but she gave no indication that it affected her. "Now go. The opening is there. Do not believe your eyes. They deceive you."

It took several moments for Trya to realize that the sorceress referred to the fact that the opening appeared to move. She jumped to another rock before it transformed into a creature. Suddenly, she realized that no one followed her. Turning around, Trya watched as Quesha stood her ground facing the onslaught of writhing beasts.

"Quesha," yelled Trya.

"Go on," shouted the sorceress. "You must continue without me. Find Galdin. Barter for his soul."

Quesha pulled a blue orb from her pocket. Gripping it tightly in her hand, she held it high above her head facing the creatures with determination. Their screeches and growls did little to sway her.

"GO!"

Trya turned and darted for the opening never looking back.

"Come now, you foul beasts," said Quesha, her voice booming throughout the chamber overpowering the shrieks of the demons. She glanced upward as one would when praying to the heavens. *I know you will never approve*, she thought, *but it must be done.*

"Come what may!"

Quesha squeezed the orb in her hand. Bright light erupted from it spreading outward, filling every crevice. A moment of stunned silence followed only to be drowned by an earth shattering explosion. The force of the impact swept through the horde of creatures vaporizing them until nothing remained.

Trya jumped from rock to rock not daring to slow down. Lightly, her feet touched the jagged edges barely leaving an impression as she leapt to the next one. Breathing heavily, she moved as quickly as she could until she touched solid ground. Not wasting a moment, Trya ran, pushing herself onward in an effort to stay ahead of the blast. She squeaked through the small opening just in time to avoid falling rocks and pelting body parts of the dismembered creatures.

Solemnly, Trya paused paying her last respects to the sorceress. No more would Quesha walk the earth.

There will be no return.

Trya remembered Quesha's words as they echoed through her mind. She had known this would be a one way trip.

Pushing all sadness aside, the elf walked onward. Ghosts of people surrounded her.

"I didn't mean to," said one in a hollow voice.

"Please," wailed a woman, "Take me away from here."

Trya wandered past them in wonderment. None of them looked at her. None of them acknowledged her presence. They were just echoes of their former selves. Slowly, Trya walked past the opaque figures searching for Galdin. This had to be the place.

"Echoes of ourselves," said a strong voice, "That is what we are. Echoes doomed to remain here until he returns."

Curious, Trya walked over to the lone figure. He was an elf killed in a war that took place long ago. She recognized the shield. It dated back to Tesnayr's day. Strangely, Trya felt as though the figure spoke to her, though he never looked at her directly.

"Echoes," he repeated, "We all come here until a far better place is made for us."

"Far better place," said Trya.

She thought back to the traditions of her people, traditions she had spurned a long time ago. The elves believed that all souls went to a dark place where they remained until purified. Some went insane forgetting who they once were. Others never lingered long in the realm of the dead. But all who died went there. A form of judgment her mother had called it. Trya had never paid much heed to it. She had found the elves' traditions too constricting; one reason why she left Belarnia.

Now she stood here before an elf repeating what her mother had taught her. Trya began to wonder if perhaps she should have paid better attention. She reached out to touch the figure. Her fingers went right through it leaving a wet, chilled feeling on her flesh. She yanked her arm back.

"You shouldn't be here."

Trya jumped. The elf looked directly at her.

"What?"

"You do not belong here," said the elf. "This is a place meant for the dead not the living."

"How—" Trya could not believe that this elf knew her. The others remained unaware of her presence; she was but a spirit to them. But this elf talked directly to her.

"Your being here violates all laws," scolded the elf.

"Please," pleaded Trya, "You must tell me where Galdin is. I must find him. War rages in the world above and we need him."

"War always ravages the land."

"Please," said Trya, "Where is Galdin?"

The elf looked up as though he listened to something.

Bewildered, Trya watched him. "Will you not help us?"

"Tell her, she holds hope in her pocket."

Frustrated, Trya reined in her temper as the elf spoke gibberish. "Tell whom? I need to find Galdin. I know he is here."

"The true heir of Tesnayr," said the elf, "She is with your friend's remains as we speak."

"Nylana?" Trya shook her head. Questions burned in her mind, but time was not her friend. Forcing her brain to focus she asked once more, "Where can I find Galdin?"

"The line of Tesnayr is not here, but further in. Walk until you see its crest. There you shall find your friend."

"Thank you," said Trya as she walked off.

"Be warned, young elf," said the elf stopping her, "A trade must be made."

Trya eyed him a moment, but the elf had gone back to ignoring her, muttering more nonsense.

"I'm sorry," said a small child as she passed more souls. He never noticed her.

Trya pushed her way through the gigantic chamber of spirits. Sometimes she paused to observe them as they stood enveloped in silver light unaware of her trespassing. No creatures came for her. No one talked to her. Only that elf had; a curiosity that plagued her mind.

Trya paused. A wooden door barred her way. She brushed cobwebs away from it surprised that such things existed here. Slowly, the crest of Tesnayr revealed itself. Excitement coursed through her veins as she pushed it open and stepped through the archway and into another room.

"Nylana!"

Trya whirled around. Galdin stood to her left wrapped in the same silver light, reliving his last moments alive.   .

"Galdin!" Trya ran to him.

"I am sorry, Nylana," said Galdin.

Tears welled in Trya's eyes as she realized that he did not see her. Like the others, he remained unaware of her presence. Unsure of what to do, Trya stood there staring at Galdin as he continued to relive those last moments before he died. *What do I do?* A headache formed as she thought about her options.

She didn't want to leave him. She couldn't. Quesha had told her there was no going back.

"Trading him his own apples."

Trya smiled as she realized that Galdin remembered the day Ryk sold a merchant his own stock to acquire money for their passage on a ship.

It hit her. Trade; that was what the old elf had meant. The true meaning of why she would never leave dawned on her. She had to choose to stay. A soul for a soul.

"Galdin," she said, "Hear me. You must return. I will take your place. The lands of Tesnayr need you."

"Protect Nylana."

Trya looked up to the nothingness above her. "Do you hear me?" she shouted, "I will remain here. Free Galdin. Take me instead."

"Trya." Galdin looked at her. "Trya, no!"

Trya stared at Galdin; a sorrowful expression on her face. The thought of leaving him ached her heart, but her desires were unimportant. She had made a promise to Nylana.

"I'm sorry," she whispered, "But the world needs you more than me."

The rings of light encircling Galdin released him as they hovered over to her. All thoughts of the world and of life left as the light enveloped her. The thought that she had one last thing to do gnawed at her. Holding on to her thoughts a bit longer,

Trya gave the elf's message to Galdin. "Tell Nylana that she holds hope in her pocket. Tell her!"

"Trya—No!"

A rift appeared above them. Fierce winds descended from the rift and howled around them seizing Galdin and pulling him to it. He hovered above the ground as his feet left it.

"Good-bye, Galdin."

The winds stopped. Galdin had gone, leaving Trya alone in death's realm muttering nonsense like the others.

Chapter II
Returned

The influx of air into Galdin's lungs told Nylana that he breathed once more. Wiping her tear stained cheeks, she helped him up. "Galdin."

Galdin breathed deeply several times before speaking. "Where's Trya?"

Closing her eyes to stop the tears, Nylana look downward telling Galdin everything he needed to know.

"So it wasn't a dream."

"No," said Nylana.

Galdin looked about him. Tabs sat in the distance watching with intense interest. "Where's Valn?"

Suddenly, Nylana realized that the Byleon had gone missing. In her emotional state she had never noticed, nor did she fully hear what Magi had told her. "I don't know. Where's Magi?"

"Valn ran after Ryk," answered Tabs, "He was taken prisoner by the barbarians. Magi disappeared soon after Trya and the sorceress left."

"We need to go after them," said Galdin sitting up. He stopped when his head spun placing it in his hands.

"You need to rest," said Nylana.

"We haven't time," said Galdin, "We can't leave Ryk to their mercy."

Nylana helped Galdin to his feet. "Are you sure you are able?"

"I'll manage," said Galdin as he checked his sword. "Which way did they go?"

"East," said Tabs.

The cat darted off through some shrubbery. Groaning at the animal's lack of consideration that they could not go through such small spaces, Galdin and Nylana chased after him hoping to find Ryk before it was too late.

*   *   *

Ryk's feet plodded along the dirt path as his captors pulled him along by the rope that bound his wrists. He counted the number of men around him: eight. Taking his options into account, Ryk wondered how he would escape. Unless a miracle happened, he knew it would be impossible.

A harsh tug on the rope practically knocked him off his feet. Two quick steps to regain his balance and Ryk continued allowing his captors to pull him along; figuring it best to be compliant for the moment.

The barbarians camped that night and tied Ryk to a rotting log far away from the fire. Ryk sat silently observing the men as they laughed and drank, confident in their superiority. He wrenched his hands within the rope trying to loosen his bounds. Something slimy whapped him on the chin. Startled, he looked up into the face of one of his captors. The man glared at him with hatred.

"Eat."

Glad that the man did not suspect him of trying to escape, Ryk glanced at the food. The bloody heart of an animal lay in his lap. Disgusted, Ryk knocked it away much to the entertainment of the man that had chucked it at him.

When the savage walked away, Ryk watched their merrymaking. Hastily, he rubbed the rope around his wrists against the rough surface of the log. A soft shuffling noise filled his ears. Making certain no one noticed him, Ryk glanced back at the men around the fire. Still drinking. He resumed his efforts of cutting his bounds.

Minutes ticked by. Sweat formed around the collar of his shirt as he continued his work. Growing frustrated at his lack of progress, Ryk redoubled his efforts. He looked at the fire again. Still safe. Desperate, Ryk rubbed the rope even faster.

Snap!

A thread had broken loose. Encouraged, Ryk worked harder completely focused on his efforts to free himself. Slowly, the rope frayed as fibers broke. Feeling its grip loosen, Ryk pulled his wrists apart as he continued to cut the rope.

Relief flooded his being when the fibers broke open and the rope fell to the earth. Ignoring the temptation to rub his wrists, Ryk glanced back at the men around the fire. They slumped in their positions indicating that they had had too much to drink.

Cautiously, Ryk stood up backing into the shadows. He bumped into something slightly hard yet soft at the same time. Dreading what he'd find, Ryk turned around. He had run directly into one of the barbarians.

Fool, he scolded himself for not counting the number of men around the fire. Only seven were there. Of course they had one standing guard.

Ryk used both hands to shove the guard away. Quickly, he turned and ran into the darkness.

"Prisoner escapes," yelled the guard at the others.

Within moments the others sprang to their feet with their weapons and chased after him. Twigs snapping and leaves crunching as he went, Ryk plowed through the small wooded area. The noise behind him indicated that his pursuers were close. He hunkered behind some dried brush, controlling his breathing. One by one the barbarians raced past.

When the last one appeared, Ryk jumped from his hiding place and tackled the man. They wrestled around the ground kicking up leaves and dust as they fought for the upper hand. A knee rammed into Ryk's stomach causing him to gasp for air. He returned the favor by slamming his fist into his opponent's jaw.

A sword lay a few feet away. Ryk scrambled for it. The barbarian grabbed his ankles yanking him back. Ryk kicked the man in the face pleased that it garnered a grunt of pain. He reached for the sword again. His fingers brushed the hilt as his opponent dove on top of him. Releasing the air in his lungs, Ryk rammed the heel of his hand into the man's throat. Backing off, the barbarian gasped for air. Ryk immediately reached for the abandoned sword. Grasping it, he swung it over his head and thrust it into the middle of the gasping man.

The others heard the commotion and turned back. Knowing he would soon be overwhelmed, Ryk hastily backtracked through the wooded area. Darkness became his ally as he raced through it hoping to out run and outsmart those who chased him. He swerved and maneuvered his way through in an effort to shake them. Slowly, their steps faded. Unsure if it was a trick, Ryk continued to run in the dead of night.

The trees thinned as a clearing lay up ahead. Ryk ran for it. Shouts and yells followed after him. He knew they would not stop until they had captured or killed him. His breathing coming in short spurts, Ryk pushed himself through the last of the trees and into an open space.

Something seemed odd about this open area. Unable to determine what bothered him, Ryk glanced back. Shapes moved through the sparse trees heading straight for him. His feet skidded to a halt as Ryk realized that he stood on the edge of a precipice. He looked down into the inky blackness. Whirling around to face his captors, Ryk held his sword before him, ready and waiting.

The savages slowed their pursuit as they realized that their prey had been cornered. Each smirking in triumph, they drew their weapons. Slowly, they formed a semi-circle around him not wanting to get too close to the edge. Ryk took a step back. His foot scraped the edge of the cliff sending pebbles clattering down to the bottom.

"You have nowhere left to go," said one of the barbarians.

Ryk knew the man was right. Dreading his prospects, he remained where he was. "I'll not go with you."

"Give us the weapon and we may let you live"

Suddenly, the place where Ryk stood crumbled. Rock and dirt fell away from beneath his feet as he plunged into the darkness below.

Two pairs of eyes watched everything from their place of concealment. Both Valn and Magi hunched low to the ground remaining in the shadows and out of sight. They waited as they watched the barbarian men look over the edge and leave.

Carefully, they left their hiding place darting to the ledge where Ryk had disappeared. Valn glanced over the edge into the black abyss. He knew it couldn't be too far down, but had no idea if Ryk survived. He would have to wait until the sun rose to know.

"Do you think he survived?" asked Magi.

"Hard to say," replied Valn. "Can you find your way down there?"

"Yes."

"Go down there and find him. I will wait here for the others."

Magi swished her tail and trotted off disappearing over the edge as she hopped down.

Valn walked back to the thicket he had hidden in earlier where he sat and waited.

Chapter III
Over the Mountains

Cold air swept through Artryl's hair, but the warmth of Trog's grip prevented him from freezing as they soared through the sky. The tops of the mountains slowly moved below him as they passed over; many of them snowcapped. As Artryl observed them with fascination, he noticed an avalanche on one. Intrigued, the boy watched as mounds of snow and ice tumbled down the mountain side into the depths below, obliterating anything in its way.

Trog's panting chest beat against Artryl's back as his thin wings propelled them forward against the wind. He knew the animal tired, but Nylana wanted that message to reach her brother before it was too late. Even by flight, it would take several days as Trog could only travel a few hours before needing to rest.

Artryl's stomach lurched as they dropped a bit. "It's okay, boy," said Artryl. "Can you make it past the highest parts of the mountains?"

In answer, Trog beat his wings harder lifting them higher. His tail swayed behind them sticking out straight as the animal streamlined his body.

Frigid wind washed over them as they moved onward while Artryl kept his eyes peeled for a safe place to land and rest. Nothing. White mountain tops still dominated the landscape below him. They lurched again.

Knowing that Trog could not go on much longer, Artryl looked ahead hoping to find something. A spot of brown caught his attention. Hoping he hadn't imagined it, he pointed it out to Trog. "See that over there?"

Trog waved his tail in answer.

"We should be able to rest there."

Banking to the left, Trog held his wings horizontal as he glided to the brown spot. Gradually, they dipped lower. With controlled movements, Trog carried them to where Artryl had indicated. He swooped low almost touching the ground. Releasing his grip, Trog dropped the boy on the small area before going back up into the sky and making a second pass. He collapsed on the ground next to Artryl. The boy patted his head and comforted him noting how exhausted the animal was.

"You did well. We'll rest here a bit."

Trog snuggled into Artryl placing his head in the boy's lap before falling fast asleep. Pleased that their trip had been uneventful thus far, Artryl rested his head on Trog's and closed his eyes. Soon both their chests rose and fell in the rhythm of sleep.

*   *   *

"My lord," said a messenger, "He is here."

"Send him in," said Vasagius.

In walked the cloaked figure. Vasagius studied the man hoping for a glimpse of his face, but never managed to get it.

"You wished to see me," said the cloaked figure.

"Yes," said Vasagius, "I have been thinking about our arrangement."

"Oh?"

"I think it is time we change the nature of our agreement."

"Do you now?" said the cloaked figure. "And what makes you think that I will accept your new terms?"

"Do not threaten me," growled Vasagius, "You may frighten my men, but I am not so easily intimidated."

"Only fools do not fear me."

"Only a fool would keep you in their confidences and I have no further use for you."

The cloaked figure stepped closer. "Really? It was I who brought you to this land. It was I who enabled you to pass through unnoticed."

"Fo which I will always be grateful," mocked Vasagius, "But I never keep a man around who might turn on me and you would certainly do so. I want you gone and if you ever show your face in my presence again, I will kill you."

Suddenly, Vasagius lost all will as he stared into the red eyes of a Nôk'ta. He hadn't seen the beast enter his tent. Frozen, the man stood still unable to move as his mind lost all control of his limbs.

The cloaked figure circled Vasagius with a malicious grin. "Did you think I would let you be rid of me so easily? You never would have made it past the shores of Sym'Dul if it wasn't for me. Now, I suggest that you listen to me well. You will do as I wish."

A flash of steel swiped across the cloaked figure's vision as Stahl entered the room and sliced the Nôk'ta's throat.

Freed, Vasagius unsheathed his sword. "Did you think I would be without my own resources?" Vasagius lunged for the mysterious man but struck only air. The cloaked figure had vanished.

Just outside of the barbarian camp, the cloaked man reappeared near the shadows. A satisfied smile crossed his lips. Perfect, he thought to himself, Vasagius is playing into our hands.

*   *   *

Tami panted as they climbed higher; the thin air getting to her. She had never been in the mountains for any length of time. Steadily, she followed Narúl as he led the way along a trail that he had found years before. The trail widened and narrowed in spots, but remained visible. The smooth incline made trekking it bearable, but Tami did not know how much longer that would last. The pack weighed heavily on her shoulders causing them to hurt. She slumped a bit, pausing for breath.

Without asking, Narúl took her pack and added it to his own. Relieved, Tami watched as he moved onward as though he had just finished a long rest. The sun gleamed on the sweat the dotted his black skin. She watched as his muscular arms used a staff to help propel him forward.

"This is no time to rest," said Narúl.

Grunting, Tami trudged onward. They had traveled two days and her stiff muscles burned with each movement she took. A sharp pull yanked her back as something snagged her skirt. Wrestling with it, Tami scared a bunch of rabbits with the noise she generated.

Annoyed, Narúl pulled her free. He used his dagger to slice off the bottom four inches of her skirt. Tami smiled gratefully and pulled away, but Narúl hadn't finished. He cut slits in her skirt so that she could move more easily.

"Hey," yelled Tami.

Narúl put his knife away. "You'll walk better this way. Now come on."

Tami glowered at the man. She wore breeches underneath, but the fact that he ruined her dress without asking infuriated her. She marched after him attempting to salvage her dignity.

The warm sun and gentle breeze accompanied them as they made their way upward. Tami began to enjoy the warmth despite the rigorous pace.

Narúl stopped.

"What is it?" asked Tami.

He pointed at the broken stone bridge before them. A gap now filled its place with two giant walnut trees forming a canopy over it.

"How are we to get across?" asked Tami.

"We'll have to find another way," replied Narúl.

"But that could take days—weeks."

"No other choice," said Narúl, "Unless you think the trees could swing us across."

Narúl immediately regretted that last statement as Tami's face brightened. She rushed over to the two trees with an idea forming.

"No. No, I didn't—"

Tami ignored Narúl's protests. She touched the tree whispering to it. Rustling noises surrounded them as the trees moved their branches and twisted around to face her.

"I am sorry for disturbing your slumber," said Tami, "But could you get us across this gorge?"

The two trees twisted around as though studying what Tami pointed to before turning back to her. Not liking this idea, Narúl backed away. Before he got far, a branch reached out and wrapped around his waist. Another snatched Tami who held her arms up for it. Narúl's stomach reeled as the trees swung him back and forth over the gorge before releasing him. Weightlessness hit him as he flew through the air before crashing into the ground on the other side and coming to a rolling stop. Tami landed next to him with a soft thump.

"Thank you," Tami called to the trees.

The trees bowed before her as they nestled back into their slumber.

"That wasn't so bad," said Tami, "You see, my magic isn't always a curse."

Still kneeling on the ground, Narúl glared at her. He forced his stomach to settle down as he rose to his feet and continued the long trek through the mountains.

*   *   *

Galdin and Nylana ran through the woods following the tracks that the barbarians had left. The deep impact in the earth told Galdin that they had run fast and hard to their destination. He picked up the pace. Glancing back at Nylana, he observed her struggling with his fast pace, but she never complained. Galdin turned back to the task at hand. He knew that the sooner they caught up, the better chance they had of finding Ryk.

Tabs stretched to his full length as he seemingly flew across the surface of the earth to keep up. His orange fur created blotches of color against the newly green landscape. He leapt and bounded over the ground near Galdin's feet. Something caught his attention. Tabs looked back quickly and noticed that Nylana had collapsed from exhaustion. "Galdin!"

Galdin stopped. When he saw Nylana he rushed to her.

"I'm alright," she panted as she tried to regain her feet.

"No, you're exhausted. We should rest," said Galdin.

"If we rest, we will never catch up to them," gasped Nylana as she panted heavily.

"You won't get far in your current state," said Galdin, "We will rest here a bit. Tabs scout ahead. Be back within the hour."

Tabs darted off.

"Here," said Galdin handing Nylana something to eat, "This should help you regain your strength."

She took a bite of the bitter substance, her face scrunching up into a wince.

"Not much for taste, but it's good for you."

Nylana took another bite ignoring the bitterness. "Do you think we will find him?"

"I'm sure of it," said Galdin noting the concern in Nylana's voice. "Why worry so much? I thought he annoyed you."

"He does," replied Nylana, "But it is my fault that he's gone."

"No, don't say that. He chose to come. Do not blame yourself."

Nylana chewed methodically on the food lost in thought. "What is happening to the land, Galdin?"

"What do you mean?"

"These barbarians. Their invasion does not make sense. First they just burn and destroy, but now they have begun taking people as slaves. And how Vasagius managed to become their leader is most puzzling. I thought he was dead."

"It isn't that puzzling at all," said Galdin, "My guess is that he left the lands of Tesnayr and found the farthest and most remote place to hide. And it isn't difficult to convince murdering cutthroats to follow you as long as you promise them wealth and power."

"There is more to this," said Nylana, "These moves by Vasagius go against his nature. When he rebelled against our father he wasted no time in attacking Norlyk."

"Except he lost," said Galdin, "Which may explain why he is taking a more roundabout way to do it. Never try the same tactic twice."

"What about the red-eyed orcs? The Nôk'ta as I've heard them called. The only one in history to control them was Galbrok. How does a man, easily subdued by their dark power, control them?"

Galdin remained silent. That was a question which he had asked himself and had no answer.

"There is something more at play here," said Nylana, "I feel it."

"You see what you want to see," said Galdin.

"Such wisdom," said Nylana with playfulness. She chucked the crumbs of her meager meal at him.

In retaliation, Galdin splashed some water from the canteen he had drunk from on her. Nylana smacked him and within moments they were in the middle of a playful fight.

Their birthmarks touched. Instantly, Galdin felt what Nylana felt; thought what she thought. He understood her skepticism of Vasagius working alone. He felt the pain she carried since she had lost her father and him. He felt the love she carried for Krispyn and him. The sense of responsibility that Nylana had for her people wafted over Galdin stunning him.

"AAAHHHH!"

A blur of orange fur raced through the air and landed atop them breaking up their connection.

"Tabs," groaned Nylana.

"Sorry," said Tabs, "I saw you two having fun so I thought I would join in."

Galdin and Nylana straightened themselves out regaining their dignity.

"Anyway," continued Tabs, "I found where the tracks lead. They end not far from here."

"Show us," said Galdin.

Tabs took off through the brush. Rising, Nylana and Galdin chased after him. They moved through the sparsely wooded area following an orange shape as it hastened away.

"Hurry up," shouted Tabs.

Galdin and Nylana ran faster to keep sight of the cat. Bits of leaves brushed them cutting their skin, smacking them. Leaves crunched under their boots as they ran; hearts pounding.

They came upon a small clearing with an ash pit in the center and an orange cat seated on a rock near it. Galdin searched around noting the footprints. An abandoned log caught his attention. He crept over there and picked up the frayed rope.

"Someone was tied up here, but managed to escape." Galdin held up the rope for Nylana to look at. "These tracks lead into the woods. They are fast and heavy. He was chased."

"Yep," said Tabs. "They lead in that direction, but then backtrack through here. I found where they end." The cat darted off again.

Instantly, Nylana and Galdin chased after him. They ran fast to keep up with the cat as the trees grew more and more sparse. Soon, a vast opening stretched before them with a deep canyon filling the area. Nylana recognized it immediately: the Whispering Canyons.

"Tell me he did not go in there," said Nylana.

"I'm afraid it looks as though he did," answered Tabs.

Galdin peeked over the edge. Nothing.

Voices trickled through Valn's fitful sleep as he turned over. A vague thought that he knew them brought his brain to full alert. He sat up quickly. As the momentary spinning abated, Valn scolded himself for nodding off. He peeked around the bush and noticed a man, woman, and one cat hovering in the area Ryk had last been seen. Recognizing them, Valn burst from his hiding place and sprinted toward them.

Galdin whirled around, sword raised.

Valn stopped just short of being stabbed in the throat.

"Valn! Where have you been?" demanded Galdin.

"Waiting for you," answered the Byleon, "I knew you would follow the tracks here."

"Where is Magi?" asked Nylana.

"In there," said Valn pointing at the canyon. "She went in there after Ryk. He must still be alive. There is no body down there."

Anger flared in Nylana at Valn's blunt manner of speaking. She didn't know why she felt angry. Nylana looked around and found a narrow trail leading into the canyon itself. "I'm going after them."

"Are you insane?" said Galdin, stopping her. "You know the tales of that place as well as I. Any who venture there are driven mad."

"Which is why I must find both of them," said Nylana, "It is my fault he is lost in there. And I will not leave him to such a fate. I'm going, whether you come with me or not."

Galdin clenched his fists over Nylana's stubbornness.

"Alright, let's go," said Tabs trotting over to the trail.

"What?" asked Galdin.

"We've been in this situation before," answered Tabs, "She is going to do what she wants and you are going to end up following after her. So in an effort to save time, let's go."

Galdin groaned as he realized that the cat was right. He hitched his pack and walked to the trail. "Be mindful of your footing on the way down."

Chapter IV
Whispers of Madness

Ryk's sweat soaked shirt clung to his back. His feet slapped the sandy dirt as he aimlessly staggered around. Heat bore down upon him causing his head to spin. Desperate for water, his mouth produced what saliva it could to soothe his parched throat. Blood trickled down the side of his head from a cut near his temple.

Ryk.

Ryk twisted around to face the nameless voice. A burning sensation seized his side. Wincing, Ryk touched the bruise that formed there after his fall from the ledge. Finding himself alone, Ryk continued on.

Ryk.

The whisper in his ear caused him to spin around again. Nothing. Shaking his head, Ryk picked at his ears thinking that he was hearing things.

"It's just my imagination," he said to himself.

His feet moved sloppily as he found it increasingly difficult to walk. He had gone without food and water before, but a day in this place felt like weeks.

Ryk. Come to me.

"Nylana?"

I am here, Ryk.

"Where are you?"

Come to me.

Ryk followed the direction of the voice. Bleary eyed, he continued on hoping to find the source. His burning throat made him cough. Hacking, Ryk forced himself to swallow the phlegm that came up.

I am here, Ryk.

A misty image of Nylana appeared before him. Smiling at the prospect of being saved, Ryk reached for the mirage. He ran for it.

"Nylana! Help me!"

Just as he reached it the image vanished.

"No! Why do you abandon me?" Ryk sank to his knees burying his face in the sand. Tears flowed as he cried in self-pity.

Danger.

Ryk jerked up. Somewhat alert, he looked all around him, but found nothing. Warily, he rose to his feet and swayed for a moment.

They are coming.

Ryk stayed where he was.

Run!

Unexplained panic rose within him as he took off across the canyon bottom. Wildly, Ryk ran in some direction not caring where he went; he just wanted to get away. A sense of danger filled his mind. He could not explain it, but suddenly he needed to get away.

His foot struck something. Losing his balance, Ryk smacked into the rough gravel rolling across the ground. Coughing, he spat out sand as laughter surrounded him.

"Leave me!" screamed Ryk to the open space before him.

More faceless laughter taunted him.

Slowly, Ryk picked himself up. He dusted his pants cursing the place that trapped him. Feeling overheated, he tore off his cloak and ditched it in the sand.

You mustn't stay here.

The voice taunted him, fueling his rage. It toyed with him the way a cat toys with a mouse. Aggravated, Ryk headed in another direction hoping that the canyon wall before him was close. He had no idea of how misleading distances could be in the desert.

Sand filled his boots with each step he took. Sweat turned the squishy substance into dead weight making it increasingly difficult for Ryk to walk. Finally, he stopped and pulled off his boots to empty them.

Onward he trekked through the scorching heat of the canyon hoping for some relief. Water was all he thought about; all he craved. Despite his light-headedness, he pushed himself forward willing his body to not give up.

Are you thirsty?

"Yes," whispered Ryk.

There is water ahead.

"Where?"

Just there.

Seeing what looked like a gray pool of water, Ryk sprinted for it; his mouth tasting the cooling freshness. With his tongue hanging out, he wasted no time in reaching it. Ryk dived into it filling his mouth with handfuls of what he thought was liquid. Soon, racking coughs choked him as he spat out sand realizing that he had been deceived.

Mirthless laughter filled his ears as the devious voices around him giggled with glee.

Oh, he fell for it.

They always do.

Silly humans.

A string of curses filled the air as Ryk ranted and raved against the teasing voices that tortured him. He shook his fists at the sky as he flung handfuls of coarse sand into the air. Minutes rolled by as Ryk continued his fit of rage before collapsing from exhaustion.

*   *   *

Magi's tiny feet trotted across the gravel as she hurried through the canyon floor following her nose. She sniffed the air every few minutes checking for Ryk's scent. A faint smell prickled her nose. He had been there.

Magi continued onward amongst the whispers. Their garbled message meant nothing to her. Being a cat made her mostly immune to them, but the incessant murmuring did annoy her. Her tan colored fur blended nicely with the landscape as she moved.

"Go away!"

Magi hunkered low. A man dressed in the furs of the barbarians wandered aimlessly yelling and screaming at nothing.

"Leave me alone!"

Realizing he had already been driven insane, Magi scurried away from him. She galloped across the sand focused on her mission. Hopefully she would find Ryk before it was too late.

Footprints caught her attention. Carefully, Magi sniffed them. Ryk's scent was all over them. Hurriedly, Magi darted off in the direction they led. She was close.

The cat quickly left the screams of the lost barbarian far behind her.

*   *   *

"Oomph," Nylana's feet finally touched the bottom of the canyon as she jumped the last several feet. Galdin helped her up. Looking at the sky, she knew they only had a few hours of daylight left. "Which way?"

"The tracks seem to go this way," said Galdin pointing north.
Welcome.

Nylana moaned. The voices wasted no time. "Let's move." She forged ahead with Galdin by her side as Valn and Tabs trekked behind.

The heat of the canyon affected them immediately. Tearing off their cloaks, they stuffed them in their packs. Their skin burned as the fiery rays of the sun turned them a bright shade of pink. Dry spit caked their mouths making them wish for water, but each knew that they needed to conserve what little they had.

Galdin.

Why do you help her?

She cares not for you.

Galdin shook his head in an effort to ignore the voices.

Did she search for you when you went missing?

She cares nothing for you.

Galdin ripped a piece of his shirt off and stuffed it in his ears. Malevolent laughter filled his mind as the voices mocked him.

You cannot shut us out.

We are inside of you.

A part of you.

She only wants you for her own desires.

Willing himself onward, Galdin trudged forward. He paused when he noticed more tracks in the sand accompanied by paw prints. Magi had been here as well. He hoped the cat would find Ryk and then bring him to them. He hoped for a lot.

Valn, why do you follow them?

They care not for you.

You are insignificant.

You should have let her die in the mud.

Valn clenched his fists as he tried to concentrate on something else. Groaning filled his throat. The sharp pricks of claws brought him back to his senses. "Thanks," he said to Tabs who seemed unaffected.

"Anytime," replied the cat. He trotted along humming to himself. "Distant voices of deceit. Leave us be or fail in your feat."

"Will you stop singing?" asked Galdin of Tabs.

"No. Leave him be," said Valn, finding Tabs' singing soothing.

The cat will not save you.

Nylana hummed Tabs' tune to herself. It did little to drown the whispers. The sun sunk lower in the sky and she dreaded spending a night there.

You who are lesser of three children. Why does your brother sit on the throne and not you?

Go away, thought Nylana to herself.

You will not find him.

Ryk is dead.

Worse than dead.

Nylana put one foot in front of the other following Galdin as he directed them onward in the direction Ryk had wandered. In a moment of weakness, she took a sip of water.

There is a lake near here. Fresh, cool water.

Shall we take you to them?

Stuffing her fingers in her ears, Nylana hummed louder to block the whispers. They pierced through her defenses as though she had none.

You are heading in the wrong direction.

He is not this way.

You will fail.

Tesnayr is lost.

"Enough!"

Nylana's voiced boomed through the canyon as fire filled her eyes. Everyone stopped and stared at her. A soft glow surrounded her body.

"Nylana?" Concern crossed Galdin's face as he looked at her.

Slowly, the glow dissipated and the fire left her eyes. "They're gone."

The others listened intently noting that the whispers had stopped for the moment. Not wasting time, Galdin pushed them forward hoping to cover as much distance as possible before night fell.

The wind stilled. An unnerving silence fell upon them. Goosebumps dotted their skin as a slight chill rose in the air. A sound resembling thunder grew in the distance drawing closer until it had surrounded them.

"Sandstorm!" yelled Valn.

Within seconds, sand blasted their faces forcing them to duck for cover as they covered their heads. Sand filled wind whipped around them pelting their flesh sending needles of pain up their arms. The roar of the wind deafened them. Disoriented, they wandered in all directions unable to see or hear.

Galdin choked as grit filled his mouth and nose making it impossible to breathe. He wrapped his cloak around his head, but it did little to protect him. Laughter mixed with the storm as it taunted them; driving them towards death.

"We need to find shelter," screamed Valn as he grabbed Tabs who had curled into a tight ball.

"There is none," Galdin shouted back.

Nylana's eyes burned as sand got in them. Unable to wash it out, she stumbled around only to be grabbed by Galdin's steady hand. He pulled her close to him. His mind raced for a solution to their predicament.

Wiping the grit from her lips, Nylana looked upward. "Uriel!"

The beating of the wind and its sandy weapons rubbed them raw, burning them. Huddled together, the four friends waited for the end.

A dark shape loomed above them. Gently, the leathery wing of a dragon enveloped them blocking out the sand, protecting them. The wind still howled, but they breathed more easily. Slowly, they relaxed a little in the confines of a dragon's guard.

*   *   *

Ryk hugged his knees as he tried to stave off the frigid cold of night. He wished he had not discarded his cloak. Shivering uncontrollably, he tried to think of other things: of warmth and fellowship.

Wish for fire and it will come to you.

The voices continued to toy with him. Exhausted, Ryk closed his eyes to sleep, but it never came. Noises and yelps in the distance woke him every few minutes. He rubbed his icy fingers together generating momentary warmth. It faded too quickly.

Give up.

Join us.

"Leave me!"

Ryk didn't know why he continued to scream at the nothingness before him. He wanted relief. All he found was torment. A snake slithered across his feet. Startled, Ryk kicked the slimy creature away suddenly fully awake. A giggle echoed nearby.

Ryk rubbed his frozen arms as he hugged himself tighter. A cold wind brushed against him causing him to shiver even more and his teeth to chatter. Feeling abandoned, Ryk looked up at the clear sky and the bright moon above him.

"Help me, please," he whispered, "Help me."

*   *   *

The fire crackled as Nylana stuck the dead rabbit in it to cook. Uriel snorted nearby. Nylana ignored the dragon as she turned the rabbit so it would cook evenly.

"There is an easier way to do that," said Uriel.

"I like my way," replied Nylana.

The small logs popped as they broke down in the flames.

"Thank you, by the way," said Nylana to the dragon.

Uriel stretched and yawned exposing his sharp teeth and forked tongue. "It's not as though I had a choice."

"How did you find us so quickly?"

"You called, remember?" Uriel flipped his head as though it should have been obvious.

"No, I mean, I did not use the horn," continued Nylana.

"No, you didn't," said Uriel. "Whatever method you used to call, I heard you just the same and knew where and how to find you. It must be the oath you made me swear."

"How did you arrive so quickly?" asked Valn.

"When a dragon swears to serve a human we are able to travel the greatest distances in the shortest span of time when called. This one made me swear to come when summoned when I asked her for a favor."

"What favor?" asked Galdin. He thought it odd that a dragon would need a human to assist him in anything.

"None of your business," replied Uriel. "Suffice it to say that your sister is my investment now and it prevents me from eating any of you." Uriel glanced at Valn. "Though you were not part of her little group at the time."

Valn backed away as Nylana gave the dragon a piercing look.

"But seeing as it would upset my investment I will refrain from making you my snack."

Nylana turned back to her work unsure about how she felt about being referred to as an "investment". She pulled the cooked rabbit from the fire and parceled it out to everyone. Galdin took the smallest of all the pieces leaving the biggest one for her.

Rotten meat for a rotten soul.

Chewing as loud as he could, Galdin managed to block the whispers that continued to plague them. "Do they not bother you?" he asked Uriel, "The whispers?"

"This is a cursed place," said Uriel, "But dragons are immune to its wretched magic. And you are welcome, by the way."

"For what?" asked Galdin.

"For saving your life," replied Uriel.

An orange ball of fur nuzzled into Uriel as loud purring echoed around them. Tabs rubbed and rubbed against the rough scales of the dragon's chin; his back arched and tale up. Uriel used the point of a talon to shove the cat away.

"Go away little runt."

Undeterred, Tabs hopped onto Uriel's nose and snuggled in, his motor going full throttle. He rolled onto his back and fell off.

"Serves you right," Uriel mumbled.

"Please, let him be," sighed Nylana, "He likes you."

Annoyed, Uriel relented and laid his head down closing his eyes. Tabs nestled into the beast's neck wrapping his tail around himself.

By morning Uriel had left. Galdin doused the smoldering embers of the fire while the others cleaned up. As usual, Tabs sang merrily to himself. "Oh, day two in the canyon of whispers. Another day of untold adventures."

"Another day of madness. Another day of being less," Galdin chimed in, not realizing that he had sung his sentiment.

"You sing! Join on in," said Tabs with glee, "Together we will sing our way through this canyon. Let's—"

"Not," interrupted Galdin.

"I will make you a champion of song yet," said Tabs as he pranced between Galdin's feet.

"We should leave," said Galdin as he pushed ahead.

Smoldering heat seared them the moment the sun peeked over the cliff face. Once again, they searched the canyon for Ryk following what tracks they found. Gloating whispers accompanied their every move.

You're going the wrong way.

Trust us.

Suddenly, Galdin bent down and touched the dirt. He brushed a section of it studying it intently. "He was here."

"Look!" Valn pointed to a lone cloak drifting over the sand as though being moved by an invisible force.

Galdin rushed to it snatching it from midair. "It is his," he said as he inspected the cloak. "He could not have gotten far without this."

Galdin handed it to Nylana who took it with care. She wrapped it carefully before running off in the direction it had come from.

"Ryk!" yelled Nylana.

Ryk is dead.

Ignoring the taunts, Nylana continued. "Ryk!"

One by one they each shouted Ryk's name as they trailed the tracks hoping to find him soon. A sinking feeling filled Galdin's insides as he called for Ryk. He feared that they were too late.

*   *   *

Panting heavily as saliva drooled from the side of his open mouth, Ryk stumbled through the canyon wandering in circles. The heat caused him to hallucinate. Often, he thought he had seen water or food only to be bitterly disappointed. His parched throat burned from the arid climate.

They are not coming for you.

The whispers plagued him constantly wearing him down. His feet shuffled along the ground kicking up pebbles and dust. His head throbbed relentlessly as he wished for relief.

You are ours now.

"No," whispered Ryk. He had no clue to whom he spoke.

"Ryk!"

The faint voice tickled his ears. He turned his head a bit, not believing what he heard having been fooled numerous times. Stopping midstride, Ryk swayed unsteadily on his feet before falling over. He slammed into the earth landing on his back. Heavy eyes stared at the bright sky.

"Ryk!"

A moist, rough tongue licked his face even as whiskers tickled him in an attempt to wake him up.

"Go away," he breathed. "Leave me in peace."

The licking grew more impatient as a paw patted his cheek.

"Ryk!"

He thought he saw a faint shape moving toward him.

"Ryk," it said.

He stared at the humanoid shape unable to focus. "Just let me die."

A rough tug moved him as the female shape bent over him. "Ryk. Ryk, wake up. Can you hear me?"

The voice sounded vaguely familiar. He thought he recognized it. "Nylana?"

Pleased that he was somewhat conscious, Nylana splashed water over Ryk's face before dribbling some into his mouth. "Galdin! I've found him!"

Quick footsteps sounded around them as Galdin and Valn ran over to her. Galdin lifted Ryk's eyelids and checked his breathing. "He's barely alive. We need to get him out of here fast before we all end up in this state."

He lifted Ryk onto his shoulders knowing that within another day the whispers of the canyon would kill them all.

They turned around and froze. All self-will left their minds as their limbs remained still. All thought left them as they stared into the mesmerizing eyes of a Nôk'ta unable to think.

Noticing their plight, Tabs and Magi jumped on the beast breaking its hold over them. The creature grabbed Tabs and flung him to the side. He turned back to the others hoping to reestablish contact. Suddenly, a black shape swooped from the sky and gobbled up the beast before landing next to Nylana.

"Uriel," said Nylana, shaking her head to clear her mind, "I thought you had gone."

"I had," said the dragon, "But as you seem to have a tendency to get into trouble, I remained nearby."

Ryk mumbled incoherently to himself.

"Uriel," said Nylana, "We need to get out of this place."

"Indeed." The dragon eyed them a moment as though he didn't understand Nylana's request. "Oh very well. Climb on my back."

Nylana scooped up Tabs while Valn grabbed Magi. They mounted the dragon with Galdin still holding onto Ryk.

"Hang on," said Uriel as he spread his wings. Dust billowed around them as he beat the ground and took off soaring high into the sky.

"Take us in the direction of Hemíl," ordered Nylana.

Uriel banked to the left in answer as the Whispering Canyons grew smaller.

Chapter V
Onward

Artryl peeked over the ridge he hid behind as he watched the marching army of barbarians heading east toward Hemíl. Though unable to count their numbers, he knew that they outnumbered any army in Tesnayr.

Strange creatures with red eyes followed after them. He did not know what they were, but shied away from them. The clanking links of their armor reverberated around him as they marched past unaware of his presence.

Artryl stretched up for a better look. His hand slipped sending pebbles clacking downward. A barbarian soldier turned toward him. Instantly, Trog dove on top of Artryl covering the boy with his body as he hunkered down.

The man crept toward where Artryl and Trog were; his weapon raised before him. He poked what appeared to be a rock with the tip of his spear. Nothing happened. Satisfied that his imagination played tricks on him, the man rejoined the barbarian ranks.

Trog opened his eyes. He rolled off of Artryl who took several deep breaths. Before the boy could speak, Trog wrapped him in his arms and ascended into the sky flying as fast as his wings allowed.

*　　　　　*　　　　　*

Ryk's eyes fluttered open as he regained consciousness. He stared straight into Nylana's face as she leaned over him dabbing his forehead with a moist cloth.

"Welcome back," said Nylana.

"What happened?" asked Ryk as he felt the bandage around his head.

"You hit your head pretty hard and apparently no one warned you about wandering the Whispering Canyons," replied Nylana. She pushed Ryk back down when he tried to sit up. "You need to rest. We're well-protected here."

"I once met a man who had survived those canyons," said Galdin. "He spent his days staring out a window. Never speaking. Never moving. You are lucky to not have lost your mind."

Ryk watched the faint firelight dance on the rock wall next to him. The shadow of a dragon snatched his attention. Frightened, he struggled to get up, but Nylana pushed him down again.

"It's alright," she said, "The dragon is a friend. He saved us all."

Relaxing, Ryk took the bit of food that Nylana handed him. "You came for me."

"Of course I did," said Nylana. "Now eat that and rest. We are not leaving until you are able."

"Sing a song of ale. Drink up before it grows stale," sang Tabs.

"Mulled mead of every spice shall cure me of any vice," Uriel joined in.

"None believe me, thinking me too free," Tabs continued the merry tune.

"Laugh and gurgle all the day. Ale's my friend I say," finished Uriel.

"Is that cat singing a drinking song with a dragon?" asked Ryk with a note of concern.

"If you mean the fur ball with a dung heap for brains, then, yes," replied Galdin.

"Hey," said Tabs. He hopped down from the dragon's paw and walked over to the group. "Singing is good for you."

"If you can carry a tune," snorted Galdin.

Tabs whacked him in the face with his tail. He noticed Ryk reaching for a cup of water. "Here," he said pushing the drink to the man, "Have a drink on me."

"There's fur in it," said Ryk.

"I said it was on me," replied Tabs.

"That's not all that's on you," grumbled Magi.

Uriel chuckled to himself.

A soft note hit Ryk's ears. He looked over and noticed Nylana cleaning the dishes while she hummed to herself, content to be ignored. "What are you singing?"

Nylana looked at him. "Nothing."

"I want to hear it, please," said Ryk.

"Please just tell him otherwise he will never shut up and I will never get any sleep," Magi blurted out.

Galdin thumped her on the head which garnered him a hiss as she stalked off.

"There is a cat that does not appreciate a good song," commented Tabs as he pointed at Magi.

"Not when it comes from you," retorted Magi.

Ryk shushed them. "Please," he said to Nylana.

Nylana settled beside him, relenting. "It is a song about when Queen Amborese married Scypher."

"Sing it for us," said Ryk.

Nylana obliged.

> "To thee I pledge my love and hope,"
> said Scypher to his queen.
> "And I to you; my love and hope,"
> quoth the noble Amborese.
> And thus was born the age of peace.

The short melody only took a moment to recite. No one said a word. Nylana stood up and walked away. "You should sleep," she told Ryk.

"We all should," said Valn stretching out.

Galdin picked up his sword prepared to take first watch when Uriel stopped him. "Sleep. No one will dare attack you this night. Not with a dragon here."

Not one to argue with a dragon, Galdin found a remote area to stretch out and fell fast asleep.

A crisp morning dawn woke everyone from their slumber. Uriel still stood over them poised in a watchful stance. He watched as they each sat up and packed their belongings.

"Morning to you all," said Uriel. "I will take my leave now. But I am certain we will meet again as you always seem to need my services."

The dragon spread his massive wings and took off without another word.

"Not much for good-byes, is he?" said Tabs. "Well, Galdin, I am famished. Rustle me up some grub."

A scowl appeared on Galdin's face at being ordered about by a cat. He remained silent as he bent down and dug through the moist dirt until he found what he looked for. Kneeling before the cat, Galdin held out his palm to Tabs allowing him to see the grub he had pick up. "Your breakfast, sir."

Tabs wrinkled his noise in disgust. "Apparently I must have a word with the cook."

The cat stalked off as Galdin dropped the squirming grub.

"Oh, a grub he thinks I shall eat," sang Tabs as he walked, "But my claw he shall meet."

The others chuckled to themselves.

Nylana handed Galdin a bulging knapsack. "You will carry this. Ryk is too weak to."

"I don't—"

Nylana thrust the bag into Galdin's hands not allowing him to finish his thought. She hurried over to Ryk and helped him up, allowing him to lean on her.

"Face it," said Valn as he walked up, "You're the packhorse."

Galdin groaned as he heaved his pack and the one Nylana had handed him onto his shoulders.

They trekked along the trail at a steady pace, with frequent stops as Ryk still had not fully recovered from his ordeal in the canyon. With Nylana's help, he managed to keep up.

"We should sing a song or something," said Ryk, "To pass the time as we walk."

"I don't know any good songs for traveling," said Nylana. "Perhaps you should save your strength."

They passed a fallen tree with branches scattered around it. Ryk picked one up as it was just the right size to be used as a staff. He tested it nodding to himself as it seemed to support his weight. "Now you may save your strength, my dear lady. This will help me walk."

Nylana looked at him doubtfully, but refused to question him.

"A song a song," sang Tabs, "My good fellow, give us a song."

"One of these days I am going to put a muzzle on that cat," grumbled Galdin to himself.

"I'll help you," added Magi.

Ryk ignored them as he thought about a tune that had been popular in his homeland. Humming to himself until he remembered the melody, Ryk began to sing.

> Indeed I am a lowly man.
> I've never owned a bit of land.
> Not a coin in either hand
> Oh, what a lowly man I am.
>
> I once desired a lady fair
> Whose beauty none compared.
> Her scorn proved more than I could bear.
> Oh, what a lowly man I am.
>
> So, on a boat I crossed the sea
> To a place where none wanted me.

"Aha," said I as I laughed with glee.
Oh, what a lowly man I am.

Far and wide did I travel;
Going where I was able.
Sleeping in a poor man's stable.
Oh, what a lowly man I am.

So here I am at last
Where I found a noble lass
Whose love is softer than the grass.

Ryk paused as he and Nylana looked at each other with tender expressions. Realizing where he was, Ryk pulled his gaze away and finished the song.

Oh what a joyous man I am!

Not to be outdone in the singing department, Tabs continued as he merrily pranced around.

But a cat you need
To keep you on task.
Need to know, just ask.
The cat knows better than thee.

"That is the only smart thing you have said all morning," Magi chided Tabs.

Galdin scanned the horizon gaging the distance to Hemíl and the time needed to get there. His brow furrowed as he realized that they had wasted too many hours in the Whispering Canyons. "We should quicken our pace," he said, "Or we will never reach Hemíl in time. Valn, help Nylana with Ryk."

Galdin moved closer to Ryk so he could speak more privately. "I know you are still ill, but we must hurry."

"Set the pace and I will keep up," Ryk said.

Galdin clasped the man's shoulder before he pushed ahead. He hoped they reached the Keep of Edrei in time for Nylana to meet with Lord Stefon.

Chapter VI
Night's Farewell

"What is this place?" asked Tami as she looked upward staring at the cliff face and the homes that were built into it. Dark holes dotted the rock wall as narrow steps led to each one.

"I assume cliff dwellers used to live here," answered Narúl as he climbed up one of the narrow stairs. "I found this place long ago. It is a good spot to stop and rest." He held his hand out for Tami who took it allowing him to help her up.

Tami eyed the ruined cliff dwellings. "How long has it been abandoned?"

"Hard to say. There was no life here when I found it. It is just as barren each time I pass through here."

He clambered up a couple more levels having to assist Tami each time.

"How far up are we going?" asked Tami.

"To the top."

Tami almost fainted when Narúl's answer registered. There were at least seven more levels to climb. Narúl caught her as she leaned precariously close to the edge. "Must it be so high?"

"Afraid of heights?"

"No," spat Tami as she climbed higher; her face getting paler with each step.

Chuckling to himself, Narúl lifted the girl over the last edge. He brushed the cobwebs away as he stepped through a dark opening and into the vacant interior. He found a discarded table cloth and hung it like a curtain covering the entrance. He lit a small fire; enough to warm them, but not too big so as to attract attention.   Noticing Tami's shivering form, Narúl wrapped his cloak around her shoulders.

"Even in the warm season, the mountains can get cold," he said.

"How much farther?"

"Maybe a day's walk," said Narúl.

"Tell me about your home," said Tami.

"This is my home," Narúl replied.

Tami glared at him. He knew what she meant.

"I come from a place far across the sea. It is filled with coarse sand. A man can wander for days before finding water.

"I was captured by a neighboring tribe that sold me to a trader. Later, I was brought to a strange land where once again I was sold before ending up here. And you know the rest."

"But why remain here?" asked Tami. "Why didn't you ever return to your home?"

"This is my home now," repeated Narúl. "My sons would be grown now. For me to return would bring shame upon my family. I will never do that.

"When a man is taken captive it is considered the gravest of dishonors. My wife would have mourned my passing long ago. For her sake, it is best if I do not return."

"Doesn't seem fair," muttered Tami.

"Our ways seem strange to you."

"I just don't understand how returning to your homeland would take away your honor," said Tami.

"And what honor would I gain by forsaking my oath to my lady?"

Tami didn't answer.

"I will meet them again, even if it is not in this life."

"She looks up to you. I can tell. I never thought that one raised in the palace would have such respect for any below her station."

"Because she believes no one is below her station," said Narúl, "Unlike most, Nylana has realized that all are equal under the eyes of the heavens. All deserve to be treated as men."

"I've been on my own for as long as I can remember," said Tami. "Mostly I get by collecting coins for a few magic tricks. At least, for the ones that don't backfire."

A noise outside caught their attention. Quickly, Narúl doused the fire before peeking through the doorway. Below them rested a contingent of barbarians. Many prepared meals over fires, while other sharpened weapons. From the way they acted, Narúl guessed that they were headed to Hemíl.

"I thought you said that no one knew of this place," whispered Tami.

"I guess I was wrong. We need to leave."

Narúl slipped outside. Darkness had fallen. He eased himself to the level directly below them. With care, he helped Tami down. A small gap stood before them. Narúl jumped across motioning for Tami to follow. Uneasy, she hopped to the other side; her feet making soft plops on the rock.

Strong arms led her to a set of steps that progressed downward. Cautiously, the two took a zigzag route to avoid the barbarians.

Tami's foot slipped. Quickly, Narúl grasped her hand before she tumbled below. Both paused, looking down to make certain they hadn't been noticed. Narúl lowered her gently to the ledge below them. He scrambled down past her and to the next level.

"Come on," he whispered.

Carefully, Tami eased herself to where Narúl stood. He hopped to the bottom level with Tami close behind. Making certain no one saw them, Narúl guided Tami away into the protection of darkness.

*   *   *

Galdin walked alone in the darkness letting only the quarter moon light his path. Events had prevented him from saying a final farewell to Trya; something he owed her. While the others slept, he searched for the necessary items hoping to find them. Unaware of a small shadow following him, Galdin carefully checked the plants for the specific ones he needed.

A twig snapped under his foot. Cursing his lack of stealth, he looked behind to make certain that the others hadn't woken. A quick glance told him that they still slept soundly. He turned back coming face to face with a pair of glowing, amber eyes.

"You won't find it here," said Magi as she stepped out of the bushes.

"I don't know what you're talking about," said Galdin.

Magi slapped him with her bushy tail. "If you insist on playing this game you will lose."

"What makes you so certain?"

"People always lose to the cat." Magi smirked in her whiskers as Galdin watched her. "I know what it is you seek and if you follow me, I will take you to it."

Galdin did not move.

"This way. Now." Magi hopped to the ground and trotted off. She moved gracefully making certain that Galdin had no difficulty following her in the dark. They pushed past overlapping trees and thick brush to a secret place that Magi had known her whole life. Galdin gasped when they came upon it.

Mounds of flowers twinkled in the darkness forming bright colors despite the dark night. A patch of sage rested in the center. Wisps of wind brushed the flowers lifting bunches of them into the air as they danced upon the breeze and swirled around Galdin whispering to him.

"What is this place?" he asked.

"I don't know," said Magi. "I found it once on my travels and have never forgotten it."

"Travels?"

"I was not always at the palace of Norlyk. I am well over seventy."

"Does Nylana know of this place?"

"Yes," came a soft voice from behind.

Galdin whirled around.

Nylana looked at him, sorrow etched on her face. "Yes, I know of it. Magi brought me here once when I was thirteen."

"I thought—"

"You were the only one who cared for Trya?" Nylana stepped past him and into the field of multicolored flowers. She reached down and grasped a handful of orange mums and yellow lilies. "Here," she handed Galdin the plants.

He laid his cloak on the ground and placed them within it. Slowly, the three meandered through the field picking irises, begonias, crocuses, and daisies. Carefully, Galdin cut away some sage tying it into a bundle.

They carried everything back to camp. Valn awaited them, which did not surprise Galdin.

"Here," said Valn pointing to a pile of granite rock. "I gathered these while you were away."

"You only pretended to be asleep," whispered Galdin to Nylana.

"Who's pretending?" yawned Tabs.

Galdin went to the granite rocks. Carefully, he placed them in a circle making certain that four of the stones marked the four corners of the earth. He placed the sage in the middle and lit it allowing it to smoke. Gently, Galdin laid the flowers around the smoldering sage. Magi pushed a stray one back into the bunch.

"Here," said Nylana handing Galdin the blue rose.

"Keep it," said Galdin. "It was given to you."

In response, Nylana plucked a handful of petals from the rose and sprinkled them upon the mound of flowers. They dotted it like confetti.

In the tradition of the elves, Galdin remained silent for several moments allowing the sage to free Trya's spirit and send it to the world beyond. "Na hak'kamin. Na-kacuwe se-serin," he said after the allotted time had passed.

A breeze rose up sending its tendrils towards them. Slowly, the flowers rose into the air swirling around them until they floated away towards the moon.

Ni'lee y'lee.

"Long ago she ran away from home," said Galdin, "Now the forests of Belarnia will await the arrival of one who will never return."

Nylana and the others watched as Galdin conducted the final rites and said one last farewell to a friend.

Soft steps echoed behind them. They all whirled around to find three unicorns; one with a badly injured leg. The injured unicorn was supported on each side by his companions.

"We are sorry to have disturbed you," said one, "We are merely passing through."

"You survived," said Nylana.

"We are the only survivors of the destruction of our home," said the unicorn. "We fled to the mountains here and are headed to Belarnia."

"Come with us," Nylana urged.

"I am sorry, my lady, but we will not. We shall seek refuge in Belarnia, from there we will leave these lands."

Nylana's downcast face did not go unnoticed.

"Do not be so disheartened," said the unicorn, "The world is changing and our time is ending."

"Everything is changing," said Nylana.

"As all things must eventually."

Galdin pointed out the injured unicorn to Nylana. He took her hand and led her to the wounded creature. "If you'll permit her."

The wounded unicorn bowed.

Gently, Nylana placed her hand upon the unicorn's leg. A breeze whispered around them as healing power flowed from Nylana and into the unicorn's leg, mending what had been broken.

"Thank you," said the healed unicorn.

"We are sorry about you friend," said the unicorn that had spoken first. "And we wish you luck in your quest. We must take our leave now."

The three magnificent beasts continued downhill, allowing themselves to be concealed by the night. Galdin watched them go feeling sorry for their plight as solemnness filled his heart. He glanced at Nylana and knew that she felt the same.

*   *   *

Trog placed Artryl gently on the stone steps of the palace of Norlyk. The animal plopped beside Artryl enjoying every second as the boy scratched his floppy ears. Refusing to waste more time, Artryl raced up the steps to the palace doors. A guard stopped him with the point of his spear.

"I have a message for King Krispyn," said Artryl.

"Move along," said the guard not believing the boy.

"I am telling the truth," continued Artryl, "The Lady Nylana sent me with a message."

"Sure she did," scoffed the guard. "Now get going."

Artryl flashed the message before the guard's face revealing the unmistakable seal upon it. The guard's expression changed as he recognized the mark of Nylana. Swiftly, he opened the door ushering Artryl inside.

"Wait here," said Artryl to Trog as he stepped inside.

The boy trotted after the guard's long strides as he attempted to keep up. The palace seemed changed since he had left; darker as if a shadowy presence had taken hold. Speeding past doorways and turning many corners, they finally arrived at the throne room. The guard held out his arm stopping Artryl.

The big man swept inside bowing low before Krispyn who sat upon the throne. His advisor, Shelwyk, stood nearby.

"My king," said the guard, "A messenger from your sister has arrived."

"Send him in," said Krispyn.

The guard waved his armored hand at Artryl who ran in. He stopped before the king and bowed clumsily unsure of how to present himself. "Krispyn," said Artryl trying to sound braver than he felt.

A sharp intake of breath snatched his attention. One of the nobles present stared at him as though he had committed the gravest of insults.

"I meant no disrespect," stammered Artryl, "Your sister always insists I use her name."

Smiling, Krispyn silenced those within the room who murmured to themselves. "No need to apologize. There is no law that forbids addressing the king by his name."

Pleased that he was forgiven, Artryl held Nylana's message to Krispyn. Krispyn took it and read it.

Krispyn,

The boy here is my personal envoy and should be treated with the respect due. Though young, he is a brave lad.

As you read this, I should be entering Hemil. There I plan to talk to Lord Stefon. Lord Belznyc has refused to send help. I regret to inform you that Lord Trisk is dead. La'nar has fallen to Vasagius, the leader of these barbarian forces that invade our land.

I implore you to contact Lord Ardryn and convince him to ride with you to Hemil. See to it that Sym'Dul is able to send their forces as well. I am sorry if I do not have happier news.

Awaiting your reply.
Nylana

Krispyn folded the note tucking it in his pocket.

"My king," said the guard reappearing a second time, "A messenger from Belarnia."

What timing, thought Krispyn. "Send him in."

The Elven messenger knelt before the king before standing straight and delivering his message. "I come from Lord Ardryn of the elves. He has requested your presence in Belarnia."

"Tell him that I shall be there within the week," replied Krispyn dismissing the elf.

"My king," said Shelwyk, "It takes at least twice that to reach Belarnia."

"I will make it within a week if I ride alone. You Shelwyk shall lead the army of Tesnayr to Hemíl. Tell my sister that I have gone to meet with the elves, but will be there as quickly as I can. Now go."

Shelwyk saluted the king and walked out.

"Artryl," Krispyn motioned for the boy to walk with him to a secluded area of the chamber. "I have a reply for my sister, but would prefer not to write it down. How is your memory?"

"Excellent, sir."

"Good. Tell her that I have left to meet with Lord Ardryn. Whatever his sentiments, I shall be in Hemíl before the month is out. And remind her to be careful."

"You don't need to worry about that. Galdin is with her," Artryl blurted out.

Chuckling, Krispyn clasped the boy's shoulder. "I shall keep that in mind." He steered Artryl back to the center of the room. "Guard, take the boy to the kitchens. See to it he is given a hot meal and a place to rest for the night."

Saluting, the guard motioned for Artryl to follow him out.

*   *   *

Narúl and Tami glanced around nervously as they were led into the great hall of the keep to meet with Lord Stefon. Narúl had not expected the Lord of Hemíl to greet them, but mentioning Nylana's name had an effect.

"Leave us," said Lord Stefon to the guards. "So you bring word from the Lady Nylana?"

"Yes," replied Narúl. "She sends word that she is on her way here as we speak. She hopes to be here within the week and desires to meet with you."

"Why did she not travel with you? Why send just the pair of you?"

"Circumstances forced her hand, sir," said Narúl. "But she wanted you to be warned that barbarian forces have overrun the five lands. Belyndril has fallen and Lord Trisk is believed dead."

"And MurDair?" asked Lord Stefon.

"He has refused her request for aid."

Lord Stefon paced to another part of the chamber pondering Narúl's message. He knew of the barbarian invasion, but hadn't realized to what extent it had affected the land. "I shall inform my guard to be on the lookout for Nylana."

"Thank you, my lord," said Narúl.

"You both look tired," said Lord Stefon, "Go to the kitchen and get something to eat. One of my men will take you to where you can rest afterward."

Narúl and Tami bowed low and left. He hoped Nylana would arrive soon.

*   *   *

Artryl chewed happily on the turkey leg in his hand. He hadn't realized just how hungry he was. Trog sat before him with a pleading look on his face hoping for a bite. Chuckling, Artryl tossed the animal some of his food. Trog snatched it out of the air never letting it touch the floor.

"I see you have a loyal friend there," said Petra as he sat beside the boy.

"His name is Trog."

Trog wagged his tail happily with his tongue sticking out of his mouth. His floppy ears waved wildly at the mention of his name. Petra tossed the creature a turkey leg.

"How is Nylana?" asked Petra.

"Well," Artryl said around a mouthful of turkey, "She misses you. She seems sad sometimes, but always tries to hide it."

"She has much on her mind," said Petra. "Will you be returning to her?"

"Yes, but Trog is very tired. I do not know if he could fly us both there."

"You should come with me," said Petra. "Shelwyk is leading some men to Nylana and I am going with him. Would you and Trog, here, wish to join me?"

In answer to the wizard's question, Trog pushed his head against the man's hand chirping merrily.

"I think that means, 'yes'," said Artryl.

"Of course it does. Would you like to see a magic trick?"

"Sure."

Petra did a swirling movement with his hand before reaching up behind Artryl's ear where he pulled out a coin.

"I know that one," laughed Artryl, "Even I can do it."

"Ah, but can you do this?" Petra held his hand out and in it a muffin appeared from thin air. He tossed it to the boy.

Artryl bit into the savory texture of the muffin allowing the crumbs to dot his chin. "Wow. Can you teach me to do that?"

"We'll see." Petra stood up. "I'll meet you when it's time to leave."

A sorrowful whine stopped the wizard. Trog looked at him with the saddest expression he had ever seen. He held his hand out as another muffin appeared and tossed it to the animal. Trog caught it swallowing the muffin in one gulp. Hastily, he searched the ground for more; his nose sweeping the stone floor as he breathed in bits of dirt.

Laughing, Petra left the kitchens.

*   *   *

The orange sun hung low in the sky as they stood on a precipice looking down upon the Keep of Edrei and all of Hemíl. "There's the keep," said Galdin, "If we hurry, we might make it there before nightfall."

Galdin glanced at Ryk who leaned heavily on his staff. "How are you doing?"

"Don't you worry about me," puffed Ryk. "I will make it."

Nylana gently touched Ryk's arm out of concern. A bit for the magic within her flowed into Ryk of its own volition, giving him renewed strength.

Ryk straightened himself. "Let's move. The longer I remain here, the more I'll want to stay put."

Galdin agreed. He helped Nylana down to the trail. "I hope Lord Stefon listens to you."

"So do I," said Nylana.

One by one, they hiked down a narrow trail to the bottom of the ravine which led to the Keep of Edrei. All of them marveled at the construction of the keep and how it had managed to withstand over 1500 years of erosion and various wars.

King Edrei must have known what he was doing when he built this, thought Nylana to herself. She only hoped that she could be as wise.

Chapter VII
Lost Hope

Nylana ran her fingers over the engraved markings on the stone wall; markings etched in time. Legend said that Tesnayr himself had put it there and that time had not the courage to wash it away. She wondered what had been going through his mind as he forever marked his name in the stone. *What trials led him here?*

"Nylana," Galdin approached, "Lord Stefon will see us now."

Regally, Nylana rose to her feet taking a momentarily glance at the twinkling stars in the blackened sky. "How will I tell him that Belyndril is lost and that MurDair has abandoned us?"

"We will tell him together." Galdin held his arm out for her. Nylana took it and together they walked to the great hall of the keep where the others waited.

The massive doors opened before them as they stepped into the firelight. Lord Stefon stood at the far end silhouetted by the torches. "Lady Nylana, what is all this? I was under the impression that you were coming alone."

"It is not safe for me to travel alone," answered Nylana. "And you will speak to both me and my brother, Galdin."

"I have already heard the news about La'nar and Lord Trisk," said Lord Stefon. "It is unfortunate."

"Vasagius leads the barbarian forces. They are on their way here as we speak," said Nylana.

"If they haven't already arrived," commented Lord Stefon.

"Krispyn, your king, asks for your help," said Nylana, "I have been sent—"

"My help?" Lord Stefon stared into Nylana's eyes. "Where was he when Hemíl needed him? For the past year he has treated us lords like vermin demanding more of our resources. We are sovereign lands who only acquiesce to the King of Tesnayr when we choose. We are not slaves to his will."

"Lord Stefon, there is more at stake than just the sovereignty of Hemíl," said Nylana.

"Unless Krispyn relinquishes some of his claim of lordship over us, I'll not help you."

"Then you will die," said Galdin, his voice carried through the chamber.

"Are you threatening me?" demanded Lord Stefon.

"Merely stating a fact," replied Galdin. "Vasagius will come here. Of that you can be certain. He cares nothing for your grievances against Krispyn. He will burn this place to the ground and the people within it. For your own sake, and for the sake of your people, you'd do well to heed Nylana's request."

"And how do I know I can trust you—you who worked as a mercenary most your life. Yes, I know of your past."

"Then trust her." Galdin pointed at Nylana.

Men disguised in the armor of Hemíl, but with barbarian crests beneath, tiptoed through the alleys of the keep remaining in the shadows. In groups of three they veered off toward the armory. Other groups darted for the gates and the outer defenses with its positioned ballistas. Each group drenched their targets with containers of grease. One by one, strategic areas within the keep burst into flames.

Satisfied, the raiders ripped off their outer armor to reveal their true identities. They slashed at the screaming masses of people around them who vainly tried to escape.

At the gate, the clinking of coins sounded as the guard was paid to walk away. Grinning with satisfaction, the barbarians turned the wheel that opened the gates to the keep. Grinding and groaning filled the air as they revealed the horde of savages waiting on the other side.   Deafening battle cries overwhelmed the area as armed men poured into the city wreaking havoc.

The wails of women resonated off the stone walls as invading forces slaughtered them and the infants in their arms.   People scrambled in every direction as they fled.   Savagely hunted by the invading force, their lifeless corpses filled the streets as blood pooled around them.

Nylana rushed to the window when she heard the screams. She flung open the glass watching in horror as a black mass of barbarian forces entered the city cutting down any in their path. She surveyed the fires that now consumed the Keep of Edrei. Ears aching from all of the shrieks, Nylana turned away.

Galdin appeared beside her.   He looked out at the keep assessing the situation.   Marking where all of the fires burned, Galdin estimated how much time they had before the flames spread. People below him fled for their lives. He noted the open gates and the empty guard tower that stood nearby.

"Narúl," said Galdin.   "See that tower with the catapults by it?"

Narúl nodded.

"Take a garrison with you.   Use the catapults to bring the tower down. Make certain that it closes off the open gate."

Narúl saluted. He whistled at a garrison of men who raced toward the courtroom chamber to protect Lord Stefon. Without argument, they followed the man to the lower level of the keep.

"Lord Stefon," said Galdin. "It appears that war has come to you."

Lord Stefon raced to the window watching in horror as his home was destroyed by savages.

"You know this keep far better than anyone here," said Galdin. "Bring all you can to the upper levels of the keep. Take Nylana with you."   He pulled Lord Stefon closer so he could whisper in his ear. "Keep her safe."

"You have my word," replied Lord Stefon.

"Now wait—" began Nylana.

"You stay with him," Galdin ordered; his tone commanded obedience. "And take Tami with you."

Relenting, Nylana followed after Lord Stefon with Tami close behind.

"Ryk," said Galdin, "You are with me."

Galdin raced out of the chamber finding cowering soldiers trying to escape the chaos.

"Cowards!" roared Galdin, "Why do you huddle together like children when your bravery is required elsewhere? All of you with me or let it be known that Hemíl fell because her soldiers had turned into withering old women."

Slowly, the soldiers rose to their feet. Galdin glared at each of them before heading out to face his enemy. The chastised soldiers trailed behind. They stormed the edges of the second level.

"Block this entrance," ordered Galdin. "Do not let them pass."

Men barricaded the entrance to the second level of the keep. They piled bits of boulders and broken sides of building as people rushed past.

Narúl slid down the rails of the stairwell hastening to the area Galdin had directed. A burly man stepped in front of him. Ducking back to dodge the blow to his head, Narúl lurched forward, straightened, and twisted around while plunging his blade into the man. He shouldered another barbarian that headed for him forcing him over the side of the stairwell.

"Put the catapults over there," ordered Narúl.

Men rolled the two catapults to where Narúl had indicated. They pushed the wheels gradually steering them away. Grunting and sweat marked their movements.

"Line them up carefully," said Narúl as the catapults were finally positioned.

Men loaded debris into the catapult bucket as they were carefully aimed. Swarms of barbarians enveloped them. One attacked those with the catapults.   Others from the garrison jumped in defending their comrades.

"Ready," yelled Narúl. "Fire!"

The boulder arced high above the fray before slamming into its target. A soft roar rumbled around them growing in intensity as the supporting wall of the tower crumbled away. Slowly, it tipped over heading straight for the open gate of the keep.

"Brace yourselves," shouted Narúl.

He and his men sprinted away as the guard tower fell over. Dust and rocks flew everywhere engulfing them as the stone turret crashed into the ground. Men gagged on the clouds of silt. Panicked shrieks rose up from the barbarians that stood in the path of the falling tower calling for help as it crushed them to death.

Coughing, Narúl turned just as one man attacked him.   He brought his sword up plunging it into the man's belly. Shaking him off, Narúl whirled around slashing at another that made for him. More came from the debris as they scrambled over it to get inside the keep.

Narúl took out his hatchet. A wild man with flaming hair headed straight for him yelling loudly. Narúl caught the man's weapon with his hatchet twisting it out of his hands. Instantly, he rammed his blade into the wild man's stomach and flipped him over onto the ground.

"Sergeant," he yelled at one of the Hemilian soldiers, "Set fire to the thing."

The sergeant snatched a smoldering piece of debris. With expert skill, he flung it toward the place where the demolished tower stood. Flames roared to life engulfing the area and any men in their way. Terrified screams pierced the night as people burned alive.

A sharp whistle caught Narúl's attention. Galdin stood in the open waving at him.   Understanding the message, Narúl motioned for his men to follow. They raced back through the streets of the keep to the second level.

"Check that building there," yelled Galdin.

Ryk ran to where Galdin had pointed hoping to find some weapons. The main armory had been burned to the ground, but smaller ones still remained. He opened the door only to have to jump back as flames lunged for him.

"These are all gone! Consumed by the fire."

Galdin kicked a barbarian away from him and over the edge. He looked about at the chaos. *How did they get here without being noticed?*

A dark shape loomed in the archway of the front gates. Galdin stared at it for several moments before realizing that this was the same cloaked figure from La'nar. Taking an arrow, Galdin aimed and fired. The arrow whizzed through the air heading for its target. Before it struck, the shadowy figure plucked it from the air and snapped it in half.

A wĕdlym climbed over the top of the outer wall settling next to the cloaked figure. Its massive head faced Galdin. The cloaked man snapped his fingers. Instantly, the creature raced across the ground trampling any in its path as it headed for Galdin; its six feet moved in unison leaving holes in the stone.

Galdin braced himself. He lunged to the ground as the creature reached him and rolled across the stone away from it before jumping back on his feet.

"Galdin!" yelled Ryk as he ran for his friend.

The wĕdlym whipped its tail catching Ryk in the middle and flinging him across the keep. Ryk crashed into a solid wall crumpling to the ground.

"Ryk!"

Galdin faced the massive creature. From a distance Narúl raced for him. The wĕdlym snapped at Galdin. He dodged out of the way swiping his sword across its snout. Focused on the beast's teeth, Galdin never noticed the claw-like tail heading for him. Within seconds, it scooped him up forcing him to drop his sword.

Narúl jumped in front of the beast with his blade up. Undeterred, the wĕdlym slammed a foot into the man pinning him to the ground. Spit dribbled from its teeth as it leered over Narúl. A whistle stopped the creature. Instantly, it took off heading for the cloaked figure still holding Galdin out to him.

Elsewhere in the keep, Nylana helped a mother with her young child escape falling debris. She and Tami had searched buildings for people directing them to the upper section of the keep.

"People of Hemíl," yelled the dark stranger as the creature held Galdin up for all to see, "I give you your hero."

Galdin struggled helplessly against the creature's grip.

"No!" Nylana's voice echoed across the keep filling every crevice.

She watched in horror as the life was slowly squeezed from her brother; fire filled her eyes. She pulled out her sword holding it high above her; the blade glowed ominously displaying all of its markings. Wind whipped around Nylana as lightning flared in the night sky. A bolt struck the blade filling it with power that coursed through her.

As though in a trance, Nylana hurled the sword of Tesnayr at the wĕdlym striking it in the heart. The hideous monster crumpled to the ground releasing Galdin as it died. Galdin snatched the sword. Its power filled him as though welcoming his touch. He whirled around to strike the sorcerer, but the man had gone.

Despite the chaos of battle, Galdin glanced at Nylana who stood transfixed; her steely eyes burned as she stared at him with a luminescent glow surrounding her. A dash of fur darted across the stone surface of the keep heading straight for her.

"Nylana!" shouted Magi.

Slowly, Nylana returned to her normal state regaining her senses.

"We have to leave. The keep is lost," said Magi.

"The cat is right," added Lord Stefon as the barbarian army continued to pillage.

"Tabs and Valn found a way out," said Magi, "Get these people to the lower levels of the keep." Magi darted off to tell the others.

Galdin watched as his sister ran off with Lord Stefon and Tami close behind. He started for them only to be stopped by a mass of scrambling, fighting savages. He arm jerked upward knocking a barbarian's sword across the ground. Unused to his movements being dictated by an object, he moved clumsily in an effort to keep up. Suddenly, the sword moved his arm in a tilted jab catching the barbarian in the stomach. Warm blood oozed over Galdin's hand.

The blade shone brilliantly dousing the night as its power surged up Galdin's arm filling his entire being. He finally understood what it wanted. Charging across the fray, he swerved and dodged attacks as the weapon guided his every move. With the expertise of a master swordsman, Galdin tore through the fight after Nylana.

"Galdin!" shouted Magi forcing him to stop momentarily, "To the lower level."

He raced away. Galdin charged up some stairs heading straight for the back part of the keep. He remembered a stairwell there that would take him to the bottom, interior level of the fortress.

Magi scurried between stomping feet and falling victims as she hurried to where Ryk and Narúl had to be. She pricked an invader's ankle as she passed. Her small form went unnoticed as she avoided people's carelessness. She scooted past the chaos stopping short when she noticed Ryk standing dangerously close to a ledge fighting against two barbarians. His feet hung over the edge as he was pushed closer.

Quickly, Magi scrambled up a post leaping onto an overhang. With great agility, she sprung upward gripping the stone ledge with her sharp claws. Just before Ryk lost his balance, the cat lunged at one of the men he was fighting. She scratched and clawed the man tearing his skin.

Using the opportunity, Ryk pushed himself away from the edge and plowed into the second barbarian. They tumbled to the ground rolling across it; each reaching for a weapon. Ryk elbowed the man in the face. He rolled away lunging for his sword. Grasping it, he raised it before him deflecting a blow. The man untangled their weapons, but not before Ryk stabbed him with his spare dagger.

The man charged him. Ryk jumped to his feet bracing for the impact. From nowhere Magi leaped over Ryk's head and plowed into the man's face. Ryk rammed his heel into the man's stomach. With speed, Ryk seized the man's hair ripping his head up so as to expose the tender part of his neck before slicing it.

"Where is Narúl?" Magi demanded.

Before Ryk could answer, a strange creature whose entire body turned into a wing attacked from behind. Spindly arms tipped with hooks shot out of its stick-like middle swiping at them. Ryk jumped back barely avoiding its attack. He slashed with his sword. The steel blade bounced off of the creature's wing as it wrapped itself up. Instantly, it unwound itself reaching out with its hooks.

The whoop-whoop-whoop of a flying hatchet sounded in Ryk's ears as it flew past his head striking the strange beast in the neck. Screeching, the creature writhed and shriveled into a wrinkled lump as it died. Narúl sprang from the fray, snatched his axe and turned on Ryk.

"It's me," shouted Ryk, holding up his hands.

Narúl stopped mid-swing.

"Get to the lower levels of the keep," ordered Magi as she leapt onto an abandoned wagon so as to match their height.

"On whose command?" challenged Narúl.

"Nylana's," answered Magi before running off.

Narúl grabbed Ryk and half-pulled, half-carried him as he followed the cat. They pushed their way through the mass of fighting men never pausing even to defend themselves.

"Here," said Magi as she squirted through a partly open door.

Narúl pushed Ryk inside and barricaded the opening. They marched swiftly down the stone corridor descending deep into the Keep of Edrei. The cat darted around a corner that led them to where Tabs waited.

"Not so fast," said Ryk.

"Learn to keep up," quipped Magi.

"There," said Lord Stefon pointing to the entrance of the inner keep. A boulder slammed into the buildings above them.

Tami leapt out of the way as debris fell around her. She muttered a spell to deflect the crumbling bits of stone. They slowed slightly before crashing on the ground around them.

"Inside all of you," yelled Nylana as she pushed people along. One by one they hurried through the doorway. "Quickly!"

A log like creature peeled away from the side of the building unwrapping itself making its body into a single wing. Darts shot out of its middle striking those around it. Men fired arrows at the strange creature and attacked with their swords. The thing just wrapped itself up spinning wildly in a circle as steel and arrows bounced off. Occasionally, the winged creature opened up shooting out more spikes before closing tight again.

Galdin flung Tami to the ground as the thing tried to swipe at her. He whipped his blade up to block the attack. The moment the steel touched the creature it cried in anguish. Realizing that the glowing blade harmed it, Galdin jumped up and rammed his blade through the creature's back. It seized up going rigid before collapsing. Wasting no time, Galdin pushed Tami through the doorway.

"Galdin!"

Nylana hunkered over a frightened child as another of the creatures whirled towards her. He tossed her the sword. She caught it and stabbed the thing in the middle. It too withered. Another fired darts at her. Dictating her movements, the sword forced her arm in a position where it blocked the deadly spikes.

Scrambling over to her, Lord Stefon seized the frightened child and hurried toward the doorway. Years spent as a soldier guided him as he dodged and blocked as he fought single-handedly while cradling the child. Galdin took the child and shoved him through the doorway to a man with outstretched arms. He whirled back around and kicked one of the creatures away from Lord Stefon.

"Go," said Galdin to the man. "Take these people to safety."

Nodding, Lord Stefon disappeared through the opening.

Galdin searched for Nylana. She still battled against the creatures and invaders. Her fluid movements mesmerized him for a moment as he watched. He readied his bow and fired striking one of the barbarians in the neck.

Unable to break away from the onslaught, Nylana pulled out the horn of Selexia. Remembering Uriel's words she blew on it. Instantly, a deafening shriek filled the area causing them to cover their ears. Not caring which dragons appeared, or how many, Nylana blew harder on the horn.

The flapping of giant wings sounded. Looking up, Nylana saw the shape of Uriel as he hovered overhead lowering himself. A winged creature lunged for Nylana. Sharp teeth appeared snatching up the beast and flinging it away. Uriel whipped his tail around sweeping an entire group of barbarian men over the wall.

"We need time to escape," said Nylana.

Uriel lowered his head in a slight bow. Spreading his wings, he rose into the air, heading for the thick of the battle. Galdin snatched Nylana's arm and pulled her toward the doorway. Just before she stepped through an explosion shook the entire area. Turning around, Nylana watched helplessly as two catapults fired at the dragon bombarding the mighty beast.

"No!" shrieked Nylana. She started for the dragon. Strong arms seized her around the middle and forced her through the door.

Once inside, Galdin barricaded it. He caught Nylana as she tried to push past him. "You can't help him."

"But I must."

"If you go out there you'll be killed." Galdin pushed her forward toward the group of people that awaited them. Sulking, Nylana went.

The dark hallway matched their mood as they hurried through to where Magi had said Tabs awaited them. They twisted around corners and sped down steps going deeper. Finally, a pair of glowing eyes greeted them.

"It's about time you got here," said Tabs. "We've been waiting a long time."

Ryk, Valn, and Narúl appeared as well; for which Nylana was grateful.

"Which way?" asked Galdin.

"This way," said Tabs.

They followed the orange tabby to a slit in the wall. The thin opening was barely wide enough for a man to step through.

"This leads to a tunnel which I believe we can use to escape this place," said Tabs.

Galdin motioned people onward. One by one, they squeezed through the small opening and into pitch blackness.

Magi took the lead. Being a cat, she had no difficulty seeing in the dark. "This way," she said, her voice echoing off the tunnel walls. Every few feet, she spoke so that the people could follow her.

"How far is it?" asked Galdin of Tabs.

"I don't know," answered the cat, "But I do not think it is very far."

"Up ahead," said Magi, "I see the opening."

A wide hole stood frozen at the end of the tunnel allowing them to escape the darkness and re-enter the world. Lord Stefon stepped through first. He looked back at the Keep of Edrei; his home for the last twenty years.

Fire consumed it as the invading forces plundered what they could. More screams echoed across the ravine reminding him that they had failed to save everyone. Glancing around, Lord Stefon realized that they were on the side of the canyon. A trail stretched out before his feet. Smoke in the east caught his attention. With a heavy heart, Lord Stefon realized that Swalya had been overrun as well.

Galdin appeared beside him. "Where to?"

Controlling his anger, Lord Stefon answered in an even voice. "This trail will lead us up to higher ground and away from here. If we move quickly, we should be gone before dawn."

"Lead the way."

As frightened refugees exited the small tunnel they formed a line that snaked up the canyon wall and over its ridge. They stepped carefully, using their hands at times to balance themselves.

Nylana turned back to the keep. A tear slid down her cheek as she felt abandonment and guilt. Memories of La'nar coursed through her mind; events that seemed far in the past.

"My lady." Narúl held his hand out or her.

"I just left him there," said Nylana; speaking of Uriel.

Somehow, Narúl knew of whom Nylana spoke. "I am certain he does not feel that way."

Gratefully, Nylana took Narúl's hand as he helped her climb up.

Busy with their conquest, the barbarian forces never noticed the small group of shadows fleeing into the darkness.

Chapter VIII
Lord Ardryn

Wisps of light danced around Lord Ardryn as he watched the three riders approach. He stood upon the top of the stairs overlooking the forests of Belarnia with the thunder of the waterfall drowning his thoughts. Noting the flag that one of the riders carried, the elf knew that Krispyn had come bearing bad news.

A brown leaf fell from a tree landing delicately by Lord Ardryn's foot. Curious, he reached down and picked it up; studying it. Sadness filled him. Never before had a leaf fallen from the trees of Belarnia. Death had entered the land. The song of the phoenix had ended.

"Na'ha salin. Res-il'han," whispered Lord Ardryn to himself.

The elf glanced at a portrait of the Lord Naganis. He wished he were here now.

After the death of Amborese, Naganis left the lands of Tesnayr vowing to never return. Some said the sea had claimed him. When he left, Ardryn was made Lord of Belarnia. It wasn't long after that that the wizard Zolo disappeared—last seen at the tomb of Amborese.

Colored leaves brushed against the floor as they crept across—another reminder that the world had changed. Glancing at the bottom of the stairs, Ardryn noted that the riders had dismounted. Krispyn walked ahead of his two guards. *Only two guards?*

"King Krispyn," greeted Lord Ardryn, "What brings you here?"

"You know why I have come," replied Krispyn.

"And you are undoubtedly aware that there are few of us elves left," said Lord Ardryn.

"Numbers are unimportant. I need your help. Barbarian invaders have ravaged the five lands. Belyndril and Hemíl are lost. I am afraid MurDair is also as none have heard from Lord Belznyc. Belarnia is next and so is Sym'Dul."

"It is my understanding that the barbarians number more than the stars in the sky," said Lord Ardryn, "How are we to defeat them if they outnumber us so?"

"I do not know."

Lord Ardryn studied Krispyn noting something that he had never seen on the man before: defeat. The once proud king seemed beaten, desperate.

"I haven't many elves."

"I will gladly accept any you can spare."

Lord Ardryn glanced at the forest he had called his home for over five centuries. *How much it has changed.* The music had dimmed. The trees had lost their luster. Many of the elves had left seeking refuge elsewhere. The last days of Belarnia.

"I beg of you, Lord Ardryn," pleaded Krispyn.

"And your sister?"

"Nylana is in Hemíl as we speak. She requests our presence."

Silence ensued as the elf mulled over Krispyn's request.

"Lord Ardryn, I know we have not always agreed on things, but if this is to be the last days of the lands of Tesnayr let us ride out together under one banner."

"Be ready to leave within the hour," said Lord Ardryn as he walked off to summon his elves.

"Thank you," bowed Krispyn with humility. He hurried down the steps to his guards and their horses.

Lord Ardryn watched the young king leave. Much had changed, he thought to himself, but I will not abandon Nylana.

Chapter IX
Uriel's Passing

A black line of soldiers snaked across the Azul Plains as they followed Shelwyk to Hemíl. He traveled at the head of the party carrying out the orders of his king. His black cloak flapped behind him as he rode erect, his face a mask of callousness.

"Where were you two nights ago while we camped?" asked Petra as he rode beside Shelwyk.

"No place that concerns you," said Shelwyk. He kicked his horse and galloped ahead away from the wizard's inquisitiveness.

The clinking and clanking of metal trailed behind as the soldiers marched. Despite their attempts to hide it, fear plagued them. They too had heard the tales of Vasagius and the savages he led. None noticed the shadows that followed them: a boy and his friend.

*   *   *

A black form caught Nylana's attention as she walked with the group to Norlyk. Recognizing it, she bolted for it; her feet pounding the earth as she ran.

Ryk tore off after her. "Nylana!"

Heavy, ragged gasps filled Nylana's ears when she reached it. "Uriel," she said.

"Hello, little runt," wheezed Uriel. "I thought you'd come this way."

Nylana noticed the gashes in the dragon's side. Holes dotted his wings despite his attempt to hide them. Gently, she touched one of the wounds wincing as the sticky blood oozed over her hand.

"It is just a scratch," said Uriel.

"Don't lie to me," said Nylana, "I can heal you."

"No!" Uriel lifted his head so he could look directly into Nylana's eyes. "There is little of me left. Save your strength. You will need it before the end."

"But—"

"No."

Nylana backed away bowing toward the dragon.

"Do not weep for me, little one," said Uriel, "I am an old dragon. Now listen carefully. The barbarians march for you. They plan to take Norlyk and if they do, all will be lost.

"Head for the Black Mountains. Those peaks are treacherous to all, but for you they may prove useful."

"But—"

"Listen!" A fit of coughing racked Uriel's body as he struggled to remain conscious a while longer. "The dragons. There are some in the Black Mountains. A wizard can get you there without delay. Convince them to help you. Though you may find that you already have one ally there."

Uriel's breathing grew shorter and more labored.

"What if they choose to harm me?" asked Nylana choking back her tears.

"They cannot for the same reason that I could never hurt you. The power that dwells within you must be obeyed for it belongs to one far mightier than I.

"Now go. Do as I have said."

Gently, Nylana touched Uriel's snout as the last bit of air escaped his lungs. Slowly, his body turned to marble before transforming into dust. Swirls of it rose into the air carried by the breeze that wept for his passing.

"And so passes Uriel, the noblest of dragons," said Nylana. She repeated a poem she had learned as a child in honor of the dragon.

When Death comes for thee
And asks of me,
  "Who is this man for whom you weep?"
  I shall reply, "My friend of friends."

Ryk placed a hand on her shoulder feeling her sadness. He held her as she wept. "Cry all you want," he said, "I will not let the others see it."

"Thank you," Nylana said.

"No need to thank me," replied Ryk.

Drying her tears, Nylana's face hardened in determination. She strode away from where Uriel had been to her pack horse. As she tied various weapons around her person, Ryk stopped her.

"What do you think you're doing?"

"To do as Uriel asked."

"Stop!" Ryk pulled Nylana to a halt forcing her to face him. "Wait for Krispyn to arrive. He deserves to hear all this from you"

"There isn't time!"

"Well, you are not going alone."

"Why do you care so much?"

Wounded, Ryk looked at Nylana; a gentleness filled his eyes. "Do you really need to ask?"

Nylana lowered her head in shame.

"Since the moment I first saw you in Pras'quel I have loved you. Though a slave, you possessed such noble character—one I had never seen before. When we came here it mattered not that you are the Princess of Tesnayr. And then there is the fact that you broke my nose—and—well—"

Nylana chuckled for a minute.

"A token," Ryk plucked a daisy from the ground and handed it to Nylana. "My love for you will always be here whether you choose to accept it or not."

Nylana took the offering gazing deep within Ryk's eyes. She saw truth and earnest within them.

"Why do you think I stay by your side?"

An arrow whizzed past Nylana's ear.

"Barbarians!" yelled a scout.

The battle cry of a man charging Nylana and Ryk caught their attention. Ryk shoved her out of the way. He grabbed a sword and brought it up just in time to block the attack. Kicking the man in the groin, Ryk untangled their weapons and bashed the hilt into his opponent's face. Quickly, he rammed the point of the blade into the man's chest.

Another attacked from behind. Ryk turned around just in time to see Nylana slice the man's head off.

"Come on," said Ryk as he took hold of her arm and led her away.

"Form a circle with the wagons," ordered Galdin as savages raced for them. "Everyone behind them!"

Quickly, those unable to fight huddled together behind the meager protection of their wagons.

Galdin looked about him gauging the situation. Grossly outnumbered, he knew they had no hope of defending themselves. "Valn, we need archers up top. Narúl, protect the rear."

Both Valn and Narúl dashed off to carry out their orders.

A winged creature plowed into Galdin sending him flying. Dazed, he rose to his knees shaking his head to clear it. The winged creature slammed into him again clipping him in the shoulder. Galdin snatched his sword. He sliced upward deflecting another blow by the beast.

The creature wrapped itself into a thin bundle twirling around Galdin as he spun around attempting to kill it. Every so often, the thing slashed at him with its claws before enveloping itself once more with its wing. Galdin stabbed at it, but to no avail. The outer layer of the wing was impenetrable.

Finally, Galdin stopped. He stood still as the thing danced around him in circles; waiting for the precise moment. Holding his sword before him, he focused his will. The creature unwrapped itself. Seizing his chance, Galdin thrust his sword into its middle until it poked out the other side. Sharp screeches reverberated around him as the creature wailed in pain. Galdin freed his blade. He watched heartlessly as the beast moaned before laying still.

Tabs hid under the piles of items in a wagon. He watched as a couple of barbarians walked cautiously beside it. Once close enough, the cat undid the buckle that held the provisions in place. Precariously piled as they were, the equipment tumbled on top of the two men burying them.

Tabs jumped up sitting erect watching the two squirm under the junk that lay atop them. "Ha! You have to get up early to pull one on old Tabs."

Narúl ducked as a barbarian attacked him forcing the man to roll over his back and crash onto the ground. He whirled around and plunged his weapon into the man's chest.

Another charged him. Ringing filled the air as the two steel blades clashed. Narúl reached behind him for his hatchet. Once he grasped it, he brought it over his head and plunged it into the barbarian's back. Stunned, the man loosened his grip on his weapon allowing Narúl to free their swords. He ripped out his hatchet while simultaneously slicing the man in the stomach.

Two more charged him. In a furious rage, Narúl raced for them. He dodged as one attacked from the left. With fluid movements, Narúl swung his hatchet upward slicing one from groin to neck before turning and ramming his sword into the other's back.

He noticed a man heading for Nylana. She did not see him. Weighing his hatchet in his hand, Narúl took careful aim before throwing it. It caught the savage in the middle of his back. Quickly, Narúl ran to retrieve his weapon.

"You," he called to a group of Hemilian soldiers, "To the rear."

They followed after him.

Nylana and Ryk stood with their backs to a wagon pinned by a wĕdlym. Splinters flew around them as the creature slashed with its tail. Suddenly, a black shape dived out of the sky plowing into the wĕdlym. It was Trog.

Trog hunkered low to the ground growling venomously at the wĕdlym. The creature lunged for him. Trog rolled out of the way before springing to his feet again.

"Hey," yelled Artryl holding a lit torch. The wĕdlym lashed out at him jumping back the moment Artryl waved the torch in its eyes. At the same instant, Trog fastened his teeth on the back of the beast's neck.

Nylana studied the situation a moment. She glanced at her sword which glowed softly. Suddenly, she knew what to do. "Throw me onto its back."

"What?" said Ryk in disbelief.

"Just do it!"

Grudgingly, Ryk held his hands out for Nylana's foot. "Ready?" he asked when she placed her foot in his grip.

"Now!"

Ryk thrust her upward as she jumped sending her flying. Nylana's stomach ached as she landed on the creature's back. Quickly, she scrambled into a seated position straddling it. Allowing the sword to guide her, Nylana plunged it deep within the beast.

Sharp screams echoed around her. She wrenched the sword in deep holding tightly to the hilt so as not to be thrown off. Moving violently, the wĕdlym swiped at any in its path as it slowly ceased its movements.

Ryk rushed over to Nylana to help her down. "That was pure insanity. Don't ever do it again."

"Next time, it's your turn," breathed Nylana.

Trog nuzzled into her licking her hand. Nylana patted his head before running off.

On the only high ground Valn could find, he lined up the archers. Standing in the middle, he raised his sword arm signaling for them to take aim. "Fire!"

Hundreds of arrows flew through the sky darkening it momentarily; each striking its target. Bewildered, Valn looked behind him. A company of elves and men approached, each armed with a bow. They reloaded and fired.

Valn glanced at the battle before him. Riders on horseback rushed toward them in a cloud of dust. Recognizing the crest of Belarnia and Tesnayr, the Byleon knew they had been saved. He smiled to himself. Perhaps, they'd live to fight another day.

"Leave none alive," ordered Krispyn over the chaos. Saluting, his men charged after the barbarians and the strange creatures that accompanied them. They chased them into the hills determined to slaughter them all.

Galdin approached Krispyn and the two clasped hands.

"Krispyn!" Nylana ran up to him and hugged him. "It is good to see you."

"I got your message," replied Krispyn tipping his head in Artryl's direction.

"I am afraid there is no time for pleasantries," said Galdin, taking charge of the situation. "Hemíl is lost. Both Swalya and the Keep of Edrei have been burned to the ground. These people must be taken to the safety of Norlyk."

"General," called Krispyn to a heavily armed man bearing Tesnayr's crest. "You and your men will lead these people to Norlyk. Once there, fortify the city's defenses as the barbarians may yet attack it."

The general saluted and rounded up his men. Slowly, the refugees of Hemíl followed after them; uncertainty etched on their faces.

"My lady," Lord Ardryn approached Nylana holding out a small item wrapped in a leaf.

Nylana took it with a small grin on her face. Unwrapping the leaf, she found a treat inside.

"I remember you used to love those things," said the elf.

"Thank you, Lord Ardryn." Nylana popped the candy in her mouth savoring the sweet texture; remembering the days when as a child he would bring her one each time he visited the palace.

"How did you get here so quickly?" asked Galdin.

"I headed for Belarnia the moment I received Nylana's message," said Krispyn, "I sent Shelwyk ahead with the army. Once Lord Ardryn agreed to join me, we wasted no time getting here. By a happy circumstance, we reached you at the same moment Shelwyk did."

"Krispyn," said Nylana, "Is Petra with you?"

"As a matter of fact I am," said the wizard approaching from behind.

"I have need to find the dragons." Nylana relayed Uriel's message to the others.

"I don't like it," said Galdin.

"Neither do I," added Krispyn.

"I must go," said Nylana, "I promised Uriel."

"And I'll go with her," said Ryk.

"Not without me, you won't," said Petra. "I can get you to the Black Mountains where they were last rumored to be, but you better hope that the dragons will agree to bring you back."

"I must go," Nylana insisted.

"I know there is no changing your mind," said Krispyn. "Take the wizard and this man with you." He placed his hand on Ryk's shoulder.

Nylana hugged Krispyn again in appreciation. "Thank you, brother."

Galdin looked at her with apprehension. Nylana pulled him aside.

"I know you don't like it, but I must go. Make certain that they reach the Black Mountains and that Vasagius follows you there."

"What are you planning?"

"I don't know for certain," replied Nylana, "But I have this feeling that it should all end there."

"Very well. I'll do as you ask," said Galdin. "And, Nylana, be careful."

Chapter X
Passing of Beasts

The small boat rocked as Ryk and Nylana paddled up the river with Petra seated on the bow directing their movements. Their muscles burned with each stroke as they moved against the current.

"How much farther?" asked Ryk. "We've been rowing for the last four hours." He wiped the sweat from his face.

"There is a hidden cove along the river that we must reach," said Petra.

"Hidden cove?" said Ryk, "If it's hidden, how do you know where it is?"

"Because such is the way of wizards," said Magi crawling out from underneath a tarp.

"Magi!" Nylana stared at the cat with surprise. She had ordered her not to come. "I thought I left you behind."

"You did," said Magi, "But I chose to ignore you."

"Typical," muttered Petra.

"Well, come on, put your backs into it," said Magi to both Ryk and Nylana.

Ryk raised his paddle out of the water contemplating smacking the cat. A disapproving look from Nylana changed his mind. He placed it back into the water propelling the boat forward.

Gradually, they glided up the river against the strong current. As the sun arced higher in the sky, their tired arms strained to continue rowing. The purple shaded water lapped at the hull of the boat taunting them.

"Why is the water purple?" asked Ryk.

"No one knows," answered Nylana, "But it is the reason why this river is called the Amythest River."

"Steer to the right," said Petra.

Ryk and Nylana obeyed, guiding the boat to where two willow trees formed an archway over the water. They moved through the leaves out of the sunlight and into a dark, enclosed area where a pool of water rested. They pulled their oars out of the water as the boat grated across the sand beaching itself.

"Quickly," urged Petra.

They grabbed their things and moved further ashore. Magi settled in Nylana's pack.

"What is he doing?" Ryk asked as Petra gathered leaves from the willow tree.

Nylana shrugged her shoulders.

"Stand close together," said Petra.

The others obeyed.

"Petra," said Nylana, "What is all this about?"

"This place is well hidden," said Petra, "And we do not need prying eyes watching us."

"And where did you get that?"

Petra glanced at the parchment he held; the one Quesha had given him. "From an old friend. Now, hush."

Petra tossed the leaves into the air as he muttered the four words on the slip of paper. His mutterings started soft gradually building in intensity. The air enclosed around them growing thick and heavy. Nylana pulled at the collar of her cloak. Wind blew around them as a bubble formed enveloping the four of them. Then, they were gone and all had stilled.

High within the Black Mountains three people and one cat appeared out of thin air. They stood on a small patch of black moss where the snow had melted. Each gasped for air relishing the crisp mountain breeze.

"What was that?" asked Nylana.

"A teleportation spell," said Petra, "Undoubtedly the way our friend Quesha manages to move around."

At the mention of Quesha's name, Nylana's face fell.

"What is it?" Petra asked.

"Quesha is dead," said Nylana.

The wizard's face softened for only a moment before regaining its composure. "That is unfortunate."

"Which way do we go?" Ryk asked looking around.

Nylana pulled out the horn of Selexia. Uriel had said to use the horn, but she had no idea what he meant. Slowly, the horn turned in her hands until the tip pointed north. An overwhelming feeling that she should head that way consumed her.

"North," she said. She took off running. "Hurry! We have little time."

The others chased after her.

Four tiny figures ran along the ridge of the mountains as they made their way to the dragons. They moved swiftly, barely pausing long enough to rest or eat. Long shadows followed their movements as the sun swung overhead until it hung low in the sky indicating the onset of evening. The golden rays of the setting sun lit their way as they raced along the ridge; Nylana in the lead.

She stopped a moment studying the horn within her hand. It swiveled for a second before pointing at an angle.

"This way."

Nylana took off again. Panting, Ryk gathered Magi into his arms and continued on with Petra taking up the rear.

Silhouetted in the last rays of the sun on the mountain top, they didn't know how much distance had been covered. Nylana continued on with renewed vigor. Her legs burned from the exertion, but she ignored them. She breathed steadily keeping time with the pace she had set.

The sun dipped lower until half of it had gone. Determined to keep going until all light had left, Nylana ran faster. She heard the ragged gasps of Ryk and Petra behind her. She refused to stop. Glancing at the sun, Nylana realized that night fast approached. She knew they could not run through the mountains in the dark. Too many dangers.

She paused on a small rise. Looking all around her, she spotted a small protected cave not far from them. "There," she pointed at it, "We will rest there for the night." Nylana sped downhill.

Ryk stared after her; hunched over with his hands on his knees gasping for air. "Does she never tire?"

Petra watched as Nylana made her way down the hill; his face unreadable. Without answering Ryk's question, he started downhill with Magi.

*   *   *

Lord Ardryn stood by a flag pole staring at the looming Black Mountains wishing Nylana had allowed him to join her. The day she left with the wizard, she had asked him to stay put. "Why?" he'd asked.

"Because I need you here," Nylana had replied, "Galdin will need your consul. Look after him for me."

"As always, my lady, you need only ask and I shall obey." Lord Ardryn pulled out one of his daggers. He had always admired its intricate designs and knew that it would serve Nylana well. "Take this."

"I don't need—"

"Please, Nylana. You may find that you do."

Nylana took the weapon with gratitude. "Thank you." An oak leaf fell into her hand as she fingered the dagger. Opening the leaf she found another candy inside. "You know I am not a child anymore."

The elf grinned. "And yet you still eat it. Indulge an aging elf."

Nylana popped the treat into her mouth savoring its sweet flavor; admiring the elf that looked as though he were forty years of age. "You know where to meet me. If I am not there in seven days continue on."

"I shall watch over them both," said Lord Ardryn referring to Galdin and Krispyn.

Nylana embraced the elf before leaving.

Lord Ardryn reminisced about their departure as he studied the black mounds of earth before him. The Black Mountains: the darkest place in the five lands. The elf whispered a small prayer asking the voice on the wind for Nylana's success.

*   *   *

They stared at the rocky cliff face before them. Fog wrapped around them concealing their view of the top. Nylana stared at the horn in her hands. "It says we should go this way."

"Very well," said Ryk pulling off his pack. "We'll have to climb."

He took out some rope and a grappling hook. Tying it securely, he stood back a bit swinging it. Once he had momentum going, Ryk thrust the hook upward. A sharp clink told him that he had hit the top. He tugged on it to make certain that it held. Ryk pulled out more rope handing a line to each of them, while Magi crawled into Nylana's pack.

"Tie them securely to the rope," said Ryk. "Petra, you go first. Then I'll climb. Nylana, you'll go last since you're the lightest."

One by one, they each took hold of the rock wall lifting themselves up. Pebbles dropped to the bottom bouncing off of the cliff. Petra reached upward feeling for a good place to grab hold. Slowly, he heaved himself up placing his feet carefully along small protrusions of rock. He moved upward making certain that enough slack was kept in the line.

In the middle, Ryk did his best to maintain their balance. He kept both lines slack while offering bits of advice to Nylana, who seemed to be struggling. "Take your time," he called to her; his voice booming through the small ravine.

Nylana barely heard him as she stretched her arm reaching for a hold. Her hand slipped on some slush that had settled there. Suddenly Nylana fell, pulling the line taut.

A sharp blast of breath emptied Ryk's lungs as the rope jerked against his stomach nearly pulling him away from the cliff face. Quickly, Ryk secured himself to the rock yelling up at Petra, "Stop! Secure yourself!"

Nylana dangled below them. She reached out for the rock before her. Her fingers brushed against it scraping the skin off. Finally, she grabbed hold and clung to the rock wall. Her foot slid an inch. She knew she could not hold on for long.

Ryk scrambled down to her sliding down his line. Carefully, he secured himself just above Nylana. "Take my hand," he said.

Nylana took Ryk's hand clasping it just as her line fall away. Together they hung in the air.

Their line lurched.

"The hook is coming loose," yelled Petra.

Ryk looked up. They dropped a bit more.

Poking her head out of Nylana's pack, Magi leapt onto the cliff face digging her sharp claw into the rock. Slowly, the cat climbed upward; her claws scraping against the rock with each movement she made. Magi calculated the time necessary to get to the top before everyone fell. She reached up pushing with her hind feet until she was level with Petra. She and the wizard looked at each other a moment before she continued on.

Ryk and Nylana dropped a bit more as the hook continued to lose its hold.

"Drop me," said Nylana, looking into Ryk's eyes.

"No," replied Ryk.

"This thing won't hold. You have to let me go or we'll all die."

Ryk stared into Nylana's determined face refusing to release her. Either they all made it, or none of them ever would.

"Don't be a fool. You have to let me go," continued Nylana.

"I'll not drop you." Ryk's determined voice forced Nylana to cease her pleas. She glanced at him and for a moment their eyes locked; each determined to save the other.

Magi reached over the top ledge hooking her claws into the black earth. She scrambled over it and rolled onto the solid ground. Spotting the grappling hook as it continued to loosen, the cat sprang onto it. She placed her entire weight upon the hook stopping it for the moment.

"Climb! Now!" Magi's voice echoed over the expanse.

The rope pulled taut as Petra worked his way up. Arm over arm he heaved himself upward towards the top; his sweaty hands slipping on the rope. His legs pushed against the rock wall as he hoisted himself over the ledge.

Quickly, Petra turned round clutching the rope that held Ryk and Nylana. With immense effort he pulled them up, while Magi remained seated on the grappling hook.

The line scraped against the razor edge of the cliff. Steadily, the wizard hauled them up as the wind whizzed past him, mocking his efforts. Ryk's hand appeared. Hastily, Petra grabbed it heaving the man onto the ledge. Together, they pulled Nylana to safety as she rolled onto the bluff relieved to be on solid ground once more. Just then, the grappling hook popped out of the earth.

"Why didn't you let me go?" asked Nylana.

"Do you not know?" replied Ryk. In an effort to lighten the mood, he changed his tone, "First, your brother would kill me. Then, Narúl would kill me. Then, your brother would kill me."

Nylana chuckled a moment, but she thought she saw something else in Ryk's eyes. Something she had never noticed before.

"When you two are done dawdling," said Petra, "We have a mission to complete."

Nylana and Ryk untangled the rope from around their waists and packed it away. They moved onward in the deepening gloom of the Black Mountains hoping that the horn led them in the right direction.

*   *   *

In a tent far away from the rest of the troops, men leaned over a map plotting. Krispyn marked the trail in which Nylana would have taken. She had asked that they head to the Black Mountains as well.

"We are at least a week from the mountains," said Krispyn, "With Vasagius close behind."

"And closing fast," said Lord Stefon. "It appears he took the bait."

"Then we will move twice as fast. We must reach the Black Mountains at the same time Nylana finds the dragons. I suggest we stage our points here and here."

"Why there?" asked Lord Ardryn.

"Because Uriel suggested it before he died," said Galdin.

"The dragon?" asked Krispyn. "You trust his word?"

"Yes," said Galdin, "And so does Nylana."

"Very well," Krispyn said, "But I believe we ought to place men here as well." He pointed at the map.

Galdin mused over it a bit. "Agreed. Lord Stefon, I want your men here on the southern side of the mountains. Lord Ardryn, your elves should be in the hills, on high ground."

"We should send word to Lord Preston of Sym'Dul," said Galdin. "He can meet up with us as we pass Drynelle."

"A wise decision," replied Krispyn. "I will have a message sent straight away."

"And what of Lord Belznyc?" asked Krispyn.

Galdin frowned. "I would not count on his coming."

"Then we shall have to make do without him," said Krispyn, "There are some ruins here in the Black Mountains. Vasagius undoubtedly knows about them. He will expect us to go there."

"A trap," said Galdin, "Good thinking. Will you take command there?"

"Of course."

"It is settled then."

"In the meantime," said Krispyn, "We should all get some sleep. I want to leave in a few hours as I have no desire for Vasagius to catch us until we are ready for him."

*   *   *

Nylana sat alone staring at the starless sky. Not even a moon provided any light. She pulled out the feather twirling it in her fingers. *What am I to do with this?* Despite the glumness of the place, the feather brought life to the area; its colors standing out among the black landscape.

A hand with a wood carved heart pendant appeared by her shoulder. Smiling, Nylana turned around and found Ryk standing there. "I made this for you," he said.

Nylana took it admiring the gift. "How—"

"I wasn't always a thief," said Ryk. "There was a time when I carved wood. I was the best wood carver in Pras'quel."

"Why did you become a thief then?"

"The king of Pras'quel raised his taxes to the point where my customers could no longer afford to hire my work. So I closed my shop finding it easier to steal than to work."

"I think you are better at carving wood."

"May I?"

Nylana held up her hair while Ryk placed the pendant around her neck. Its intricate design mesmerized her.

"It is you who make it beautiful."

A loud snort caught their attention. Both turned around in time to see a bushy tail disappear.

"Nylana," said Ryk, his tone serious, "In all my years I have never met a woman quite like you. From the moment I first saw you, I have loved you. Slave or princess, you are the noblest person I have ever known. And though I am just a lowly thief, will you do me the honor of becoming my wife?"

Tears welled in Nylana's eyes. Her entire life she had awaited a proposal from a man who cared nothing for her crown. Yet, something held her back. She glanced at the pendant that Ryk had given her. "I—I don't think I can."

Disheartened, Ryk wrapped his fingers around hers.

"With this war—with all that is happening, it would be wrong for me to think of a wedding."

"But that makes it all the more important."

"I—I'm sorry."

Nylana ran away hiding her face and the tears that dotted it. Ryk watched her leave. Slowly, he turned and walked away.

Concealed in the branches of a nearby tree, sat Magi. She twitched her whiskers as she watched them.

Fog greeted them the next morning as they awoke. It floated around them soaking their clothes with its dampness. Nylana held the horn out letting it point them in the correct direction. "I think we're close," she said.

They walked throughout the morning with the sun hiding behind dark clouds. Only the fog remained; even it looked black, matching the surroundings.

"You seem gloomy today," said Petra as he walked beside Nylana.

"It is nothing," said Nylana.

"Then why do you cry?"

Nylana glanced at Ryk who walked ahead with Magi trailing after him. "Ryk asked me to marry him."

"And you do not love him?"

Nylana stared into Petra's eyes unable to conceal her true feelings.

The wizard's face softened as he looked at her. "So you do love him."

"I turned him down," said Nylana.

"Why? The man was willing to fall to his death yesterday to save you. And as I understand it, he has chased after you since the day you met him."

"But how can I focus on my own happiness when so many are suffering at the hands of a madman? Besides, he probably only sees the crown."

"Do you really believe that?" asked Petra.

Sobbing, Nylana shook her head.

"And I suppose you are going to tell me that you do not love him."

"No, I don't."

Petra touched the heart shaped pendant she wore. "Somehow, I don't believe you. Take the advice of an old wizard: don't throw his love away because you are afraid. I have watched you your whole life. You are stubborn to a fault. Do not let the world prevent you from having even the smallest amount of happiness."

Nylana embraced the wizard crying on his shoulder. He allowed her to.

"Your whole life you have carried the weight of other people's sorrows." Petra lifted the pendant before her. "I do not think it is your position he wants."

A whistle brought them out of their conversation. Ryk waved them over. Beside him stood a giant skeleton: the skeleton of a dragon.

The mist shifted slightly revealing that they walked among the remains of dragons. Giant bones littered the area as they stepped over skulls and rib cages. Ryk carefully walked around the vertebrae of what was once the spine of a dragon. Fragments lay everywhere dotting the black dirt.

"What is this place?" asked Ryk.

"A graveyard," said Petra.

"I hope this is not what is left of the dragons."

"Indeed it is," boomed a deep voice.

They all froze as a dragon walked out of the mist and into view. "What are you doing here?"

Nylana stepped forward reining in her earlier emotions. "We've come to seek an audience with the dragons. Uriel sent us."

Other dragons appeared. They moved slowly as though age had taken them. The ground vibrated with each step they took as they formed a circle around them. Nylana watched their movements. Uriel had not exaggerated their circumstances.

"And why would he have sent you?" said the one who had spoken earlier. "Unless it was to provide a snack."

Suddenly, the dragon opened his mouth wide exposing all of his sharp teeth as he dived for Nylana. Thunder roared as a powerful force knocked the dragon backwards sending him flying until he crashed into the dark earth on his back. Shocked, the others just stared at her unsure of what had just happened.

"What lives within you?" asked the dragon.

Nylana did not answer right away. She had no idea what had happened or how to respond.

The dragon approached her carefully. His snout hovered before Nylana as the great beast sniffed her. "HMMMM," he growled, "I can see why Uriel sent you. Something otherworldly resides within you. Tell me, why are you here?"

"The five lands of Tesnayr need your help," said Nylana. "Uriel said that you would provide it."

"He was mistaken," said the dragon.

"Barbarians ravage the land. They are heading here as we speak. They care nothing for the dragons and will kill all of you where you stand," said Nylana.

"Let them," spoke the dragon.

Nylana could not believe her ears. She had heard stories about the fierceness of dragons. But the ones staring at her resembled relics more than warriors. "Do you not care?"

"You are young, Princess of Tesnayr, but we dragons have been dwindling a long time. What you see here is what is left of us. Soon even we will lie in this place as mere bones for the scavengers."

"We need you," pleaded Nylana. "You are all still a part of this world. Why not fight one last time before death claims you? Why do you cower here?"

The dragons roared in anger at Nylana's words. "We are not cowards!"

"Then why do you refuse me?" said Nylana. "You are not dead yet. Will you not honor Selexia's promise?" Nylana held the horn of Selexia out to the dragon that spoke.

"That promise was made long ago when we numbered more than the stars. Queen Amborese freed us from it. We are no longer bound to honor the horn."

"It meant more than the bonds of magic," Nylana scolded the dragons, "Selexia's oath means more now than it did the day she made it. If you were to honor it now, it demonstrates more courage than the dragons that kept it only because magic forced them to."

The surrounding dragons stared at Nylana. She saw defeat written on their faces; they had quit the world and wished only to leave it behind.

"Will not a one of you help?"

"I will join you," said a strong voice from above.

Everyone whirled around. A fully grown, gold dragon stood upon a small rise. Nylana could barely believe it. It was the same dragon whom she had saved from the trolls only months earlier.

"Mishkunn," whispered Nylana.

The gold dragon walked toward them, proudly displaying his scales. "As you have saved my life once, I shall return the favor and go with you."

"Mishkunn," said the older dragon, "Why do you go with these people? You owe them nothing. We dragons—"

"You dishonor the dragons' name," interrupted Mishkunn. "And you are wrong. I owe them everything." Mishkunn knelt to the ground. "Climb upon my back."

Knowing when not to argue, Nylana and the others climbed upon the gold dragon settling themselves between his spikes. His glittery wings spread wide and with the strength of ten elderly dragons, Mishkunn took to the sky leaving the defeated group behind.

Chapter XI
Great Loss

"There," said Nylana to Mishkunn when she spotted Lord Ardryn and Narúl on the ground. The gold dragon banked to the right lowering himself gently. He landed beside the two on the ground with a grace neither had ever seen.

"Thank you, Mishkunn," said Nylana as she climbed off of the dragon's back.

"Where will you go, little one?" asked Mishkunn.

"The army is headed north," replied Nylana. "Away from Drynelle and Norlyk."

"Take them deep within the Black Mountains. Dragons always fight when threatened." Mishkunn rose into the air. "I will meet you there." He disappeared.

"My lady," said Lord Ardryn as he embraced Nylana. "I am pleased that you have all returned safely. Galdin and Krispyn both lead our forces. They are half a day's ride from here."

"We should head there immediately," said Nylana.

Lord Ardryn saluted her and walked off with the others.

Narúl pulled Nylana aside, away from the others. "Is everything alright?"

"I'm fine," answered Nylana.

Narúl eyed her questioningly.

"Am I that readable?"

"Only to those who know you best. And I noticed this." He pointed at the necklace she wore. "Do you love him?"

Nylana nodded.

"Then I approve."

"You—what?"

"As aggravating as he is, I am certain he will treat you well," said Narúl.

Nylana smiled. "Thank you, Narúl."

Shouts and the clanging of swords summoned their attention. Hurriedly, Nylana charged over to where they came from. Barbarians burst through the brush straight for her. She whipped out her sword cutting one down while blocking an attack by another. Swiftly, she rammed her shoulder into the man's throat before killing him.

Nylana noticed a barbarian heading for Ryk. Spotting an abandoned bow on the ground, she dove for it raising it up. With expert aim, she fired striking the man in between the shoulder blades.

"Ryk," shouted Nylana as she ran for him.

Ryk threw his opponent off of him killing the man. He turned toward Nylana as she approached.

"Are you--"

"I'm fine," he interrupted her.

Relieved, Nylana gave him a quick peck. "Get them out of here." She whirled around until she found Petra. "Head for the army, then, lead them to the Black Mountains."

Nylana searched about her for Narúl but found no sign of him. She took off to where she had last seen him.

"Nylana, wait!"

Nylana didn't listen. She charged through the bushes until she spotted Narúl who was surrounded by Vasagius' men. She watched as he struggled to fend them off. A dark shape streaked through the trees heading straight for Narúl: Artryl.

Narúl spun on his heels with a hatchet in one hand and a sword in the other. He blocked with his blade before bringing the hatchet up and bashing the man in the face. He turned around bringing his hatchet low, striking another in the belly.

A blunt force knocked his hatchet from his hand. Recovering quickly, Narúl grasped his sword with both hands and blocked another attack. With a strength few possessed, he used one hand to maintain the locked position, while using his other to wrench his opponent's hand from his blade. Suddenly, Narúl head-butted the man before killing him.

Something struck him in the face. Stunned, his weapon fell rom his grasp as a savage moved in for the kill. Unexpectedly, the man stopped with a confused expression on his face as a sword poked through him from behind. When he fell to the ground, Artryl stood there.

"Narúl," said Artryl as he shook the man.

Slowly, Narúl regained his senses. He spotted Artryl and seized him by the shoulders. "I thought I left you with Galdin."

"I had to come," said Artryl. "Where you go I go."

Softening his manner slightly, Narúl hugged the boy. "Stay behind me."

"Narúl!" yelled Artryl, pointing behind him.

Narúl whipped around and knocked the bow out of a charging man's hands, but not before he fired. He stabbed the man in the neck.

"Narúl."

Narúl turned around. Artryl stood there with an arrow in his chest; blood poured from the wound. Instantly, Narúl ran to the boy and caught him before he collapsed. "Stay with me."

"Narúl, I'm sorry."

Nylana ran up from behind and stopped when she noticed Artryl in Narúl's arms. Slowly, she walked up to him.

"No," said Narúl, "You've nothing to be sorry for."

"But I disobeyed your orders," coughed Artryl.

"I'm glad you did. You have saved all our lives."

"I'm so tired."

"Sleep," said Narúl reining in his emotions, "Just close your eyes. When you wake, you will be in the most beautiful of places and will know only peace."

"I love you," whispered Artryl.

"And I you, my son."

Artryl's eyes closed as his head rolled to the side. Narúl clutched the limp body tightly.

Gently, Nylana placed her hand on Narúl's shoulder.

"Leave me," said Narúl.

Understanding his pain as she choked back tears, Nylana backed away to give her mentor and friend some space.

Narúl laid Artryl gently on the ground placing the boy's hands on his chest and a sword within them. "Rest well, my son."

Screams pierced the solemn moment as men grabbed Nylana from behind. She elbowed one, but he wrenched her weapon from her and knocked her unconscious.

Narúl jumped to his feet. He rushed for Nylana when something slammed into him knocking him to the ground. Narúl lay unconscious as the barbarians dragged Nylana away.

Chapter XII
Back with the Army

Sullenly, a line of people walked along the narrow trail; heads hung low. They had lost their princess. Narúl took up the rear with Artryl's lifeless form in his arms.

"I'm going back for her," Ryk turned around and tried to march away.

Petra's strong arm stopped him holding him firmly. "Use your head, boy. If you go after her now, you will also be killed."

"We cannot just leave her!"

"Nylana ordered us to meet up with Galdin."

"But—"

"Think of the bigger picture," said Petra, "If we do not heed her request, we will lose this war. What difference will saving her make if Vasagius wins?"

Ryk yanked himself free of the wizard. "I don't like any of this."

"Do you think any of us do?" demanded Petra.

"They approach," said Magi, darting for them, "We've found them."

Out of the mist came the army of the five lands of Tesnayr with Galdin and Krispyn riding in the lead. Krispyn held up his hand stopping them.

Galdin leapt off his horse heading straight for the small group. "Where is Nylana?"

"Vasagius has her," answered Lord Ardryn. "I am sorry, my lord."

"How did this happen?" demanded Krispyn as he approached.

"We were ambushed," said Lord Ardryn, "But she gave express orders that we come here regardless. She has word from the dragons: continue to the Black Mountains. There we shall make our stand."

"Then that is where we will head," said Galdin. "Fall in. We will ride until sunset."

Krispyn's face flashed to anger before softening immediately. "You heard him."

Petra and the others obeyed, taking their place within the ranks of men.

*   *   *

Narúl knelt next to a mound of dirt. Tears dotted his cheeks; the first in a long time. The army had camped an hour after dusk. Soon after, Narúl carried Artryl's body to a secluded place for burial. He had refused offers of assistance from others.

Moisture from the ground seeped through his pants chilling the skin. He ignored it. A breeze rustled the leaves around him and Narúl faintly heard Nylana's name.

Resolve burned through him as he rose to his feet and marched to his tent. Ryk waited for him there.

"I am going with you."

"You are staying here," said Narúl.

"I will not let you go alone," Ryk closed the distance between him and Narúl.

Without warning, Narúl grasped Ryk's hands wrenching them behind his back. With great speed, he snatched a leather strap and tied Ryk's wrists together. Before the man could call for help, Narúl shoved a gag in his mouth.

"You are staying here. When I return, it will be your duty to care for her," said Narúl.

He secured Ryk in a corner before grabbing his things. Narúl tied a dagger around his waist. He checked his bag. Frowning, he knew he only had enough food for two days. No matter, he thought, if I do not find her by then she will be dead and so will I.

Galdin entered just as Narúl pulled his cloak tight. "Where are you off to?" He glanced at Ryk who struggled against his bonds. "Should I ask?"

"Do not try and stop me," said Narúl.

"Narúl," Galdin stopped the man as he tried to leave, "I cannot let you go alone."

"If you get in my way, I will kill you."

Galdin and Narúl locked eyes each reading the other. Galdin knew Narúl would do as he had promised.

"We need you here," said Galdin.

"No, you do not. I abandoned her once before. I'll not do it again."

"At least let someone—"

"No." Narúl's voice silenced Galdin. "I'll not leave her to suffer at the hands of that madman. I can travel faster alone. I will find her. She's—"

"Like a daughter to you," interrupted Galdin.

Narúl's features softened slightly. "From the day her father put me in charge of her safety, I have never let any harm come to her. When he died, I taught her everything that a father would teach his child. It is my responsibility to rescue her."

"Let me come with you," said Galdin.

"No," replied Narúl, "You are needed here. Lead them, Galdin. You must lead them." Narúl held the tent flap open as he paused. "Do not follow me." He left.

Galdin stared after him sighing heavily. "Good luck."

*   *   *

Deep in the forests of Belarnia, three unicorns walked carefully always watchful of their surroundings. The silent forest plagued their nerves as they longed for the chirping of birds or the buzz of insects. The silence meant that even the trees had felt the change in the world.

Go back.

"Did you hear that?" asked one of the unicorns.

The other two paused twitching their ears as they searched for the voice that had summoned their companion's attention.

You cannot hide here as they will come.

All three unicorns turned in circles searching for the source of the voice, but found none.

"Who said that?" asked one.

"The trees," said a second. "They are warning us."

"Warning us of what?"

"Were we not hasty in our decision to leave the five lands?"

The other two unicorns pawed at the grass in shame.

"Perhaps our time is ending, but we can still help those who need us while we are able."

Go now to the Black Mountains.

The unicorns turned and headed north away from the forests of Belarnia and to the darkness of the Black Mountains. They broke into a gallop letting their limbs stretch into long strides.

"Will we make it in time?" asked one.

"I do not know," answered the leader.

Chapter XIII
Meeting the Enemy

Nylana's knees throbbed from being dragged across the rough ground and into Vasagius' tent. The men carrying her dropped her unceremoniously before his feet. Angrily, Nylana stood glaring at him with pure hatred.

"The Lady Nylana," said a man.

"Thank you, Stahl," replied Vasagius. "It is customary to kneel before your master."

Nylana spat in his face.

Vasagius wiped the spittle off of his nose and mouth before backhanding her. He seized her roughly by the shoulder forcing her to the ground. "I said kneel," he whispered in her ear.

Nylana did as ordered keeping her mouth shut.

"What I need from you is information," continued Vasagius, "Why are you heading to the Black Mountains? There is nothing there, unless—of course. It's a diversion. No matter. I will crush it and then destroy Norlyk. And any other settlement along the way."

Nylana remained silent. She scanned the area with her eyes hoping for some means of escape.

"And I know about Galdin."

Nylana's face jerked towards his. A sneer crept across it.

"You thought I didn't know. The Lost Prince returned to Tesnayr; found by his sister. How poetic." Vasagius circled around her. "Tell me of your defenses."

"I'll die first," growled Nylana.

Vasagius nodded at Stahl. Pain ripped through Nylana as Stahl grabbed her hair and forced her head backward.

"One way or another I get what I want," said Vasagius. "Now tell me, why the Black Mountains?"

Nylana refused to speak.

With another nod from Vasagius, Stahl took his knife and plunged it deep within Nylana's chest. She doubled over gasping for air.

"Perhaps, I will just serve Galdin your heart," Vasagius said.

A soft glow filled the area. Grasping the handle of the knife, Nylana gritted her teeth and pulled it out. Smooth flesh remained where the blade had been.

Not believing what he had just seen, Vasagius gaped at the spectacle. Nylana seized her chance. She smacked Vasagius in the face before charging Stahl. She knocked his weapon from his hands before jamming her knee into his gut. Within moments, Nylana pinned Stahl against a post with the sharp steel of the knife against his throat.

"You have more fight than your father," said Vasagius wiping a trickle of blood from his mouth. "Go ahead. Kill him. He tried to murder you, so take his life instead. Take your revenge."

Nylana looked into the frightened eyes of Stahl who glanced between Vasagius and her. She pressed the blade against the skin drawing a small amount of blood.

"Do it," said Vasagius. "I know the hatred that burns within you. He would not hesitate to kill you. Prove to him your superiority."

The desire to end the life within her hands burned within her, but something else reigned there as well. Fire filled her eyes as she lowered the knife. "No. I'm not like you."

Vasagius snatched the knife from her hands. "Pathetic." He whirled around and slashed Stahl's throat without a moment's hesitation; callously watching as his faithful servant sunk to the floor gasping for air. Vasagius turned on Nylana.

Shouts came from outside as men hurried about. Distracted, Vasagius ran out of the tent. Flames spread throughout his camp consuming his armory and catapults.

"Get those fires out," shouted Vasagius. He grabbed a man running past. "Watch her."

Soon after Vasagius left, a black shape grabbed the man about the shoulders and bashed his face in.

"Narúl," called Nylana.

Narúl pulled a cloak out from under his own and wrapped it around Nylana while pushing her outside. Together they ran along the edges of the encampment past men trying to put the fires out. One noticed them. Quickly, Narúl grabbed his weapon wrenching it from the man's hands before dispatching him.

Nylana pulled them to a halt. She had noticed a man stripped to his waist tied to a beam.

"Lord Trisk." Nylana ran to him with Narúl close behind. "He still breathes."

Narúl pushed Nylana back while he pulled out his sword. With great strength he hacked at the bonds until they fell away. Hastily, Narúl put Lord Trisk around his shoulders while directing Nylana to the nearby woods. They bolted through the camp going unnoticed by those battling the spreading fire.

"Do not stop," said Narúl as they ran.

Nylana obeyed following Narúl's directions until they had left Vasagius' camp far behind.

*   *   *

Ryk yanked on the strap as he fastened a saddle to a horse in the dead of night refusing to stand idly by while Nylana was in danger. He did not know Vasagius, but he understood how men like him thought. He knew well what Vasagius would do to her.

"Going someplace?" asked Tabs as he appeared from the shadows.

"What makes you say so?"

"Oh, I don't know. A packed horse. You saddling it while others sleep," replied Tabs, "I'd say that you intend to disobey Galdin's orders and go after the fair princess yourself."

"No one is stopping me this time." Ryk finished securing the strap.

"Are you sure?" asked Tabs.

Ryk eyed the cat warily.

"What if I were to do this?"

Instantly, Tabs leapt at the horse landing on the rump of the animal digging his claws in. The horse reared up on its hind legs neighing loudly and ran off. Tabs let go before it got too far.

The cat burst into song, as was his custom. "Oh, I stopped the foolishness of Ryk—Please don't hit me with that stick!" The orange tabby squirted away a few feet just as Ryk snatched a stick and headed for him.

"What are you doing here?" demanded Ryk.

"Galdin asked me to keep an eye on you," replied the cat. "I know you feel that you need to rush off and save your beloved, but I implore you to remain here. Magi says that Narúl will find her. You must trust him."

"It appears I have little choice."

Ryk tossed the stick away and stalked off in frustration.

Tabs watched him go twitching his whiskers as he pondered the behavior of people. "Humans are so frustrating," commented the cat to the night sky.

                *   *   *

"Please stop," Lord Trisk begged as they ran through the valley. Gently, Narúl laid him on the ground.

"We're almost there," said Nylana as she held her flask for the man to drink from it.

Coughing, Lord Trisk shook his head. "It is too late for me. Go. Leave me."

"I left you behind once," said Nylana, "I'll not do it again."

"You don't have a choice." Lord Trisk seized Nylana's arm with his bony fingers. "There is something strange at work here.

Vasagius is not the one leading this invading force. Another is in charge—one close to you. One whom you all trust."

Another fit of coughing racked Lord Trisk's body before it stopped suddenly. Nylana held his face toward her finding only his lifeless eyes. Carefully, she brushed her hand over them closing them. "I'll not leave you here."

She stood up, lifting Lord Trisk's body onto her shoulders. Narúl stopped her with his hand. With great care, he put the man upon his shoulders motioning for Nylana to walk ahead of him.

"I will carry him," Narúl said.

Chapter XIV
Ambushed

Nylana and Narúl walked into camp welcoming the sounds of hammers and whetstones. People ceased their work to observe the two carrying a corpse. Many bowed in Nylana's direction. She returned their gestures.

Galdin burst from a nearby tent running straight for her, enveloping her in a warm embrace. Krispyn wasn't far behind.

"You need to quit disappearing on me," Galdin said with a smile.

Nylana returned the grin. "Lord Trisk is dead."

Krispyn looked at the body in Narúl's arms. With a wave of his hand two men took Lord Trisk's remains carrying them away. "Come. We've much to talk about."

She followed her brothers into a tent while Narúl went to gather food. Lord Stefon, Lord Preston, and Lord Ardryn awaited them.

"My lords," greeted Nylana.

"We will make our stand here," said Krispyn pointing at a map. "We can hide in the hills and the trees here. Lord Ardryn, you and your elves will be in the lower hills here. Galdin will be here with a contingent of men and I shall be at the other end. Lord Preston, you will hide in the trees here."

"If you can call them trees," muttered Lord Preston.

The others nodded knowing what he meant. The trees in the Black Mountains resembled dead, scraggily wood that stuck vertically out of the ground.

"Lord Stefon," continued Krispyn, "You will be in the valley here with your men acting as a decoy."

"That is suicide," said Lord Stefon.

"I'll do it." Ryk stepped out of the shadows. No one had noticed his presence. "I will lead a group there to lure in Vasagius."

"Very well," said Galdin before Nylana could protest.

"We will do it together," said Lord Stefon not wanting his courage to be in question.

Nylana looked around at the cul-de-sac they were in. "If this goes poorly, we will have nowhere to retreat to."

"True," said Galdin, "Their numbers are too great for us to face on an open field."

"And where will I be?" asked Nylana.

Everyone stared at her in silence.

"Well?" urged Nylana.

"My lady," said Lord Preston, "The battlefield is no place for you." Nylana's piercing glare made him wish he had not said that.

"Up in the highest reaches of the hills," said Galdin. "You have remarkable skill with a bow. Petra and Tami will be near you."

"I don't think—" began Krispyn.

"Agreed," said Nylana.

A messenger burst into the tent. "Vasagius and his army will be here by morning."

"Thank you," said Krispyn. "You are all dismissed. Get the men in position."

"Before you all leave," said Nylana, "We should bury Lord Trisk. I want it done before dusk."

"As you wish," said Krispyn.

They all filed out of the tent. Nylana and Ryk brushed each other on their way out. They looked into each other's eyes before Nylana broke contact and left. A strong hand jerked Ryk back.

"You better come out of this alive or I will hunt you down in the underworld itself," said Galdin.

"Is this your way of saying you like me?" asked Ryk.

"Petra told me about your proposal," said Galdin. "I'll not let you break her heart."

"But she refused me."

"Try asking her again," said Galdin as he left.

Galdin carried the lit torch to the funeral pyre on which Lord Trisk's body had been laid. The men from Belyndril had all gathered around to say farewell to their beloved leader. Even a few elves and had gathered to pay him honor.

Nylana watched with controlled emotions as Galdin lit the dried wood. It instantly went up in flames. Sadness tugged at her heart at the loss of a noble man.

The man next to her bearing the crest of Belyndril sang a solemn tune. The words matched her own sentiments.

Farewell, Lord Trisk, of Belyndril.
Of your courage we sing still.
Go now to the halls of your fathers;
May your spirit be at peace forever.

Nylana turned back to the writhing flames. *How many more will have to die?*

*   *   *

Nylana checked her gear before setting off to where she was to be positioned during the battle.

"Good luck," said Narúl as he walked up. "You take care of yourself."

"I always do," said Nylana.

Narúl lifted up her cloak revealing her sword. "I thought you were to be with the archers."

Ripping her cloak from his hands, Nylana glowered at him. "You never know when you'll need a blade."

Chuckling to himself, Narúl pulled out a dagger and handed it to her. "Here, you may need this."

Nylana took it gratefully. She embraced Narúl before turning to make the climb to the upper hills.

*   *   *

The beating of the drums reverberated off the mountain sides dancing around them as they waited. Morning had dawned and so had the arrival of Vasagius. Slowly, the barbarian army approached drawing closer to where Ryk and Lord Stefon waited with their men.

Nylana watched from her vantage point as the mass of well-armed savages drew closer. She stole a quick glance at Tabs and Magi who both waited with her. She hoped that luck was on their side.

Nylana raised her bow. She pulled the string taut listening to it creak a bit as she took aim. She released. The arrow arced through the sky with a soft whistle as it flew toward the approaching barbarian army before striking one in the neck.

Ryk kept his face impassive as he watched the approaching enemy. He stole a quick glance at Lord Stefon who stood proud; his face set in a firm expression. He looked up at where Nylana stood silhouetted in the light of the sun. The wind caused her cloak to billow behind her as she maintained an erect posture. *Always the regal figure.* Ryk momentarily wondered if she felt the same fear he did.

The ground vibrated beneath his feet as the barbarians moved closer. He observed the mass of bulky, bare-armed men as they neared.

Two boulders flew over his head as they sailed through the air striking the mountainside. Dirt and rock crumbled and burst outward as it fell. Ryk turned back to the approaching army as the front lines broke into a charge heading straight for him.

"Brace yourselves!" yelled Ryk as he raised his sword.

The men behind him widened their stances. The cries of the barbarians neared. Steeling himself, Ryk swung his sword upward striking one man in the neck as the line of barbarians plowed into him and his men.

Krispyn watched from up high as the army of Vasagius took the bait. The throng of men moved into the cul-de-sac entrapping themselves. Perfect, thought Krispyn.

"Ballistas!" he yelled.

Men armed the ballistas lining them up. Upon Krispyn's signal, they fired. Across the way, Galdin gave the same order. Together, two spears shot from the hills toward the invading army.

"Again," shouted Krispyn.

Another barrage of spears struck the enemy forces.

Lord Ardryn watched from where he stood with his elves. As master archers, they were positioned in the best place for firing arrows. He waited for the signal. Once received, he held up his blade and brought it down. Instantly, dozens of arrows left their bows racing through the sky, darkening it. Screams of pain filtered up to him as each arrow struck their target.

"Fire!"

More arrows shot from their bows wreaking havoc on the ones below.

Lord Ardryn studied the damage left below. He pulled back his bow and fired an arrow at the branch above Galdin's head.

"That's the signal," said Galdin. "Time for Lord Preston and his men to enter the fight."

A nearby soldier blew on his horn. The note resounded through the hills with an eerie stance.

Well hidden in a patch of trees near the enclave waited Lord Preston and his men. Next to him stood Valn. "That is the signal," said Valn.

Lord Preston nodded. "Charge!"

With wild screams, the army of Sym'Dul burst from the scrawny trees running for the battle below them. They pushed their way into the fight.

Valn ducked under a barbarian blade. He stabbed the man as he jumped back to his feet. Darting around men's feet, he moved unnoticed by those twice his height. He swiped his blade across the calf of one. The man screamed in pain and doubled over. Taking advantage of the situation, Valn rammed his weapon into the enemy's throat.

Valn noticed Lord Preston pinned between two men. He raced for him. Squirting between fighting men, Valn reached Lord Preston just in time to jump upon one of the men. He grabbed the man's back jabbing his sword into the base of the neck. As he fell, Lord Preston threw the second man off of him. Together they finished the savage.

Lord Preston nodded his head in appreciation before charging off. Valn turned and spotted Ryk. Seeing that the man was in danger, the Byleon raced for him.

The stale breath of a barbarian wafted over Ryk as he was pinned against a sharp rock. The savage leered over him knowing he had the advantage. Desperately, Ryk pushed against the bulky man as the blade of his knife neared his throat.

Out of the chaos a small figure ran straight for him. Sweat poured down Ryk's face as he struggled to keep the knife away from his flesh. It lowered another inch. Suddenly, the figure struck the man in the back. As his opponent reared up, Ryk seized his chance and threw the man off of him. Snatching his knife, he plunged it into the man's chest.

"Thanks, Valn," gasped Ryk.

"Don't mention it," said Valn.

The two parted and dove into the chaos of the battle.

A twig snapped. Curious, Magi snuck away trekking down the hill behind them away from the battle at hand. No one should be here, she thought to herself. She crept through the underbrush listening for the sound that had attracted her attention.

Something shiny caught her eye. Padding closer, Magi poked her head through the thicket. Men in barbarian armor walked up the hill planning to attack from behind,

Betrayal!

Magi leapt away bounding up the hill to where Nylana stood overlooking the fight. She squirted under logs and bushes as she hurried to the top. Huffing, Magi reached the ledge where Nylana shot off more arrows.

"Barbarians! Behind you!"

Nylana turned around just as a man poked his head over the crest of the hill. She quickly fired an arrow striking him in the throat. Another burst over the pinnacle charging her. His strong hands seized her wrists as a malicious smile of broken teeth filled her view.

Suddenly, Tabs jumped for the man's leg digging his claws in deep. As the barbarian roared in pain and hopped on one foot, Nylana kneed him in the stomach. She kicked the man over the edge of the cliff just as Tabs let go of his leg.

More approached from behind. With a sinking feeling, Nylana realized that Vasagius had somehow outsmarted them. She backed toward the edge. As her heels hung in the air, Nylana looked all about her finding no escape.

Magi glanced down. A flash of gold caught her attention. "Nylana, step off."

"What?" breathed Nylana in disbelief.

"Trust me," said Magi. "Just step back."

As the anxiety of certain death took hold, Nylana scanned the line of barbarian men heading for her with greedy expressions.

Closing her eyes, she took a deep breath steeling her nerves and took one step backward allowing herself to drop with Tabs and Magi right behind her.

Her back hit something hard. Opening her eyes, Nylana realized that she and the cats had landed on the back of a dragon.

"Hold on," yelled Mishkunn.

Nylana grabbed one of the spikes on his back and pulled herself into a seated position. The dragon shot into the sky high above the clouds before banking to the left. With sudden exhilaration, Nylana watched the people below her as they headed for them.

"Take out their catapults," said Nylana.

Mishkunn's body dipped as he headed for one of the catapults. The great machine released its ammo just as the dragon plucked it from the sky dropping it on top of a group of savages. The sun glittered off of Mishkunn's gold scales as he turned around. His claws ripped into another catapult.

Shouts rose all around them as men fired arrows and spears at the dragon. The metal tipped missiles bounced off of his scales. Dragon fire covered the ground encasing many of the barbarians in flame. They stamped and screamed in agony as they vainly attempted to escape a burning death.

Nylana watched the swarm of Vasagius' army. The realization that they could not win filtered through her mind. "Make for Krispyn," she said to Mishkunn.

The dragon turned around in indication that he had heard her orders.

Higher up Tami and Petra watched as the battle went ill. Despite the protective spells they had cast, Vasagius gained the advantage.

"Take hold of my staff," said Petra.

Tami did.

"Together, we can combine our magic and take these men out of here to safety."

Tami barely nodded in confirmation that she heard; her eyes filled with fear. She watched as the barbarian army poured over the hills attacking from behind. More came from the front. In the distance Tami observed strange creatures thirsting for blood. Her skin paled.

"Just repeat after me." Petra recited the words to his spell.

Tami glanced at him her face betraying the panic that rose within her. She heard something behind them. Four savages approached.

"I'm sorry." Tami let go of the staff and darted away ducking behind a thick overgrowth as she headed for safety.

"Tami!"

Saving his anger for later, Petra faced the four that drew nearer. He held his staff before him. The four men laughed at such an act.

"You should know better than to corner a wizard," Petra said.

The men laughed even more.

A bright, white light shot from the staff enveloping all of them. Terrified screams filled the air as the light slowly dissipated. Once gone, all that remained was Petra and four melted bodies.

Narúl stood next to Krispyn as they watched the chaos below. Something gnawed at him. The feeling that all was not right wafted over the man.

The sound of a blade being secretly pulled from its sheath caught his attention. Narúl glanced at Shelwyk who stood nearby. In a flash, Shelwyk charged Krispyn with his drawn sword. Narúl pushed the king to the ground blocking the blade with his own. He wrenched his sword disarming Shelwyk.

A satisfied smile crept across the man's face as Shelwyk took them all in.

Krispyn stared at Shelwyk in shock. "Shelwyk?" gasped Krispyn. "What is this?"

"You know perfectly well what this is," spat Shelwyk.

"I trusted you," said Krispyn.

"Ha!"

Narúl swung his sword at Shelwyk but struck nothing as the sorcerer dematerialized.

The crunching of dirt caught their attention. Everyone looked up to find barbarian soldiers approaching from the rear.

"Sound the retreat," shouted Krispyn. "We've been betrayed!"

A horn reverberated around them as Narúl grabbed one of the savages. He snapped the man's arm in half before splitting open his stomach. Lifting the now lifeless corpse over his head, Narúl flung it at those who headed straight for them.

Arrows rained from the sky; each striking a barbarian soldier. Looking up, Narúl saw a gold dragon hovering above with Nylana and two cats seated on its back.

"Krispyn," shouted Nylana, "They have surrounded us. We need to head for the caves. Narúl, with me."

Narúl hopped onto Mishkunn's back behind Nylana. The dragon flew away heading for the other side where Galdin stood.

Galdin twisted just in time to see the barbarians that approached from behind. "Behind you! Turn around!"

Swords clashed as his men turned in time to block the incoming attack. Within seconds each of his men found themselves locked in armed conflict with the very people they had thought they had outflanked.

Something crashed into Galdin from above knocking him to the ground. He rolled in the black dust losing his sword. Looking up, Galdin stared into the face of a muscular man holding a hatchet in each hand. He lunged for Galdin. Quickly, Galdin rolled to the side avoiding a deadly blow. He lunged for his sword. A hatchet landed beside his hand barely missing it.

Leaping to his feet, Galdin stared at his enemy. A wicked grin spread across the man's face. The man lunged again for Galdin. He sidestepped to avoid the blow, but tripped over a rock plummeting to the ground. Within seconds he found himself facing a raving lunatic as the barbarian charged him; hatchet raised.

Suddenly, Narúl fell from the sky crashing into the man and taking him to the ground. Narúl jumped to his feet placing the heel of his boot on the savage's hatchet arm. With a harsh kick, Narúl rammed the toe of his boot into the man's face breaking his jaw. He reached down grasping the barbarian's head with his strong hands. One quick wrench snapped the man's neck.

"Are you alright?" asked Narúl as he helped Galdin to his feet.

"Galdin," yelled Nylana, "We have been—"

The blunt force of a boulder flung from a catapult rammed into Mishkunn. Nylana and the two cats tumbled from the dragon's back. Magi and Tabs landed safely on solid ground while Nylana continued over the edge.

Desperately, Galdin lunged for her. He snatched her hand just before she fell away. Hanging in midair, Nylana looked into Galdin's eyes. He pulled her to safety just as Narúl reached for her.

"Mishkunn," yelled Nylana.

"I am here, princess," said Mishkunn as he hovered beside her. "That hurt."

"I need you to be my eyes in the sky. Find out the position of Vasagius' men."

Mishkunn flew away.

Nylana turned to Galdin. "I do not know how Vasagius did it, but he managed to sneak up from behind."

"But those rock cliffs are impossible to climb," said Galdin. "How—"

"Shelwyk," interrupted Narúl, "He is the sorcerer."

"Shelwyk?" Nylana looked down at the enclosed valley where Ryk and Lord Stefon fought.   Vasagius' men closed in around them.

Movement caught her eye.   Armed men on horses rode straight for the fight within the valley.   Dust rose behind them covering the land in black filth as they charged into the fray.

"We need to—" Nylana cut herself off. Savage men closed in around them. Grossly outnumbered, she knew they could not fight their way out of this.

An angry shout sounded from afar.   Immediately, the area filled with dwarves as they charged the barbarians. Surprised, the savage men gaped at the short stature of those that killed them with ease barreling through their lines.

Nylana pulled out her sword and ran for the fight. With one smooth strike, she lopped off the head of a barbarian before striking another. The power of the sword fueled her movements.

"Lord Belznyc!" exclaimed Nylana as she literally ran into him.

Many barbarians fled from the onslaught of the dwarves unsure of how to respond.

"Cowards!" yelled Lord Belznyc. He turned to Nylana. "Did you think I wouldn't come? We saw these men climbing the Black Cliffs."

"But how did you—"

"There is no rock that we dwarves cannot climb," said Lord Belznyc. "Captain! Take a charge and chase that yellow — bellied filth 'til the last man is dead."

Two blasts of a horn stopped them in their tracks.

Ryk and Lord Stefon stood back to back as they fought the barbarians that surrounded them. The sound of galloping hooves caught their attention.   Armed men on horses burst onto the scene wearing a different crest. Ryk recognized it immediately.

"Stop," he shouted at a Hemilian soldier aiming an arrow at the new arrivals, "They are here to help."

The soldiers of Hemíl watched as those on horseback cut down the barbarians, but left them alone. With renewed vigor, they charged their enemy joining the strange horsemen.

Two bursts from a horn sounded in the distance. Slowly, the fighting died down as Vasagius' forces pulled back. Ryk and Lord Stefon watched them leave.

"Remain here," Lord Stefon shouted at his men.

A man on horseback rode up to them. He jumped off of his mount pulling his helmet off. "King Krispyn?"

"My name is Lord Stefon and this is—"

"Ryk!" The man shook Ryk's hand with enthusiasm before turning back to Lord Stefon. "I am King Orrin of Pras'quel. I wish to speak with your king immediately."

Just then, a loud voice boomed over the valley and hills. "People of Tesnayr, I am Vasagius, your conqueror. In an effort to avoid more bloodshed, I have called off this fight for the moment. I give you a choice: continue this futile resistance of yours and die, or accept my lordship over these lands and live. I will give you the night to think it over."

Vasagius' words bounced off of the hills around them as they slowly faded.

"This way," said Lord Stefon to Orrin.

Chapter XV
Decisions

Nylana carefully wrapped a bandage around the cut in Ryk's arm. Her nimble fingers unraveled the cloth with each pass she made.

Ryk watched each movement of her hands never wincing once. "You do that well," he said.

"I learned to long ago." Memories of watching her mother dress wounds after Vasagius' rebellion flashed through her mind. "You should be more careful."

Ryk lifted Nylana's chin peering into her green eyes. "This is not like the last time."

"I'm not sure what you mean."

"I know of Vasagius' rebellion and of how he murdered your father. This is not like before."

"Are you certain? Whenever Vasagius appears I lose someone I love."

"Well, you will never be rid of me," said Ryk.

Nylana shot him a surprised look.

"You do a poor job of hiding it."

"I suppose I do."

Nylana allowed Ryk to wrap his arms around her for a moment. She noticed Tami skulking through the encampment away from prying eyes. Excusing herself, Nylana followed the girl.

Nylana found Tami seated alone in the moonlight; her knees drawn close as she hugged herself. Curious about the girl's behavior, she moved closer.

"You should not sit so close to me," said Tami, downcast.

"Why not?" Nylana took a place beside the girl.

"I ran away," said Tami, "I don't know why. I saw the army of Vasagius and the men sneaking up on us and I got frightened. I always thought that I was brave, but the sight of those men—I just couldn't face it.

"I am so useless. My magic nearly always fails. And now I have let you all down."

Nylana listened carefully. She understood. "Tami, you are no coward. You are not the first to flee at such a sight, nor will you be the last. You can regain their respect."

"How?"

"All men feel fear. You must face it. When we meet Vasagius again, you will stand on the front lines."

"I don't think I can," whispered Tami.

"You will. Use the power that I know you have within you."

"But I failed you all," said Tami.

"You will only have failed us if you refuse to face Vasagius' men tomorrow."

"I am a simple girl," said Tami, "I was not raised to be brave and face dangers like you were. It is difficult."

"And so it is with me," Nylana replied. "Courage is never taught. It is something you choose."

Tami turned away hugging her knees even more tightly.

Leaving the young girl to her thoughts, Nylana moved away feeling sorry for Tami.

A commotion caught her attention. She hadn't realized that Krispyn and Galdin had called a meeting. Knowing why she wasn't informed, Nylana marched toward the tent.

Tami stared after Nylana as she walked to the tent where the men had chosen to meet. Perhaps she is right, thought the girl. Tami hugged her knees even more. She felt like a failure.

Fur brushed her leg. Tami reached down and stroked Magi's soft fur. "You shouldn't be alone," said the cat.

"I desire solitude for the moment," said Tami.

"In that case I will sit with you." Magi nestled into Tami's side purring loudly. "What you need to do, young lady, is decide how you wish to be remembered."

"What do you mean?" asked Tami.

"Well, do you want to be remembered as the girl who ran away, or the girl who faced a charging hoard of barbarians?"

Tami remained silent.

"I know what Nylana said to you and she's right."

"Eavesdropping again?"

"Of course," said Magi as though it should have been obvious. "Just think about it. And scratch my ears."

Tami rubbed the cat's ears as purring filled the small space around her. *Perhaps there is hope.*

"How did they manage to surround us?" demanded Krispyn.

"Have you forgotten Shelwyk?" said Lord Preston.

"No, I have not. It is unfortunate that he is the one behind all this. But the only way they could have snuck up from behind is by climbing the Black Cliffs—impossibly sharp rocks even for a dwarf to climb."

"Magic was at work there," said Petra.

"And you," Krispyn turned on Orrin, "How did you know to come here?"

"I received instructions," replied Orrin. "Soon after Galdin and I had parted, my father died and I was made king. And I received this note." He pulled out the paper that Quesha had sent him.

Petra took it, examining it. "There is only one person in the world who would have written this. I'd recognize that witch's handwriting anywhere."

Krispyn reached for the note. "And you obeyed these instructions from one you did not know?"

"She was very persuasive," answered Orrin.

"She usually is," chuckled Petra. "My king, you have little to fear from this man. If Quesha sent him, she had a reason."

"And he saved all our lives," said Galdin.

A cough sounded around them.

"As did you, Lord Belznyc," Galdin added with a slight bow.

"What should we do about Vasagius' offer?" asked Krispyn.

"Surrender," said Lord Preston. "It is the only way."

"But that would be—" began Lord Ardryn.

"Foolish!" Nylana burst into the tent.

"My lady," said Lord Preston, "We did not see you standing there."

"Nor would you be expecting me to since I was not informed of this meeting," Nylana said.

"Nylana," began Krispyn, "We were merely discussing—"

"I know what it is you were discussing," interrupted Nylana, "If you give in to Vasagius' demands there will be no hope for the rest of us. He will kill us all."

"But we have his word," said Lord Preston.

"And you trust the word of a man who burns entire villages and kills without remorse," said Nylana.

"I am always for a good fight," said Lord Belznyc. "We dwarves refuse to give up our arms."

"I must agree with the dwarf," said Lord Ardryn.

"Lord Stefon?" asked Krispyn.

Stefon looked up for a moment. He shook his head slightly remaining silent.

"If we fight we will die," said Krispyn. "I propose a choice. We will let the men decide if they wish to continue this war or leave."

"Are you—"

Petra squeezed Nylana's arm forcing her into silence. "What say you, Galdin?"

Galdin unfolded his arms as he pulled himself from his musing. "You all have valid points. We cannot win this fight through strength of arms. But surrendering entirely is unwise. Vasagius will most likely kill us all despite what we do.

"You can offer the men a choice, Krispyn, but you best hope they make the right one. I for one believe we should take a stand even if it means annihilation."

"What is your decision?" Petra asked Krispyn. Something in the back of his mind clawed its way to freedom.

"I cannot order them into annihilation. If there is a chance we might live, then we should take it. Let the men choose their own fate."

Krispyn noticed the troubled look on Petra's face. "Something troubling you, wizard?"

Petra looked directly into Krispyn's eyes keeping his face unreadable. "What isn't to trouble me when we are facing a madman with an army bent on our destruction?"

The note in Petra's voice indicated that he had just learned something; but what no one could guess.

The four remaining lords of the five lands saluted and left the tent with Krispyn and the wizard.

Nylana rounded on Galdin. "Are you just going to let them sell themselves into slavery? If we are to die we shall die as men. Will you not try to convince them?"

Galdin faced his sister. "If there is one thing I have learned from you, it's that you always find a way of taking a stand and convincing others to follow you. They will not follow Krispyn."

"He is their king. How can you be so sure?"

"Because you convinced me not to." Galdin left Nylana alone to stew in her frustration.

She stormed out of the tent running right into Orrin.

"Never struck by a slave indeed. If only I had known you were the Princess of Tesnayr."

"I—"

Orrin cut her off. "I know why you never told me. You had no reason to trust me. I wish to apologize for my father's actions."

"There is no need."

"I beg to differ. And when this conflict is over, I hope that relations between Pras'quel and Tesnayr can be restored."

"They were never lost," said Nylana.

"Perhaps not," said Orrin. "Shall we?" He motioned for her to follow him. "We have much to discuss."

Chapter XVI
Hope Restored

Dawn peeked over the horizon as Nylana sat alone staring at the armies before her twirling the feather in her hand. She had been sent to find something that would restore hope and found it. She had no idea what it was for. The first rays of sunlight glittered on the feather as it turned a brilliant gold.

A tune escaped Nylana's lips as she pondered the mysterious feather. She sang the same song that all children learn in the lands of Tesnayr. The song that Quesha had recited when she appeared in Norlyk that day they met with the council.

"A coin for your thoughts," said Petra as he sat beside her.

"Here," said Nylana, "This is what you sent me after."

Petra took it examining it. "An odd feather. What are we to do with it?"

"That is what I am asking you. You sent me after a lost relic and this is what I found, but I have no idea what to do with it."

"I'm sure you'll figure it out," Petra handed her the feather again.

"Armies of the five lands; men of Tesnayr," said Krispyn as he stood above everyone.

Nylana and Petra jumped to their feet and joined the gathering crowd around Krispyn.

"We have been faced with a difficult choice," continued Krispyn, "Vasagius has offered sanctuary if we surrender to him now. If we refuse, he has vowed to kill us all. Since this goes beyond the confines of any kingship, I lay this choice before you: whatever you choose, no one will think ill of it. If you wish to return home, then leave now and good luck. If you wish to stay and fight, then remain."

"It is too dangerous," said a soldier. "It is not worth the sacrifice."

"Then what is?" asked Nylana, her voice echoing throughout the hills and the valley. "What shall we fight for? If we turn away now, who will take our place?"

Nylana walked regally before the men. She scanned their faces noting the fear and hopelessness that dwelled within them. "All of you have sworn oaths to the lands of Tesnayr—to my brother! And yet you cower here. Where is your honor? Where is your courage? Will you not take up arms to fight for those you swore to protect?"

"But we will die," said a voice.

"Yes, death is certain," replied Nylana. "And let us meet that end head on and with honor. Confront it like the men you are. I ride to meet Vasagius. Who will ride with me?"

"I will," said Galdin, stepping forward.

"Will you say, yes, if I come?" Ryk stepped forward.

Nylana smiled at Ryk's question. "If you survive."

"Then I am yours to command," said Ryk with a bow.

A harsh clearing of someone's throat forced Nylana to turn around. "You know I'm in," said Lord Belznyc. "I'll go anywhere where there's a good fight." He looked foreboding with his battle axe resting against his left shoulder.

"Are there no others?" shouted Nylana.

Narúl stepped forward, his hand on the hilt of his sword. "I have been by your side our whole life. I will not abandon you now, or ever."

Krispyn placed his strong hand on her shoulder. "You will always have me." He glanced around him. "Men of Tesnayr, will you not answer your lady's call?"

Shouts and cheers went up thundering around them as men found the courage to follow Nylana to the end.

Nylana shoved her hand into her pocket where she touched the feather. She pulled it out into the growing light of dawn twirling the feather in her hand and letting the soft silk caress her fingers. She studied the meshing of gold and red. An idea occurred to her as she pulled the blue rose out of her pocket and stared at it admiring how the feather accentuated the rose.

A gift he needs from its glen.
And a tear from old lore.

"When two become one," whispered Nylana to herself.

It hit her.

Nylana rushed toward Petra. "Petra, the journal, what did it say again?"

The wizard turned toward her pausing in his conversation with the captain. "Now isn't—"

"Tell me!"

Upon the determined look on Nylana's face, Petra acquiesced. "The gift of the phoenix, its tears, and something that hasn't been seen since the days of Tesnayr are needed to restore what has been lost. It's almost like that children's rhyme."

"Like this?" Nylana held up the feather. It glittered gold in the morning sunlight.

The wizard took it carefully realizing where Nylana was going. "Fool of a wizard I am. I must be getting old."

Nylana snatched the feather and darted off.

"Nylana—"

"I know what to do." She marched to the man with the horn. "Sound the horn," she ordered, "I want all eyes upon me."

Nylana ascended the rise above both the forces of Tesnayr and those of Vasagius. Along the way, she grabbed Galdin pulling him with her. He started to protest but the determination in her movements silenced him. She stopped at the side of a cliff overlooking the black valley below as the man blew his horn to summon the army's attention. Everyone looked at this woman on the hill.

"People of Tesnayr," said Nylana, "Vasagius wants you to believe that he has won. That there is no hope left. We have suffered much. Our homes destroyed. Our loved ones murdered before our very eyes. But I stand here this day as testament to the will of Tesnayr: the will to fight! I give you hope."

Nylana yanked Galdin's sleeve up exposing the birthmark, matching and asymmetrical to hers. She placed her arm against his. Instantly, the two marks on their skin turned gold. Gradually, light surrounded them as Galdin watched the fire in his sister's eyes once more. With her other hand, Nylana wiped tears from her eyes and held up the rose and feather muttering strange words. "When two become one."

She released them. The breeze caught the feather and the rose twirling them around in circles. They spun faster and faster spinning around each other until they became a blur. Gold and silver light spilled from Nylana as a great cry escaped her lips and the gold light around her and Galdin formed the shape of the phoenix.

Sparks flew from the whirling feather and rose. An explosion rocked the earth as the light surrounding Nylana and Galdin disappeared and flames burst from the rose and the feather. A great cry filled the air. The phoenix had been reborn.

The majestic bird shot from the flames cawing fiercely as it swooped through the sky dipping low among the gathered armies. The people of Tesnayr cheered with renewed fervor. Fear filled the faces of the barbarians.

Galdin caught Nylana as she fell unconscious. Gently, he laid her on the ground.

"Nylana!" Ryk ran up to them.

Steel rang out everywhere as the armies of Tesnayr restarted the fight. "Stay with her," ordered Galdin. He grabbed Nylana's sword and plunged into the fray; the blade leading his way.

A red eyed orc charged for the unconscious Nylana. Ryk jumped in front of it making certain not to look in its eyes. He swung his weapon splitting the beast's head from chin to brow. A wĕdlym appeared from nowhere leering over Nylana. It swiped at Ryk catching him in the stomach and flinging him into a tree. He grunted as he hit the ground.

Suddenly, the phoenix barreled into the wĕdlym. The force of the impact sent the massive beast flying through the air until it caught fire and turned to ash.

Carefully, the phoenix landed beside Nylana. It eyed her with sorrow. It placed its beak upon her forehead giving her a gentle peck. "The world has need of you yet," the phoenix said. It flew off.

Stirring, Nylana opened her eyes. It took her several moments to remember where she was.

Ryk rushed to her. "Nylana!" He held her tightly kissing her on the cheek. "I thought I lost you."

"Thought you were rid of me so easily," said Nylana. "My sword!"

"Galdin has it," said Ryk. "Use mine." He handed her his weapon while he snatched a nearby one from the ground.

Together, Nylana and Ryk charged down the hill and into the battle for the five lands.

Deep within the Black Mountains the dragons ignored the clashing of swords and ringing steel having no interest in the affairs of humans. The dragon that had tried to eat Nylana grunted in annoyance.

Caw!

The dragon peered to his left and noticed a strange bird poised on a rock staring at him with eyes that pierced his soul. Instantly, he knew what creature it was.

"Will you not answer the call?" asked the phoenix.

The dragon turned his back to the bird. "The others may go if they wish. I want to be left alone." He sauntered off into a cave allowing the blackness to consume him.

The phoenix cawed again and took off with only a handful of aging dragons behind him.

On the sidelines of the battle, Shelwyk stood with a group of Nôk'ta watching the proceedings. How did she bring back the phoenix, he thought to himself as he watched the magnificent bird fly overhead. He glanced over at one of the red eyed beasts.

"You know what to do," Shelwyk said to the creature. "Leave none alive."

A wicked smile spread across the Nôk'ta's face. He raised a bow taking aim at Galdin. Pulling the string back, the creature never noticed the rock that crept up from behind.

Suddenly, Trog unfolded himself and lunged for the Nôk'ta clenching his jaws around the beast's arm. Growling filled the area as Trog ripped the flesh from the orc's arm. The creature swung at the animal, but Trog jumped out of the way; his movements quick.

A boulder rammed into Trog's head sending the animal flying and garnering a yelp of pain. Trog lay sprawled on the black earth.

"Stupid creature," sneered Shelwyk. He leered over Trog raising his weapon for the deadly strike.

Without warning, Trog swiped his tail across the ground sweeping Shelwyk's feet out from under him. The sorcerer crashed into the dirt. He watched as Trog leapt for him. Muttering a spell, Shelwyk disappeared just as Trog reached where he had been finding only dust. Disappointed, Trog spread his wings and took off as the Nôk'ta dispersed.

Amidst the chaos Lord Belznyc noticed that Lord Preston was in trouble. The distance between them was too great. Lord Belznyc noticed a winged creature flying overhead. Quickly, he took some rope and made a loop. Swinging it over his head, he flung it at the winged creature catching it around one foot.

Instantly, his feet left the ground as he held on with one hand; his axe in the other. Flying through the air, the dwarf kept his eyes fixed on Lord Preston as he struggled against two other winged creatures.

Once there, he let go dropping onto one of the beasts. Before it could react, Lord Belznyc hacked its middle with his axe. He whirled around to face the second one. Instantly, the winged creature wrapped itself up spinning like a top as it fired spikes. Lord Belznyc and Lord Preston dodged the sharp spears.

Lord Preston tapped a stone with his sword. Distracted, the winged creature stopped. It relaxed slightly eyeing Lord Preston greedily. Suddenly, Lord Belznyc leapt onto its back digging his axe deep into its neck. Meanwhile, Lord Preston stabbed the beast in the middle as it writhed and crumbled to the ground.

A harsh screech reached their ears. Lord Belznyc shoved Lord Preston out of the way just as a third winged creature appeared taking the brunt of the impact. He rose to his knees staring murderously at the animal.

"Come on you foul beastie!"

The winged creature stepped toward the dwarf. Before it moved far, a rock hit it in the head. It whirled onto Lord Preston. Seizing his chance, Lord Belznyc moved in jamming his weapon into the creature's middle at the same instant that Lord Preston did the same.

"You are wounded," said Lord Preston.

"Tis a scratch," Lord Belznyc waved off the man's concerns. He noticed more wĕdlym skulking under a precipice. "Is there a catapult nearby?"

"Yes."

Together the two wove their way through the melee as they ran for the nearest catapult. Once there, they heaved a boulder into its holder. Breathing heavily, Lord Belznyc strained under the weight of the rock as blood oozed from his mortal wound. They lined it up and pulled the lever.

The rock sailed through the air crashing into the precipice sending heaps of debris below. The screeching of the wẽdlym as they were crushed to death filled their ears rendering a satisfied smile on the dwarf's face.

Lord Belznyc collapsed. Quickly, Lord Preston caught the dwarf, concern etched on his face.

"I guess it was more than a scratch," said Lord Belznyc. He handed Lord Preston his axe. "Get them for me."

Lord Preston took the axe as the dwarf released his last breath. Gently, he laid him on the ground. Rising to his feet, Lord Preston caught two of his men and led them to the thick of the battle.

Tami stood upon a precipice overlooking the battle below. That same fear rose up within her. She pushed it away, summoning her courage as she remembered Nylana's words. *Summon the power I know is within you.*

Magi walked up from behind. "Nylana believes in you. Why do you not believe in yourself?"

Tami held out her hands stretching them wide. Muttering words in the ancient language of the fairies, her hands shook. The ground vibrated beneath her feet and rumbled as dirt rolled over the surface. Slowly, figures rose from the ground transforming into humanoid shapes. Giant rocks rolled across the earth stopping before the newly formed soldiers. Gradually, each rock grew in size until it took the shape of a horse. Some of the dirt soldiers mounted the horses. They all faced Tami awaiting her command.

"The people of Tesnayr need your help. Defend them! Destroy those red-eyed beasts and all who fight under Vasagius' shield."

Thunder roared as they took off charging down the hillside and into the valley below.

Grit filled Valn's mouth as he crashed into the ground. He snatched a nearby shield bashing a barbarian in the jaw with it. Hurriedly, he leapt to his feet and slammed the tip of the shield into the man's throat.

His limbs froze. Despite his will, the Byleon's limbs refused to move as a red-eyed orc bore down upon him. It growled in victory as it moved in on its prey. Valn's mind raced, but he remained frozen.

A dirt soldier appeared behind the red-eyed orc. The beast turned around freeing Valn as it did so. Fear filled its face as the strange dirt soldier grew in height before striking the orc with its weapon.

It neared Valn. The Byleon remained still as the strange creature studied him. As quick as it came, it disappeared.

Valn picked up his sword and noticed Tami poised on high ground overseeing the battle. He smiled to himself as he realized that the thing that saved his life came from her.

"Valn," said Tabs as he ran up. "Look!"

Valn peered at the sky as a handful of dragons flew overhead with Mishkunn in the lead. In formation, they banked to the right and dived to the ground plowing into the mass of barbarians that charged across the field.

"In all my days, I have never seen such a sight," said Valn.

"Nor I," added Tabs.

Valn looked out across the field and noticed a group of winged creatures surrounding Orrin and Lord Stefon. A bit of white caught his eye as three unicorns raced across the field toward them. I hope they make it in time, the Byleon thought to himself.

A winged creature plowed into Orrin knocking him off his horse and into Lord Stefon. The two men rolled across the ground. When they stopped, they eyed the winged creatures that surrounded them. One creature wrapped itself up spinning fast as it fired spikes at them clipping Orrin in the shoulder. He raised his shield blocking more.

Lord Stefon stabbed at a nearby winged creature, but his sword bounced off its wing. A creature sliced at him. Lord Stefon rolled out of the way stopping at the feet of another.

"There's too many of them," Orrin shouted.

He slammed his shield into the face of a winged creature. It squealed in anger as it slashed at him catching him in the arm once again.

One of the creatures seized Lord Stefon from behind. Orrin leapt up ramming his weapon into the thing's neck forcing it to let the man go. Once freed, Lord Stefon whirled around and shoved the limp body of the winged creature into another.

Orrin and Lord Stefon stood back to back watching warily as the creatures closed in. The mind of each raced as they tried to find a way out of their predicament.

A blur of white appeared as a unicorn rammed its horn into one of the winged creatures. It screeched in anguish as it shriveled in a crumpled mass and lay still on the ground. Quickly, the unicorn swung its head catching another of the creatures. Lord Stefon and Orrin watched in amazement as two more unicorns appeared and systematically vanquished the winged creatures.

"Where is Nylana and her brother Galdin?" asked one of the unicorns.

"I do not know," replied Lord Stefon. "She could be anywhere."

The unicorn nodded its head at the other two who followed.

Nylana lay sprawled on the ground; her sword out of reach. A wēdlym slowly approached her as she lay there. She watched as the creature moved closer, saliva dripping from its rotted teeth. Unable to reach her weapon, Nylana waited for the inevitable.

Mishkunn landed over Nylana in a protective stance releasing a tremendous roar. The dragon scooped the wĕdlym in his jaws swallowing it in one bite. Just as quickly, he took off.

Nylana picked up her sword. She noticed Petra just below her fighting a barbarian savage. She watched as the wizard dodged a deadly blow smacking the man with his staff. Balls of fire shot from one end striking two other barbarians. Deftly, Petra struck his opponent in the throat.

Nylana noticed Galdin racing for the wizard, the sword of Tesnayr glowed brightly in his hand. His legs stretched in long strides as he hurried to Petra's aide.

Shelwyk appeared beside Petra. Before the wizard could react, the sorcerer stabbed him in the stomach. Helplessly, Nylana watched as Petra collapsed to the ground clutching his wound. Shelwyk sneered maliciously before vanishing.

"Petra!" screamed Nylana.

Nylana started for the wizard. Narúl's strong arm immediately wrapped around her waist yanking her back as he appeared from nowhere. She struggled ferociously prying his arms off of her. Despite Narúl's and Ryk's protests, Nylana charged down the hill for the wizard.

Galdin reached Petra as he lay there gasping for air. Carefully, he lifted the wizard's head, cradling it. "You'll be fine."

"You can't lie to a wizard," coughed Petra, "There is more here than meets the eye. Everything you see is an illusion."

"Don't talk," said Galdin.

Petra grasped his shoulder with a bloodied hand. "Take care of Nylana. She is strong, but vulnerable. You must be the one to make the sacrifice."

"I will," said Galdin unsure of what the wizard was talking about.

"Kr—" Petra's head dropped back.

Carefully, Galdin laid the wizard on the ground. He looked up. Not far from him stood Shelwyk with a triumphant look. Furious, Galdin ran for him.

Krispyn stood amongst the chaos of the battle as fighting men swarmed around him; each preoccupied with their own opponent. One barbarian attacked from behind. Krispyn ducked avoiding the deadly blow while allowing the man to smash into the hard earth. With expert ease, he twirled his sword and plunged it into the barbarian.

Another headed for him. Krispyn callously grasped another barbarian and yanked the stunned man around to take the full brunt of the attacker's charge. Coldly, Krispyn tossed the dead man aside and finished off the other.

Metal clashed around him sending its ringing tone everywhere. Shouts and screams rose up from every corner of the battlefield. As though temporarily cut off from the events around him, Krispyn surveyed the carnage gaging his next choice of action.

Movement caught his eye. On a small rise stood a lone figure cradling someone. Krispyn recognized Nylana instantly. A black shape sped toward her trying desperately to push his way through the throng of fighting men. Narúl, thought Krispyn.

A riderless horse galloped for him. Bracing himself, Krispyn seized the reins flinging himself into the saddle. Hastily, he kicked the horse and sped through the melee and to his sister. The horse snorted as it tired. Krispyn kicked it again spurring it on; keeping his eyes fixed on Nylana.

Nylana reached Petra's body just as Galdin hurried away. She dropped to her knees.

"Petra," she choked.

Gently, Nylana closed the wizard's vacant eyes. Her mentor, friend of her father, gone.

"So the wizard is dead," laughed Vasagius as he stood over her.

Anger coursed through Nylana. She jumped to her feet and charged Vasagius. He deflected her strike easily knocking her to the ground. She glared at him a moment; rage implanted on her face.

Nylana charged again. With ease, Vasagius parried her strike forcing her to drop her weapon.

"You know, you should really learn how to fight." He handed her her sword.

Nylana took it and grasped it tightly. Suddenly, one of Narúl's lessons entered her head.

Always control yourself. The emotional opponent is easily defeated.

"You still wish to fight?" teased Vasagius with amusement.

Nylana held her sword before her, calming herself. Vasagius, lunged. Swiftly, she stepped to the right wrenching her sword downward clipping his blade. Nylana took her posture again. Surprised, Vasagius stared at her. He swung again. Nylana jumped backward forcing him to lose his balance. Quickly, she jumped forward striking him in the arm.

Checking his cut, Vasagius eyed her carefully. "It appears you do know a bit about swordplay. More than your father at least."

Vasagius kicked dirt into Nylana's eyes. Momentarily blinded, she swung helplessly. A sharp blow forced her to spit out some blood as her jaw throbbed. Blinking repeatedly, Nylana managed to clear her vision enough to see Vasagius attack again. She brought her sword up, deflecting his strike and kicked him in the shin unlocking their blades. Whirling around him, Nylana dodged blow after blow.

Vasagius punched her in the gut. She doubled over gasping for air. Just in time, Nylana avoided a fatal strike by hitting him in the face with the horn of Selexia; breaking it into pieces. Bringing her sword up, she clashed with Vasagius'. With great strength, he unlocked their blades kicking her away from him. He charged. Nylana swung the hilt up bashing him in the face.

"That is for my father."

Vasagius charged again. Nylana ducked striking him in the side.

"That is for my brother," she said.

Enraged, Vasagius lunged for her. Nylana somersaulted on the ground before knocking his feet out from under him.

"That is for Petra," Nylana said.

Vasagius swung his fist to the side catching her in the face. Stunned, Nylana stood still long enough for him to disarm her. He backed her against the scrawny trunk of a leafless tree; his blade to her throat.

"It appears you are out of tricks," sneered Vasagius in her ear.

Remembering the dagger Narúl had given her, she plunged it deep into Vasagius' side hitting the lung.

"And this is for me." Nylana pushed Vasagius off of her watching callously as he fell to the ground.

Krispyn, Ryk, and Narúl reached her as she bent to reclaim her sword.

"Are you alright?" Krispyn asked. He looked down on Vasagius' dead form. With one smooth strike he cut off the man's head. Grasping it by the hair, Krispyn raced for high ground. Once there he held Vasagius' disembodied head up high.

"Army of Vasagius," he bellowed, the rocks carrying his voice, "Look at your leader now!" Krispyn tossed the head away allowing it to roll down the rocky cliff and land in the valley below.

Frightened, the barbarian army turned to flee running in every direction; their escape cut off by Tami's army of dirt and rock.

"Leave none alive," said Tami.

Screams filled the air as her army cut through the lines of Vasagius' men killing as they went.

Galdin chased after Shelwyk following him deep into the Black Mountains where caves dotted the landscape. He stopped before the mouth of one knowing that the slippery man had gone in there. Grasping the sword of Tesnayr tightly, he marveled momentarily as the blade glowed slightly.

Slowly, Galdin entered the dark cave. He stepped lightly making certain to not make a sound. As his eyes adjusted to the darkness, Galdin searched about him for any sign of Shelwyk. He crept further in.

"You will never find me," said Shelwyk disembodied voice.

Galdin ignored the taunts.

"I am here!"

Swiftly, Galdin turned around swinging his weapon and hitting only air. Maniacal laughter echoed around him.

Biding his time, Galdin delved deeper into the earth. He listened to every sound, every clink. Water dripped nearby. Turning in small circles as he walked, Galdin kept a constant awareness of his surroundings.

Suddenly, Shelwyk appeared. He knocked Galdin to the ground. His sword clinked as it landed away from him. Rolling onto his back, Galdin brought his arm up just in time to block an attack from Shelwyk. The sorcerer crashed on top of him pointing a knife at his throat. Galdin rammed his fist into the man's neck. He threw the sorcerer off of him and darted for his sword.

He grabbed it just in time to bring it before him as Shelwyk shot lightning at him. The sword of Tesnayr deflected the lightning sending a return shockwave that knocked Shelwyk off his feet. Galdin ran for him. Suddenly, the air was sucked form the area. Gasping, Galdin stopped holding his throat struggling for another breath. The sword glowed gold telling him what to do. Allowing the blade to guide his movements, Galdin swung his sword behind him striking Shelwyk on the cheek.

A yell reverberated around him as the sorcerer called out. He touched his bloody cheek eyeing Galdin with a menacing glare.

Though grateful that he could breathe once more; Galdin had no time for resting. Shelwyk charged. Galdin brought his sword up. Sparks flew as their blades clashed sending a piercing ring through the underground tunnels.

Galdin grasped Shelwyk's wrist and head-butted the man. Without losing a moment, he unlocked their blades and cut off Shelwyk's sword hand. A painful cry bounced off the cave walls.

Shelwyk dropped to his knees not bothering to cradle the stump where his hand had been. "You may think you have won here, son of Glasaf, but you have achieved nothing. Everything here is an illusion."

Shelwyk pulled out a dagger with his other hand. Before Galdin could stop him, he jammed it into his own throat. Gurgling, Shelwyk's body slumped to the side before settling on the bloodied floor of the cave.

Galdin eyed the lifeless corpse before him. He wiped his sword clean. Callously, he poked Shelwyk's body with the toe of his boot. Satisfied that the man was dead, Galdin left the cave heading back to the battlefield. *The animals can have him.*

Upon reaching it, Galdin paused. He looked out at the expanse below him in awe as Tami's army of dirt and rock swept across the field. Rain fell from the sky washing away the filth of bloodied corpses as the phoenix soared overhead.

Chapter XVII
A Union

Farewell, dear friends buried here.
Of this day will all sing far and near.
To thy ancestor's halls may you be
guided for your sacrifice and noble deed.

Slowly, the voices died as the song ended and the people of Tesnayr honored their departed friends with one last farewell. Fires sprung up as those from Belyndril burned their dead. Nylana watched the dancing flames; Petra's death weighing heavily upon her heart. She felt a hand on her shoulder. Turning, she looked straight into the eyes of Galdin.

Nylana looked back upon Petra's burning form with sorrow. "Farewell dear friend," she said, "You were noble to the end."

"He would not have wanted you to mourn."

"You're right," said Nylana, "But he was my teacher. Like Narúl, Petra was there when my father died. Without his guidance, I would not be here. Whom will I look to now?"

"You could try listening to the cat," Magi quipped. "I have been around for quite a while and know a thing or two."

"Well there you go," grinned Galdin, "A cat's wisdom."

       *   *   *

A week passed before the council of Tesnayr met to declare the name of their king. Nylana stood in a corner watching the proceedings as the members of the council debated among themselves. She stole a glance at Petra's empty chair. *Who will fill his place?*

"I say that Krispyn remain as king for the courage he displayed on the battlefield," said one of the members. "It was he who destroyed Vasagius."

"That was Nylana's doing," yelled Magi from the shadows as she watched the proceedings with disgust. "Imbeciles," the cat muttered to herself.

The man that had spoken looked around for the source of the voice, but finding none, assumed that one of the other members had spoken. "If that is so then—"

"You know my feelings on the matter," said Nylana.

"Indeed," said Byron rising from his chair. "In that case, I believe that Krispyn should remain as the king, but Galdin will be his general. Together, they will share leadership which will be tempered by the council."

"A wise plan," said the representative from Belarnia. "Krispyn, may you govern wisely."

Krispyn bowed before the elf in acknowledgement of the sentiment.

"Might I make a suggestion?" said Orrin who had been invited out of courtesy in an effort to maintain relations with Pras'quel. "It appears you have an empty seat on the council. Perhaps Nylana should be the one to fill it."

"I agree," Byron said.

"But—" began Nylana.

"It is settled then," said another member of the council. "Nylana will fill the wizard's seat."

"My lords," said Nylana, her voice rendering all of them to attention. "I must refuse your offer of the seat on the council. I am honored, but my place is elsewhere.

"We are sorry to hear that," said another member of the council. "But, might I congratulate you, my lady, on your proposed marriage."

"Thank you," said Nylana.

"Marriage?" asked Krispyn. "Could it be that you have finally chosen a husband?"

"Yes."

"My sincerest congratulations," Krispyn embraced his sister, "Long have I prayed that you would find a man worthy of your company."

"When will the wedding take place?" asked Byron.

"Within the week," said Krispyn. "A joyous event like this should not be delayed."

The council chamber burst into excitement as everyone congratulated Nylana on her impending marriage to Ryk. Each took her hand and voiced the happiness they had for her.

"I know he will treat you well and make you happy," said Galdin as he hugged his sister.

"Thank you, general."

Galdin winced at the title. "I prefer Galdin."

*   *   *

Ryk studied himself in the mirror admiring how handsome he looked. He tugged a bit at the starched collar of his tunic. If only looking well-dressed didn't mean wearing itchy clothes, he thought.

Narúl strolled into the room. He took one look at Ryk and straightened the scarf around his neck. "So, she has accepted your proposal."

"It appears so," said Ryk, unsure of what to think.

"You will take good care of her."

"Yes."

"In my homeland," said Narúl, "There are these ants as big as my finger. Their hills can dwarf a building. It would pain me to have to bury you in one of them."

Ryk gulped. Narúl's stony face betrayed nothing. "I swear on pain of death to always treat Nylana as the queen she is."

"Then we will get along fine." Narúl clapped Ryk on the shoulder. "Relax. This is your wedding day."

Relax he says, thought Ryk. He straightened his clothes and left the room where he ran into Galdin.

"Ready?" asked Galdin.

"Yes. You don't think Narúl would really bury me in an ant hill do you?"

Galdin gave him a quizzical look.

"Never mind."

A hush fell over the chamber as Ryk and Nylana stood at the front.

Krispyn stood before them with a broad smile. "Who gives this woman to be wedded this day?"

"I do," said Galdin.

"And who gives this man to be wedded this day?" asked Krispyn.

"I do," said Orrin.

Krispyn wrapped Nylana's and Ryk's hands with a purple cloth. "Nylana, do you accept this man as your husband, to know only him and to be bound to him for the rest of your days?"

"I do," said Nylana.

"Ryk, do you accept this woman as your wife, to know only her and to be bound to her for the rest of your days?"

"I do," answered Ryk.

"As you have pledged yourselves to each other, drink of this cup and become one." Krispyn handed them a goblet of wine.

Ryk and Nylana each took a sip from it.

"People of Tesnayr," said Krispyn, "I give you Lord Ryk and the Lady Nylana."

A series of claps, shouts, and cheers rang throughout the room as people celebrated the marriage of their beloved princess.

"Let the feast begin!" said Krispyn amidst the cheers.

Chapter XVIII
Bitter Sting

Galdin strolled through one of the many corridors of the palace of Norlyk deep in his own thoughts. Petra's last words to him plagued him. He hardly knew the wizard, but the man's desperate pleas stuck with him, mingling with Shelwyk's taunts.

Nothing is as it seems. This is all an illusion.

Repeatedly, these words flowed through his mind.

"You must make the sacrifice," Petra had told him before he died.

Sacrifice, thought Galdin, what sacrifice?

Petra's dying breath was what bothered Galdin the most. "Kr—" Petra had breathed.

Galdin barely registered the servants that passed him in the hallway. *Kr—Kr—Whom was Petra referring to?* Galdin pondered over it until he could think no more.

The singing of a cat pulled him back to the present. "Hello, Tabs," said Galdin. "Where is Nylana?"

"With Krispyn," replied Tabs.

Krispyn? Krispyn—of course! "With Krispyn?"

"Yes," said Tabs as he lapped from a goblet of mead. "They're in his chambers."

Galdin sprinted through the corridor for the nearest set of stairs. He had to get to Nylana before it was too late.

*   *   *

"Here," said Krispyn handing Nylana a goblet of honeyed mead. "A little celebration to our success in saving the lands of Tesnayr."

"This isn't necessary," said Nylana.

"I tire of grand celebrations," said Krispyn. "I just wanted to talk with you. I see so little of you lately."

Nylana sipped her beverage.

"Have you thought about what you want to do?"

"No, I haven't."

"You could stay here as a co-monarch," suggested Krispyn.

Nylana eyed her brother. His demeanor seemed different; too questioning. "I never wanted the throne. You know that."

"An advisor then."

"Sorry, Krispyn, but after all this, I just want to settle down to a quiet life. MurDair has offered Ryk and I a small manor. We thought we'd go there."

"From princess to farmer."

"Worse things have happened," said Nylana. "You do not need me, little brother."

Krispyn moved to the window and stared out at the courtyard below. The moon shown so bright it almost resembled daytime. "No doubt you need a rest. And to think that all your troubles began in Pras'quel when a tree knocked out the road."

Slowly, Nylana lowered her goblet placing it quietly on the table. A puzzled look crossed her face as she thought back to the day slavers had captured her by knocking a tree over and forcing her carriage to stop. "Yes," she said, trying to sound normal.

Turning from the window Krispyn looked directly at her. "But then you never mentioned the tree did you?" He put his goblet down. "From the moment you returned, I was afraid of making this mistake. At least it waited until after I had achieved my goals."

Nylana backed away bumping into another table.

"Those stupid men were paid to kill you. Apparently their greed got the better of them. You can't even imagine my surprise when I saw you enter Norlyk. My own sister whose death I was assured of."

Nylana stared at Krispyn in disbelief.

"You seem surprised. It never occurred to you that I would want to be rid of you. But why would it? You always did think the best of people."

"Krispyn, why?" breathed Nylana not believing her ears.

"I always wanted the throne. I knew the council would never approve of my remaining king so I needed a way to prove to them that I should remain as their king. I just needed to get rid of my competition."

"But you know I never wanted—"

"Doesn't matter," spat Krispyn. His eyes had gone cold. A menace Nylana had never seen filled them. "The war was my doing. After being rid of you I still needed to prove to the people that I was a warrior. A hero like the ones told about in stories. But then you showed up. And with him.

"Of all the people to rescue you from your fate, it had to be your long lost brother. The true heir to the throne of Tesnayr. Oh, but I can always count on you to make certain that both your brothers have a chance of proving their worth. Though a crimp in my plans, I just moved up the invasion of the five lands."

"And Shelwyk? He worked for you?"

"A most loyal servant if there ever was one. He will be difficult to replace, but he did his job well."

"Krispyn, this isn't you. You were always so kind, so quiet."

"I played my part well," sneered Krispyn, "You never suspected? All this time you still believed that I was the sweet, little boy from our childhood. Our mother never loved me the way she loved him. You either. Deep down, I knew that you both missed Galdin; the child lost forever due to a madman's rebellion."

"I always loved you. You are my brother!"

"I never was. Merely a poor replacement. I watched as you and Galdin grew close. You've barely known each other but a few months and already you share the bond of twenty years." He ripped a knife from under his belt.

"Why?"

"I was content to just let you and that Ryk ride away to MurDair. But, obviously, I can't allow that now. I can't let you tell others the truth."

Nylana looked about her thinking of a way to get free. She dodged just as Krispyn lunged for her. The screeching of a cat filled the room as a mass of fur dropped from above landing on Krispyn's neck. Furious, he flung the cat off of him. Magi slammed into the wall and lay unmoving.

Nylana dodged again knocking over trays, candles, and papers. She snatched a paperweight and smashed it into Krispyn's shoulder. "Krispyn, no! Don't do this."

In answer to her pleas, he charged again knife held high. Pinned between the wall and his knife, Nylana grabbed hold of his hand. She tried to push it away. Her muscles strained as she struggled against Krispyn's strength. Closer the knife came.

An explosion racked the room as the door burst open. In rushed Galdin. He seized Krispyn and flung him away from Nylana. The fierce movement, and Krispyn's hold on her, forced Nylana to fly across the room slamming into a wall of shelves. She lay crumpled on the stone floor buried under debris.

Releasing a bloodcurdling cry, Krispyn darted for Galdin with his dagger poised for the kill. Galdin stepped to the side catching Krispyn's wrist and wrenching it back. The sound of crunching bones filled his ears. Krispyn retaliated. He whirled around ramming his gloved fist into Galdin's jaw. Momentarily stunned, Galdin took the knife from Krispyn and threw him against the wall.

A crazed look crossed Krispyn's face as he glared at Galdin. He raced forward his hands outstretched. Galdin stood his ground. Planting his feet firmly, he brought up the knife and plunged it into Krispyn's diaphragm. Blood trickled out of the dying man's mouth and down his chin as he gradually slumped to the hard floor.

"You think you've won," hissed Krispyn, "You just murdered a hero of Tesnayr. A king." A long, slow gasp escaped Krispyn's lips as he breathed his last.

The door slammed into the stones behind him as guards charged into the chamber with their weapons raised. Taking one quick glance at Krispyn's dead form and Nylana unconscious in the far corner, they pointed their weapons at Galdin.

"Clap him in irons," said the Captain of the Guard.

Instantly, shackles snapped around Galdin's wrists knocking the blade from his bloodied hand. They shoved him out of the room and down the long steps to the dungeons below.

"Take her to her chamber," said the Captain of the Guard pointing at Nylana.

Two men rushed to her making sure that she still breathed. Gently, they lifted her up and carried her away.

Pain engulfed her head as Nylana groggily opened her eyes. Narúl's face greeted her. "Back from the netherworld I see," he said placing a cool, damp cloth on her forehead.

"Krispyn! He's—you've got to get Galdin!"

"Settle down," soothed Narúl as he pushed Nylana back onto the pillows. "I have taken care of everything."

"You don't understand."

"Galdin has been imprisoned for murder. Unfortunately, your brother is dead."

"Murder? He's innocent! Krispyn—Krispyn is the one in the cloak. He started the war! He did all this."

Narúl's brow furrowed at Nylana's rambling. He held up his hand to silence her.

"Narúl, please. You must listen to me before another innocent man is killed."

"The guards saw what happened," said Narúl.

"They saw what Krispyn wanted them to see," said Magi walking slowly into the room.

"Magi," exclaimed Narúl, "Where have you been?"

"In that room buried under rubble. No one ever notices the cat even when the cat wants to be seen." Magi hopped on the bed placing herself beside Nylana. "Nylana speaks the truth. I heard everything. Krispyn planned the invasion. He orchestrated all of this to make the people believe that he should remain as their king."

"I can't believe it," sobbed Nylana, "He betrayed us all. Why would he do that?"

"Some will do anything for power," said Magi.

"But this is too fantastical," said Narúl, "None of it makes any sense."

"You humans never do anything that does," said Magi. "But believe it. Krispyn allowed the barbarians to invade the five lands. Then he declared war on them and destroyed them. Afterward, we crowned him as our king. People are singing his praises in the street. It was a perfect plan."

"But how—"

"Narúl, it's true. He tried to kill me when I found out. If it wasn't for Galdin, I would be dead and the kingdom would be in the hands of a madman," said Nylana. "He tricked us all."

"It just doesn't make sense," whispered Narúl still not wanting to believe that anyone was capable of such treachery. "To incite a war against his own people for a throne."

"Narúl," said Nylana, "In all the years you have known me, have I ever lied to you?"

Frowning, Narúl stared at her. "No."

"We need to free Galdin. Tell people the truth." Nylana jumped to her feet. She wavered a bit as a wave of dizziness passed over her.

"Hold on a minute," said Narúl taking hold of her arm. "You have been unconscious for two days. A lot has happened since then."

"What?"

"Word of this has already spread to the farthest reaches of the land. Everyone believes that Krispyn is a great hero and that Galdin murdered him in cold blood. They would have hanged him already if it wasn't for Ryk."

"What do you mean?" asked Nylana.

"Judgment has already been passed on him. You cannot release Galdin. He has already been declared guilty."

"But he is innocent!"

"Think of the riot that will ensue if you do not act accordingly."

"What are you saying?" asked Nylana.

Narúl took hold of her hands and sat her on the bed. "To try and convince people of Galdin's innocence will be of little use. No one will listen. Their emotions are too high; too convinced of his guilt."

"But he is innocent! The truth is—"

"Of little importance at the moment," said Narúl. "Nylana listen to me. Krispyn is still being worshiped as a hero. They sing of him even now in the streets. Galdin was found standing over his dead body with the knife in his hand. He did kill him. No one will care why, not at this time."

Singing filtered through the window reaching them with its faint chorus.

> *Krispyn! Krispyn! Noble to the end.*
> *Twas he that killed Vasagius*
> *Instead of receiving a hero's praise*
> *Foul death he met by the hand of Galdin.*

"But—"

"You cannot convince people of something they do not want to believe. You are now the Queen of Tesnayr. The throne is now yours. Krispyn is dead and innocent or not, no one will allow Galdin to be crowned. We have laws. Murder is punishable by death. The murder of a hailed king even more so. As queen you must uphold this law."

"He is innocent," whispered Nylana, "I can't do it."

"He is right, Nylana," said Magi, "Think of what will happen if you release Galdin."

"So you think I should just go along with a lie?"

"I think you should talk to Galdin," said Magi. "I'm sure he would want to speak with you."

"This is too—" began Narúl.

"Outrageous?" said Magi, "It's a tragedy. Now come along all of you. There is one person we need to speak to." She squirted through the slightly ajar door.

Ryk walked in. "Nylana!" He ran to her giving her a giant hug. "For a moment I thought I had lost you."

"Help me up," said Nylana.

Ryk allowed her to lean on his shoulders as he helped her to her feet.

"Come on," said Magi waving her tail impatiently.

Nylana and the others followed once again taking orders from a cat.

Water dripped from the ceiling as they entered the darkest depths of the prison chamber. Puddles of murky water littered the cracked, stone that made up the floor. Damp, cold greeted them. Nylana shivered.

"Halt," said the guard. He noticed Nylana for the first time. "I'm sorry, my lady. I did not realize it was you."

Nylana noticed Magi squeeze between the guard's feet unnoticed. "I wish to see the prisoner."

"I have orders to let no one in."

"And who gives those orders?" demanded Nylana.

The guard's demeanor wavered as he mulled over what to do. His captain had given him specific orders and yet here was the queen changing all of that.

"I am certain that you do not wish to disobey a superior officer," said Narúl, "But as she is now your queen, her command supersedes your captain's. And would you deny her the right to see the man who murdered her brother?"

The guard lowered his weapon. "Of course. I am sorry, my lady. Of course you may see him."

"Narúl," said Nylana, "See to it we are not disturbed."

Narúl pushed the guard into an empty chair. "Sit."

Nylana and her party walked toward the long hallway that housed the prison cells. In the far end sat a lonely figure. She ran to it. "Galdin!"

Instantly, the figure stood up clutching the bars to his cell. "Nylana. You shouldn't be here."

"I had to see you." She did her best to hug him through the bars.

Narúl stood a few feet away near a torch keeping watch with Magi.

"Are you alright?" asked Galdin.

"No permanent damage," replied Nylana, "Galdin they want you to hang. According to our laws murdering the king is punishable by death. We need to tell everyone the truth. We must—"

"Do nothing," said Galdin.

"What?"

"You cannot help me."

"But you're innocent. It was all Krispyn. We must tell them."

"No," said Galdin with finality, "Krispyn deceived us all. In the two days that I have been down here I have listened to the singing and chanting. People in the streets praise his name while cursing mine. Think of what would happen if you told them that the man they love; the man they believe saved them is responsible for the death of their husbands, their wives, and their children."

"But they celebrate a lie."

"Yes, they do. They believe in Krispyn so much, think of what would happen if they learned the truth now. It will crush them. They will never believe in anything again."

"But they need to know the truth!"

"They will. Someday." Galdin placed a finger under Nylana's chin raising her head so he could look her in the eyes. "One day, they will be ready. And when that time comes they will learn the truth and accept it. Do not take their faith away. It is all they have left. If their hope dies, then Krispyn will have truly won."

"I can't do it," sobbed Nylana, "I cannot order your execution. I can't go through with this. You saved my life and now you are asking me to condemn yours."

"Enough people have died for the greed of one man," said Galdin. "Let it end with me. Let them hate me. Let them have my blood. Let them have their justice so that they can carry on."

"I can't."

"You have a strength deep within—a strength no other possesses," said Galdin.

Nylana shook her head as more tears dropped onto her cheek.

Galdin gently wiped a tear away. "The phoenix entrusted you with its power so that it could be reborn. It trusted you and no other. You can do this. You must do this."

"But—"

"I will always be here," Galdin pointed to Nylana's heart, "Ni'lee y'lee."

Gently, Galdin took Nylana's hand in his own. He sang the lullaby that his mother had sung to him; that he had sung to Mira. The melody filled the prison chamber as Nylana cried tears of sorrow.

> Sach le ge-lan, mac wehyn
> Fear not my child.
> This storm shall pass.
> Terrible and reviled

> It will not last.
> Now, dry those tears.
> Give me a smile.
> Despite its long years
> Dawn will light the isle.
> Sac le ge-lan, mac wehyn

"You have a strength that I will never possess," Galdin told her when his song had finished. "You are the one that they truly praise. One day they will realize it.

"You gave me something to believe in. Something to fight for. Now fight for your people. And someday long after we have gone, they will learn who truly saved the lands of Tesnayr."

"But I can save you."

"You already have," said Galdin, "That day when you were running from the slavers; it was not I who rescued you, but you who saved me."

"I don't want to lose you," said Nylana as tears streamed down her face making her eyes puffy and her nose red. "I lost you once before and then found you. I don't want to lose you again."

"You must let me go."

Nylana kissed his hand. "I just wish I did not have to make this decision. If only there was some way to free you."

Magi's ears turned in her direction.

"You set me free long ago. Now go. Do your duty as the queen and do not look back."

Ryk wrapped his hands around Nylana's shoulders and helped her to her feet. "It's time we go."

"Look after her," Galdin said to him.

Ryk nodded in Galdin's direction. "I will."

He led Nylana through the dark corridor and back to where the guard waited with Narúl. Slowly, they made the long trek to the outside world.

Chapter XIX
Krispyn's Funeral

The heels of Nylana's shoes echoed with each somber step she took circling the throne that stood alone in the chamber. Her eyes focused on the mosaic that covered the floor: an eight point star with the crests of the five lands circling around it and the crest of Tesnayr resting in the center.

For years Nylana had admired the mosaic never quite understanding it. Now, its meaning became all too clear.

Belarnia

Belyndril

Hemíl

MurDair

Sym'Dul

Tesnayr

"My lady," said a messenger. "It is time."

Nylana managed a weak smile to let the messenger know that she had heard.

Silence ensued as the funeral procession made its way to the burial ground. Despite the sun's warmth, Nylana's heart remained cold and broken. Even the birds refused to sing sensing the passing of a beloved son of Tesnayr.

Nylana eyed the gathered crowd. If only they knew the truth, she thought. But how could she tell them that the man they worshiped as a hero had actually betrayed them? Another secret she must carry deep within her heart.

As she watched Krispyn's body being placed within the mound of earth, the song her mother used to sing to her filled her mind. Nylana had sung the same melody to Krispyn when he was a small child, back when they were still friends.

She remembered asking her mother about the first verse. Her mother had replied by simply stating that the first verse of the song conveyed the sorrow of parting and a breaking heart. If it were to ever be translated to the common tongue, the sadness within it would consume whomever heard it.

As she thought back, Nylana suddenly thought it strange that such a thing would be considered a child's lullaby. The more she considered it, the more she realized it was a parent's way of preparing their children for the pain that life sometimes brings. She also understood the pain that the first verse was said to convey.

As people silently said their farewells to Krispyn, Nylana began to sing the lullaby that she had sung for him long ago. She sang it for Krispyn, the brother she had helped raise. She sang it for Galdin, the brother she had lost and found, and was about to lose again.

> Ni'lee y'lee ni se le'han
> Bok a san la'na
>> Ni'lee y'lee ni se le'han
>> Se ma'hak ana
>
>> Farewell my friend. We'll meet again
>> Far down River's way.
>> Farewell my friend. We'll meet again
>> Long before end of day.
>
>> Save your sighs, the dawn is nigh.
>> Time to move on.
>> So, say good-bye. Don't ask why.
>> Go, before morning's gone.

Now, kiss me sweet. Take my love.
Close to your heart
Forever keep. In heaven above
There we'll never part.

Farewell my friend. We'll meet again.
Sure, as Mountains rise.
Farewell, my friend. We'll meet again.
Soon, in sun strewn skies.

Hush, don't you cry. Dream of stars,
Light and feathery.
The blue jay cries from afar;
Such sweet melody.

Let gentle wind hum softly
And melt your cares away.
There will I be by your side,
Here, where you lay.

Farewell my friend. We'll meet again.
Soon, in Meadows new.
Farewell my friend. We'll meet again.
Down in rosy hue.

Now go to sleep. Please don't weep.
Time for eternal rest.
The time has come with setting sun.
There forever blest.

Your spirit free, don't cry for me,
Here on earthly tomb.
I sing for thee with happy glee.
My time will come soon.

Farewell my friend. We'll meet again.
Down in Valley's fold.
Farewell my friend, we'll meet again.
Far from winter's cold.

Ni'lee y'lee ni se le'han
Bok a san la'na
Ni'lee y'lee ni se le'han
Se ma'hak ana

Once the song was finished, Nylana wept silent tears for herself. She wished someone could remove the knife buried within her heart. The phoenix cried overhead. Gradually, Nylana glanced at it. It flew over everyone giving its own lament as though it understood her torment.

Chapter XX
A Woman Crowned

Music floated through the labyrinth of sarcophagi weaving their way to Nylana. She stood before the grave of Amborese staring at the blue roses swaying in the breeze. Many times she had come here seeking solitude and found solace before the tomb of one of Tesnayr's greatest heroes. But not today. Her heavy heart swept over any ounce of fulfillment she might have had.

A somber whine drew her attention. Trog stared at her with sad eyes.

"I'm sorry, Trog," said Nylana.

A blue rose broke free of its vine and glided to Nylana landing delicately by her foot. She scooped it up. Twirling it in her fingers, Nylana studied the flower remembering a time when it had happened before; when her life changed. The soft cry of the phoenix echoed around her pulling her from her self-pity.

"They are waiting for you," Ryk stepped up beside her.

"I'll be there in a bit."

"There is still time to release him."

"I can't," said Nylana, "They will know it was me, or you. No, Galdin made his last request. The least I can do is abide by it."

"But you are about to be crowned queen. You can change the law."

Nylana smiled wanly at her husband. "It does not give me the right to do as I please. Narúl is right, even I have to obey the law. And with no evidence to prove Galdin's innocence, his fate is set."

"Someone should convince him to escape," muttered Ryk.

"You are welcome to try."

Ryk frowned. He knew well Galdin's stubbornness. Like Nylana, when his mind was made up there was no changing it.

"Let it go," whispered Nylana. "This must end."

She walked gracefully to the throne room where all of Norlyk, and many from the other lands, awaited the coronation of their new queen; their beloved lady. Nylana strode to the front of the chamber where Orrin and the five lords waited for her. Taking her place before him, she knelt.

"Lords of Tesnayr, do you each swear to serve Nylana as your queen?" asked Orrin.

One by one each of the five lords stepped forward declaring their oath to Nylana. A small stab of pain touched her as she listened to the newly appointed lords of Belyndril and MurDair.

"Nylana, daughter of Glasaf, do you swear to protect the lands of Tesnayr, uphold its laws, and respect the sovereignty of the five lands?" Orrin asked her.

"I swear it." Nylana's crisp voice echoed through the chamber.

"Then I, King Orrin of Pras'quel, recognizing your claim to the throne and in accordance with your laws, declare you, Nylana, Queen of Tesnayr. May you lead the five lands justly and righteously. May your days be long and blessed."

Orrin placed the crown upon Nylana's head, as it had been placed upon so many others. As it was once worn by Tesnayr, and a thousand years later by Amborese, now it rested upon Nylana. Regally, Nylana rose to her feet facing the throng of gleeful faces before her.

"People of Tesnayr," boomed Orin's voice, "I give you your new Queen."

Ryk ran to his wife planting a big kiss upon her lips and hugging her tightly. Despite her mood, Nylana smiled. At least she had her husband.

Cheers echoed around them hailing their new queen and king.

"Ryk," Orrin's voice silenced the room. "Do you vow to serve the lands of Tesnayr, protect them, and uphold their laws?"

"I do," said Ryk.

"And do you also swear to serve their queen?"

Ryk gulped. "Yes."

"Then, by the fact that you are married to her and I have little choice, I declare you the King of Tesnayr." Orrin unceremoniously plopped a crown upon Ryk's head.

More cheers went up as applause and gleeful shouting filled the room.

"Open the kitchens," said Nylana, "Let drink and food flow freely. Let us celebrate as peace reigns in the land once again."

More cheers. The band played music as cooks and servers from the kitchens brought out a variety of meats, breads, cakes, and ale.

Nylana waved a man over. "See to it that those in the kitchens work in shifts so that they may also enjoy the festivities."

"Yes, my lady." The man darted off.

                    *   *   *

"Tabs," said Magi, interrupting the orange tabby as he dove into a glass of mead. "Get away from that drink and follow me."

"But—"

"Now!" Magi skittered between people's dancing feet and into the outside corridor. Knowing he would probably regret it, Tabs followed. The two cats trotted through the castle and to the prison chamber entrance.

"It's shut," said Tabs.

Magi placed her paws on the wooden door. It opened under her weight just enough for them to squeeze through. "You have much to learn."

Magi walked briskly through the dark hallway to the room where the guard sat with his feet on the table.

"What exactly are you—"

Magi smacked Tabs in the mouth with her bushy tail. "Do as I say. Distract the guard. Keep him occupied while I free Galdin."

"Magi, don't you think it will cause a commotion. What about when they notice he is gone?"

"With the celebration going on, Galdin can slip out easily. By the time anyone notices his absence he will be long gone."

"Why are you doing this?" asked Tabs.

"An innocent man does not deserve to die for the crimes of another. And because Nylana has suffered enough."

Magi darted into the room where the guard sat placing herself within the shadows.

"That Krispyn is a hero," said Magi.

"Hear! Hear!" said the guard raising his empty tankard to no one in particular. "A great hero."

"Actually I think he was a no good rat," said Tabs, his voice reverberating through the hallway.

The guard smacked his boots onto the floor. "Who said that?" He stood up and poked his head into the corridor. "What scum said that?"

Stealthily, Magi slipped the keys from around the man's belt.

"Come and get me you big louse," yelled Tabs.

"Why you—" the guard dashed into the hallway running straight to the end.

Quickly, Magi dashed through the room for the hallway at the other end that led to the individual cells. She padded through the darkness with the keys in her mouth.

Deep within the dungeons the celebration vibrated through the stone walls and to Galdin's cell. He rested on a mound of hay awaiting his fate. He didn't care that he was about to die. Peacefulness surrounded him.

Clink!

Galdin glanced over to find Magi seated in front of his cell with the keys.

"Are you going to sit there all day?" The cat pushed the keys under the door.

Galdin picked them up jamming them into the lock and opening the cell. He shut it behind him and handed the keys to Magi. The cat darted down the corridor, placed the keys on the table, and ran back to Galdin.

"You need to learn to be lighter on your feet," echoed Tabs' voice as he led the guard on a wild goose chase.

Galdin headed for the exit.

"Not that way you idiot," hissed Magi. "Follow me."

She ran in the other direction deeper within the prison chamber. Galdin followed. His boots clicked on the hard floor as he chased after the cat to his freedom. Magi stopped. Hastily, she sniffed a brick in the wall searching. Galdin was about to question her when she stopped.

"Press this brick here."

Galdin pushed against it. To his surprise it sank into the wall as a hole the size of a dwarf opened.

"In."

Galdin trailed after Magi as she led him into the secret room and the door closed behind him. Swords and axes lined the walls around. "What is this place?" he asked.

"The armory," replied Magi, "Now grab what you need and get going."

Galdin selected a sword from the wall. He balanced it in his hand a moment satisfied that it was of good quality. He put on some armor, grabbed a shield, bow, and quiver of arrows. A glint of steel caught his eye. On the wall as though placed so he would find it, hung the sword of Tesnayr. Galdin traded the first sword for it. "Ready."

Whipping her tail, Magi hopped to the door peeking outside. "Clear."

She squeezed through.

Galdin slipped into the hallway. *No one.* A furry shape trotted down the corridor. Hurriedly, he chased after the cat.

Music filled his ears as they reached a stairwell. Taking the steps two at a time, he reached the top within seconds and paused. Still no one.

"This way," said Magi. She swerved around a corner.

Galdin trailed after her; alert for signs of being discovered. The entire place seemed vacant. *They must all be at the celebration.* He moved carefully through the maze of hallways and the many twists and turns that Magi led him through. Finally, a wave of fresh air greeted him. He breathed deeply.

"The stables are just over there," said Magi. There is a horse already saddled. Head straight to the Fiery Caves in Belyndril. No one will bother you there."

"Thank you," said Galdin.

"And, Galdin, I hope we meet again."

Voices reached their ears. Two men moseyed through the castle talking loudly.

Instantly, Magi darted away. "Hey, you two," she called, "Free ale in the kitchens."

The two men stopped midstride, turned, and ran to the kitchens with a satisfied cat watching them.

"Take care of yourself," she said to Galdin before bounding away and disappearing around a corner.

Glancing in all directions, Galdin ran for the stables. He hugged the shadows keeping careful watch for prying eyes as he darted through the courtyard. *Empty.* Within moments he was in the stables. The saddled horse stood right where Magi said it would be. He inspected the harness noting the food and water in the saddle bags. The horse snorted as he jumped upon it. Kicking hard, he sped into the city streets.

The horse's hooves clopped on the cobblestone roads as he steered it through the various levels of the city and to the gates. No one paid him any heed. He soon reached the gates of Norlyk knowing that was where he was most likely to get caught. They stood open and the guards had gone. Magi had thought of everything.

"Come on," he told his horse.

Together they galloped through the gates and into the open plains beyond.

*   *   *

Hours passed as the celebration continued. Some still danced while others sat in chairs too full to even think about eating another bite. Nylana surveyed the dwindling crowd. Soon, people would trail away to sleep. She stifled a yawn.

A guard ran up to her. "My lady! The prisoner! He has escaped!"

Silence hushed everyone as the news spread.

"Escaped?" asked Nylana.

"Yes, my lady," puffed the guard. "I don't know what happened. I went to inspect the cells like I do every evening and he wasn't there."

"Search the grounds," said someone.

"No," ordered Nylana. All eyes rested upon her.

"My lady?"

"Galdin will not be in the city," said Nylana, "He is no fool. By now he will be leagues away."

"Then what do you propose we do?" asked Lord Stefon.

Though ecstatic that Galdin was free, Nylana contained her emotions masking her face with a cold expression. The sternness in her voice surprised even her.

"Let it be known that henceforth Galdin is exiled from the lands of Tesnayr. Let no one offer him quarter. Should he be captured, he is to be brought here for execution."

Nylana turned away before her emotions could betray her. She left the chamber, wove her way through a throng of hallways until she reached a place of solitude. Open doors caught her attention. Nylana stepped through them to a veranda and into the open air.

The winds of summer tickled Nylana's hands as she stood upon the balcony overlooking the great valley beyond Norlyk. Much of the city rested behind her. But she was more interested in the grassland beyond and the lone figure upon it. Bittersweet emotions roiled within her heart. She had saved the lands of Tesnayr from a man bent only on its destruction and his own gain. But at a heavy cost. For the second time in her life, she had lost her brother.

Soft footsteps sounded behind her. Narúl had followed.

"Why did it have to end this way?" she asked.

Narúl placed a gentle hand on her shoulder. "Galdin did what had to be done. Just like you did."

"Duty before happiness."

"Would you have preferred Krispyn remained king?"

Nylana pursed her lips. The thought sickened her.

"I thought not," said Narúl, "One day, when the world is ready, Galdin will be hailed as the hero that he is. He saved the lands of Tesnayr. He saved you. But for now, let the world believe what it will. You, Nylana, were always meant to have the throne."

Narúl left Nylana alone on the balcony.

The cry of the phoenix echoed from above. She glanced up at it. You knew this would happen, she thought. The majestic bird sang again to provide comfort to her.

Nylana's hair swayed in the breeze. A touch of coldness dotted her cheek. Slowly, Nylana dabbed the tears from her face. Sorrow clenched her heart as the lone figure galloped away into the horizon. She inhaled deeply when it paused on a hill to look back at her. She knew that he did so to say one last good-bye.

"Farewell, Galdin," whispered Nylana, "Good-bye, brother."

*   *   *

Hooves clopped softly on the ground as Galdin steered his horse over a small rise and out of sight of Norlyk. His horse stopped suddenly and snorted.   A peculiar rock caught his attention. He studied it closely. The rock blinked.

"Hello, Trog," said Galdin in greeting.

Instantly, Trog jumped up spreading his wings and letting his tongue hang out of his mouth. He jumped on Galdin giving him a huge, slobbery lick.

"You really shouldn't do that," said Tabs poking his head from Galdin's pack.

"Where did you come from?" demanded Galdin, surprised.

"Oh, you know. The guard was busy, you were making your great escape; I thought I'd tag along," answered Tabs, "Oh, and you might want to stop for some supplies. The jerky is gone."

Frowning Galdin popped the top off of his flask. "So is the water."

"Is it?" came Tabs' innocent tone.

Galdin steered his horse onward away from a life that could never be. "Come along, Trog."

Trog sprang to his feet settling beside Galdin's mount matching its pace. As they disappeared over the crest of the hill, the phoenix flew overhead wishing them good fortune.

Epilogue

Gina tossed the bucket of scraps into the alley. Cold mist prickled her skin.

"You can go now, girl, and be here all the earlier tomorrow," said the baker's wife.

"Yes, ma'am," replied Gina.

She trotted down the alleyway hurrying to a small space underneath the innkeepers lodge that she called home. Orphaned at eight years of age, Gina spent the last two years learning to survive on the streets. She was pretty good at it, and the odd jobs provided some money for buying food. However, her life wasn't without its risks.

She darted down another alley as the rain picked up and bumped into a man who kept his cloak pulled up. His piercing gaze held kindness and Gina immediately knew who it was: the old hermit who lived outside of the town. No one knew his real name and he kept to himself.

"I'm sorry," said Gina.

"No need to apologize," said the hermit.

"You should adopt her," hissed a voice that Gina swore came from the man's pack.

The hermit shifted his bag getting a meow in response.

Gina continued on her way. Strange tales surrounded the hermit. Some said that a rock followed him around. Others spoke about a cat who frequented the taverns singing tales about the valiant Galdin for the price of a mug of ale.

Lost in her thoughts, Gina never noticed the three youths following her. A hand seized her from behind yanking her feet off the ground and pinning her against the side of a building. "Let me go!," she screamed.

"Give us what coins you have," said one of the boys.

"I haven't got any," wailed Gina.

"No coins, eh? You know what that means don't you lads?"

The hungry look in the three youth's eyes frightened Gina. "Please let me go," she pleaded.

The hermit appeared from around the corner creeping towards the ruffians. He walked up behind them without a sound. Unnoticed, he reached for the hilt of his sword gripping it tightly, prepared to fight if necessary.

"Let her go," he commanded.

The three hooligans spun around. They eyed him suspiciously. "What do you want, hermit?" demanded one.

The hermit stared at them coldly. The steel in his eyes made the three youths falter in their bravery. "I said release her."

The conviction in his voice forced the three boys to obey.

"Let's go," said one.

They released Gina who slumped in the mud coughing. They ran from the alley relieved to getaway from this strange man who demonstrated neither bravado, nor fear.

"Thank you, mister," said Gina.

"Are you alright?" asked the hermit.

"Yes."

"What is your name, girl?"

"Gina."

"Where are your parents?"

The girl looked down at the mud in response.

The hermit understood immediately. "I'm sorry," he said. He turned to leave.

"Wait," called Gina, "Who are you?"

"Just an old hermit," replied the man.

"I know you have a name, aside from what everyone calls you. What is it?"

The hermit turned to leave.

"Please let me come with you," pleaded Gina.

The hermit shook his head and started to leave. A small tug at his heart forced him to glance back at the girl and her downtrodden face.

"Have a heart," whispered a voice from his bag.

The hermit walked back to the young girl. "This bag is terribly heavy, and my place is such a long way—"

Gina snatched the bag from the hermit and heaved it onto her shoulders; a broad smile covering her face.

The man grinned as he and the girl walked the lonely trail away from the village. They soon came upon a small, one room cabin with smoke rising from the chimney. The man opened the door and held it for Gina who hurried inside. She gently placed the bag on the table and gasped as Tabs darted out of it.

"Thank you, my dear," said Tabs as he jumped onto Trog who lay sleeping by the fire.

"You talk!" said Gina.

"It's getting him to shut up that's the problem," said the man.

Gina studied the old man whom everyone called the Hermit. She spotted the sword and her eyes opened wide.

"I know you! I know who you are! You're Galdin!

"I've heard all of the tales about you. About how you saved the Queen Nylana. About how you have helped many villages and farmers from terrible dangers as you wandered the five lands despite your banishment.

"The stories of you killing King Krispyn have to be lies. I told the baker's wife so just yesterday."

"And what makes you so certain that I am he?"

Gina reached for the sword and held it up. "This."

Galdin laughed a hearty laugh. "And what makes you believe that the story about my crime is not true?"

Gina looked Galdin in the eyes. "Your eyes are too kind."

"Many of those stories are exaggerated," said Galdin. "And that was thirty years ago."

"I may have embellished a few details," mumbled Tabs around his drink.

"This proves that you are Galdin," exclaimed Gina.

"Unfortunately, one tale is true," said Galdin, "I did kill Krispyn."

Gina eyed Galdin. His demeanor, his rescuing of her, no heartless murderer would do such a thing. "Why?" she asked with pure innocence and curiosity.

"Because he intended to kill someone I cared about," answered Galdin.

Gina absorbed what Galdin had said, but it did not bother her in the least.

"Do you not wish to contact the town magistrate?"

"No," replied Gina, shaking her head. "I've heard tales about Krispyn as well; that he was not as great of a king as people believed."

"And I bet I know where those come from," said Galdin.

Tabs pushed his face further into his mug drinking loudly.

"Well, my dear," Galdin said to Gina, pushing a chair towards her, "As you seem to know my story, why don't you tell me yours."

Glossary

Amborese	am-bore-eese
Ardryn	Are-dren
Ársa	are-sa
Artryl	are-tril
Belarnia	ba-lar-knee-a
Belyndril	ba-lynn-drill
Belznyc	bellz-nick
D'arr	dar
druloc	drew-lock
Drinylle	dry-knell
Edrei	eh-dree
Galdin	gal-din
Gorganof	gore-gan-off
Hemíl	heh-mill
Krispyn	kris-pen
La'nar	la-nar
Magi	ma-jye
MurDair	myrr-dare
niht'anda	nit-on-da
Nok'ta	knock-ta
Narúl	nah-rule
Ni'lee y'lee	nee-lay e-lay
Norlyk	nor-lick
Nylana	nuh-lawn-a
Orrin	or-in
Perili	pur-ill-e
Petra	peh-tra
Pras'quel	pras-kell
Preston	press-ton
Quesha	k-sha
Ryk	rick

Sac le ge-lan, mac wehyn   sack-lay-gay-lynn-mack-way-lynn
Selexia   se-lex-e-uh
Shelwyk   shell-wick
Stahl   stall
Sym'Dul   sim-dull
Stefon   stef-on
Tesnayr   tez-nay-air
Trisk   tri-sk
Trog   tr-ahg
Trya   tree-a
Uriel   yer-e-ul
Valn   val-n
Vasagius   va-sag-e-us
wẽdlym   wed-lim

About the Author

Nova Rose is a pen name for author Janet McNulty. She began writing the *Legends Lost Trilogy* twelve years ago. *Galdin* is the third and final book.

The story began when she watched her cat playing one afternoon. There she got the idea of a talking cat who once was a queen telling her story to a girl named Amborese. From then on, Ms. McNulty delved into the world of fantasy and adventure.

She published the first book in the series, *Amborese*, in 2011. Upon completion, Ms. McNulty knew that the story of the lands of Tesnayr did not end there. So she sat down and wrote the remaining books: *Tesnayr* (2012) and *Galdin* (2013); eventually publishing them as well. A unique trilogy, Ms. McNulty said that *Legends Lost* was more of a lost history of a place that existed long ago.

Ms. McNulty has always enjoyed writing, penning stories since the age of eight. After years of public education and college enlightenment, she decided to make a career of it.

Follow on Twitter: JMRUL
Follow her blogs: Books and Legends

More From the Lands of Tesnayr

Learn about the first king of Tesnayr and the man who started it all.

1,000 years before the birth of Amborese is a far greater story. The legend of Tesnayr. Before the lands of Tesnayr existed, there were five distinct kingdoms. Each proud and constantly at war with one another. But all that changed... A stranger washes upon the shores of Sym'Dul, beaten and barely alive; the only survivor of a devastating war in a land far across the sea. Nursed back to health, Tesnayr makes a new life for himself and begins to think that his past is behind him. Then the orcs arrive led by Galbrok. They quickly ravage the land. Faced with a terrible choice, Tesnayr forms his own army to stop them and quickly draws the attention of each of the five kings. Yet, Tesnayr's past refuses to release him. Can he unite the five kingdoms before Galbrok annihilates them? Can a lone man from across the sea achieve what all believe to be impossible?

The second great legend of the lands of Tesnayr.

Amborese thought she was a peasant's daughter until one night dark creatures murdered her parents and pursued her into the forest. Saved by a talking cat and her friend Zolo, she fled for her life only to learn that she had a bigger destiny than she once believed. Pursued across the five lands of Tesnayr by an evil wizard's army, Amborese must overcome her doubts and unite the dragons, elves, dwarves, and the five lands themselves. But will they follow a mere girl?

More by Nova Rose under the name Janet McNulty.

The Mellow Summers Series

Mellow Summers moves to Vermont to attend college, accompanied by her friend Jackie. They soon find themselves running into ghosts and one mystery after another.

Available on Amazon, IBookstore, and Smashwords.

illusion, food is rationed, and everything you do is tracked by a chip implanted in your arm. This is Dana Ginary's world.

At age seventeen, people receive their career assignments chosen for them by a government body. Forced to work at the Waste Management Plant because she was declared too individualistic, Dana finds herself surrounded by death and brutality. Knowing her days are numbered, she looks for a way to leave the plant before she, too, becomes one of its causalities..

It is then she meets a man named George and soon finds herself caught up in a cat mouse game between the resistance and the Dystopian government. Dana finds herself faced with an agonizing choice of whom she will betray and whom she will save: her friend George, her parents, or herself.

www.ingramcontent.com/pod-product-compliance
Lightning Source LLC
Chambersburg PA
CBHW030752260626
47169CB00001B/16